HOSTILE BID

Peter Cunningham

MICHAEL JOSEPH
LONDON

MICHAEL JOSEPH LTD
Published by the Penguin Group
Penguin Books Ltd, 27 Wrights Lane, London W8 5TZ, England
Viking Penguin, a division of Penguin Books USA Inc.,
375 Hudson Street, New York, New York 10014, USA
Penguin Books Australia Ltd, Ringwood, Victoria, Australia
Penguin Books Canada Ltd, 2801 John Street, Markham, Ontario, Canada L3R 1B4
Penguin Books (NZ) Ltd, 182–190 Wairau Road, Auckland 10, New Zealand

Penguin Books Ltd, Registered Offices: Harmondsworth, Middlesex, England

First published in Great Britain 1991

Printed in England by Clays Ltd, St Ives plc
Typeset in 11/13½ pt Photina

A CIP catalogue record for this book is available from the British Library
ISBN 0 7181 3474 5

For JOANNA, for MORY
and for JESSICA
With love from fathoms deep.

I too have groped
In utter darkness.
Someone else must decide
Which it might have been –
Whether dream or reality.

   – Kokinshū Poems, tenth-century Japan.

Preliminary

It was always going to be a memorable day. It had been cold in London the morning before, but as he rode the ferry from Staten Island to Manhattan there were still the warm breezes of an Indian summer in New York Harbor, ruffling his dark hair as he stood on the forward deck. The city suddenly appeared through the morning mists like the magic towers of a child's fairytale. His city.

The day came to represent everything. The best and the worst. He would later devour the minute details of those first few hours with the fervour of a vagrant counting his last pennies: the skyline of Wall Street, the walk up a sunny Broadway and into Beaver Street, the breakfast in the panelled dining room of the banker where everything was crisp and solid silver and where anything was his in exchange for a nod.

Back at his desk in the big office with unrivalled views in both directions over city and sea, he had looked out at the trading room and felt an exhilaration that nothing could surpass. It was the clarity of his mind that had pleased him most: he had had a perfect vision of where they were going and how they were going to get there. He had felt blessed.

'*Ross!*'

He looked up in surprise as the door to his office flew back.

'Hold on,' he said to the telephone. 'What . . .?'

'*Quick!*' said the man, a gold trader.

1

It was exactly 11.00 a.m. In the trading room everyone was standing, unspeaking, straining to see a door at the end of the room. They looked at him as he strode through.

'Oh my God! Oh Jesus Christ! Get a doctor!'

Jim Morales's secretary was staggering from the men's washroom, her hand to her mouth. The crowd surged silently forward.

'Holy shit!' someone said.

Ross shouldered to the door. Two traders squatted either side of a body. On a bright red sheet.

'He did it pretty good,' one man said. 'Both wrists to the bone.'

'Can't you stop the bleeding?' Ross asked.

The trader looked up as if Ross had not understood.

'This guy is dead, Ross.'

Ross realized he was kneeling in blood. Blood on his hands was warm and sticky. How could Jim Morales be dead if his blood was warm?

'Why?' he asked, utterly perplexed.

Among the faces at the door that of the accountant stood out grimly. Ross got up, a terrible tension in him. He walked the man over behind a desk.

'What happened here?'

'You're not going to like this,' said the accountant, his eyes afraid.

Was that the worst moment, the hearing of a timeless, hackneyed phrase?

'What?'

'Klinch has filed for bankruptcy in Chicago within the last hour,' the accountant said.

Ross closed his eyes.

'Our money,' he said calmly. 'Has he got any of our money?'

'Jim made a transfer yesterday. I told him you said the word on Klinch was bad. I told him, Ross, but you know Jim and Klinch go way back, I couldn't stop . . .'

The accountant's voice dried up. Ross realized he still had the arm in a vice, that Jim Morales's blood had now made its way to the sleeve of the accountant's shirt. Fifty people were staring at them.

'How much?' he asked.

'Twelve million.'

'Twelve million?'

That was the worst moment, worse than any other, worse even than that awful moment two weeks later when after days and nights of alternating hope and despair and sleeping beside his desk, he had finally given up and come home to the house in Staten Island and read the note, that she had gone, that she had scented the air and smelled the stench of failure, carried through those narrow streets and canyons quicker than a bullet from the barrel of a gun.

BOOK ONE

THE YAKUZA
1995

One

Intense heat percolated the leaves of the few trees that had been left and fried Tetsuya Kikuchi's bald head. He stood watching the little plane bump twice as it put down, then he ran out across the compound to be there when the door opened. It was three years since Rokuo Chiyaha had flown into Mindoro.

A giant heaved out of the plane and exchanged bows with the plant manager. Kikuchi had heard of Ō-Otoko of Kobe but had never seen him. Kikuchi now stared openly as Ō-Otoko held back the door. A small sized man stepped to the ground, dusted himself off and surveyed his surroundings. He was bespectacled, aged forty. His head was forward set, his mouth large and prominent. He frowned in Kikuchi's direction, then delivered a short bow; Kikuchi responded by bending himself double. As bird sound echoed from the surrounding jungle, Kikuchi led the way back across the open compound and indoors to an office where a noisy ceiling fan was attempting to raise air currents.

'We are most honoured by this visit,' Kikuchi began expansively, wiping imaginary dust from a chair and placing it beneath the fan. 'As your excellency can imagine, life in a place like this, thousands of miles from civilization . . .'

Rokuo Chiyaha did not indicate whether or not he was listening. He sat down.

'The most recent figures show that the output of shabu in

Mindoro is still far behind the plants on Panay and Negros,' he stated coldly.

Kikuchi let out his breath in a long shudder. 'To compete in today's amphetamine market we need more modern equipment . . .'

His voice dried up under Chiyaha's stare.

'The issue, although grave, is not why I am here,' Chiyaha said. He tapped his briefcase. 'I have read your report.'

Kikuchi nodded, eager to be of use. 'His name is Tran Dinh Thack, but they call him Rex, excellency. He's twenty-three. His father's identity is unknown, but as you will see he was obviously a Westerner, probably a GI stationed near Saigon. His mother then married a Vietnamese farmer and the boy was brought up in the extended family. When he was nine they were dispossessed of their land by the banks and Rex was sent to live with an uncle in Manila.'

Chiyaha listened impassively.

Kikuchi continued: 'He became involved in juvenile crime and was sent to a detention centre where his physique brought him to the attention of a martial arts enthusiast. Later, Rex's uncle arranged for his instruction in a special camp operated by a Korean ex-army officer on Cebu. He teaches a technique known as sul sa – it is the art of killing without weapons.'

'I know,' Chiyaha said.

'Rex got five years for assault and robbery when he was eighteen,' the manager said. 'He was paroled fifteen months short of his full term and came to our attention.'

'Contract work,' Chiyaha said.

Kikuchi inclined his block-like head.

'Filipino agents who were slow in paying for their supplies of shabu, excellency. In one case over a hundred thousand US was involved.'

'I remember,' said Chiyaha dryly.

'Rex gained access to the house when the agent was away,' Kikuchi babbled. 'He spent five days and nights in the rafters; on the sixth day the agent returned and was dead before nightfall.'

'But after three of these contracts . . .?'

'He needed somewhere out of view,' Kikuchi raced on. 'I gave him a job, here in compound security.'

8

Chiyaha looked down at his file.

'What motivates him?'

'Money, excellency,' Kikuchi responded. 'He has this dream that one day he will come home, the wealthy man, buy back the farm and reinstate himself and his brothers.' Kikuchi made a dismissive expression, distancing himself and Chiyaha from a half-caste, Vietnamese peasant. 'In some things he has the mind of a child.'

Kikuchi watched as Chiyaha looked out the window. There were other reasons than lack of investment why Mindoro was not making the grade, reasons which Kikuchi had long considered his personal reward for working in such a hellhole . . .

'Does he speak good English?' Chiyaha snapped.

'He grew up on the backstreets of Manila,' Kikuchi swallowed.

As Chiyaha got to his feet and walked most discourteously out the door in front of him, Kikuchi knew it was time to be planning his departure from Mindoro.

In the full heat of the Philippine day, Chiyaha saw Ō-Otoko jump to his feet and fall in behind as the party walked down the back of the factory, towards the perimeter fence. A footbridge ran over a ravine where sulphurous red dye was piping into the Mongpong. Chiyaha saw an insect the size of a prawn settle on the cheek of Kikuchi. The weasel-like manager slapped it. Chiyaha frowned. Flesh noise.

Kikuchi was jabbering: 'Excellency, there is one thing . . .'

Chiyaha looked at him.

'You know we fly girls in here from Manila on weekends for the men . . .?'

Chiyaha nodded.

'We have a job to get them nowadays,' Kikuchi said, 'mainly due to Rex. He's hard on them, roughs them very badly. I just thought you should know.'

They followed the fence to a tower and guardhouse of rough wood. Kikuchi rapped with knuckles on the door. Again Chiyaha frowned. Noise. Of bone on wood. Before flesh noise.

Slowly the door swung out and a man in a crisp blue shirt, blue jeans and clean, white training shoes stepped out. His hands rested lightly by his sides. Chiyaha saw a Westerner:

9

round, blue eyes, an oval face, hair that was more brown than black with no Oriental gloss. Perfect.

'Leave us together,' Chiyaha said and entered the guard-house.

The seating was a stool and an upturned crate; Chiyaha chose the crate. He watched as Rex pushed the door closed and stood there with an expression of mild interest.

'Please take off your shirt,' Chiyaha said in English.

Rex blinked once, then he slowly unbuttoned his shirt. The upper body was exceptional: powerfully rounded shoulders over straining pectoral muscles. The chest below the neck and the arms down to the elbows were completely covered in elaborately decorative tattoos: flowers that blossomed at the nipples of the chest and supernovas that exploded on the hard muscles of the stomach.

Thirty minutes later the heat had turned Chiyaha to a swamp of sweat.

'Can you do it?' he asked in Japanese.

'I can do it,' Rex replied, 'but the terms are unacceptable.'

Chiyaha's head went forward and his mouth opened in disbelief. 'Unacceptable?' he said. 'I offer you half a million US dollars in cash and you tell me that is unacceptable? I am sorry but I cannot do anymore.'

Rex got to his feet.

'Then I am sorry too, Chiyaha-san,' he said, moving to the door, 'but you have made a wasted journey.'

'Wait!' Chiyaha said. 'Tell me what you consider acceptable.'

'One million US,' Rex spoke. 'Payable one third now, two thirds on completion. The first payment to be made immediately into an account in the names of my brothers in Ho Chi Minh City. An irrevocable letter of credit for the balance to be opened in their names, payable the day after the completion of the contract.'

Chiyaha looked into the blue eyes which at this distance were empty, translucent pools.

'What if you fail?'

The ghost of a smile flicked across Rex's face.

'A true ninja does not fail. Not when he values his own life less than the mission he has undertaken.'

Chiyaha nodded once.

'Very well,' he said, rising to his feet and bowing, 'I agree.'

Out in the sun, Ō-Otoko stood by the perimeter fence; Kikuchi crouched, chatting to a camp guard whose lightweight sub-machine-gun rested across his knees. As Chiyaha emerged with Rex, plant manager and guard stood.

'Ask him for his weapon,' Chiyaha said to Rex in English.

Rex spoke an order and the guard passed over his gun. Chiyaha put out his hand, took it, then tossed it to Ō-Otoko. The big man caught it hard. Noise. Flesh on steel. Chiyaha frowned.

'I have never seen Sul Sa,' he said in English, to Rex.

Chiyaha saw the smile that had crossed Rex's face in the hut, now tug a corner of his mouth. He stepped one pace back and pointed to Kikuchi.

'Korose,' he said in Japanese. 'Kill him.'

It took a second for everyone to comprehend what had been said. Kikuchi turned, then abruptly halted as Ō-Otoko clicked off the sub-machine-gun's safety catch and levelled the snout at his chest. The man's jaw went slack.

'Ah . . . ah . . .'

Rex seemed to turn. There was a hiss of air, he took a sideways step, then his whole body was in mid-air and Kikuchi was falling backwards, face to sun, hands flapping.

The three men walked to the airstrip and squeezed into the small plane. They taxied down to the end of the strip and took off over the long, tin-roofed buildings, up into the breathless, Mindoro sky. No noises, just the drone of engines. They wheeled once, always climbing. In the yellow-brown compound below, Chiyaha could see a group of insects lifting an inert object on to the back of a cart.

*   *   *

Blue the sea. Blue the sky.

Fresh the air.

Haunting the cry of a gull.

Magical the solitude.

Wondrous a world empty of man.

Ross stood, one big, gloved hand held for balance on a halyard. Rise and fall. Mesmerizing, each wave, exactly the

11

same and utterly different to the one before, each unique in its sameness. He would never leave the sea, he swore. She had been a mother to him when he had left everything, when he had left the old man with those blue-lantern eyes and run.

Spray flew in over the pitching bow to wash and rewash the places where the pain still lay. The water was an anointing. It washed his caked lips and chaffed skin. It dripped from the black thickness of his beard and ran in yellow rivers down his oilskin. He turned his head at the sound of a clanking as the nets began their winching out over the stern. He smiled.

He felt at peace.

*   *   *

The long, black sedans began arriving at 6.00 p.m. Through a mist which tumbled down all the way from the peak of Funagata Yama, they crawled up the winding mountainside and in through the gates of the hotel at Jōgi Spa.

Senko Okuma looked down from the roof of the five floor building. He was fifty-six, low sized and thickly built. His face was round and open but at times like this when great responsibility was his, it crinkled under the pressure. The hotel had been paid 500 million yen in cash and closed for five days. Every inch of it had been swept for explosives and listening devices. Men with sub-machine-guns patrolled the roof and the gardens below and three jeeps constantly reconnoitered the approach roads. Special cooks from Tendo were installed in the kitchens. A helicopter stood by with a precautionary flight plan cleared to Sendai National Hospital. Even so, the things that you failed to anticipate were usually those which occurred. Senko heard the cars and his face furrowed even more.

The first to arrive was Ichirō Abe, the oyabun or godfather of northern Honshu. Abe, who for years had cast longing eyes southwards on Senko's territory, controlled a syndicate based mainly on prostitution with tentacles all the way to Tokyo's Ginza. From the roof Senko watched through binoculars as the doors of the first car flew open and four kobun, soldiers dressed in dark, three-piece suits, jumped out. Ichirō Abe was an old man now, something of a father figure among yakuza. Dressed

12

in a greatcoat, he was ushered quickly in from the unfriendly night. On the roof, Senko could hear the doors of the hotel flapping to close.

Up the driveway simultaneously came the retinues of Kanji Egusa and Shigeru Ōmori, from Nagoya and Yokohama respectively. Egusa, the sarakin, the fat loan shark, emerged smiling benignly from his car, as then did Ōmori, the great bakuto, the handsome prince among gambling bosses in Honshu, his hair slicked back and shining.

At seven it was the turn of Kazuhiro Kasumi. No one was more powerful in southern Honshu. Notorious for his women, the fifty-year-old, bearded Kasumi ducked under an umbrella and hurried inside.

It was nearly seven-thirty when Chiyaha arrived. Senko, who had never left his place on the roof, knew he would be last. Six black BMWs drew up slowly. Over twenty kobun deployed before a back door was opened and a huge man stepped out and straightened himself. As Senko held his breath, Chiyaha emerged. He stood for a moment, looking about him, then he looked suddenly upwards and found Senko on the roof. The little boss felt a sudden chill. Chiyaha bowed. Senko put down his binoculars and bent his body in two. As half a dozen of the men from Kobe closed in behind them, Chiyaha and Ō-Otoko made their way inside.

The flapping noise of the hotel's doors ceased. The engines of the cars restarted as the kobun brought them off for parking. Senko sat on the parapet of the roof and looked into the night.

He was a simple man, happily married for forty years to a strong and sensible woman known to everyone in Sendai as Mama Yayoi. Their only daughter – he called her Mio-chan – the joy of Senko's life, was now reared and working in a good job in Tokyo. Senko would always be a provincial boss, working a mixed business, protection rackets on shops and nightclubs, a rake-off from amphetamines, a little bookmaking, a little pimping. He had come up the hard way; he knew his territory and he stuck to it. But this was the stuff he had heard about; these were the big boys. And yet, following the arrival of Chiyaha, he felt more uneasy than before.

*

13

Chiyaha paced his suite as one male secretary handed him the messages that had awaited his arrival, and another scribbled down the oyabun's responses. His bid for a speedboat racing franchise south of Tokyo was under official scrutiny: his lawyers required urgent instructions; and a plum gambling slot near Kobe was under threat from local, small-time yakuza: immediate action was required.

'Is that all?' Chiyaha inquired when he had finished dictating the faxes.

'That is all, Lord Chiyaha.'

'What word from Tamon Hara?'

'None, I regret,' the secretary whispered.

Chiyaha looked away lest the man would see the worry on his face. So much depended on Tamon Hara now.

At 10.00 p.m. the first session began. The six oyabun sat cross-legged on tatami mats, facing each other across a long, low table which was empty save for a vase with a single yellow chrysanthemum. All were dressed in traditional house clothes: yukata, light cotton robes, and haori, padded half-coats worn over the yukata. On their feet they wore sandals. By special agreement all kobun and wakashū, captains, were excluded.

Ichirō Abe looked down the table at Chiyaha from old, hostile eyes that peered through the blue veil of smoke from his perpetual cigarette. Five years before, Abe's brother had fallen foul of Rokuo Chiyaha in the struggle for control of a number's racket in Kyoto.

'To the glory and purity of our country, to the happiness and industry of our people,' said Abe as father of the meeting. 'Three banzai for our beloved Emperor.'

The cheers reverberated around the room.

With infinite courtesy the oyabun began to inquire of each other's personal well-being, family health and general business prosperity. The exchanges were part of a traditional etiquette, which, no matter what enmities might exist, could never go unheeded. The oyabun of Miyagi, Senko Okuma, was complimented on the efficiency of the arrangements and the suitability of the chosen location.

'To come south to such luxurious surroundings is reason enough for any journey,' said old Abe obliquely.

14

Rokuo Chiyaha took the opening and bowed low towards the oyabun.

'Although there are others who have not accepted my invitation to come here to Jōgi Spa, the fact that even we six sit round this table tonight marks the occasion out as memorable,' he began. 'For when all the rice has been weighed and sold and the money counted, are we not all on the same side?'

The silence was broken by old Abe's harsh cough. Senko Okuma stared in open awe at Chiyaha.

Chiyaha continued: 'We are yakuza. Ours is an honourable profession. We trace our roots back into the mists of history.'

The oyabun nodded impassively.

Chiyaha continued: 'But we have not been treated kindly. A Socialist government rules Japan. Whereas in the old days we could rely on the loyalty of politicians, today we are beset with new laws at every turn, senseless regulations, a crusade to drive us out. Look around you: think how many kobun you commanded ten years ago, then count how many are loyal to you today.'

When Kazuhiro Kasumi spoke, it was bluntly; the oyabun of Kasumi-rengō was known for his distaste of circumlocution.

'Yes, our numbers have shrunk, Chiyaha-san,' he growled in his deep voice, 'but show me an industry that hasn't streamlined it's operations and I'll show you one that's going out of business.'

'I agree with Kasumi-san,' said Ichirō Abe. 'We're leaner and fitter nowadays. And if what I read in *Asahi Shimbun* is true, these Socialists will not be in power in twelve months. They bicker among themselves like dogs following a bitch.'

Kanji Egusa laughed but Chiyaha's head went forward relentlessly.

'Be honest,' he said 'I will not try to hide the figures for Chiyaha-gumi: in real terms we're down ten per cent on last year; last year was down ten per cent on the year before. I no longer recruit new men. I have a problem in providing pension and prison benefits. I can no longer afford the bonuses of even three years ago. Be honest! What man here can say that this new government is not hurting yakuza as never before?'

There was a brief, uncomfortable silence.

'I once employed a clerk to count my money,' said Shigeru Ōmori. 'Now I count it myself.'

'I am not ashamed to be as candid as Chiyaha-san,' said fat Kanji Egusa. 'I don't mind saying that the crackdown on money-lending is a disaster. Yes, times are different – and difficult since power changed on Kasumigaseki.'

'So we have problems,' rumbled Kazuhiro Kasumi from the depths of his beard, his thick eyebrows colliding. 'Who hasn't? We'll find new ways to make up lost ground. What are you telling us, Chiyaha-san, that we don't already know?'

'Unfortunately, these problems are just a beginning,' Chiyaha said. 'You may have heard rumours of new legislation that will be put before the Diet in the next year – legislation that will attempt to squeeze the very blood from our veins. The rumours are true. All the traditional areas from which we draw our strength are coming in for special, new scrutiny. Public prosecutors are to double in number and the power of magistrates to hand down severe sentences on yakuza will be greatly increased.'

Chiyaha leaned forward and plucked out the yellow chrysanthemum; the knuckles of his hand stood out.

'We will be disgracefully impoverished,' he whispered. He opened his hand and crushed petals fell to the table. 'Our shame will be paraded for the world to see.'

'*Never!*'

Kazuhiro Kasumi's bearded face had flooded purple.

'Never whilst I have breath in my body! We will have slaughter! I will tomorrow send ten of my best men to exterminate the vermin who propose these laws.'

'Hai!' responded old Ichirō Abe, his eyes bright. 'To your ten men, Kasumi-san, I add five, men who will not flinch or value their own lives higher than a pickle.'

'We must have blood,' muttered fat Kanji Egusa.

Senko Okuma simply nodded his concerned face.

Chiyaha spoke: 'Where are your brains? In your fists? Or in the point of your swords? Have you the minds of simple bosozoku, fools on hot rod bikes, whose reaction to every crisis is the knife and the chain?'

Kazuhiro Kasumi bristled. 'Don't play that game with me,

16

Chiyaha-san,' he rasped. 'The fish in Kobe Harbour have fed for years on your enemies.'

'My apologies, Kasumi-san,' bowed Chiyaha. 'Perhaps I should have said that your brains lie in the fearsome weapon between your legs that still opens half the golden gates in the Ginza every night.'

Kanji Egusa was unable to suppress a snort of laughter which travelled around the table. Kazuhiro Kasumi swallowed and decided to take the remark as a compliment.

Ichirō Abe: 'You are wasting our time with old washing, Chiyaha-san. I have heard nothing here to make me think that I would not be better off at home, seeing that my girls are not cheating me.'

'Your time has not been wasted,' Chiyaha said. 'To prepare for the lean years ahead – to weather the storm until these Socialists are driven from power – we need money to keep our organizations intact. To survive. But it is no longer possible for us to make such a fortune in Japan. We must look outside.'

*　　　*　　　*

Tamon Hara was tired. Another metal scrapyard north of Tokyo, another blank. The fourth that week. The twentieth that month. He was an expert on Japanese backstreet garages and metal yards, he thought ruefully. He'd been in them all now, as far north as Niigata and south to Kita-Kyushu. Hara-san, the amiable, second-hand car buff, smiling, courteous. The man who had placed the small ad in half a dozen national papers in the used car section.

Easy Money; BMW 323i; top price paid for old car no matter what condition.

Hara yawned and rewound the answering machine in his Kobe apartment; a voice saying it had read the ad, advised him of a BMW 323i available in a scrapyard east of Yokohama. As one of Rokuo Chiyaha's three top captains – a wakashira-hosa – Hara well knew the penalties for failure in Chiyaha-gumi. Thus as he clicked off the machine and stretched, he knew he would catch only two hours' sleep before having to hit the road again.

*　　　*　　　*

17

Morning was Chiyaha's best time. As a young boy in Kobe, he had crept at dawn from the apartment with its rice-paper walls, escaping from the man smell and the noises. He had gone to sit by a waste lot and watch the sun rise over Osaka-Wan. In a world of plunging shadows, of noise he had to plug his ears to kill, the rising sun was an ally, always dependable, always warm.

As first light etched the outline of pines, he finished applying his jitsu-in, his signature seal to correspondence. He looked up.

'Lord, the oyabun of Yokohama,' announced a kobun.

Like Chiyaha, Shigeru Ōmori wore a yukata. Both men bowed their foreheads deeply, then sat on two large cushions beneath the window as green tea was served. There was no tension between them: Ōmori was a proven ally of many years, the only oyabun in Funagata Yama who was not in some way a threat.

'The first sun inspires all men,' Chiyaha opened.

'But some men can use that inspiration like a sword,' replied the bakuto, 'whilst for others it is just a gift with which they have grown complacent.'

Chiyaha bowed to show his respect for his brother oyabun's words.

'Last night I spoke thoughts from my very core,' he said, 'in the fervent hope that each man would grasp the sense of great danger that I know to be upon us.'

'Your words, Chiyaha-san, kept intruding on my sleep,' Ōmori responded as he waited for what he knew would be an unfolding.

Chiyaha sipped tea.

'Have you ever imagined, Ōmori-san,' he said softly, 'what would happen if Japan stopped, even for a short time, buying the Treasury Bills of the United States?'

Shigeru Ōmori's lips pursed as he weighed the question.

'Financial chaos in America,' he replied eventually.

'Yes,' Chiyaha nodded, 'certainly. And how would such chaos manifest itself?'

Ōmori drew in his breath.

'The yen would soar, the dollar would collapse,' he replied.

'Yes, yes.'

'US bonds would fall apart.'

'Yes.'

Ōmori screwed up his face like a schoolboy in class under Chiyaha's expectant stare.

'Precious metals would go through the roof,' he said.

'*Yes!*'

Chiyaha rocked himself back and forth.

'Gold, silver,' he said quietly. 'And platinum. The whole world would scramble for them in a panic never before seen.'

'But . . .' Ōmori began and licked his lips cautiously, 'why would Japan ever make such a move, Chiyaha-san?'

'In the event of a great confrontation between Japan and the United States,' replied Chiyaha simply.

'Such a . . . confrontation is hard to see, Chiyaha-san,' said Ōmori, his handsome face set in a puzzle.

Chiyaha spoke: 'It is the old promise of the Socialist party that when elected they would banish all US troops from Japanese soil,' he said quietly. 'When that promise is fulfilled, a confrontation with the US will certainly arise and chaos will follow.'

The oyabun of Yokohama was frowning deeply.

'You are talking about Japan suspending the Security Treaty with America?' he asked. 'What would cause the Socialists to take such an action?'

'An outrage by the US on Japan's pride,' whispered Chiyaha, burning. 'That is all that is needed for the Socialists to fulfil their promise, for Japan to stop buying the debt of the US and for platinum to soar to the moon.'

At 4.30 a.m., Kanji Egusa had already breakfasted on pickles, seaweeds and green tea and flanked by three kobun was making his way down the corridor towards Chiyaha's suite.

Egusa fretted over the split that was developing. The yakuza would divide on any vote into the supporters of Chiyaha and those of Kazuhiro Kasumi respectively. But which to support? To openly support Chiyaha Egusa risked making an enemy of Kasumi, the most powerful oyabun of the old school. Egusa licked his lips as one of his kobun knocked on the door. Why had Chiyaha asked for a meeting at such an early hour? How would Chiyaha try to compromise Egusa? Kanji Egusa felt himself at the top of a slippery slope and wished he had stayed at home in Nagoya.

The door swung in. Egusa saw Ō-Otoko, the Kobe giant, standing to one side, his hand in the pocket of his coat.

'Irasshaimase, Egusa-san,' said Chiyaha, rising and bowing low. 'You are most welcome.'

'Ohayō gozaimasu, Chiyaha-san,' responded Kanji Egusa, returning the courtesy.

As both men sat on cushions, a lacquer tray with tiny cups and a teapot was brought, and little bowls of rice crackers and miso biscuits.

'I have always valued your skills in the world of money,' Chiyaha began. 'I would be most honoured if you would do me the favour of sharing your experience with me so that later, when I put my thoughts to our brother yakuza, I can do so with the comfort of your expertise.'

'My limited knowledge is at your disposal,' said Kanji Egusa warily.

Chiyaha took out a folder.

'Here is the target,' he said.

For twenty minutes Chiyaha explained and Egusa, warming to his role, responded.

'It could be done most cleverly,' said Egusa with enthusiasm. 'First, we sell the underlying metal; then, we buy the stock. But the limiting factor Chiyaha-san, apart from the reason that will make these metals rise – a reason you have not yet shared with me – the limiting factor is a man.'

Chiyaha raised his eyebrows.

'Someone has got to be in place,' Egusa nodded vigorously. 'Someone who knows Wall Street and markets and how the gaijin work, someone on the spot who can implement the strategy I have just outlined. But where you find such a man . . .'

Chiyaha had taken a quarto sized photograph from a file and placed it on the table. Egusa had to blink to hide his surprise.

'You recognize him?' Chiyaha smiled.

'Ahh, yes,' Egusa replied and swallowed.

The subject had a domed head which was bald back to halfway, wore heavy-rimmed spectacles and had a tight, banker's face.

'He has the credentials you describe,' Chiyaha observed.

'Ahh, yes,' Egusa agreed, 'but . . .'

Chiyaha's head came forward.

20

'Is he still on the files of the police, the omawari?'

Egusa licked his dry lips as he tried to wonder how Chiyaha had come into such information.

'Probably,' he replied, 'but the charges were not pursued. The files will be cold.'

'The basis of your loans to him?'

'Five points over the average, overnight, Tokyo interbank rate,' replied Egusa in despair. 'He lends on at anything up to five years – but my loans to him are repayable on demand.'

'Demand,' said Chiyaha, savouring the word.

'Please, Chiyaha-san,' sputtered Egusa as he felt control of events slipping fast, 'this man has taken years to develop . . .'

'And I want to respectfully ask that you free him to work for our new consensus,' Chiyaha said, adding, 'after all, your loan terms to him will make it impossible for him to refuse.'

Kanji Egusa's hand went to his forehead in a gesture of difficulty.

'You appreciate, Chiyaha-san, that someone like this represents a valuable asset,' he said. 'To transfer him, to sell his debt as it were, is a serious transaction – I would only sell such an asset were it to help an ally – or future ally.'

Chiyaha smiled coldly.

'By transferring the person in question so that he can work for the greater good, you will have made me your closest ally, Egusa-san,' he said.

Kanji Egusa knew he was beaten; he decided that a quick decision would enhance his position with Rokuo Chiyaha.

'Then, in that case, there is no problem,' he said importantly. He took out a pen and scribbled down a figure.

'I assume you wish to make a provision for interest unpaid,' Chiyaha said.

'The provision is already made in the sum mentioned,' bowed Kanji Egusa and licked his lips.

At six, O-Otoko came to Chiyaha's door.

'The oyabun of Aomori has arrived,' the big man announced.

Ichirō Abe entered cautiously. As two of his kobun remained in the outer room, he slipped off his shoes, exchanged correct bows with Chiyaha, then crossed his legs stiffly and sank down.

21

'I know you don't like me,' Chiyaha said, businesslike. 'If it helps you to appreciate the way I work, please understand that I have no such feelings about you.'

'What do you want of me, Chiyaha?' asked Abe hoarsely. 'Why have you brought us all together here? Why have you asked to see me alone?'

'I want you to know how much I value your support, Abe-san,' Chiyaha said. 'The oyabun respect you as an elder. Last night they were following your lead – later this morning they will again be swayed by what you say.'

Ichirō Abe's lips drew back so that all his gums were revealed.

'I have not come here to listen to your attempts at flattery, Chiyaha-san. If you think I'm going to support you in some scheme which sees you ending up with power at my expense, then forget it. I am not alone in that view. Kasumi-san is a more powerful man than I, and he hates the very loins that bred you.'

Chiyaha closed his eyes briefly and swallowed the deep insult. He heard the steady noise of a ticking clock.

'I have a favour to ask you,' he resumed.

At Chiyaha's signal, Ō-Otoko activated a television screen. She was at most fifteen and sat on the side of a bed, dressed in a white kimono. Her face on the screen combined innocence and sexual knowing. Her raven hair slicked over one shoulder, a blend of child and whore, she sat with one foot on her knee examining her bare toe, a cigarette in her lips. A man appeared. Also kimono clad, he was fit looking, caucasian, mid-fifties. The kimono failed to cover his big chest from which great sproutings of blond hair sprang. He carried a doll in his hands and when he reached the bed, he slowly went down on his knees and presented it to her. The girl took the doll in both hands and smiled radiantly. The man had begun to kiss her feet. With a childish lack of ceremony, she propped some pillows behind her, pulled the knot which held her obi, then as the two sides of the kimono fell apart like curtains, she took her cigarette from her mouth and lay back, stroking the doll. Her body was as beautiful as her face: long and teenage and freshly supple with replete, rose-tipped breasts.

22

'I need the man, Abe-san,' said Chiyaha. 'She owns him, that is obvious; thus, I need to own her.'

'You are mad!' old Abe sneered, his eyes spilling venom. 'You think I would hand you the highest paid whore in Tokyo, no matter what you needed? No matter how much you paid? Never. I said it last night: you've wasted my time.'

The old man made to get up, but Chiyaha was in no hurry.

'I have often asked myself, how does an oyabun as venerable as Abe-san leave his mark on history?' he said quietly. 'Through his wealth? Through his reputation? No, I suddenly realized, Abe-san will be remembered through his family, through his children . . . and his grandchildren.'

Ichirō Abe's eyes narrowed at the first scent of danger; he crouched, one knee beneath him.

'I congratulate you, Abe-san,' Chiyaha went on. 'Yours is a family to be proud of. Your grandchildren who impress me most are the twin boys and little girl of your daughter, Yumi, yes, the one who lives in Fukuoka and who has, understandably, changed her maiden name from Abe to Yoshida to avoid being linked to yakuza.'

Abe's mouth went slack.

'The twins are my favourites,' Chiyaha said. 'So manly, even at eight, the way they catch the school bus every morning at the corner of Kiyose-dori. And they're so glad to see their old grandfather, Ichirō-chan when he arrives in Fukuoka from wherever it is he lives.'

'Chiyaha . . .'

Ichirō Abe had long since lost the ability to bluff his way through a major shock. Now he looked like any other old man short of breath.

'I just wanted to make it clear how much I value your support, Abe-san,' Chiyaha said.

*   *   *

The farmhouse was on the side of a sloping valley, overlooking a marshy river delta that most of the original inhabitants had forsaken over the last twenty-five years for the comforts of industrial Miyazaki.

The old peasant woman saw the ad. Not that she read newspapers – far from it – this one had been used to wrap the cod fillet which she had bought that morning from a hawker out of Sadowara. It was the words, *Easy Money* that caught her eye.

Easy Money . . . old car . . . no matter what condition.

'Listen to this,' she called to her husband who was feeding carp ten yards away in an irrigation channel. She read him the ad. 'You remember three days ago you passed marshland behind Tano being drained by men from Miyazaki? You told me that you came across a BMW car that had appeared in what used to be a creek.'

Her husband made a dismissive gesture.

'Oh, I just remarked on it. It's a wreck.'

'But the ad here says "no matter what condition."'

'You!' he scoffed. 'Next thing we'll be going to Tokyo in a limousine.'

'What have you to lose?' she asked indignantly. She read out the ad again. 'Are you too feeble to make a simple phone call from Sadowara?'

The old man straightened himself. She would keep this up right through the day until she got her way. She always won. He would go into Sadowara and make the call just to shut her up. When he was there he would drink two beers and pay for them out of the housekeeping account.

'Give me the paper,' he said.

*   *   *

At 8.00 a.m. Chiyaha entered the conference room. Ichirō Abe again sat at the head of the table. The old man looked haggard and drawn; he must not have slept, thought Senko Okuma.

'Last night Chiyaha-san gave us all a great appetite for his words,' said Abe heavily. 'Let the banquet begin.'

Chiyaha spoke without interruption for an hour. Halfway through his unfolding he distributed the same glossy, annual report that earlier he had shown to Kanji Egusa. It was printed in English with a translation in Japanese.

When Chiyaha had concluded, the debate began. Each man

24

had his say, some arguing with fierce passion, but those oyabun who had expected a strong contribution from Abe, father of the meeting, were disappointed.

'This plan is an outrageous blasphemy,' said Kazuhiro Kasumi hotly. 'It offends the very flesh and blood of all Japanese and besmirches the honour of our ancestors.'

'So, yakuza remain the victims of events outside their control and in order not offend some of their fellow countrymen, allow themselves to be put into penury? Is that your proposal, Kasumi-san?' asked Chiyaha.

Kazuhiro Kasumi turned to Ichirō Abe.

'You are the father of this meeting, Abe-san,' he said pointedly. 'What is your opinion?'

Ichirō Abe's eyes could not disguise his fear.

'If the . . . event will not occur on Japanese soil,' he whispered, 'then I support it.'

Senko Okuma could not believe what he was hearing; but in the presence of these city men whose presence he was coming so much to regret, he was tongue-tied.

Noon came and went. Then only Kazuhiro Kasumi was left.

'Two years ago,' he said, 'when Chiyaha-san's eye fell on a gambling franchise in Yokkaichi that had been mine since my father's time, four men were dead before he eventually settled for half and stopped the bloodshed. He is a man of boundless ambition. He will stop at nothing to extend his control over us all.'

The yakuza looked down the table at Chiyaha.

Kasumi continued: 'He lures in our money with the promise of huge dividends, but the reality is that the money required is so big that he cannot proceed alone. He talks of uniting us, but the reality is that he wishes to unite us only as party to his crime, and then as a unit with himself at its head. That can only happen if he gets us all in, otherwise his principal objective of securing power cannot succeed. He will use our resources and our wealth for his own purposes and when it suits him, he will discard us like pea shells. I will never vote for something that Chiyaha-san proposes.'

'I believe that Kasumi-san's caution is prudent,' said Kanji Egusa, avoiding Chiyaha's eye.

25

Kazuhiro Kasumi nodded vigorously.

'Everyone has had his say,' he said, addressing Abe. 'I suggest we put Chiyaha-san's plan to a vote.'

Abe looked in Chiyaha's direction.

'All decisions must be unanimous,' he said warily.

'I beg for an adjournment,' Chiyaha said.

Shigeru Ōmori stood by the window.

'We can proceed without Kasumi,' he said.

'We cannot,' Chiyaha said. 'He was right. There is so much we can borrow, but to implement the strategy in full, I need all the oyabun here behind me with their cash.' He clenched his thin fist. 'Remember earlier we spoke of platinum soaring as Japan stops the buying of US T-Bills? Now you see how it can happen, Ōmori-san! Now you see how!'

'It is a plan of genius,' Ōmori murmured.

A telephone rang in the suite. Chiyaha stared as Ō-Otoko came towards him, a triumphant expression on his face.

'Chiyaha-san,' he said as if he scarcely believed. 'Hara-san has found the car.'

Chiyaha walked along the corridor, two kobun in front, two behind and Ō-Otoko at his side. The door opened on the first knock. A wakashira-hosa of Kasumi-rengō indicated that only Chiyaha and Ō-Otoko could enter.

'Please,' the wakashira-hosa said. 'Against the wall.'

Chiyaha spreadeagled himself as Kasumi's man, expertly and none too gently, frisked him, then Ō-Otoko.

'Please,' the man said. 'Only the oyabun may go through.'

Ō-Otoko moved to protest, but Chiyaha cut him off with a gesture.

Kazuhiro Kasumi had made sure that he would feel at home in the Funagata Mountains. A large, heavy bed had been installed near the window of the room. In the alcove there was a small, Shinto altar with burning incense, comfortable cushions were dotted about, and scrolls of calligraphy hung on the walls. The oyabun of Kasumi-rengō sat in a specially raised chair from which he rose with minimum grace as Chiyaha appeared.

'Ohayō gozaimasu,' Kasumi bowed.

'Ohayō gozaimasu,' Chiyaha bowed in return.

The seating was contrived so that Chiyaha sat at Kasumi's feet. The larger oyabun sat back in his chair, relishing the moment.

'I have come humbly to beg your help,' Chiyaha began. 'Without it I can go no further.'

'Save your breath,' Kasumi said. 'My position is no different. Nothing you say or offer, or should you be foolish enough, threaten, will change my mind.'

Chiyaha took a deeply regretful breath, then he reached into his pocket and withdrew an envelope. He fanned out three photographs. The shots were head and shoulders of children, three girls aged between seven and twelve.

'Who can forget the rumours about the oyabun of Kasumi-rengō?' Chiyaha murmured.

Kasumi began to sneer.

'This little girl is Haru,' Chiyaha said, pointing to the first picture. 'She was found strangled near Urawa. She'd been raped first, of course, full penetration. Pretty little thing, isn't she?'

Kasumi's face was a mask.

'And this one is Kaori,' continued Chiyaha, going to the next photograph. 'Kaori's a real angel, you'll have to agree. Left school on a Monday, never got home. A week later she was found on a vacant lot out in Tachikawa. Smothered in sand. What monsters do these terrible things?' Chiyaha sighed. 'And finally, poor little Reiko. Everyone has heard about Reiko, haven't they? Her parents were on that programme the other night, I saw it myself. They were just begging someone to come forward and tell them what had happened to little Reiko.'

'Get out!' Kasumi roared. '*Get out!*'

Kasumi's wakashira-hosa sprang into the room, his hands around a gun.

'I will go when I am ready,' said Chiyaha dismissively. 'The biggest manhunt ever followed the disappearance of these kids, Kasumi-san. Then the police computer popped out something very interesting. Following the taking of literally thousands of statements, it emerged that a black BMW, model 323i, was seen by someone in each case. The car became the key. The whole country was alerted. Every BMW 323i ever imported into Japan was traced to its current owner – or otherwise accounted for.'

Kazuhiro Kasumi was shaking his head.

'You're bluffing, you bloodless little rat,' he sneered. 'I've been through all this with better men than you.'

'The forensic people found tiny fabric particles on the bodies of the two recovered children,' Chiyaha went on. 'In Kaori's case they said she had bled very extensively and that they were sure blood traces would still be in the car, no matter what efforts had been made to remove them.'

'You're finished, Chiyaha,' Kasumi snarled.

'Only five cars never turned up,' Chiyaha went on without concern. 'One of them belonged to none other than the renowned oyabun of Kasumi-rengō, Kazuhiro Kasumi, who reported his black BMW 323i stolen the day after the car story was broken by the Press.'

'*You're a filthy liar!*' Kasumi roared, quivering. 'The car was stolen! It was never found!'

Rokuo Chiyaha's hand went to his brow.

'Ahh, so sorry, Kasumi-san,' he said. 'I should have told you. The car has been found. Half burned, it seems, and buried in marshland just freshly drained near Miyazaki. Don't worry, nothing will happen, we've brought it safely back to Kobe.' He passed a piece of paper across to the trembling oyabun. 'Please, here is the chassis number.'

Kazuhiro Kasumi's face went from purple to deathly white. He held both arms of his chair as if, to let them go, might precipitate disaster. Chiyaha leaped up, his face inches from Kasumi's.

'I was in Sugamo prison fifteen years ago, you piece of filth,' he hissed. 'The guys who were there for doing little kids all died before their term from shitting blood.'

'Are we ready to vote?' asked Ichirō Abe.

The men around the table nodded and looked at both Chiyaha and Kasumi.

'I would first like to make a statement,' Kasumi said.

To Senko Okuma it looked as if the oyabun of Kasumi-rengō had lost weight since the morning session.

'I believe in admitting a mistake,' Kasumi said tonelessly. 'I made a mistake to mistrust Chiyaha-san. I have listened again

28

to the arguments for his fine plan and I am now happy to say that I will vote for them.'

Kanji Egusa looked at Kazuhiro Kasumi as if expecting a trap. Ichirō Abe had become a sickly grey as the significance of the moment sank home.

'Those in favour of the solution proposed by Chiyaha-san, raise your right hand,' he said shakily.

Kasumi's hand was up first. Then Chiyaha's. Ōmori's followed, then Egusa's. Abe looked coldly down the table, then his hand went slowly into the air. Only Senko Okuma was left. He took a deep breath.

'For what we are about to do, may the goddess Amaterasu forgive us,' the little mobster said and put his hand up.

Abe spoke: 'We have all agreed on a sacred solution. Now let us seal it with the traditional ritual of yakuza.'

Chiyaha withdrew a gold pin from his lapel, punctured the tip of his middle finger and squeezed a drop of his blood into a glazed cup. Each oyabun did likewise, adding his blood. When the cup again rested at Chiyaha he took a flask of sake and filled the cup to the brim.

Ichirō Abe intoned: 'The ritual of brotherhood on even terms, uniting us in our purpose to save the honourable tradition of yakuza will now commence.'

Chiyaha drank. Each oyabun followed suit till it came around to Senko Okuma. Again the little man hesitated, then he drank.

Ichirō Abe spoke: 'The sake cup ritual is now over.'

Getting to his feet, Senko Okuma led the way to double doors and pushed them open to reveal a traditional Japanese banqueting room. Okuma took the host's place as women in traditional costume appeared to serve them flasks of chilled sake, the best of the Miyagi crop. The food followed: Sendai Miso, the red, salty soup of the area, and oily Shiroshi Umen noodles, and platters of succulent oysters from Matsushima Bay.

'To our host, the oyabun of Miyagi,' proposed Shigeru Ōmori. 'That he continues as fortunate in life as we have been today in food.'

The seated yakuza toasted Senko Okuma who glowed like a pint-sized icon at the head of the table.

There was the sound of chopsticks tapping glass.

29

'To the oyabun of Kasumi-rengō,' Chiyaha said. 'His support means that we yakuza can go forward from this place together.'

Chiyaha held Kasumi's eyes and both men drank.

Fresh flasks of the excellent sake were brought. A soldier of Okuma-kai went to a raised stage at the back of the room and turned on spotlights. The oyabun broke into spontaneous applause. A karaoke machine, a musical synthesizer complete with microphone and audio-visual cue, stood centre stage, pulsing out a low beat.

'Okuma-san!' cried Ōmori. 'As host, it is proper that you go first!'

'I could not presume . . .' protested Senko Okuma.

'Okuma-san! Okuma-san!' sang out the oyabun and Senko Okuma got to his short legs and rolled up on to the stage.

The kobun worked the lights so that only the little man's face was visible. He took the mike, pressed out his choice and then began to sing.

'I left my heart . . .

In San Francisco . . .'

The oyabun sighed and clucked their tongues appreciatively. Chiyaha watched Senko Okuma's face. Chiyaha had heard the reservation spoken by the little mobster before he voted; Chiyaha had seen Okuma hesitate before he drank the sacred cup.

The last long sedan disappeared through the hotel gates and down the mountain. It was just twenty-four hours since everything had begun, and again dusk was creeping into the valleys.

The men of Senko Okuma's command were decamping. The oyabun of Miyagi had seen off each dignitary from the door; rather than return inside, he walked alone on a narrow road, high up into the mountains, hoping to clear his buzzing head. He sat on the trunk of a fallen tree, staring down into the misty void. He felt unreal. He could see himself sitting on the tree trunk, way down there, a tiny figure alone in the vastness of the world. He had drunk the sake cup, he knew. Yet would it not be even braver to follow his own instincts? To abjure any thoughts of self and to do what he thought was right? But was he right? Had not the arguments been skilfully and convincingly presented by men who knew far more than he, Senko Okuma?

Desperately, Senko looked for a sign. Sworn to secrecy, perhaps in nature he might find an ally. In the forests around there were the echoes of dripping water. Crows and pigeons flapped in branches as they began to settle for the night, and miles below, in the valley where night had already been a reality for thirty minutes, lights glowed up like beacons from the belly of a vat. All at once, Senko looked across and westwards. For the briefest moment the cloud thinned and the top half of the plunging red sun was visible. Then like the curtain in a Kabuki theatre, it was gone. Senko nodded his stout head and smiled. Suddenly he knew the answer.

He would tell Mama Yayoi; Mama Yayoi would know what to do.

Rising from the log, courage rising from the mountain into his short, thick legs, Senko began the walk downhill.

BOOK TWO

THE FISHERMAN 1996

Two

An enormous bowl: the Santa Cruz mountains its one side, the purple Diablos its other. A building, thrust up from the floor of the bowl: an indian tepee in design, eight graceful floors to a point. At the highest level of the tepee, a penthouse, it's sides tinted glass. Four men in dark suits on a sweeping leather couch beneath a vast chimney-breast of cut stone, a fifth man, standing, facing them. Air-conditioning of the near-chill variety making it difficult to believe that outside even the iguanas had made for the shade.

'In conclusion, gentlemen, we are now an ever-diversifying trading company, producing and handling raw materials and minerals on a worldwide basis.'

Freeman Oxx swept his piercing blue eyes over the four, hard faces with their East coast pallor.

'We have a growing presence in the engineering, textile and freight business in over a hundred countries. But we will always value our origins as an African mining company. Our platinum mining operation in Bamolisi, Bophuthatswana is the jewel in our crown, the foundation stone on which everything was built, and which still contributes over thirty per cent to overall earnings.'

Freeman Oxx brushed back his white hair and leaned towards the seated men.

'The future of Industrial Oxx is in your hands. You control

35

over twenty-five per cent of the equity. Of course Sun Valley's bid seems attractive: it values Industrial Oxx at over two and a half billion dollars; of course you must act in the best interests of your shareholders. But I have asked you here today to consider the other dimension. The human dimension.'

Freeman's eyes shone like night-lights through slits in canvas.

'Oxx's success is founded on the mutual trust established between myself and the Masisi people. Forty years ago pledges were given that sacred lands in and around a hill called Gotsube would never be mined – nothing in writing, just a handshake between men of honour. Now forty years later, modern geological surveys show the earth beneath Gotsube to be platinum rich. But to mine such ground would be to violate the preserve of the Masisi's ancestral spirits.'

The money men exchanged glances.

'All our representations on this matter to Sun Valley have been ignored,' Freeman continued. 'They have no intention of honouring the agreements between myself and the Masisi. Sun Valley will fully exploit the platinum beneath Gotsube and treat the Masisi's centuries old beliefs with contempt. They must be stopped.'

A banker wearing black rimmed glasses cleared his throat.

'What are your, ah, counterproposals?'

Freeman Oxx: 'With your support, to raise the cash for a counterbid that will place Oxx in trust. I'm seventy-four, I don't need the cash anymore, I don't have anyone coming after me.' He paused as if for the ringing of a bell; he resumed: 'The Masisi go on as they have done since before recorded time. The trust will be for them. But to achieve all that I need time, gentlemen. You can give me time.'

The manager of a pension fund in the top five on Wall Street spoke.

'There's less than a week to go, Freeman, and you've already thrown more delaying tactics into the works than most people ever knew existed. This is a fair bid. Maybe the Japanese will sell you the platinum business when they're in control.'

'If I thought there was a chance that would happen, would I have flown you out here to listen to an eleventh hour plea?' Freeman asked.

'You ask us for time,' spoke a grey suited, oily skinned man whose bank directly owned over two per cent of Industrial Oxx. 'You've had time to raise the finance for a counterbid but the truth is that your lead banks pulled out and your junk issue aborted. A further delay is guaranteed to achieve nothing and increases the risk that the Japs will go away.'

'Not a risk we could be accountable for,' said his pension-fund colleague.

Freeman Oxx's face was criss-crossed with lines of fatigue.

'There is more to life than assets on a balance sheet,' he said. 'I'm giving you an opportunity you'll never get again. I'm asking you to make an investment in your own souls.'

The four men looked away uncomfortably.

'Will you at least think about it?' Freeman asked.

'Sure, Freeman,' said the banker and they all stood up. 'Sure we will.'

Freeman walked them out, shook their hands and stood until the elevator doors had closed. He walked slowly back. Too old for this, much too old. If only things had worked out differently; if only the years could be rolled back. In his mind he saw the photograph of an earnest, broad shouldered boy in a 1960's news story, looking out from the dereliction of a Los Angeles slum . . .

'Goddam,' he said aloud.

'No hope, sir?'

Freeman turned. A man in his late twenties with sun-bleached Californian hair, stood attentively to one side of the fireplace.

'They want their cash,' Freeman said grimly. 'The meeting will go ahead.' He turned intently. 'Anything on the Macau shipment? Anything at all?'

Orem Williams had been Freeman Oxx's personal assistant for five years.

'I'm sorry, sir.'

Freeman punched his hand.

'Your visitors are waiting, sir,' Williams said.

Freeman closed his eyes. Too old to gamble anymore, too old to go on. He had to go on. The reason he had to go on was walking into the room.

He seemed impossibly tall. His skin was ebony black and

lustrous. His head was topped like a mountain cap with white snow. You knew immediately that his clothes – a shapeless, grey suit, a white shirt, a tie – were wrong, that his person had been conceived for the wearing of regal robes.

'Chief Tshubisi,' Freeman said, stepping forward and clasping the black man's two hands in his. 'You have made a long trip. I am honoured.'

Chief Tshubisi's face was impassive. Behind him was a younger man of equal bearing but despite his youth of lesser build.

'And your son, Stephen,' Freeman said, repeating his hand clasp. 'The boy I met last year in Bamolisi has become a man.'

They sat and Orem Williams carried a tray with small cups and a pot of coffee to them. Serving the coffee he sat to one side of Freeman.

'I am deeply sorry that your visit takes place at such an uncertain time,' said Freeman quietly.

'So it is true.'

Chief Tshubisi's voice came as from the depths of a well.

'It is true,' Freeman said. 'I cannot raise the funds for a counterbid – the people who own our stock will sell to Sun Valley. Nor can I persuade a court to block the bid. Nor can I get any assurances from the Japanese that they will not mine Gotsube.'

'And you . . . .?' the black man began.

'I cease to have any function,' Freeman answered grimly. 'I will no longer have even a key to the door of this office.'

Chief Tshubisi turned to the younger man.

'Tell Mr Freeman Oxx what you have been brought up to believe.'

'My father is the head of a proud people,' Stephen Tshubisi began. 'We have lived in Bamolisi since the beginning of time. We live and breathe the same air as our ancestors, walk the same land as did they, hunt the same animals. When my father's body dies, his spirit will continue to live in Gotsube where it will walk every day with the spirits of his father and with my spirit when my body dies, and my son's spirit, we all will walk and hunt and live with the people yet unborn. That is the way of the Masisi.'

'For ten thousand years no one has touched Gotsube,' Chief

Tshubisi said. 'Of course we will fight, but I know we will lose the fight because we lack the weapons and this will not be a war that we can understand.'

'It is possible that after the bid goes through, that the Japs will listen,' Freeman said. 'I will of course make myself available to talk to them, if required. I'm sorry I've failed you . . .'

His voice flickered like a weak candle. What use? This black man in his awkward suit had surrendered his people's rights forty years ago in exchange for a handshake and a promise. He looked at the proud face, empty of guile. In the plains and rivers of Bamolisi where men and spirits ran free there was no such thing as a hostile bid.

Chief Tshubisi spoke: 'We never spoke of failure forty years ago, Mr Oxx, you and I.'

Freeman looked up. Although older than he, the chiefman was still a fighter in the true warrior mould. His words might have been spoken in the recent past by someone Freeman knew very well – the legendary Freeman Oxx, the man who, with his own hands had taken raw earth and built it into something proud; Freeman Oxx, the warrior, who would have lined up fifty of the grey bankers who had just left the room and floored them all with a single blow! The photograph of the boy intruded on his mind's eye again.

'Chief Tshubisi,' Freeman heard himself say, 'you may go home with an easy heart.'

Williams's face began to screw up in disbelief.

'Industrial Oxx will not fall into the hands of men who will defile Gotsube,' Freeman was saying. 'I will not let that happen. I will go to New York. Somehow I will succeed. The mines in Bamolisi will be worked only as you and I agreed; and the unborn generations of the Masisi may sleep in peace. You have my word.'

The face of the black chiefman shone; he turned to his son with an expression justifying their twelve thousand mile odyssey, then got to his feet.

'I was not wrong,' he said. 'All those years ago I took a chance, but I was not wrong.'

Freeman stood as Williams escorted the two men out. The distant Diablos looked near enough to reach out and touch. Williams, as he came back from the door, was a study in doubt.

39

Freeman spoke each word in a voice Williams had not heard before.

'I've got to find who sold that platinum and I know of only one man in the world who can do it.'

He's losing his grip, Williams thought.

'Sir?'

Freeman whirled. 'Find Ross,' he snapped. 'I don't care how you do it or how much it costs. Find him and bring him here.'

'Jesus, sir,' said Williams in a rare lapse of protocol, 'where do I start?'

'Probably in hell,' said Freeman, turning once more to stare at his mountains.

*   *   *

'*Magee!*'

The skipper's voice sang through the Grand Banks fog like a cheese-wire.

'*Any minute now!*'

Ross Magee half turned and stuck his thumb up at the dim wheelhouse. Three feet away, luminous green net was winching in over the stern. Where the top and bottom of the mesh met the boat, two arc lights picked out the white-bellied cod, hopping back into the submerged cod-end. The *Isobelle* pitched beneath him. He rode the swell, solid and broad as the cross-beam of her mast. Nodules of ice formed on his eyebrows and six-day beard, black like his knitted cozy. Black hair licked over his collar. His grey eyes which probed the fog were weather-beaten cracks, his skin charred and chaffed by salt and wind. He looked older than thirty-five. His yellow oilskins were smeared with scales and blood of fish whose gills had snagged a mesh. He blinked; six days since Lunenburg with only snatches of sleep.

It didn't matter. Sleep didn't come easy any more.

The *Isobelle's* engine groaned as the weight-angle of the catch became acute. Ross could hear the radio chatter over the skipper's tannoy, other French-Canadian boats swapping positions and details of the night's catch. A gaping cod with the eye of a cow trundled upwards in the mesh: Ross tore it out with his

40

gloved hand and flung it forward into the open hold. The boat's engine screamed and the head of the cod-end broke the surface.

'*Fais attention!*' rasped the skipper, lapsing into his first language.

The swell was rolling the hundred-foot *Isobelle* as Jean-Claude swung the derrick aft. P'tit Pol from Quebec rode every movement with the reflexes of thirty years; he stood beside the hold, a flat shovel in his hands. Grabbing the hook from the derrick, Ross took it out over the stern.

The skipper watched the big man balance precariously on twenty tons of heaving fish and slip the hook into the steel sleeve. Who was he, Ross Magee? An American, that was all the skipper knew. An American who had showed up two and a half years ago. Who spoke little but who worked harder than two men and who knew the sea. From whom was he hiding? The skipper shrugged. What did it matter? Many men came into the Newfoundland fog to hide. The skipper caught his breath as the *Isobelle* pitched violently to starboard. He swung the wheel instinctively to bring her more head-on, then let his breath out in a long hiss as the big figure hopped nimbly back on deck.

'*Espece du con!*' the skipper swore over the tannoy and saw P'tit Pol look at Ross then grin up through the fog at the wheelhouse like a hamster showing off its dentures.

Ross watched rivers of water cascade back into the North Atlantic as the cod-end come slowly up: fifteen tons of big-eyed cod, many already dead from the pressure change in their last ascent. He leaned against another roll. Jean-Claude began to swing the cod-end, a water-spewing black mass the size of a truck, towards the hold. P'tit Pol yawned; the little deck hand had played poker all night with Xavier, the galley cook.

Already, three hundred tons of half-frozen cod came up to within fifteen feet of the hold's lip. The cod-end swung across the afterdeck; the skipper gave a little thrust to bring them around. The radio chattered, a comforting fixed-point in a foghound world. Quivering, the cod-end hung over the dark mouth, Ross and P'tit Pol either side. Ross had unlashed a six-foot steel bar from the gunwale. He crouched, readied, and struck the release-pin at the exact moment that the *Isobelle* was caught square-on. She lurched crazily, her bows shooting skew-ways for the blind sky. Ross tumbled on his back as the thousands of fish poured hold-wards. The boat righted. Ross pulled himself up. The limp cod-end stood dripping over the dark hold, but P'tit Pol had vanished.

Ross vaulted in. The skipper was screaming '*merde!*' It was pitch black in the hold as Ross sprawled lengthways, fish kicking beneath him. He tried to judge from a look up at the hatch frame where the little deck hand might have fallen in; anxious faces appeared, blotting out the brightness.

'Light!' Ross shouted. 'Get me light!'

He began to dig feverishly. There would be some air, but not much. He dug, flinging fish either side of him. Those fish he threw up slid back again; after ninety seconds he stood waist-deep, his big chest heaving, his eyes blinded with sweat. Jean-Claude was also in the hold. There was the sudden blinding of an arc light.

'*Ave you found 'im?*' cried the skipper over the tannoy, as the *Isobelle* pitched violently and Ross's face met cold cod. '*Magee, 'ave you found 'im?*'

'Tell him to hold the fuckin' boat steady!' Ross called up.

He filled his lungs and began to cleave deeper. His arms screamed, as did his legs, now lifting hundredweights with each further inch. He tore off the gloves: he wanted to feel. He could be going in the wrong direction and if he was then the little deck hand was dead. He felt the weight increase, but these were still fresh fish, some were alive and flapped in terror as he met them, eye to eye. As long as he was in fresh cod there was hope. Somehow he made it to within ten feet of the wall, buried in over his chest, but still moving forward. He heaved his arms upwards and dug himself another three inches down and forward. The skipper, now at the hold's lip, was screaming at him. Ross dug, hands raw and numb.

'Magee! *Tu est fou!* You are crazy!' shouted the skipper.

Just one more step to the wall. P'tit Pol was dead. Ross stretched out his left hand in a final gesture, one last probe. His blunted fingers touched something smooth. Something like an oilskin. Ross attacked. The trawler heaved and he went under, but kept going. Now he had a fistful of oilskin, now he felt thin shoulders, now he had a neck and a skull. He saw a face ashen as a cod's belly. He got one arm around P'tit Pol's chest and with a last, supreme effort burst them both upwards. He was caught, then he and P'tit Pol were pulled up to the surface of fish.

The air, though dank, seemed pure and welcome as a day in Spring. He heaved, trying to answer the demands of his heart.

'You OK, Ross?'

Ross battled to take in oxygen.

'Is he alive?' he panted.

P'tit Pol was in Jean-Claude's lap. Breathing.

'He's alive,' Jean-Claude said.

Ross lay on the mountain of fish, drained. He felt the swell beneath him; all at once he was on another boat in another place.

Misty. Lovely Misty.

Water had slapped the hull.

'Ross, are you asleep?'

He opened one sleepy eye and saw the outline of her head. It was a shape he could remember from his earliest memory; she was his perfect friend, his sister by adoption, his lover . . .

'You have the face of an angel and the body of a lion,' she smiled.

Could all those years have really passed? The lee of Nantucket; beneath a makeshift canopy; naked on the hot deck. She propped and looked down, her face freckled from sun.

'I'll bet Ashley doesn't tell you things like that,' she said.

'Come on.'

'I'm sorry.' Her head on his chest. 'She's your wife. I guess that's the way it's meant to be.'

His finger on her lips.

'Sssh.'

She brushed his hair.

'How is Wall Street?' she asked.

'It's fine, it's good. I have a good team – it's going to happen.'

'Why don't you get in touch with Freeman?' she whispered. 'I know he wants so much for you two to be close again.'

His eyes had narrowed in the hot sun.

'I will one day. When I can look him in the eye as my own man, then I will.'

43

There was a paragraph, tucked away at the end of the page like an afterthought . . .

'Ross?'

Jean-Claude was looking down in concern.

'You're exhausted. You must rest.'

Ross nodded. He allowed himself to be helped up. Suddenly, he very much wanted to sleep.

*   *   *

The office screamed bad taste: carpet of very deep pile in loud, zigzagging purple, long framed rectangular wall hangings which looked the work of a psychotic, and a central table made of glass which meant that even at conference the carpet would not go away. Incorporated into a wall was a bookcase with glass doors through which, amongst books, trophies and framed scrolls, a sculpture in gold stood out most clearly, two unambiguous testicular orbs clutched in a man's fist with, on a plague beneath, the legend: 'The Other Guy's'.

Freeman Oxx hated Wall Street. It was full of men with offices like this, men like Tyler Wrixon, head of corporate finance at Isaac Watson Securities, who had just concluded the lighting of a baton-sized cigar despite the fact that it was still only 8 a.m. Wrixon at thirty had black hair retreating behind a high forehead, a fleshy face and a deserved reputation for abrasiveness. Having reached for a document fronted in heavy, black type, he tossed it into the middle of the table.

'It's all there, Freeman. Twenty-four bucks a share, cash. Values Oxx at two point five billion.' He made a face of resignation. 'We're on auto-pilot from here in.'

Two faces turned on cue to Freeman. He saw James Lascalla, a board member of Industrial Oxx and the managing partner of Portfolio Trust, the firm's brokers on Wall Street; and he saw Rudi Meshnick, small and clever, a bearded gnome, senior partner in the firm of Bastin and Nazareth, attorneys. Neither of them was laughing.

'What you mean is, we've failed.'

'What else can we do, Freeman?' asked Lascalla, a thin man with a black, pencil-thin moustache. 'God knows, we've counter-attacked. We've appealed directly to our shareholders. You yourself have held countless meetings with the fund managers and institutions who hold the strategic stakes; you've asked them for more time; you know the score.'

'The score is that they're selling out a company that has given them a decent and steady return on their investment for over thirty years,' said Freeman heavily.

'So we're dealing with shits,' Wrixon said. 'Welcome to the world, Freeman. Nowadays "decent" and "steady" don't figure. Read "sexy" and "fast" instead. Twenty-four bucks a share for stock that even as we speak is trading at twenty-three is sexy – they want it, fast.'

Oxx looked around the table. They reminded him of the vultures in Santa Clara County, gathering around a coyote in its death-throes. He decided the vultures had more dignity.

'I look around me here and I see millions of dollars of fees,' he said tightly, 'but still, four months after the bid, none of you can even tell me who Sun Valley is.'

'Sun Valley, incorporated in New York, is a wholly owned subsidiary of Sun Valley Holdings, registered in Kobe, Japan,' said Meshnick, the lawyer, patiently. 'The chief executive in New York is Eiichi Eda whose résumé reads like a page from the Securities Exchange Commission textbook.'

'He's fronting a shell,' Freeman said. 'Tell me who's behind him. Tell me!'

'Sun Valley is owned by pension funds and trusts – we can go no further under Japanese law,' Meshnick said. 'As for your other allegations about them ...' His voice trailed off and he threw his hands in the air.

Tyler Wrixon spoke quietly with the corners of his mouth downturned: 'Even if you had counterbid they'd have raised the ante. Gerry Bacik is personally handling it for them, something that rarely happens. Reeson Rhoades have to be on two per cent. Bacik only gets into a situation like that if he's going to win.'

'Aren't you being unduly apprehensive about the Japanese plans for Bamolisi, Freeman?' asked Rudi Meshnick reasonably. 'The Japs play by different rules to us. In a hostile bid situation they're not going to give any assurances or guarantees they think may weaken their hand or restrict them when they're in control. And anyway, the Masisi tribe can always take legal action if they think their rights are being infringed.'

Freeman shook his head.

'Not worth a shit. The Supreme Court of Bophuthatswana are interested exclusively in the employment and taxes side of the issue. The Masisi won't have a chance.'

Tyler Wrixon's eyes rolled in exasperation.

'Wall Street isn't interested in witch doctors,' he said and looked at his watch. 'I'm sorry it's worked out this way, we're all sorry. We fought and lost. We tried to finance a counterbid and failed. It's time to accept the facts.'

There was a knock at the door and a woman came in. She went to Tyler Wrixon.

'Seems there's an urgent call for you, Freeman,' Wrixon said.

The secretary brought a telephone from a side table, placed it in front of Freeman, pressed a key and handed him the instrument. Four people saw his hand shake as he took it.

'Yes, Orem?'

'I've found him, sir,' said Orem Williams, two thousand miles away.

'*Good!*' Freeman stood up, jaw set. 'Now bring him home!'

'I'm not certain that . . .' Williams began, but in Wall Street, New York, Freeman had hung up.

'*You!*'

Rudi Meshnick of Bastin and Nazareth froze as Freeman levelled his index finger like a pistol.

'I'm paying you guys two million.'

The lawyer's gnome-like face was a picture as he fought to refind balance.

'Buy me more time,' Freeman said.

'Jesus, Freeman, we've done everything,' Rudi Meshnick swallowed. 'Moved your registered office to Delaware, got temporary restraining orders against Sun Valley in the chancery court there, commenced proceedings in the Federal District Court of New York, made representations to the SEC . . .'

'Give me an option, however wild,' Freeman snapped.

'Look, Freeman . . .' Wrixon began.

'Shut up, Tyler!' Freeman snarled.

46

Meshnick began to shrug reluctantly. 'Hypothetically . . . I suppose . . . if someone believed that there was . . . vital new evidence about to emerge concerning Sun Valley's SEC filing, for example, then we could go back into the Federal Court of New York, and enter affidavits testifying that we needed more time . . .'

'How long could it buy?'

'Two weeks, maybe, three at the outside, but . . .'

'Freeman!' cried Lascalla. 'As a member of the Oxx board, I must protest!'

'Let him talk!' Freeman snapped.

'. . . but we're talking perjury here,' Meshnick whined, 'the court would skin us alive, I couldn't appear on such a basis . . .'

'Add a million to your fee,' Freeman shot. 'Do it today.'

Rudi Meshnick blinked.

'This really is playing craps with good money!' Tyler Wrixon rasped. 'I want it on record that I am voting against this latest delay.'

'You don't have a vote, Tyler,' Freeman spoke. He turned to the lawyer. 'Have the necessary papers at my apartment within an hour.'

Tiny blue flints shone out at the room. Three weeks.

'Good day gentlemen.'

*   *   *

There was fog all the way home; the weather faxes coming into the wheelhouse promised more of the same for twenty-four hours. The *Isobelle* nosed into the Front Harbour in Lunenburg, leaving Battery Point to starboard. Ross stood alone near the cream bows, savouring the solitude. This was now his life and what he had earned in thirty months had gone to a shipyard in St John's, Newfoundland, downpayment on a trawler in need of much paint and attention, but whose sleek lines he could see quite clearly, riding the Atlantic swells under his hand like a little mermaid. He had found her first and beaten three others to the deal. The Credit Union in La Have had come through with a $150,000 dollar loan and in twenty-four hours Ross was meeting the Bank of Commerce for the short-term he needed to get

47

up and running. All indications were that he would take delivery as planned on May 10th. His lips cracked in a smile as he thought of the shipyard owner in St John's, the legendary Captain Belliqueux.

'You 'ave me stolen blind, Monsieur Ross, but she goes to a good 'ome, so I say "yes".'

They had shaken hands across the bows of the little mermaid that would start Ross back.

He rubbed his hand over his chin. He wanted a hot bath, a shave and a change into light fresh clothes. He wanted a home-cooked meal and a drink. He saw pier lights and the outlines of wharfage slipping by: it might have been midnight instead of twelve noon. Silent gantries reared up suddenly from swirling fog. Ross did an instant retake: Wall Street; the Twin Towers reared up at you like that on winter mornings, coming in from Staten Island. Ross winced as the old excitement surged. That was another world now. Action from another time. He closed his eyes as if the reed-like cranes poking from the fog might see him and sneer. But when he closed his eyes he could hear voices.

The voice of Henry Babbage, his attorney.

'It's true Ross.'

Ross took a step back and sat down heavily.

'I'm sorry,' Henry said gently. 'The only reason it came out is because Morales Magee are bankrupt. The million you owe to Chase has been secured all along by a secret deal on collateral provided by Freeman Oxx. The bank lose nothing.'

Ross wanted, there and then, to die.

'All along,' he whispered, 'when I thought it was me, all along it was Freeman they were looking to.'

Henry's face showed he understood emotion.

'You know banks,' he said, trying to make light of it, 'they want it on both sides and toasted too, if they can get it.'

'Jesus!' said Ross and clenched his fist so tight he thought it would burst. 'Now he's taken away every ounce of pride that I had left.'

He slowly opened his eyes; the voices subsided until all that remained was the sound of the *Isobelle's* prow whispering through the water.

They tied up alongside the factory and stripped the holds.

Immediately, giant claws began to grab out the cod into hoppers for weighing. There was a-rumbling and a-banging of a great fishing port at work. Ross shouldered his gunny sack and climbed the gangplank.

'Around ten at Le Bon Bock, if you're interested,' Xavier called.

'Maybe,' Ross called back. Ten was ten hours away. He reached the quay and looked towards the sky as the fog turned to drizzle. He roomed with an old Irishwoman off King Street, just beyond the Park, fifteen minutes by foot.

The quay felt momentarily unsteady after the *Isobelle*. He passed lorries tending trawlers, forklifts carrying fish boxes, small groups of dock hands standing, smoking. Lumps of factory ice littered the ground. He saw the red cab from the corner of his eye. It had been parked fifty yards from the factory berth; it drove diagonally across the quayside until it was beside him and a man got out. Ross kept walking. The man was everything he was not: blond, smooth-shaven and tanned in California.

'Mr Ross Magee?'

Ross kept walking, straight for the gate. They drew looks from the dock hands: the big fisherman, the clean-cut Californian and the red taxi, all moving in a line down Bluenose Drive.

'Mr Magee, I work for Mr Freeman Oxx,' said the trotting man. 'My name is Orem Williams.' He showed a card and slowed to allow Ross through.

It was raining in earnest as they walked two-a-breast past the Compass Rose.

'Can I give you a lift to wherever you're going?' asked Williams. The rain had darkened his hair and streaked his face.

'I'm busy,' Ross said and lengthened his stride.

'He just wants to see you, Ross,' said Williams. 'He wants to talk.'

'I told you I'm busy, Williams,' Ross replied. 'Now get lost.'

'It's important,' Williams said. 'Industrial Oxx is being taken over. He needs your help.'

Ross wiped his nose and mouth with the back of his hand and spat in the kerb.

As he picked up the phone, Ross's eyes were drawn to the trading room below him where removal men were at work.

'It's Mr Babbage, Ross.'

Ross could hear Henry take a deep breath.

49

'Ross, have you spoken recently with Freeman Oxx?'

'No, Henry, I have not.'

'Ross, I don't quite know how to present this, but this morning I got a call from a banker I've known for many years,' Henry said uncomfortably. 'It seems that Freeman Oxx has approached this bank, unilaterally, and that they have agreed to a five year, twelve million dollar loan to you, secured against future earnings, with you as the sole chief executive of a new setup. It sounds good. You keep your premises, your employees . . .'

Ross's fist hit the table so hard that the removal men stopped in their work and looked up.

'No, dammit!' he had hissed. 'No!'

Williams's voice cut through.

'He's sent up his plane, Ross. It's standing by with two pilots up at Halifax.'

'Get lost, Williams,' Ross repeated and jumped from the kerb into traffic on Cumberland Street, dodging across the road to blaring horns, leaving the cab marooned behind.

'Be reasonable, Ross,' Williams pleaded. 'The plane will have you back here tonight with a fresh crew, if that's what you want. Come on! He just wants to talk!'

Ross set his jaw and kept walking. The rain, now driven from the harbour by an ice-cold wind, was enough to put anyone off boats and fishing ports for life. In his mind's eye he saw the paragraph on the bottom of the page, all too easy to have missed. The taxi had caught them again and coasted level, splashing water on Williams's legs.

'What are you afraid of, Magee?' asked Williams, changing tone. 'You think you can hide up for ever in this shithole? You think the United States is waiting on the edge of it's chair for the great Ross Magee to make his move? I've got news for you mister, you're nobody anymore, so if you're worrying what people think, then quit worrying. They forgot you existed the day you ran away.'

Ross's mouth turned down in distaste. He turned off King Street and took the first left. The lodging house was twenty yards from the corner. He took a key, walked up six steps and opened the front door. Williams was right behind him.

'Ross!'

'Sorry, not available,' said Ross shortly.

'He said to give you this.'

Williams thrust a white envelope at Ross, then threw it over his shoulder into the narrow hallway behind.

'Ross, this is going to cost me my job,' said Williams forlornly.

'Go to hell,' Ross snarled and slammed the door.

Restless Ross plunged backwards and underneath the steaming water. He rose and lathered his chin, kneading cream into his beard. His body glowed in the hot water; black chest and loin hair floated up like dark, silken weed. He began to draw the cutthroat across his jaw, feeling the beard lift, little by little. He heard Henry Babbage speaking again.

'Mr Ross Magee has authorized me to say on his behalf that despite the fact that he has no personal, legal liability to any creditor here, he will issue personal notes guaranteeing the repayment of all amounts up to twelve million dollars.'

An outburst of disbelieving laughter.

'Will these notes carry coupons?'

Further laughter and cries in the overfilled hall.

'Mr Magee is acting contrary to my advice!' shouted Henry Babbage over the uproar. 'My counsel to him has been that he is no way responsible for the collapse of Morales Magee and that he should not feel obliged to pay anyone a red cent!'

Goddamn it.

Ross dashed water on his face.

'Mr Magee.'

There was a knock.

'Your meal.'

'Five minutes,' he said and knifed out. He towelled himself quickly, wrapped the towel around his waist and padded down the corridor. In the bedroom with the floral wallpaper, the corner basin and the bed with the bulging eiderdown, he parted the lace curtains. The lights and dusk and fog were scenes from Dickens, except for the red roof of the cab. Ross lay back, his hands behind his head on the pillow.

There were silk green sheets on her bed, green for her eyes.

'Why not take what he can give?' she wept.

The tears in her eyes made the green in them change colour like the green in a misty sea.

51

'*From as far back as I can remember,*' he whispered, looking at her face so as to never forget it, '*everyday, he took away a little more of my pride. I thought that in New York I had escaped, but I was wrong. He secured the bank without whom I could never have started. He now wants to bail me out and set me up again.*' He caught her hands. '*I can't be owned, Misty!*'

'*You have spent your whole life running away from him because you are too proud to admit that everything you have is due to his kindness,*' she said miserably. '*Are you now going to run again? Away from him? From me?*'

'*I'll come back for you,*' he had said. '*I swear that.*'

On the bed, the ripped envelope and it's single sheet of paper lay where he had left them. The words were strung out across the otherwise blank page. They read:

'*If not for me, then for Misty.*'

Ross threw away the towel and began to button on a clean, white shirt. He dressed quickly and went downstairs to eat.

The Nova Scotia sky was wallowing in its trough between the night and the coming of the dawn. Lights through the barred cellar window clutched up like the fingers of a desperate hand at the sidewalk.

Inside, there wasn't any air to talk of, just a haze of smoke and sweat and stale beer. Ross skimmed the five cards from the table and gently nudged out a corner of each. Four warm hearts pouted at him; the lone spade was like a dog turd in a harem.

'*Oui.*'

Xavier had won when it mattered most; mounds of dollar bills cluttered the table in front of him and the floor space around his chair. Now he made a point of counting out the pot.

'*Quatres milles,*' he said, 'she'll hold four thousand,' and he added a wad of dollar bills to the $8,000 in the centre.

'Oh-la-la,' said a big bellied man from St John's with the name of Pot de Vin. Nevertheless, he pitched in.

'*Non.*'

'*Non.*'

One by one they dropped out. Even Jean-Claude couldn't find the courage at this late hour.

'Ross?'

Ross's cheek muscles tensed in and out. Seven thousand in cash left. He'd been up twelve at one stage. Light years ago. This was the big hand.

'I'll play.'

Xavier was dealing. *'Les cartes pour messieurs.'*

'One,' said Pot de Vin.

Two pairs, thought Ross, Pot de Vin would never bet four grand on a broken hand. Pot de Vin was sane.

'One,' said Ross, discarding the spade and sweeping the new card in behind the others.

'I'll play these,' said Xavier with the air of a man forced to do his duty.

Ross's heart thudded as he squeezed the edge of his bought card out: another red-tongued kiss flirted at him. His face was a mask. Pot de Vin was beaten now. Even if the fat man had filled his house, Ross's flush would still win. That left Xavier. No cards bought, could be a bluff, but probably meant a full hand. A flush? Maybe, but Ross's flush was ace high, so the likelihood was . . .

'I'll bet five thousand,' Xavier said in English.

Pot de Vin took all of a second to decide: he threw down his cards and relit a soggy cheroot.

Ross studied the ship's cook's face: Xavier was giving nothing away. The odds were either on a flush or a straight – or a full house, now that Pot de Vin had faded. Ross scribbled a note on a scrap of paper for $2,000 . . . and tossed it with $3,000 cash into the pot.

'Seen.'

Xavier turned up his cards and fanned them out like a fairground magician.

'Four eights,' he beamed. 'Dealt cold.'

The other players looked at Ross. He shook his head and threw his hand in, face-down.

'Not good enough,' he said. He took a deep breath. 'Thanks, fellows. Good night.'

Up the cold steps and outside, Lunenburg had begun to gear up for another day. A yellow sun was lighting up the sky somewhere out over the Labrador Sea; the wind had gone about and taken the rain and fog with it. He felt empty of everything. His limbs might still have been wading through tons of fish, they were so leaden, so uninspired. He needed sleep but as always that would be difficult. Crossing diagonally he caught a glimpse of his face in the glass of a shopfront; at that moment a ship's hooter blasted from somewhere out beyond Kaulback Head.

Twenty years melted instantly. A soft knocking at his cabin door. It was past midnight, way past the time that Freeman had said they should be asleep. He was tired but he couldn't sleep. They'd waterskied all day and he could still see Misty's body, glistening with water, the first time he'd really noticed . . .

The knocking again, urgent.

'Who is it?'

'It's Misty.'

'What do you want?'

'Let me in.'

He slipped out of the bunk and unlocked the door; Freeman's master cabin was at the other side of the galley; Ross was scared he would hear.

'What do you want?' he asked again, but this time something was stuck in his throat. She was wearing a T-shirt and bikini bottoms just like she had worn that day. He felt himself surge in the darkness.

'What do you want?'

She laughed. 'I saw you looking at me today, don't pretend you weren't.' She caught him in her hand and pressed him back on the bed. 'I was right, wasn't I?' she whispered.

She began to lick his chest.

'Jesus, you're gorgeous,' she said. 'Every girl on this yacht would eat you without a fork.'

'Misty . . .'

She went astride him and sank down, infinitely slowly. Suddenly he lost all control and was pumping with madness. She had to bend down and cover his mouth with both hands to stop Freeman hearing his cries.

Later, she sat on the side of the bed, running her hands through his hair, but Ross's eyes were somewhere else.

'You're a strange guy for thirteen,' she said. 'Tell me, what do you want from life?'

54

'I dunno . . . to be myself.'

'Meaning?'

'Oh, nothing.'

'Come on, Ross! That statement meant something. What's the matter?'

For the second time in minutes he could not stop himself.

'I want to be myself,' he blurted, 'not someone picked by Freeman Oxx from a photograph in a news magazine.'

'He gave you everything when he fostered you,' she whispered. 'Is that not enough?'

'No!' he cried. 'It's not enough!'

She looked at him, her face screwed up in puzzlement.

'You can't just take and accept, can you?,' she said. 'You're a person whose pride won't let him do that. You need to feel you've given him something in return when all he wants is your love. Why don't you give him that?'

Ross turned his head away.

'I hope someday there'll be something you can give him,' she had quietly said.

At that moment the hooter of a boat had sounded so near that she had grabbed and clung to him as if to life itself.

Ross walked without turning around to see who he knew would be there. At Bluenose Drive he watched the cold tide lap upwards over the green, slime-covered jetty piers. Suddenly, like a hot knife, he recalled the lost paragraph.

'Daughter of well known millionaire . . . Died instantly when her car . . .'

In his chest a screw was turning.

'Ross.'

He closed his eyes.

'He just needs to talk,' Williams said.

Ross turned around. He knew that the years had so conditioned him that now his reflex, even to thoughts of the old man, was to turn away. The old man was cunning. He could own you even when you didn't know he was around, as the bank episode in New York three years ago had shown. He gave, gave, and he took away your pride. But what if Williams was telling the truth? What if Freeman really did need him?

I hope someday there'll be something you can give him.

Freeman Oxx didn't *need* Ross, or anyone. Ross saw him as he always had: impregnable, a powerhouse of wealth and strength that no one could topple, powerful and all-giving. But what if Williams was for real? It could be a trick . . .

If not for me, then for Misty.

Ross focused. Williams looked exactly as he had eighteen hours ago: his face, his white shirt, his smoothly tanned face were as neat as a graduation photograph.

'Ross . . .'

'On two conditions,' Ross said suddenly.

Williams nodded eagerly.

'First, that at nine o'clock, somebody calls Harry Warren, the manager of the Bank of Commerce here, and tells him I can't make it in today,' Ross said.

'No problem,' Williams responded. 'I'll set it up.'

'And second that we take a lot of very good strong coffee on board,' Ross said.

'You got it,' Williams grinned.

They walked together in the brightening morning towards the town hall where there was always a cab to be found. He felt a weight lift off his chest. Pride was a funny thing.

Three

The G-VI caught a tailwind over the Great Lakes and touched down in San José Municipal Airport at ten in the morning Pacific time. Ross had eaten and tried to sleep; for the last hour of the journey he had read from a thick file. They opened the door in California and as he squinted through the warm dancing air at the purple Diablos, he suddenly realized he had come home.

North on 101. Glistening San Francisco Bay to the west, as different from the sea Ross had left as a turtle from a Nova Scotia crab. The headquarters of Industrial Oxx came into view and Ross thought of the time he had come here as a child, with Misty in Freeman's limousine, watching in awe as the giant girders of the massive triangular skeleton were manoeuvred into place.

Freeman's familiar voice.

'This will be yours one day, laddy.'

'I don't want it.'

Even the driver had turned round in surprise. Freeman managed to laugh, but there had been anger in his eyes, blue flames in blue ice.

They walked through the cool, marble-floored atrium to the elevator removed from the others. Williams inserted a plastic card and the doors of the car glided open: the brass rail, the hand-tooled leather on the walls, the prints of old coaching scenes from England.

'Does he still work a sixteen hour day?'

Williams's small smile could have meant anything. Out into a small lobby.

'Go right through, he's expecting you,' Williams said.

Ceiling-to-floor doors swung inwards to reveal the inside of a tinted glass pyramid. The air conditioning hit Ross in the face like a cold douche.

'Hello, Ross.'

Shirtsleeves half-rolled showing forearms bushy with blond-white hair; but less fullness across the chest, Ross thought; and an extra veil of age over the face since the five years they had last met, a single brushstroke of advancing time, not dramatic but none the less apparent. Neither had Ross fully remembered how much bigger and broader he was than the old man. We have both changed.

Ross nodded. 'Freeman.'

They stood there, metres apart, each man taking up the part last played, neither willing to be the first to give. Freeman came slowly forward, his hand out. Ross shook it briefly and felt the iron still there, like a blacksmith.

'They look after you on the plane?'

'Sure.'

Ross saw the blue flames in their beds of blue ice. Were these the eyes he didn't trust? Had his love for Misty now lulled him into lowering his guard?

'Good,' Freeman said and led the way to the leather couch beneath the chimney-breast. The burnished copper table was as Ross remembered; as were the vivid tapestries overhanging the cut stone.

'I'm sorry about Misty,' Ross said. 'I should have called. Or written.'

Freeman scanned Ross's face.

'A waste of a life.'

'What happened?'

'A drunk ran her off the road.' Freeman's face was expression-less, his eyes almost invisible. 'End of the line. That's vanity for you. Funny thing is, I thought things might have worked out different, even though you married someone else.'

Ross felt a jolt. He knew about us. He's always known.

Freeman asked: 'Ashley . . .?'

'We split three years ago.'

The two men assessed each other in the cramped silence.

'That whole business on Wall Street – it can't have been easy,' Freeman said eventually. 'I tried to keep in touch . . .'

'I haven't always been easy to find,' Ross replied.

Freeman made to say something, then changed his mind.

'You read the file?' he asked.

Ross nodded. 'What happened? Your shareholders were due to vote two days ago.'

'I paid a lawyer a million dollars to go into court in New York and lie his ass off,' Freeman replied. 'I bought three more weeks – until May 17th.'

'What's the story?'

Freeman told him. 'The money is irrelevant to me. I wanted to buy the company myself and give it to the Masisi. More goddam vanity, I expect you'll say, but what the hell.'

He got up and went behind a bar where he put up two highball glasses, clinked in ice and filled them with water from a bottle. Ross watched him. So familiar this man: he had always been there: with his planes and his yachts and his women.

'We noticed someone buying stock as far back as last December,' Freeman said, putting a glass in front of Ross and sitting down. 'We forced them into the open at the end of January and two weeks later they made the bid.'

'Who are they?'

'Sun Valley is owned by a private corporation of the same name registered in Kobe, Japan. It in turn is owned by nominees. I've spent a fortune trying to find out who the beneficial owners are, but under Japanese law I can't.'

'Someone must be calling the shots,' Ross said.

'They've got a guy in New York named Eda who seems to check out fine,' Freeman said. 'He's low profile, won't talk to the media, never appears. He leaves the nuts and bolts to Reeson Rhoades, the hostile bid specialists. Their top guy is Gerry Bacik, he's running the show.'

'I know him,' Ross said.

'He's on a reputed mega retainer for this contest,' Freeman said.

59

'Why don't they reply to you about Gotsube?' Ross asked. 'They know your concern, they must realize that's the main reservation.'

'They won't reply because Gotsube is what they're after,' Freeman replied. 'They'll break Oxx up, keep the mines and double the output by mining Gotsube and everything around it.'

Ross ran his hand through his hair.

'So they want the platinum mines. Doesn't that tell you who they are?'

'That's the question I keep coming back to,' Freeman said tightly. 'They don't act like any of the Jap autocatalyst buyers we know; the big Japanese jewellers would buy a shipment of the finished product, not goddamn mines. That leaves someone who wants to buy a company that has platinum mines.'

'Could be anyone,' Ross said, watching the old man closely.

Freeman sat forward on his chair.

'As big producers of platinum, we watch the movement of platinum stocks very carefully,' he said. 'Starting last December – when Sun Valley first started to buy our shares – quantities of platinum have been shipped from Macau into New York Mercantile Exchange warehouses as deliveries against short contracts.'

Ross raised his eyebrows.

Freeman continued: 'That in itself is unusual, I don't have to tell you – someone owning platinum in the Far East would sell it over there, not bring it halfway round the world and then sell it on a futures market where very few physical deliveries ever take place. Even at four hundred and sixty dollars an ounce as the price was then.'

Ross nodded.

'How much was involved?'

'In total, more than two hundred million worth. The sale had two effects: it depressed the price of platinum, and that in turn depressed the price of platinum mining companies, including Oxx. Our shares came back from thirty bucks to twenty-four – the price the bid was made at.'

'You're saying somebody sold platinum to get it's price down, then used the proceeds to bid for a devalued Oxx?' Ross asked.

'I am,' Freeman said grimly. 'I called up a guy I know in

Macau. It took him a week and cost ten thousand dollars. Macau was simply a trans-shipment point for the platinum; a very elaborate smoke screen had been put in place to disguise the actual origin; there were dummy bills of lading, dummy invoices, the works; but the platinum came from Japan and the reason that so much trouble was taken to disguise its origins is that it had been assembled by figures in Japanese organized crime.'

You walked up four steps from the business area of the office to a small mezzanine, a curtained corner, where a table was set up for lunch. A tall black youth in a white tunic served them salads.

'This is John Mamorema,' Freeman said and Ross shook the man's hand. 'John is a Masisi over here to learn catering. Damn it he's only been here a month but he can make the best French dressing I've tasted anywhere outside Lyons.'

John Mamorema smiled broadly and offered the wooden bowl to Ross.

'Tell Ross about the bowl,' Freeman said.

'I make,' John nodded to Ross. 'For Mr Oxx.'

'He made that with his own hands,' Freeman said. 'Feel it, it's wafer thin, goddamn it.' He smiled at John who left the bowl and withdrew. 'These people are uniquely equipped. They're in touch with their past – their present *is* their past – in a way that modern man should envy, not ridicule. They have a oneness with their surroundings and with life and death which is a vital link with the natural world of a thousand years ago. Unarmed against the modern world they're going to get wiped out. It's happened in Australia and the Amazon, it'll happen in Bamolisi. We have project groups of them come over here under different headings every year. The boy you just met never wore shoes before he was fifteen. But next year two Masisi doctors will graduate from UCLA and the year after that two engineers. They'll go home to Bamolisi and we'll start to see infant mortality coming down and bridges being thrown across tributaries of the Obobo. It's their only chance. Otherwise they'll be devoured.'

Ross held the eyes. Did men really change? Was this genuine, this cry for help, or was it simply another manoeuvre from a master of the art? It was as if years ago those eyes had made Ross bleed into a dark crevice and the blood had lain there ever since, congealing. Maybe Freeman had changed; after all, Ross had.

He said: 'How are you going to stop it happening? The bid.'

Freeman pushed away his empty plate.

'If there are criminals involved, then under US law, they can be stopped taking over my company,' he said and looked at Ross intently. 'The proof is on Wall Street, Ross – but it's not my territory.'

'You've got highly paid advisors,' Ross said, ignoring the suggestion.

'They're interested in two things: money and now,' said Freeman bitterly. 'I can't trust them, any of them. Tyler Wrixon put Industrial Oxx into play in the first place, I'm sure of it.'

'What about your own board? Some of the heavyweights of American industry are in there.'

'And if this was a straightforward financial problem, then they'd be able to understand it. But take a few hundred human beings in a place called Bamolisi and a little tribal belief in an African mountain and see how far you get.'

'Your contacts in Washington?'

'I'll give you that file too. It's four inches thick. I'll also give you the correspondence with our Commercial Attaché's office in Tokyo. These people are all too busy, they don't want to know.'

Ross looked out to the foothills of the Santa Cruz mountains. He felt himself being dragged in a way that made him want to lash out.

'I can't help you,' he heard himself say. 'I can give you names of people I know, contacts, but . . . everything has changed for me. I came here because you asked me to – out of respect for Misty. I want to go back now.'

'What is it?' Freeman asked softly. 'What is it between us? What went wrong? So help me God, I don't think there was ever a moment since I fostered you that I didn't show you all the genuine love and kindness that my heart could give.'

Sunlight caught a cross-member of the giant window and exploded there.

'You gave me everything,' Ross spoke slowly, 'but you also took away my pride. No matter what you did I'll always be a ghetto kid you saw in a news story and picked up like a piece of merchandise from K-Mart. That's why I ran. You followed me to Wall Street where I wanted nothing more than to make it on my own. When I failed, you showed me up for what I was. Nobody. I look back now on those days and I want to crawl. It wasn't me they were lending money to – it was you.'

Freeman's head went forward on his chest.

'I know,' he said quietly. 'It's a little late, I guess, but now I think I understand.' The blue flames became suddenly soft. 'I never had a son. I wanted you to be everything I was, to have everything I had.' He shook his head. 'I never realized that the harder I tried, the more I was pushing you away.'

Ross heard his own voice again, strangely.

'Is this just another play to get me back here? An attempt to sabotage the boat deal you probably know I'm just completing? To get me back where you think I belong?' He looked at the older man with concern. 'You see, I don't know, I can't tell. I just can't tell.'

Freeman's voice was a desert breeze whispering over scrub and sand.

'Laddy, if you can't tell, then for just this once, let your old man tell you. It's as simple as the air we breathe. If ever a guy needed help, I need your help now.'

*   *   *

The media rarely focused on Tyler Wrixon of Isaac Watson Securities without the description: '. . . son of a cab driver from Red Hook.' The meteoric ascent of a twenty-year-old bond salesman was made all the more dramatic if mean streets were in the near background, particularly when New York art circles and United Cerebral Palsy now had new patrons in, respectively, Mr and Mrs Tyler Wrixon.

Wrixon felt lousy. He reached for a foil packet from the shelf in the bathroom adjoining his office and peeled open two tablets. Three days ago he'd gone to Mount Sinai and swallowed green shit and sat and watched as the pipes and conduits of his guts flashed on to a screen like the plans for an emerald sewage works. An ulcer, but containable with managed diet, minimal stress, and drugs. Like fuck. Gagging, he chased the tablets with water, then leaned gasping on the basin as two-edged blades nicked whole sections of his stomach away.

The curt summons to come immediately to the fortieth floor of the bank had arrived five minutes before and it meant trouble. Up to that time Wrixon had thought that Guy Kallman, the Chief Executive Officer of Isaac Watson Banking Corporation was still sailing his asshole boat in the Anadaman Sea.

Wrixon hurried from his office and down a glass-sided corridor which seemed in danger of falling into New York's afternoon traffic. A place in society's firmament cost: a $2.5 million Connecticut mansion; a lot of pictures that did nothing for him; and expenses that grew exponentially.

Patting his pocket to verify the presence of the tablets, Wrixon made his way into the main bank building and, while waiting for an elevator, concentrated on the man he was going to meet.

Guy Kallman was fifty-nine. With just six quarters to go before his retirement, his face looked from the cover of IWBC's annual report and defied anyone to better the thirty-two quarters of unbroken growth over which he had presided.

Wrixon stepped from the elevator, lit a fresh cigar and walked through to Kallman's office. Stopping at the open door he began to clap his hands.

'Hey, look at this! Look at this!' he cried. 'I got eighteen-year-old traders downstairs who don't look as good as you, Guy! Welcome home!'

Guy Kallman never moved from behind his desk.

'I got in four hours ago,' he said coldly. 'IWS is indebted to IWBC for three hundred million dollars, that's a hundred and ten million on top of what it was when I left this place. I want to know what's going on and I want to know right now.'

Wrixon set his jaw, although his face had gone white.

'What's going on is that you've got a bunch of fairies in your audit department,' he shot back, 'guys whose idea of financial rectitude is to over-provision the fuck out of every transaction they lay their eyes on. They came in two weeks ago and insisted we write down over a hundred million dollars worth of IWS business. It's a book entry. It's a joke.'

'I fail to see the humour,' said Kallman icily. 'I've looked at the provisions and give or take ten million, they'll have to stand. That means this bank has to take the whole hit on the chin for the second quarter, the first hiccup in IWBC profits for eight years.'

'You can't open two hundred investment boutiques and not bruise when the market downturns,' Wrixon said uncompromisingly. He took his cigar from his mouth and contrived to smile. 'But, look, what would you say if I told you that far from taking a hit, IWC is going to have its best ever quarter?'

Kallman stared unwaveringly.

'Go on.'

'The Industrial Oxx takeover?' Wrixon said.

'I know the deal,' Kallman said. 'Your fee has already been taken into the figures I've just read.'

Wrixon sat back.

'You know IWS has a shelf company in Liechtenstein?' he asked. 'Well, recently it went halves with some guys down in Grand Bahama in a pretty interesting position.'

Kallman went rigid as if he'd been electrocuted.

'What's that meant to mean?'

'Would you believe forty million Oxx at twenty?' Wrixon asked and put his cigar into the corner of his mouth.

'*Jesus Christ!*'

'Come on, Guy,' Wrixon wheedled. 'Look – a forty million share position in Oxx will yield a net profit of one hundred and sixty million bucks. Our share takes nearly eighty straight to our bottom line.'

'You bought the stock, then put the poor bastard into play!' Kallman gasped.

'Do you think I'd do that?' Wrixon asked with wounded pride. 'The guys in Grand Bahama are dealing with a broker in Panama and have never heard of IWS. The money to fund our part of the deal came to them from a bank account in Austria. Relax.'

'You're dirt, Tyler,' Kallman said and shook his head. He got up and walking slowly to a window which went from floor to ceiling, he looked out over deserted Wall Street.

'What else?' he asked.

'Reeson Rhoades are managing the Sun Valley bid,' Wrixon said. 'For a participation in their fee, we've agreed to underwrite a hundred million of the Sun Valley bond issue at a discount of fifteen bucks on the hundred. That exposure comes into our balance sheet at cost and we've already off-loaded over eighty million to our own customers at an average discount of fourteen and five-eighths.'

'We're meant to be representing Oxx, for Christ's sake!' Kallman cried.

'Twenty-five million gets paid over as an underwriting bonus,' said Wrixon patiently. 'Where's the fraud? If we retail out all the junk at the same discount we net another thirty-six million. That totals sixty-one, plus eighty is a hundred and forty-one million. That's before we talk about the clients we put into Oxx, clients like Mid West Star who are going to make a killing when this bid goes through, and who have promised us their entire portfolio.'

'If the SEC prove this they'll see you behind bars for five years,' Kallman said. 'Have you ever paused to think about the downside for this bank? What happens to Mid West and the others if the bid doesn't go through? What will happen to the banking business we've cultivated with them over twenty years? What's that going to cost if they pull it, you stupid son of a bitch?'

Wrixon drew in his breath.

'I deal in realities,' he said confidently. 'The Oxx bid goes through.'

'I know Freeman Oxx,' said Kallman grimly. 'Besides being a decent man, he's also smarter than you, Tyler. He'll not let you deliver him on a plate to any Japanese sons of bitches.'

*   *   *

Past the old man's shoulder Ross could see the merciless midday sun, its white heat firing the desert floor like an anvil.

'I guess it's a little late to say I'm sorry for that bank business,' said Freeman quietly.

'You don't have to apologize,' Ross said.

66

Freeman drew in his breath.

'I'm not asking you to like me – just to believe me.'

'Sure,' Ross nodded. 'Sure.'

'This is the end of a gigantic gamble,' Freeman said. 'It was a gamble to mine Bamolisi forty years ago; it was a gamble to try and make my own bid for Oxx. I've paid a million bucks for three weeks' space to try this wild shot – it's another gamble but the prize is more than money can ever buy.'

I hope someday there'll be something you can give him.

Ross looked at the creased, intense face. There was a time to take and a time to give, there had to be, otherwise men might never have left the jungle.

'I'll call the shipyard and I'll call the bank,' he said slowly. 'If the guy who's selling the boat agrees to a delay, and if the bank don't think I've lost my mind then I'll give it two weeks. After two weeks, whether I find something or not, I'm out.'

Freeman nodded his craggy head.

'A deal,' he said. 'Thank you, sincerely.'

'Thank Misty,' Ross said. 'For both of us.'

Four

It was only nine-thirty but already it was a sweltering, heat-pricking New York day, more suited to August than late April. On the cab radio someone was garboiling on about the greenhouse effect. Traffic on Broadway was nose-to-tail, bad tempered and noisy. The lights had gone down at Park Row and Broadway and a lone sweating, swearing cop was trying to cope with the endless honking, foul-mouthed torrent of cars and trucks locked in hopeless confusion all the way south to Battery Park and north to the Brooklyn Bridge.

Ross paid off the cab and walked east on Maiden Lane to William Street. Eerie. The cold phantom at the window, seeing but unseen. He'd had the same feeling the night before, standing at the big window of Oxx's south-facing penthouse on East Seventieth Street. He didn't belong here anymore, the other men and women were alien, even his shirt and tailored suit and gleaming black leather shoes were strangers.

Captain Belliqueux had nearly decided the matter.

'It's impossible, Monsieur Ross, impossible. I could 'ave sold 'er fifty times over.'

'Nothing's impossible, Captain. I just need ten days more.'

'Ten days is money lost to me, Monsieur Ross.'

'How much?'

'Fivesousant.'

'Two,' Ross had said, 'and the new closing date is May 20th.'

The money had been wired from Lunenburg to St John's.

Babbage and Kellaway, Attorneys at Law, occupied the same suite of offices in the same building on the corner of William and Pine Streets as they had on the first day Ross had come to see Henry Babbage ten years before.

'Ross Magee!'

Henry Babbage trundled from his office, hand outstretched. He was a little barrel whose white head seemed to lack a neck for joining with his body. He wore a three-piece suit in gingham check and, his trademark, a bow tie, this morning blue silk with tiny red stars.

'My God, you look so healthy!' he bubbled. He turned to the lady receptionist whom Ross remembered as a fixture of the place, a middle-aged woman with thick, curly black hair and purple spectacles framed like devil's eyebrows. 'Have you ever seen anyone looking so healthy, Miss Z?'

'Never,' confessed Miss Z pinkly.

Henry bowled along ahead of Ross and pushed open the doors to his office. There were rows of green-backed tomes and law reports, and a sweeping cluttered desk and two long tables piled high with files. Henry sat, profiled by the light from two windows.

'Find yourself somewhere to sit. As you can see, everything is the same. Now, nine-fifty; you'd like coffee.' He pressed a button on his phone. 'A coffee for Mr Magee and the usual for myself.' He looked up at Ross. 'Mrs Babbage has me on oath to drink camomile. She has her spies at every corner.'

Ross smiled. It had always been Henry and Mrs Babbage.

'It's good to see you, young fellah,' Henry said.

'I know you were mad at me,' Ross said quietly.

'To issue those personal notes?' Henry said. 'You were crazy – but I understood why you did it.'

'Thanks,' Ross said. 'That meant a lot.'

Henry made a dismissive gesture.

'It's what we're here for.' He looked up sideways. 'You over it? You took quite a lashing at the time.'

'I think so,' Ross replied. 'I won't ever forget what it is to be on the wrong side of a prosecuting attorney – or a bunch of ham-fisted cops for that matter – but I think time has helped.'

69

Pots of coffee and tea were brought in by Miss Z and served. Henry slurped his tea.

'What brings you to fat city?'

Ross told him. Henry Babbage didn't just listen, he absorbed, topping up his cup every few minutes from his teapot.

'There's quite a split in Oxx, it would seem,' Henry said at last. 'Lascalla of Portfolio Trust came out yesterday with some pretty dark things to say about the chairman. He's got two other heavyweight board members behind him: Butler of Ford and the GE's Artabiche.'

'Not for the first time Freeman finds himself in a minority of one,' Ross said.

'If I remember correctly,' Henry said, 'Freeman Oxx already has gotten himself a top level team in Bastin and Nazareth – by all accounts it took all Rudi Meshnick's courtroom skills to get the latest delay.'

'You want to know the truth?' Ross said. 'Meshnick went into court with nothing. It's a last, desperate fling of the dice.'

Henry Babbage's eyes twinkled.

'Intriguing,' he said and crossed his hands on his midriff. 'The market's puzzled, I can tell you. Oxx shares have traded down to twenty-two bucks.'

'Legally, what do we have to find to stop the Japanese?' Ross asked.

Henry made a face and put his feet up.

'You don't have much time, do you? From what you tell me and from what I recall, everything that could be done has been. Mind you, I'm not unsympathetic. These Japs come over here, buying up what they like and they could be anyone. But that doesn't answer your question. Essentially, if you can establish that their SEC filing contained material errors, that they lied, if you like, then that would be enough to cause any judge to have profound reservations. But from what I've read you'll need heavy artillery: the court is already out on a limb.'

'Say these guys were really criminals, hiding behind nominees?' Ross asked. 'Say they had manipulated down the share price of Oxx by selling platinum on NYMEX?'

'That would be very material. Japan is the main world buyer of platinum. You could claim they were going to manipulate the

70

platinum market upwards once they had bought Oxx. They'd get thrown out.' Henry scratched his ear. 'Have you thought about going to Tokyo? It might be worthwhile.'

'I'll first see what I find in New York, then I'll decide,' Ross replied.

'Have you seen the list of stockholders in Industrial Oxx?' Henry queried.

'The bigger ones.'

'Then you'll have noted that Mid West Star own nearly five per cent. Mid West fired Chase as their portfolio managers six months ago. They're being courted by half the Street, including IWS, Isaac Watson Securities. Now I wonder when that five per cent was acquired, heh?'

Ross shook his head.

'Wall Street hasn't changed. IWS are meant to be advising Oxx, but Freeman thinks they put him into play.'

'Wrixon of IWS is a particularly obnoxious human being,' Henry nodded. 'I was on the other side from him a year ago – I kept wanting to go out and shower.'

'I'm keeping well clear of him,' Ross said. 'Assuming he did the dirt, it's better he doesn't hear I'm in town.'

They stood up and walked to the door.

Ross said: 'I'd like to keep in touch if that's OK with you.'

'You don't have to ask,' said Henry brightly. 'The door here will always be open.' He paused. 'By the way, two and a half billion bucks is still big money. Big money brings out the worst in people. Be careful. I'm serious.'

'I will.'

'And as a fisherman you don't need to be reminded, if you don't fill your nets in deep water, then try the shallow. It's something I've always believed in.'

'I never knew you were a fisherman, Henry,' Ross smiled.

'One way or the other, we're all fishermen,' said Henry Babbage.

Early morning on Wall Street. A freshness in the air, flitting through the towering canyons on a little breeze from the Hudson, mingling the scents of seawater with those of the bustling city.

71

Ross turned briskly off Whitehall, entered the lobby of the building on the corner of Stone Street and took the express car to the thirty-sixth floor. The discreet wallplate hadn't changed in a year. It read: 'Cresswels – Brokers'. Ross smiled at British understatement. Cresswels were the ultimate insiders in precious metals; the firm were represented wherever gold, platinum and silver were seriously traded: London, Johannesburg, Hong Kong, Singapore and Zurich as well as in New York.

The reception area was subdued. Occasionally someone came through the doors of the trading room and Ross could see shirtsleeved figures, phones jammed between chin and shoulder, trading desks crammed with flickering monitors and electronic gadgets. There were shouted orders and executions. He'd enjoyed every minute of it: the cut and thrust, the instant calculations in different currencies. All you needed were telephones, a mind like a steel trap, and balls.

'Well, I never.'

Timothy Manners was a miniature-sized Englishman of forty-something, whose new suits, pointed nose and swept back, black moustaches all combined to give him the look of a vole who had somehow made it in the world.

'Just the other day we were talking about you,' he said in a nasal accent that had its origins in London's East End. He led the way to doors the other side of the lobby. 'Someone said you were working on a trawler somewhere. A trawler? I said. Ross Magee working on a trawler? What a lot of rubbish!'

The boardroom transmitted tones of quiet respectability at odds with Manners's appearance.

'Coffee?' he asked, depressing a button on an intercom. 'Two coffees in the boardroom.' He faced Ross, his little, blue eyes searching. 'So, how's life been treating you then, chum? Better than us, I hope. These precious metals markets are just piss awful at the moment.'

Ross shrugged. 'I'm not complaining, Tim.'

Manners looked at him.

'You haven't forgotten my offer, have you? We can always do with talent around here. Anyone who knows his arse from a pumpkin knows that the Morales Magee débâcle was all down to Jim Morales, not you.'

'Tim, I've been retained to do a one-off job,' Ross said. 'I'm looking for someone. He's Japanese and in the last few months he's sold a lot of platinum.'

Manners's mind went from rewind to fast-forward and back. Coffee was brought in and served.

'What sort of platinum?'

'Physical. Delivered here against short positions on NYMEX.'

'Quantity?'

'Four hundred thousand ounces, maybe more.'

'Worth over two hundred million,' Manners said thoughtfully. 'What's so special about the selling?'

'It's irritating my client,' Ross said. 'He has a long position in the metal but he can't work out who in Japan is selling – the Japs are buyers, after all.'

'So they are.' He looked at Ross shrewdly. 'What's the deal, chum?'

'With this seller out in the open, or better still, out of the way, my client wants to increase his position,' Ross said. 'I'll do my best to see you get the business.'

When Manners sniffed, his upper row of teeth flashed. He reached to his pocket and took out cigarettes. He offered them to Ross and lit up, head back, twin smoke trails whistling out.

'We didn't act,' he said quietly. 'On the level? We'd like to have – I can't tell you how pissy business is; really bad, believe me. Anyway, we're aware of the deliveries, of couse we are. We first thought it might be flight capital from Hong Kong ahead of the takeover there, but the word came back that we were wrong. Then we thought it might be Taiwan – but through Macau? No way. Who's left? The platinum came in all right, warehouse stocks are up at an historic high, the price has collapsed. In the end, we put it down to the Russians; you know the lengths those bastards go to to make a quiet sale.'

'You keep some pretty good files on holders of platinum,' said Ross.

Manners sniffed.

'Why not?'

Propelling himself on his chair across the room to an adjoining table, he switched on a computer and made a series of rapid entries. Rows of amber figures flashed up.

73

'Supply and demand. Mining, South Africa, Rustenburg, Lebowa, Oxx. How do I get out of this? Here we go. Platinum holdings. Press enter. Holdings by region. Far East, enter. Taiwan, Hong Kong, Burma and Laos. Bollocks. Japan. Enter. These things drive me mad. Japan, here we are, then. As you can see the Jappies are by far the biggest holders of platinum. Over five million ounces. Makes sense. They use as much of the stuff as the rest of the world put together, do our little yellow friends.'

'And their stocks are actually marginally up on last year,' Ross observed.

'Yes, which technically means their purchases for investment purposes would have had to have been up by at least four hundred thousand ounces to allow your mystery seller to make his deliveries to New York. So let's look.' Manners tapped the keyboard again. 'Japan, demand by application. Autocatalyst, electrical, glass, investment. No, mate. Their investment in large bars was actually down fifty thousand ounces for the period.'

'So where did four hundred thousand ounces come from?' asked Ross.

'You're making the assumption, from Japan,' Manners murmured and his nose twitched like a hungry mouse's. 'You sure?'

'As sure as I can be,' Ross said.

Manners let his breath out, rubbed his moustache with a finger and bared his teeth.

'It's quite probable that our figures only reflect activity on the surface,' he sniffed. 'It's the same in gold. People hoard and have done for thousands of years. Precious metals attract tax flight money as well, so taking all with all, if you insist that the metal came from Japan, then I would strongly suggest that it was undeclared. Someone is being a shit and hasn't paid their taxes in Japan, maybe. I don't know. Makes that person difficult to find.'

'The sales were made on NYMEX.'

'All right, so there are trade houses and brokers. He had to use one of them – or he may have used twenty, split the business up.' Manners shook his head. 'The information you want is in the NYMEX computer, but how you get your hands on that God only knows. They're tighter than Welsh crumpet in there.'

'I knew it wouldn't be easy,' Ross said. 'But thanks for your help.'

'Any time,' Manners said, switching off the machine. 'For what it's worth, chum, I'd put a serious question mark over the origin of your mystery seller. If he's Japanese he went to a lot of trouble, didn't he, bringing his stuff all the way to New York? No, for my money this is a Ruskie transaction. If I were you that's what I'd tell my client – who did you say it was?'

'I didn't,' Ross smiled.

'You always were a tight shit,' Manners smirked, getting to his feet and leading the way towards the lobby. 'You sure you don't want to come back and work on Wall Street again? Maybe you'd change our luck.'

'Maybe someday,' Ross said.

They shook hands.

'Let me know if you find out anything,' Manners said with a little wave.

When the elevator doors had closed, he turned back for his office. Quietly closing the door, he sat into his chair and swivelled round to the keyboard beside his desk. August platinum was $405 an ounce bid, $406 a seller. Manners sniffed. He liked New York. He was someone over here; in London he was nobody, just a boy from the East End with trading smarts. He stabbed the intercom button.

'Get me everything that's been written in the Wall Street Journal for the last three months with the word "platinum" in it,' he snapped.

'Yes, sir,' said the voice of his secretary.

'And bring me the file on Ross Magee.'

The shuttle landed in Washington National at 2.30 p.m. The cab went in over the Rochambeau Bridge, past the Jefferson Memorial and pulled up outside Coco's Palace off Thomas Circle at 3.05. A dark headed man looked up from a back table.

'I think I got it right,' said Kyle Spicer, pointing to a steaming pot on the table. 'The coffee comes from the eastern cordillera, near Bogotá. The beans were stored for at least five years before they were roasted. It's been sitting seven minutes, no more I swear to God. I haven't tasted it, but I've run my nose past a few times, and I don't think you'll be disappointed.'

They both laughed and Ross sat down.

'How do you remember these little things?'

Kyle screwed his face up.

'You join the Marines the same day as a guy, you sail with him, chew the cud night after night, you learn little things like he mainlines caffeine.'

He filled their cups with the rich aromatic coffee; Ross allowed its fumes to bathe his face before he took a mouthful.

'Wonderful.' He looked at the other man: lean, alert, light green eyes, a slightly bookish face, the correct white shirt and dark suit of a Washington career man.

'How have you been?' Ross asked.

Kyle Spicer shrugged. 'As good as ever,' he replied, tapping out a cigarette. 'The new Treasury Secretary seems like he has some vague idea of how to manage the country's finances, I flog the bonds that keep the country afloat. How are things in the Magee household?'

'The collective noun can no longer be used. Ashley and I split. My business went down the tubes nearly three years ago.'

'I heard a bit,' Kyle said, flicking alight. 'I didn't want to ask.'

'It's past history.'

'That's the only way to look at it. You can't be the victim all your life of what, I understand, was very much someone else's mistake.'

Ross raised his eyebrows. 'You heard more than a bit.'

'You can't help hearing a lot of things on the fifth floor,' Kyle said. He looked at the brown eyes. 'I visited my parents in Queens six weeks ago,' he said quietly. 'You've still good friends there, Ross. I know you took your fall hard, but you should keep in touch.'

'I will,' Ross said.

Kyle poured coffee.

'So, how is life?'

'You remember in the Marines we went fishing for a week off Newfoundland?' Ross asked. 'Can you remember the boat, about a forty footer? Well, I'm buying one ten foot longer with more across the beam.'

76

'Sounds fantastic,' Kyle said. 'I envy you. So are you here as a one-man lobby for the Newfoundland cod?'

Ross put down his cup.

'I know better than to ask a Deputy Assistant Secretary to find out something for me that's maybe off-limits. But it concerns platinum. I'm trying to find a big new seller on NYMEX who delivers against his shorts. He's Japanese.'

The light green in Kyle's eyes could give way to a harder colour when he locked on something.

'Japanese?'

'Right. Someone keeping his head down. Probably using a commission house. Sold in the high four hundreds before the price came down.'

'How big are the sales?'

'Four hundred thousand ounces, maybe more.'

'Sounds like CFTC business,' Kyle said. 'The Commodities Futures Trading Commission monitor platinum futures.'

'Would they know my seller?' Ross asked.

'Maybe, maybe not,' Kyle replied. 'No further details?'

'Just that the metal was shipped ex-Kobe, Japan,' Ross replied. 'And that it doesn't figure in statistics.'

'What's your interest?' Kyle asked.

Ross told him.

'Freeman thinks they sold platinum, then when the price of Oxx fell as a result, they put in their bid, using the money from their platinum sales,' he said. 'It's a great strategy, but if they're yakuza, we can stop it succeeding.'

'Has Oxx talked to Congress?' asked Kyle.

'He's talked to everybody,' Ross replied. 'He's even tried to get the White House to invoke an amendment called Exon-Florio: it blocks transfer of ownership in a company where strategic defence considerations are involved. No joy.'

'There was a lot of sweat here over Japan eighteen months ago,' Kyle said. 'You were a nobody in Washington if you hadn't produced half a dozen "What If?" scenarios involving the new Socialist government. What if they stop buying our bonds? What if they stop importing rice. What if they become Fortress Japan again? They should all have been called "So What?" Nothing happened.'

'What if the yakuza are moving into US corporations?' Ross asked. 'Wouldn't that send a shiver down a few spines?'

'Bet your ass. We have enough trouble trying to contain South American drug money as it is – the last thing we want is the Jap mafia.' Kyle leaned back. 'Isn't old Freeman jumping the gun just a bit? I mean, it's a great leap in the dark to connect everything as you've told me.'

'Perhaps,' Ross replied. 'When I nail down the seller of this platinum I'll be able to give you an answer. Can you make some inquiries?'

'Sure,' Kyle nodded. 'I'll feed it in and see what comes out.'

Ross smiled. 'Thanks,' he said as they stood up. 'Next week I'm probably in Tokyo, so I'll call you.'

'You remember a lawyer you once dated named Helen Torr?' asked Kyle thoughtfully.

'Of course,' Ross answered. 'She used to work for Merrill, then went to the Federal Attorney's office.'

'She left the Feds two years ago,' Kyle said. 'She now heads up the surveillance department of NYMEX, New York.'

A smile spread over Ross's face.

'I came across her name in a routine report some months back,' Kyle continued. 'It has to be the same lady.'

'How do you remember these little things?' Ross asked and they both laughed.

'I'll expect an invitation to fish northern waters again very soon,' Kyle said.

'That's easily arranged,' Ross smiled and waved as the cab drew away. 'National,' he said to the driver.

*   *   *

Moonlight swam in exquisite reflection on the surface of the lily pond. Carp occasionally broke the surface, hopeful of some morsels from Chiyaha's hand.

He sat crosslegged in his night robes, head bent. For over six months of every year he spent the nights in this place. Here were no noises except those of carps' mouth at water and his own shallow breathing. Nothing hard or sharp was heard. Or seen.

A feeling of warm comfort crept out from Chiyaha's centre. Tamon Hara had brought his oyabun good news: a youth in Osaka had been arrested for selling a small quantity of marijuana. He was far from home, this young blood – he came from the north, from Sendai, where his father was in the employ of the venerable oyabun of Miyagi, Senko Okuma. The father's distress at his son's predicament had reached Kobe. All these things were Tamon Hara's job to know.

Chiyaha watched the moon's circle in the water. Most luckily, the omawari in Osaka in charge of the case was an old friend of Chiyaha-gumi: had not his old, peasant mother been driven to the doctor every week for five years by a car supplied by Chiyaha-san? And when the officer himself found his pay packet inadequate when it came to furnishing his new apartment, had he not found that he could borrow money at rates better than any bank could offer, simply due to an introduction from Chiyaha?

Chiyaha smiled and the moon smiled back at him. The case against the boy had been dropped for lack of evidence. One favour was called in from Osaka but a great debt was now created in its place. In Sendai.

In the household of Senko Okuma.

The warmth crept right through Chiyaha and the feeling was almost as pleasant as the silence.

*   *   *

Through the window of the Second Avenue restaurant Ross could see the red and green lights of a plane, banking over the city, waiting for its slot to put down in La Guardia.

The flickering gaslights on the walls picked out flecks of grey in Helen Torr's eyes. She was mid-thirties, petite, with a small, round face, gleaming brown hair and a good figure. Ross remembered her directness best of all: Helen had always said exactly what she thought, sometimes to her cost. Perhaps it was the reason she had never married. He poured red wine into their glasses.

'Here we arc, two old traders,' he said. 'Now one's a bureaucrat and the other's a fisherman.'

79

Helen put both elbows on the table and held her glass at mouth level.

'Life is all down to key decisions,' she said. 'At the time they appear a great deal less than momentous, but a kid out of high-school decides one day, for God knows what reasons, that he wants to be a dentist and condemns himself there and then to spending the rest of his life looking into other people's mouths. Help!'

'You're trying to tell me something,' Ross said.

'You made a decision to go into partnership with Jim Morales,' Helen said candidly. 'At the time that was a good decision; what was not a good decision was to stick by him, loyally, as things got bigger and hotter, and everyone could see that the pressure was getting to the guy.'

'You're right, as usual,' he said simply. 'The road forked several times in the three years before it happened; I should have cut him out, but I didn't. If I had, I would have saved his life.'

'Do you feel guilty about that?' Helen asked.

'Sometimes,' Ross replied. 'Sad and angry more than guilty.'

Helen took out a cigarette; Ross held a candle for her to light from.

'Why are you in New York, skipper?' she asked, blowing smoke sideways.

'Would you believe it if I told you it was to see you?'

'No.'

They both smiled.

'Can you keep a secret?' Ross asked.

'It depends.'

He smiled at her, then he told her. Helen shook her head.

'Tyler Wrixon,' she said. 'I think I became a lawyer to exterminate guys like that. Youthful naïvety, of course. He now owns one of the better collections of modern art around and I'm a glorified clerk. Such is life.'

Ross topped their glasses.

Helen said: 'The link is the platinum, right skipper?'

Ross nodded. 'It was sold through NYMEX,' he said. 'I need to know a broker who has, over the last three months, made substantial deliveries of platinum against short positions.'

Helen narrowed her eyes; her small face was intense and worried.

'Can I tell you something, straight up?' she asked.

'Sure.'

'I think you were too good for this place,' Helen said. 'What's done is done and can't be changed, but I'll always think of you now as a fisherman, hauling in your nets. You were never meant for juggling fractions on telephones and making a fortune out of the illusions that Wall Street has created. You were always going to make your deal with life at the core of things.'

'Thanks,' Ross said.

'I didn't say I'd do it, skipper.'

'I didn't say I thought you would.'

Helen's smile had an edge of loneliness.

A solitary musician coaxed something sad and lonely from his sax. Ross stood on the platform at Columbus Circle, waiting for the Seventh Avenue local. The call had come through that morning at 7.15.

'Ross?'

He could hear traffic noise in the background; Helen Torr was on a payphone.

'Hi, Helen.'

'Thank you for a lovely evening.'

'It was fun,' Ross said. 'Let's do it again, but let's not wait five years.'

'Sure.' Helen had to raise her voice over the noise. 'Guess who I saw this morning on my way to work?'

Ross held his breath; this was Helen's way.

'I give up,' he said, wide awake.

'Gerry Bacik of Reeson Rhoades. Just thought you'd like to know.'

'Reeson Rhoades.'

'See you around, skipper,' Helen had said.

Ross boarded the downtown local. The broking arm of Reeson Rhoades. It was so obvious. Ross had dialled the next number from memory.

'Reesons.'

'Metals desk,' Ross said.

The transfer connection rang once and his eardrum was assailed.

'Bertolini,' shouted a voice over the background swell of a busy trading office.

'Tommy Klein,' Ross said.

'Tommy Klein don't work here anymore. He works in T-Bonds. Hold on.'

There was a series of clicks.

'Klein.'

'Tommy, this is Ross Magee.'

'Ross Magee, well I'll be damned,' Tommy Klein had said.

The doors of the car opened and closed at Thirty-fourth Street. Ross smiled. Tommy Klein. He had hired him as a runner for Morales Magee when Klein was no more than a scrawny kid of nineteen, fresh out of school and wearing ties by Hieronymous Bosch. In six months there had been the sort of transformation that only Wall Street can make happen: out went the gangling kid, in came a guy wearing worsteds and trading metals with a savvy that cannot be taught. He stayed four years, then took the top metals job at Reeson Rhoades. He went with Ross's blessing. They'd drunk a lot of beer that weekend.

Ross got off at Chambers Street and came up into the noonday sunshine of downtown Manhattan. He walked uptown on West Broadway, feeling apprehensive: a one-to-one with Timothy Manners was one thing; lunch in Riki's Napoli Café was another.

Riki's, set in the surrounding dereliction of West Broadway, was a marble-floored, Art-Deco luncheon haunt of midtown real estate men and Wall Street brokers who made the trip into wasteland to savour the mixture of 'fifties nostalgia and arrested decay. Tommy Klein was late. Ross stood at the counter with a Vermouth and Perrier. The place was filling up; the neon lights of the jukebox flashed in rhythm to something by Buddy Holly. Maybe Freeman had been right, maybe you always had to confront the thing that's chasing you or it never goes away. Had he finally confronted the spectre that hung over his relationship with Freeman? Would he and Freeman ever be as friends? Deep down Ross was sure both of them wanted it to happen. He sighed. He had made the effort, but now he felt nothing but doubt.

In the bar mirror Ross saw a face; then he heard a voice.

'"I am the resurrection and the life".'

The broker's name was Grattan Ellis; Morales Magee's failure had cost his firm $20,000.

Ross turned and nodded. 'Grattan.'

'"Mary, the mother of Jesus, went to the tomb on the third day",' Ellis intoned.

Ross could smell bourbon on the man's breath.

'"But lo! The stone had been rolled back and in the entrance she saw a wondrous angel!"'

'Go fuck yourself, Ellis,' Ross said.

The broker's eyes were venomous.

'What are you doing in here, Magee?' he asked in a stage voice. 'This place is for folks who work for their living, not screw others for it.'

Ross could see people's faces at nearby tables.

'I don't go for all this shit about Jim Morales being the fall-guy,' Ellis hissed. 'Anymore than I go for your sanctimonious little address to the creditors get-together three years ago.'

Ross faced the counter.

'The only person connected with you who showed any taste was your old lady,' said Ellis at Ross's ear. 'She left you.'

Ross slammed back his elbow jack-hammer-like. It's point caught Ellis at the apex of his stomach and folded him noiselessly double, just as Tommy Klein, fedora in hand, walked into Riki's unusually quiet Napoli Café.

Ross took him by the elbow, turned him around and walked him back on to the street.

'Come on,' he said. 'This place is right out of pastrami.'

'What happened?' cried Tommy Klein as he was steered down West Broadway. He was short and stout and wore a double-breasted seersucker. 'I had a table reservation.'

Ross stopped at red lights.

'I need clean air these days, Tommy,' he said.

Tommy Klein repositioned his hat on his head. He had deep brown eyes set in a smooth, babyish face, and when he smiled an endearing, crooked grin.

83

'It was my fault for choosin' Riki's,' he smiled, then clapped Ross's arm. 'Who gives a fuck, eh? Good to see you, Ross Magee. Come on, let's go someplace they can make a bullshot.'

The girl in the place on Park Street added Campbells clear broth to two vodkas on the rocks. The bar was designed to repudiate daylight.

'Cheers,' Tommy said. 'Great to see you.'

'And you,' Ross said, drinking. 'Seems like I have a lot of catching up to do. Up to this morning I thought you were still top cat in precious metals at Reesons.' He grinned. 'Has Gerry Bacik finally got to you?'

Tommy made himself shudder. 'That tight-ass,' he said grimly. 'Jesus, is he tough. He runs an investment bank employin' eleven thousand people and he knows what the lunch voucher position is. Take metals. You hold a position for more than twenty-four hours and he's on your back. Commissions, we gotta have commissions to live, Mr Klein. Inhuman. I'm twenty-seven, right? I come home one night after tradin' twelve hours straight, my head is full of metals and numbers, I'm like a fuckin' unexploded bomb. Annie, my wife she says to me, Tommy, I'm pregnant. She might as well say, Tommy, it's rainin' outside. I fix myself a drink and sit down and there she is, the tears pourin' down her face. I say, this is all I need, honey, please tell me why you're cryin'? She looks up and says, I tell you I'm pregnant and you go on as if I'd said nothin'. What's wrong with you? I say, you never told me that. She says, Tommy, when you can't even hear the special things in life, then it's time to get out.'

The girl put up a plate of hot meatballs on the counter and two fresh drinks.

'That was eight months ago,' Tommy said. 'I told Bacik I wanted out and he persuaded me to stay on in Bonds.' Tommy shook his head in disgust. 'I should have known better. We all have wives that are pregnant, Mr Klein, but we got to have commissions. I got another job, in real estate with a firm in Midtown, then I told Bacik. I've never met a person who gives less. If he picked his own mother up off the subway track she'd be lyin' on a dime. He insisted I work out my contract – and

84

that's how you find me. Two weeks from now and it's goodbye Reeson Rhoades, fuck you, Gerry Bacik, and hello, world.'

'I didn't even know you'd got married,' Ross said. 'Tell me about your wife – and, kid, I guess.'

'Annie, I've mentioned,' Tommy said. 'She's beautiful and she's mine, as the song says. Our daughter's name is Jane. She's two months old. I call her Sunny. We live on the Upper West Side, not far from Riverside Park. I bought myself this old Pontiac, real leather interior, on weekends the three of us go on trips up along the Hudson.'

'Here's to Annie and Jane,' Ross said.

'You'll have to come and see us. I want to introduce them to the guy who gave me my first job.' Tommy's face became concerned. 'How have things been for you? We don't have to talk about it if you don't want.'

Ross shrugged. 'I don't keel over and froth at the mouth.'

Tommy shook his head impatiently. 'Mind if I say somethin'? OK, you went down the tubes – but Jim Morales had lost his mind, it had nothin' to do with you. So why the hell did you stand up like an asshole and tell everyone you'd give them their money back? I mean, this town has no time for decency – look what happened, for Christ's sake, two days later they tried to arrest you.'

Ross drained his drink. 'It had something to do with pride, I guess. People had trusted me. But I didn't want to work on Wall Street anymore, so I went north to fish, now I'm buying myself a boat. The route will be a long one, but I'm pretty sure it's the one I want.'

'You're crazy,' Tommy said. 'With your talent, you're crazy. Sooner or later you'll realize that the world is full of assholes – you can never get away from them so you might as well stay and fight.'

Ross shrugged 'maybe'.

Tommy wiped his fingers with a napkin and signalled the girl for more drinks.

'Ross, I'm a fan,' he said quietly, looking down at his drink. 'I owe no one more than you – and I mean it. If there's anyway I can help, just tell me.'

'What do you think of platinum?' Ross asked.

Tommy's eyelids flickered. T-Bonds or real estate notwithstanding, Tommy Klein knew his markets.

'It's a disaster,' he said. 'It took nearly three years to get from four hundred to four-hundred seventy-five an ounce – it lost nearly all that gain in the last six weeks.' He shrugged rhetorically. 'Why buy platinum when there are so many other investment opportunities around?'

'In a weak paper market, platinum would be king,' Ross said.

Tommy thought for a moment, then shook his head.

'What's going to make it go up? Seriously. I mean, is there a holocaust coming up that we haven't been told about on Riverside Drive? Nah, look, I spent four years writin' newsletters about platinum. "We may have been premature before, but we now believe that a major upside move is probable." With Bacik screamin' for business you end up believin' the shit you write.' He looked at Ross. 'Why the interest?'

Ross told him.

'Four hundred thousand ounces?' Tommy whistled. 'Who did it go through?'

'A commission house, I believe.'

'What are you going to do? A mail shot? There are a lot of commission houses on the floor.'

'Including Reesons,' Ross said.

Tommy's eyes locked sideways. 'You think the business went through Reesons?'

'I'm saying it's a possibility,' Ross said.

Tommy picked up his glass, revolved the ice cubes around and drained the contents. He signalled the girl.

'Ross,' he said, 'clients are the most precious thing a broker has, and that includes his balls, you know that.'

'I don't want you to tell me something you can't,' Ross said.

Tommy's face was dubious.

'When were these deliveries made?' he asked quietly.

'Over the last three months.'

Tommy threw his head around.

'Why would they bring platinum to New York?' he asked. 'They've got a ready market in Japan; they've also got a futures market. This all sounds wrong; Japs come over here to buy things, the United States of America, for example, not to sell platinum bars.'

'They did it, Tommy,' Ross said, 'and Reesons acted, at least for some of the action.'

Tommy took a deep breath.

'This sounds like something I don't need in my last two weeks,' he said. 'How important is this to you?'

'It's important,' Ross said.

'It'll take time.'

'I'm in Tokyo for the rest of this week. I need the information before I return to Halifax,' Ross said.

Tommy shook his head from side to side.

'We better have two more of these,' he said to the girl, up-ending his glass.

Five

The cab crawled in from Narita on a busy expressway. Except for the signs in kanji and the green netting of golf ranges, the hinterland was like anywhere in the world: hotels near the airport; industrial proliferation for mile after mile broken by forlorn patches of flat farmland whose owners were undoubtedly real estate millionaires. There were wooden houses built within inches of one another and high-rise housing as far as the eye could see. They reached Tokyo proper at dusk: Ross looked out at train lines crisscrossing overhead and multiple, sagging power lines and two- and three-tier flyovers making the vast city seem like a concrete monster whose stitches had burst.

The hotel was at the heart of a neon web. The cab turned and twisted and doubled back so often on alleys and streets and sudden avenues of multi-shaped and -coloured, incandescent kanji, that Ross had long since lost any sense of direction. He got in and registered and was shown to a room on the tenth floor the size of a trawler's galley. There was cool beer in a refrigerator and he drank a bottle looking out the window at the building opposite which, if the window could open he could touch. In New York it was still 8.30 that morning. Ross's jaw was dark and rough and his scalp tickled. He finished the beer, got out of his clothes and showered in a bathroom modelled on a payphone box. Peeling back crisp sheets, he slid into bed. The air conditioner exhaled at intervals. He thought of a little boat with laughing eyes skippered by a blue eyed man and a crew whose eyes were uniformly green. Tokyo slept.

'First time here?'

Kerry O'Brien had a cleancut, square-jawed face, reddish blond hair and steady, blue eyes. Commercial Attaché at the US Embassy, he was over fifty, but his big, fit frame suggested regular work with weights. The breakfast room was at street level and was the scene of half a dozen other early meetings as outside, the city went about its business.

'First time,' Ross said. 'I appreciate your seeing me so soon.'

'Always happy to try and help,' Kerry said.

'How long have you been in Tokyo?' asked Ross.

'Too long,' the older man replied with a faint smile. 'I was a commercial advisor in Rio up to ninety-one, then I got posted here as Attaché. Been here ever since.'

'Sounds OK.'

'It has its moments.'

A waiter brought a pot of coffee and plates of scrambled eggs and toast. At other tables Ross could see Japanese businessmen eating seaweed with chopsticks.

'I guess you know why I'm in Tokyo,' Ross said. 'I've read the file between Freeman Oxx and your office.'

The Commercial Attaché nodded reasonably.

'I thought the whole saga would be over by now,' he remarked. 'Then I was told they got another delay.'

'To May seventeenth,' Ross said.

Kerry looked at his watch. 'Doesn't give you much time.' He cut the egg into neat squares. 'I don't want to start your day on a negative note,' he said, munching. 'I'm happy to give you all the information at our disposal, introduce you to whoever you want to meet – but don't pin your hopes too high on going back home with any more information than we've already come up with.'

'I never thought it would be easy,' Ross said.

'What do you know about how Japanese company law works?' Kerry asked.

'In a word, nothing,' Ross replied.

'OK,' Kerry said, sitting back. 'There are two kinds of company structures here: one for big public companies and another for small family businesses. The small ones are called yūgen kaisha. Like the big companies, they are limited by shares; unlike the big companies, they're incredibly easy to form. You just fill up a document, get a set of standard bylaws, swear them up, then send them into your local Company Registrar.' He refilled their coffee cups and broke open a small jar of jam which he decanted on to toast. 'Sun Valley is a yūgen kaisha.'

'Registered in Kobe?' Ross asked.

'Registered in Kobe. We sent someone down there, looked it up, everything is in order. It's shares are held by nominees in the office of Hirano-Maeda, the most respectable accountants in Kobe.'

'The file mentions a capital of only a hundred and fifty million yen,' Ross said, 'less than a hundred thousand dollars. That's pin money for an outfit bidding two point five billion for Industrial Oxx.'

'As I understand it, the actual bid is being made by a US subsidiary, also called Sun Valley,' Kerry said, eating. 'But either way, so what? In the US tiny outfits have been making hostile bids for giant corporations ever since junk bonds were invented.'

Ross nodded.

Kerry wiped his mouth and said: 'These yūgen kaisha have almost zero reporting requirements compared to companies back home. They're not obliged to file any financial information whatsoever – as they see it over here that's protection against competition – and there are no requirements about disclosure of who owns the action.'

'So how does anyone find anything out?'

'Through shinyō chosa, credit investigating companies. For a big fee, they'll question customers and suppliers and buy a lot of sake after work for people like bank clerks.' He held up the coffee pot to a waiter. 'On Oxx's behalf we hired one of the best shinyō chosa in the business, but all they could come up with was information we already knew.'

'Which is,' Ross said, 'that Sun Valley, a company making a multi-billion dollar bid through it's US subsidiary, is owned by nominees in an accountants office in Kobe. We've got to be able to find out more.'

Kerry O'Brien made a sympathetic face.

'Let me tell you about one of the cases I had to deal with last year,' he said. 'It concerned a group of well known US financiers who spent over three billion dollars on a thirty per cent stake in one of the largest electrical component manufacturers over here. They wanted seats on the board and the dividend raised – the company wouldn't even talk to them. They tried to sue, but no lawyer here would take the case. They came to Tokyo and went to the annual general meeting to raise hell, but the company's chairman refused to let them ask questions – and they owned more of the company than all the guys on the board combined! They went home having learned a very expensive lesson: back home, you may think you're a heavyweight, but over here, unless they want you, you're nobody.'

The waiter poured them fresh coffee and Ross sat back; he thought of Freeman looking out at the Diablos, then he thought of Captain Belliqueux and his heart plummeted the same way it had over a week ago when he had first set foot again on Wall Street.

'There's another possibility, not covered in correspondence between your office and Oxx,' Ross said quietly. 'It concerns the appearance in New York of a quantity of platinum, shipped in the last few months through Macau but in reality originating in Kobe. I'd like to try and identify the shipper – there may be a connection to Sun Valley.'

'Mind if I ask the relevance?' Kerry asked.

'Freeman Oxx's information is that the platinum was sold by Japanese yakuza,' Ross replied.

The older man made a doubtful face and lit a cigarette.

'OK,' he said slowly, 'we can start with tariff statistics and see where they lead. You guys don't give up easy, do you?'

'Mind if I ask you something?' Ross asked.

'Go right ahead.'

'Do you think yakuza could be behind Sun Valley?' asked Ross.

Kerry leaned back and blew smoke into the air.

'Do you know what an old guy told me when I first got here? He said: when Man starts going to Mars, Japan will be used as the decompression chamber.'

Ross must have looked puzzled.

'In other words, I haven't the faintest idea,' Kerry said.

It was a warm and sunny afternoon on the Chiyoda Line which snaked north past Ueno Park into Arakawa-ku.

'So you threw in the whole thing and went fishing?' said Kerry O'Brien in admiration.

'I guess you could say that,' Ross answered. 'Soon as I'm through here it's back to New York, then up to Nova Scotia and the Banks.' He shrugged. 'It's a long way from Mars, that's for certain.'

'I wasn't exaggerating,' Kerry said. 'Look at what's happened already this morning. We dug out the breakdown of the official export figures for platinum and it appears that no bars were exported during the period in question either to Macau or the United States. We then went to the Tokyo Chamber of Commerce who referred us to the Japan Federation of Commodity Exchanges. They, in turn, referred us to the Tokyo Precious Metals Association who sent us to the Japan Noble Metals Co-operative Society, where we're now going to. The Japanese call this game tarai-mawashi, giving the runaround. I spend half my life in Tokyo shuttling between Ministries on Kasumigaseki, their Capitol Hill.'

Nishi-Nippori station was a catch-point for a number of lines; the two big Americans towered head and shoulders over scurrying commuters as they made their way down to street level and east for two blocks. The Noble Metals Society was on the third floor of a cramped building and overlooked a cemetery.

'Kochira wa Magee-san desu,' Kerry said, having bowed and exchanged business cards with the Society's secretary. 'This is Mr Magee.'

The man at the helm of the Japan Noble Metal Co-operative Society was a shade over four feet, young and cheerful with twin dimples in his chin which popped every time he smiled. He and Ross bowed and the Japanese spoke.

'Mr Gotō apologizes for his lack of English,' Kerry translated as they all sat. 'He asks how he can be of help.'

'I'm looking for a large consignment of platinum in bar form,' Ross said, 'exported from Japan to the United States by way of

Macau in the last six months. It doesn't appear in Japanese Customs records – they show no exports of platinum bars for the period. Who might help me find the seller?'

Kerry translated at length and Mr Gotō said 'Ahh' several times, returning his light brown eyes with interest to Ross's face.

'He says if you know the bars were imported to the States, surely you can find the information out over there?' Kerry relayed.

'It's not that easy,' Ross answered. 'They were delivered against NYMEX contracts and broker-client information like that is confidential.'

'Mr Gotō asks are you sure the shipment was not just ex-Macau?' Kerry translated. 'He says the Chinese government sometimes ship precious metals by that route.'

'It was made to look like a Chinese delivery,' Ross said, 'but we have seen bills of lading.' He watched Mr Gotō's face closely. 'The platinum came from Kobe.'

Mr Gotō simply shrugged.

'If you saw the bills of lading, then you know the shipper,' he said through Kerry.

'We saw the bills of lading but were not shown any names,' Ross replied.

'How about the ship?'

'Neither were we shown the name of the vessel.'

Mr Gotō looked very doubtful, then spoke lengthily.

'Japanese are buyers of platinum for investment purposes, the biggest in the world,' Gotō explained through Kerry. 'They rarely export bars of the metal, therefore the Customs figures you refer to are correct. He cannot see why someone would do something like you have described.'

'Tell him the person who sold the platinum this way did so to keep his name out of sight,' Ross said. 'He either didn't want anyone to know what he was doing – or alternatively, the platinum represented wealth he shouldn't have had in the first place.'

Mr Gotō listened attentively.

'He feels, with great respect, that you are mistaken and that the platinum must have come from some other country,' Kerry said.

Ross sighed.

'Platinum to the value we're talking about – two hundred million dollars – would have been warehoused somewhere prior to shipment,' he said. 'It was probably on the premises of one of his members. There would therefore have been a corresponding decrease in stocks. Does he have any figures we can check this hypothesis against?'

Mr Gotō appeared uncomfortable.

'Any figures are confidential and can only be shown to members of the Society,' Kerry responded for the Japanese. 'He regrets he cannot be more helpful.'

'Does he have a list of warehouses in the Kobe region accredited to the Society?' Ross asked.

Mr Gotō nodded.

'No problem,' Kerry said.

They bowed to each other and were shown out to the elevator. Mr Gotō's smiling chin dimples were the last thing Ross saw as the door closed.

The silver, shinkansen bullet-train was following the line of a curving bay.

'I feel I'm monopolizing all the talent in the Department of Commerce west of Honolulu,' Ross said.

'I'm fascinated, believe me,' Kerry said. 'I wouldn't have missed this for the world. Mind you, if by any chance yakuza are involved, I don't think you quite realize what you're up against.'

'The mob, as I understand it,' Ross replied. 'People whom a Stateside court would throw right out the door.'

'With respect, to understand it completely you would need to forget everything you ever learned about our laws, or ethics, or values,' Kerry said. 'Our rules back home don't apply here.'

The train flashed through a tunnel and when they emerged after thirty seconds the bay had disappeared and they were hurtling between mountains.

'In Japan, yakuza investment is often indistinguishable from so called legitimate investment,' Kerry continued. 'Unless there's a big, public issue involved, you don't find teams of fearless attorneys running around trying to squeeze the bad pips out of companies. In some cases there would be no shareholders left.'

94

'All I need is enough information to convince a court back home,' Ross said. 'The mask may have slipped enough in this platinum deal to let me do that.'

'These aren't two-bit con artists we're talking about,' said Kerry gently. 'They're very sophisticated men with huge operations and numerous legitimate investments. They've been around for generations. Separating their cash into "good" and "bad" is not possible. General MacArthur tried to do it in forty-five and gave up. If the Sun Valley case is indeed what you say, then yakuza will have laundered their cash so carefully and put so many dummy companies and trusts between them and Sun Valley that making the link you refer to will simply not be possible. There comes a point in Japan when you simply can't see any further.'

They pulled into Kobe Central just after noon. The only warehousing company in Kobe on Mr Gotō's list capable of storing large amounts of platinum had been identified by Kerry after numerous telephone calls the evening before. It was set back from the port area in a locality called Sakagura.

'It means sake cellars,' Kerry said as their cab crossed a bridge and Ross caught a glimpse of open sea. 'In the old days they stored the hootch here before shipping it out to Shikoku Island.'

The address was a modern, windowless building with a concrete roof and walls topped with inward-leaning strands of wire and television cameras every fifteen yards. At a reception area tacked on to the front, Kerry showed his card and they were ushered into an office. Mr Sakada, the fifty-year-old chief executive of the storage firm, may have been glad to see them but his face gave no hint of this.

'Over to you,' Kerry said pleasantly.

'Tell him why I'm here and what I'm looking for,' Ross said.

Mr Sakada's reactions were those of a non-lip-reading deaf mute.

'Has he heard of such a shipment being made from Kobe to Macau?' Ross asked.

'He knows no details about such shipments.'

'But ask him has he *heard* of such a shipment.'

Mr Sakada's face was glacial as he shook his head.

'He has heard nothing, he knows nothing about what you are asking,' Kerry transmitted.

Sakada spoke impatiently.

'He says he's very busy,' Kerry said. 'If there's not anything else . . .'

Ross looked at Mr Sakada intently; the storage manager looked away.

'He's lying, the son of a bitch,' Ross exclaimed. 'Ask him if he declares his client's holdings of precious metals for tax purposes. That may be a way we could check.'

Kerry raised his eyebrows a fraction, then passed on the message.

'He says he reveals nothing about his clients or his business to anyone,' Kerry said. 'He says the business has been in the family for four generations and has always been run correctly.'

'Ask him if, hypothetically, I were to store platinum here and wanted him to ship it out to Macau without anyone knowing, whether he could do it?' Ross asked.

'Mr Sakada says his warehouse is full, he could not store metal for you,' Kerry relayed.

'Did you say it was a hypothetical question?' Ross asked.

'I sure did,' Kerry replied.

'The guy is stonewalling us every step of the way,' Ross said. 'Ask him where the yakuza store their platinum in Kobe.'

'I can't ask him that,' Kerry said.

'Of course you can,' Ross said. 'It's not you asking, it's me.'

Kerry translated and Ross watched Sakada's face: it began to twitch as Kerry said his piece, then the little man jumped to his feet behind his desk, shrieking.

'Come on,' Kerry said, getting up. 'If this guy gets back on to my boss in Tokyo I'll be in the manure business.'

Sakada was shouting and gesticulating.

'What's he saying?' Ross asked as they made for the door.

'What's he *not* saying?' Kerry replied. 'He's accusing us of insulting him and his family and forbears. He says we have no right to come in here questioning him like a criminal.'

The cab had waited out front.

'That guy was lying!' Ross said and hit the seat with his fist. 'Lying, then acting. That tantrum was a smokescreen – someone who genuinely knew nothing would never react like that to a reasonable inquiry.'

'They're funny guys here when it comes to concepts such as shame and honour,' Kerry said. 'People are very touchy about yakuza.'

Ross ran his hand through his hair and looked out as they neared the harbour mouth.

'Son of a bitch,' he said. 'OK, I'll go home empty handed, but hell, I'll never be in Kobe again.'

Kerry looked at him.

'Kobe is where Sun Valley is registered, isn't it?' Ross said. 'Let's go and see if we can talk to the owners.'

Hirano-Maeda were listed in Motomachi, the commercial centre. Ross and Kerry found the firm in a spanking new, L-shaped building one block south of Motomachi Station, just west of the Daimaru Department Store.

'If you don't mind, this time I'm going to say I've left all my business cards in the office,' Kerry said.

'That's fine,' Ross smiled. 'I promise: tomorrow I go home.'

The lobby was low-ceilinged, clean and staffed by a security guard who directed them to the third floor. Kerry led the way out of the elevator, right, down a long corridor, then right again until they came to double doors. A middle-aged woman sat at a desk, knitting. Ross heard the words 'Sun Valley', as Kerry announced them.

'I'd give us two chances here,' the attaché remarked, coming to sit down.

'It might work,' Ross said. 'Sometimes you get results by just dropping in out of the blue. I remember in my early days as a broker when we had to hustle like you wouldn't believe for clients. You'd spend months trying to set up appointments to meet guys – if you suddenly appeared without warning they got such a shock they often saw you on the spot.'

'Do you miss all that?' Kerry asked.

'I think there's a part of me that misses it,' Ross replied. 'I guess if I was honest I'd have to admit that there are few things in life that compare to the thrill of matching both sides of a big deal. It's incomparable – you soar. It's the best drug there is, but like all drugs, you want to get back up there again as soon as you can.'

'Do I detect a moralist?' Kerry asked lightly.

Ross was thoughtful.

'I don't know. I'd prefer to be a moralist than a bad loser,' he replied. 'I mean, like I told you, I flunked – bad break and all the rest, but still, I flunked. I genuinely believe that the system is wrong where you need a fresh hit in the form of another deal everyday to keep you up there. It's like hunting big game: it's all right when you do it for food, but when you kill just to put a trophy on your wall, then . . .' A man in shirtsleeves came through from an inner office, spoke quietly to the woman at reception, then disappeared. The woman knitted impassively.

'How about you?' Ross asked. 'Where do you get your highs from?'

'Oh, here and there,' said the older man, looking away.

Ross thought he caught a note of sadness.

'I admire your guts,' Kerry said quietly. 'In my job the rungs of the ladder are defined, there are no risks. We're measured by efficiency, ability to delegate, how we get on with the guy one rung above. When I retire I'll have been all over the world in a cocoon – if I was your age again, God, I'd do it differently I can tell you. Everything.'

A man in a suit came out and looked at them. Five minutes turned into ten. Ross and Kerry exchanged glances; the attaché shrugged. Ross got up and walked across to the window of the office. The decompression chamber before you went to Mars. Whatever chance he had on Wall Street, over here he was lost. Was the trip completely wasted? No. He'd had to try for Freeman. He'd had to try and put something back.

There were vertical-slat blinds on the window. Idly, Ross parted them with his thumb and finger so that he was looking out over downtown Kobe. Straight ahead he could see the harbour which they'd just left; beneath him, at right-angles was the entrance door to the building through which they'd come twenty minutes before. Ross blinked and parted the blinds with a jerk. Walking briskly out and over to a waiting cab was Mr Gotō of the Japan Noble Metal Co-operative Society.

'Jesus Christ – quick!'

Kerry O'Brien was at Ross's side. Below, a head ducked into the cab.

'What is it?'

'Gotō!' Ross cried. 'The little guy we met yesterday in Tokyo! He's just walked out of this building!'

'Gotō?' Kerry said. 'The precious metals guy?'

'He's in that cab!' Ross said incredulously, pointing to the car which was making it's way slowly out into the Motomachi traffic.

Kerry's face creased up in doubt.

'Are you sure?' he asked.

'Goddammit, I'm sure!' Ross cried.

At reception, knitting had ceased.

'It's the connection!' cried Ross. 'It *can't* be coincidence. How many people are there in this country? A hundred and fifty million? And the guy we question about platinum stocks in Tokyo yesterday turns up today in Sun Valley's registered office in Kobe? It's all inter-related – Sun Valley's backers and the sellers of the platinum are one and the same, Godammit, they're mob, yakuza. We've got to get someone to talk!'

Kerry looked at the woman, then back to Ross.

'If you're right, it's one hell of a coincidence . . .' he said dubiously.

The receptionist answered her phone, then addressed Kerry.

'They're very sorry,' he said, turning back to Ross, 'but all the people here who might be able to help us are out of town.'

'It figures,' said Ross.

'Look, Ross,' said Kerry gently, 'a lot of Japanese look alike to Westerners.'

'It was Gotō,' said Ross firmly. 'He'd come down here to warn them that someone was asking questions.'

Kerry walked to the window.

'Where are we? Third floor up? Looking down on a guy, almost on his head, isn't it possible you could have made a mistake, Ross?'

Ross set his jaw. It had been no mistake. On the bridge of the *Isobelle* on a clear day he could make out another boat at ten miles. He suddenly put his hand into the top pocket of his jacket and came out with a sheaf of business cards.

'Here,' he said, handing one to Kerry. 'This is Gotō. Call him in Tokyo. Now. He won't be there.'

Kerry looked for a moment at the card, then nodded and walked to reception. The woman put up a telephone on the counter and Ross watched as Kerry pressed out the number.

'Ahh, Gotō-san desu,' the attaché said, his eyes on Ross.

The lady receptionist was watching both of them.

'Ahh, Gotō-san, chotto matte kudasai,' said Kerry O'Brien. He put his hand over the mouthpiece and looked at Ross. 'It's Mr Gotō. Do you want to speak to him?'

The New York flight took off at seven in the evening. They banked over Tokyo Bay and then began the slow climb north-east, out over the barren wastes of the Bering Sea for the long, fourteen hour arc that would end in Kennedy.

Kerry O'Brien had stuck by him all the way; he'd treated Ross to a meal the night before in Roppongi; he'd collected him from his hotel at two and insisted on driving out to Narita.

'I'm sorry for the goose chase,' Ross said as he watched his bag wobble along a conveyor and plunge out of sight.

'You want my opinion?' Kerry asked. 'Mr Oxx got caught with his pants down – now he's got to take his medicine. These people in South Africa got along just fine for a thousand years without him. They'll be able to handle new faces whether they belong to Japanese or Taiwanese or Irishmen. He should take his money and stop worrying.'

'You could be right,' Ross said.

'Give me a call if you need to know anything more,' Kerry smiled. They shook hands. 'Good luck with the fish. Maybe we'll meet again someday – if I ever get out of here in one piece, that is.'

'I'd like that,' Ross had said and walked through immigration.

The seatbelt lights went out and a stewardess came by with drinks. He had called the phone answering machine in the Oxx apartment in New York but there had been no feedback. He had said two weeks to Freeman; had it taken only eleven days to burst the old man's dream?

Ross bit his lip. Without Freeman's promise to the Masisi, he would never have come home. Freeman and he had both rolled back time and suddenly found themselves again as they had once been. It was too much yet to say that things between them were mended, but a huge leap had been made and now there was the possibility of time together where previously there had been none.

He listened to the drone of the engines, powering them ever eastwards, negating time. Time was a little understood concept, a benchmark of the body but not of the spirit. The body was a drag-anchor: without it the spirit could soar free, come and go, dip swallow-like into its own precious memories, reliving them to the full. Maybe the Masisi had it right. Our lives cross like shooting stars, some continuously, others no more than once or twice. Which stars were out there now, waiting for him? Could he discern them if he looked hard? Was that what drove Freeman, the fear that his star might never shine if his word to a Masisi chieftain were broken?

The vista outside the plane was changing as he beheld it: the sky was a swirling mixture of ink and deep red, bordered above and below with candles; stars flickering over the sunset and the twinkling lights of some city whose name he would never learn.

A girl across the aisle was sizing him up with frank interest. She was a blonde with lazy, sexy eyes and a kissy mouth. Ross smiled at her, then looked away. She reminded him of Ashley. Where was Ashley now? Still in New York, or gone back to the Coast as she had threatened so many times? Thoughts of Ashley provoked twin emotions in Ross: cold, a deep wound of hurt that would always fester coldly, the ice of hate that had gone deeper than he ever guessed was possible; and warmth, the recall of Ashley's warm, rounded body which at times like these reminded him how long it had been.

You have the face of an angel and the body of a lion.

Ross shook his head as he felt himself stir. Misty and he under that deck awning, now just one of them alive, and still she could move him. How long would he feel that? Would she still do it to him when he was fifty? Seventy? In the northern sea where each star in the sky was as bright and vigorous as she had been?

Pulling down an eye-mask, he tilted back his seat.

*

101

They touched down in Kennedy at 6.40. The girl was still interested as Ross smiled at her and disembarked. The cab came in through the Midtown tunnel and on to Park Avenue where the flowers up the central divide bloomed all the way to the horizon. At a little after nine, Ross let himself in and saw the machine flashing a single green blip.

'Welcome back from your world tour,' said Tommy Klein's voice. 'Whilst you were entertaining geishas in Tokyo, some of us here were risking life and limb.' Pause. 'I've found the seller of your platinum.'

BOOK THREE

SATORI

Six

Senko Okuma looked out from the back seat of the Mercedes as an exit sign flashed by. They had made the decision together at noon; it had taken Mama Yayoi another four hours to get through to the man she wanted in Tokyo.

Mama Yayoi. Her very name was music. Like himself she was no longer young, but for Senko she would always be the most enchanting, most beguiling creature in the world. She had seen his broad chest when she was seventeen and he twenty. He had denied his yakuza connections so that she would marry him; straight out she had told him he was a liar. He had gone down on his knees for her forgiveness and she had given him her consent on one condition – that he never lied to her again.

The car hummed south on the Tōhoku. Senko looked back briefly and saw the car carrying Toshihiko, his top wakashū, and three kobun, no more than thirty yards behind. He looked forward again and saw the yellow flecked eyes of Tada, his driver of fifteen years, looking at him from the rearview mirror.

'Less than an hour, Okuma-san,' Tada said.

'Hai,' Senko responded.

Tokyo. The nearer he got to the great city, the more certain Senko became that he was doing the right thing – and the more fearful that somehow word might have got to Chiyaha that he was doing it. He had drunk the sacred cup and felt the mortician's icy knife in his stomach wall. Now he was going against everything his whole life had stood for. Without Mama Yayoi he would never have found the courage. Wait and see their true intentions, she had said. Their hearts may yet triumph over their greed, she had said. So Senko had waited. Until tonight.

They passed the exit sign for Kanuma, white on a blue background. Senko turned to check the Nissan; he turned back to again find Tada's eyes on him. Tada had very prominent cheek-bones, a legacy from his forbears who came from the Kitami region of Hokkaido. Senko bit his lip. If there was a scrap, would these country boys be able to look after their oyabun? Senko calmed himself. His meeting was scheduled to take place at midnight. After that he would return directly to the safety of Sendai.

The sign for Kuki went by and Senko felt the car slowing.

'Why are we slowing?' he asked.

'We need gas, Okuma-san,' Tada said, eyes ahead now.

Senko peered at the dash.

'We still have a quarter tank,' he said.

'Toshihiko said to fill up here. It's the last station before Tokyo, Okuma-san,' Tada said. 'Toshihiko wants to travel the rest of the way with us.'

Senko could see the lights of the gas station. Toshihiko didn't make mistakes. Toshihiko would die for his oyabun.

'Very well,' Senko said, sitting back. He was too nervous. Mama Yayoi had wanted to come with him but he had forbidden it. This was not work for women. But for some reason, he now wished she was in the car.

The forecourt of the gas station was brightly lit and deserted. Display dials and hoses with nozzles hung down from a central, overhead gantry. Straight ahead was a small building housing toilets and an office; to the left, a garage. Music blared over a loudspeaker. They pulled in between the garage and the gas hoses; Tada switched off the engine and got out. Senko looked behind and saw the support car pulling in. He turned back and frowned. Tada was walking briskly for the toilets. Senko mouthed his displeasure. Tada should not have left the car unattended. If he needed to urinate he should have waited till the other kobun were in position.

Senko was making a mental note of Tada's sloppiness when night became day.

106

At first he thought someone in the garage had activated a welder. A brilliant flash was followed by a loud thump. Senko turned in time to see the Nissan flip over. There was a second star of light and the Mercedes nosed four feet into the air, turned 180 degrees on its tail and crashed down pointing for Sendai.

Dazed, Senko clawed up from the floor. Tada! The bastard and all his family would pay for this treachery! And Chiyaha! There was the rapid noise of sub-machine-gun fire and a smell of burning. Senko realized that the window in the driver's door had collapsed into the frame with the impact. The Mercedes had a belly-plate of eight-inch steel which had saved it; the Nissan had not. It lay upside down, wheels spinning as two figures in black stood over it, shooting into it's smoke-blackened interior.

Like thick ice cracking, the rear window of the Mercedes frosted over. Senko's fingers tore at a long panel where the back seat of his car met the floor. He thanked the gods for his foresight: if he could only now get out and away into the night he could hide and survive. His fingers touched cold steel as he dragged out the Uzi. His will to live transcended everything. He squeezed off two, three second orange bursts through the open window, then ducked low behind the front passenger seat as his fire was returned. Calling the wrath of the gods down on Tada's treason and on Chiyaha, he made it over and under the front window, between the driver's seat and the wheel. Lead hit the reinforced steel. Senko shoved the Uzi out, came up behind it and took down a black figure who had been zigzagging for him across the forecourt.

'Straight to hell, bastard!' Senko cried.

He ducked to change the clip. He felt an exhilaration he had not experienced for twenty years, an intense pride. If only Mama Yayoi could be watching this! If only she could see him and tell Mio-chan who in turn could tell her own children! Senko threw out the old clip and fumbled the new one into the breech. Outside, music blared weirdly in the lull. Senko shoved the Uzi into the night and let off half the clip in a ricochetting crescent.

He had to get out, had to preserve his firepower. He edged from the open window to the passenger's side. He chanced a look. It seemed clear. He would hit the ground on the roll – again the sense of exultation! – and keep going until he was in shadow. Two things happened: a sustained burst of gunfire raked the Mercedes, and the gushing nozzle of a gas hose was thrown through the open window.

Senko felt petrol spatter on his hands and face. He knew what they were going to do. His free hand fumbled for the door handle as the flaming torch came through the open window. He fired through the flying flame at the black, receding figure and kept his finger pressed to the guard even as the man fell.

Mama Yayoi would have been so proud.

*　　*　　*

The commuter train on the Yamanote loop line sat in Meguro Station as people packed on board. From his seat at the window which he had secured at Mejiro, Inspector Nobuo Imai could see children arriving for class at a school across the tracks.

The bump of the restarting train brought Inspector Nobuo back to the task at hand. He concentrated hard on the relationship between lips, teeth and tongue.

Will you . . . meet me for . . . coffee next week?

Coffee was a problem, English word, calling for the front, top teeth to meet the bottom lip, an awkward task for a Japanese.

Will you meet me for . . . co-FFEE next week?

Inspector Nobuo was forty-three. Short, squat and broad, he had thick, oily black hair that went straight back leaving a wide, sincere face open to the world. In this face, different people saw different things: his wife of twelve years saw the loving father of their two boys whose every free moment was spent kicking football with them in the park in Ikebukuro; the English teacher giving the class Nobuo had just left saw intelligence; Nobuo's colleagues in Keishicho, the Tokyo Metropolitan Police headquarters saw determination, although there were criminals in Kobe and Tokyo who had encountered him on his twenty-four-year climb of the ladder who would probably have called it something else.

Osaki Station came and went; a tiny lady was now wedged at Nobuo's knees.

. . . Sorry . . . next week I'm going to . . . America.

Two difficult words: *Sorry, America.* At six that morning the teacher had tried to convey the English 'r' to his class. *R-r-r.* Roll the tongue. Avoid the temptation to speak the Japanese 'l' sound. Bare the teeth like a tiger, and if it helps, prefix a 'g' to make an animal sound: *G-r-r-r.*

Inspector Nobuo kept fit with twice-weekly sessions at the police gymnasium where he practised kendō, face to face combat with long, bamboo staffs. Perfection in kendō was like the knowledge gained in the step by step building of a case. The getting to the true nature of things. Technical precision. Spiritual perfection.

G-r-r-r-r-r-r.

The tiny lady raised her eyebrows as Inspector Nobuo sighed and stood up to squeeze towards the doors: he doubted if he would ever master the cumbersome language, although at home he had a box crammed full of tapes and could even follow English language films on television. But speaking it . . . speaking it was something else.

Traffic was nose-to-tail from the Sakuradamon Gate to the ginkgo trees in the gardens of the National Diet. Inspector Nobuo crossed over and walked into the soaring, white marble lobby of Keishicho. Pinning an ID badge to his lapel, he made his way to the elevators.

'Inspector-san!'

A white-gloved duty officer was beckoning.

'Superintendent Iseki asks can you go straight away to eighteen and meet him in the Deputy Chief's office?'

Nobuo hit the button for the eighteenth floor. On Saturday afternoon Superintendent Junpei Iseki had presided over a meeting of the Criminal Investigation Bureau, but nothing had arisen which led Nobuo to expect another meeting so soon. Certainly not on the eighteenth floor. Junpei Iseki was Nobuo's sort of man: shrewd yet open; big hearted and humorous, especially late at night after sake; and at nearly fifty, still someone to be reckoned with at kendō.

The eighteenth floor was soft carpets and walls done in subdued pastels. Outside the office of the Deputy Superintendent-General sat a pair of uniformed secretaries. One of them bowed to Nobuo, looked pointedly at her watch, then preceded him in.

'Inspector Nobuo Imai,' the woman announced.

Deputy Chief Amemiya was a small, clerkish man, dressed in full uniform and standing behind a desk that looked far too large for him ever to have touched both ends of it at once. On Inspector Nobuo's side of the desk were two men in dark suits: one was Nobuo's immediate boss, Superintendent Junpei Iseki; the other man, well groomed, white haired and in his late fifties was a stranger to Nobuo.

'Ohayō gozaimasu, Inspector-san,' the Deputy Chief bowed.

'Ohayō gozaimasu, sensei,' Nobuo replied.

'Inspector, this is Superintendent Nishikawa, head of the Imperial Palace Security Division. Nishikawa-san, Inspector Nobuo.'

'Dōzo yoroshiku,' Nobuo bowed. 'Pleased to make your acquaintance, sir.'

'Likewise, Inspector,' Nishikawa bowed.

'Ohayō, Nobuo,' boomed Superintendent Iseki. Big by any standards, for a Japanese he was positively enormous.

'Iseki-san,' Nobuo bowed, trying to read a reason for the meeting from Iseki's face.

'Gentleman, please,' the Deputy Chief said, gesturing to chairs. 'I've been telling Nishikawa-san about your successes against yakuza, Inspector,' he said to Nobuo.

Nobuo bowed respectfully. Over Superintendent Nishikawa's shoulder, the lakes and lawns of the Imperial Palace shone like green jewels in a desert.

Junpei Iseki went to a projector as the Deputy Chief turned the slats of the windowblinds flush bringing the room into semi-darkness. The broad head and shoulders of a round faced man in his sixties flashed up on the wall screen.

'Senko Okuma,' Iseki said. 'Until last night, oyabun of Miyagi, the dominant yakuza syndicate up there.' The picture changed and the less clear likeness of a woman appeared. 'Married for forty years to this woman, Yayoi Okuma, known as Mama Yayoi. They have one child, a daughter, thought to be living in Tokyo.'

A picture of a motorway service station came up.

110

'The Kuki-exit service station on the Tōhoku Expressway when it was opened,' Iseki said. 'At approximately nine last evening, six men took over the station at gunpoint, bound and gagged the three employees and transported them out of the area.'

The screen changed and what looked like the outcome of an air raid came up. Nobuo cursed himself for not having read the morning papers.

'What remains of the Kuki-exit service station,' Iseki said. 'Sometime after nine, two cars travelling south to Tokyo pulled in. One carried Senko Okuma, the other, four of his kobun.'

The bombed service station was replaced by a row of eight, charred bodies.

'This is what police from Saitama prefecture found,' Iseki said. 'Forensic say a rocket launcher of some kind was used.'

'The gas tanks went up,' the Deputy Chief said. 'The fireball was visible in Tokyo.'

A shot of a close-eyed man appeared.

Iseki continued: 'Because of the heat, all the dead haven't yet been identified – but this one has and he's of particular interest. He's Moto Takizawa, up to last night a ranking lieutenant on Rokuo Chiyaha's staff.'

'Chiyaha,' said Inspector Nobuo softly.

'An old adversary of yours I believe, Inspector-san,' said Deputy Chief Amemiya as the projector was turned off and he allowed daylight back into the room. 'So why are we here discussing what is obviously a case of yakuza genocide?' he asked and turned to the head of Imperial Security. 'Superintendent Nishikawa may have the answer.'

Nishikawa tilted his well groomed head.

'I am from Kogota, gentlemen. I began my work as a young policeman with the Miyagi prefecture. Forty years ago I was on the beat in Sendai and one of the young hoodlums I came across was Senko Okuma.'

'You knew him?' Nobuo asked.

'In the way that a cop on the beat gets to know these people, yes,' Nishikawa replied. 'There was something different about Okuma – integrity would perhaps be too strong a word to use, but he had something more than the others. I think he was grateful to me for seeing that. When I came to Tokyo he wrote me a letter – quite a feat for an uneducated man – saying how much I would be missed.'

Nobuo tried to see behind the coiffured head, tried to get a glimpse of the young cop pausing at a corner for a brief chat with a young, streetwise yakuza, forty years ago.

'Yesterday morning I received a call from a woman,' Nishikawa said. 'She introduced herself as Okuma's wife, the said Mama Yayoi. She sounded very agitated, saying that to call omawari went against everything she stood for – but the situation warranted it and she had persuaded Okuma to meet me. I pressed her to say what about. Yayoi-san declined. I said I could not meet Okuma unless I had some idea what was involved. She then said it involved the life of someone at the very highest level in the land.'

Nobuo and Junpei Iseki exchanged glances.

'I agreed to meet Okuma last night here in Tokyo,' Nishikawa said. 'We all know what happened.'

There was silence, broken by the soft tapping of typewriter keys from the outer office.

'Therefore the threat to the palace, if threat it is, is by inference,' Nobuo said.

'Exactly,' Junpei Iseki nodded.

'The very highest level in the land?' said the Deputy Chief. 'That's pretty specific, Inspector.'

'But yakuza?' said Inspector Nobuo. 'I could understand a yakuza threat against someone in the government, but not against the palace.'

'Precisely, Inspector-san,' said Nishikawa smoothly. 'I knew that had there been any rumblings from organized crime which even indirectly involved the royal family, your section would have briefed us long before now.'

Nobuo saw Junpei Iseki avoid the strafing stare of Deputy Chief Amemiya.

'Has anyone tried to contact Mama Yayoi?' asked Nobuo.

Nishikawa's face showed polite indulgence. 'When I heard what had happened to Okuma, I immediately got in touch with the police in Sendai, but Yayoi Okuma has disappeared.'

'I see,' said Inspector Nobuo.

'What do you make of it, Nobuo-san?' asked the Deputy Chief.

'It is hard to know,' Nobuo replied. 'Last night's attack is the first serious incident of yakuza warfare in over a year.'

'The crackdowns must be hurting them financially,' the Deputy Chief said. 'A man like Chiyaha doesn't lie down, he fights to the end in ways we never thought of.' He scratched his head as if pondering the puzzle he had just set. 'What does the royal itinerary look like at the moment, Superintendent?'

'Their Majesties have routine court and civil functions this week,' Nishikawa replied. 'Next week they rest prior to their departure to Washington for a State visit. Although we will inform the US authorities of this matter, the last thing we want is for the royal family to be upset at such a time by a silly, baseless rumour.'

'Of course, of course,' said the Deputy Chief as all the men got to their feet.

Nishikawa bowed low; the Deputy Chief indicated that the men from CIB should remain.

'Iseki-san,' he said as soon as the door had closed, 'you should learn why this hoodlum was killed on his way to see the head of Imperial Security, don't you think?'

Junpei Iseki flinched under the bland tone. The Deputy Chief continued: 'We should learn why, before –' he leant on the word '– before Imperial Security find out, would you not agree?'

'Certainly, sensei,' said Iseki correctly. 'All I can say at this point is, we have had no warning of anything.' He looked to Nobuo who nodded in support. 'We will initiate inquiries without delay.'

'No unseemly fuss,' said the Deputy Chief, raising his finger. 'We want to get to the bottom of it, but we don't want to cause a panic in the process, is that clear?'

'Perfectly clear, sensei,' said Iseki as he and Inspector Nobuo bowed and left the room.

The Criminal Investigation Bureau on Keishicho's fifteenth floor hummed with quiet activity. Iseki and Nobuo walked past uniformed women, busy at keyboards, directing information into computers. Nobuo saw Sergeant Bando, his heavily be-spectacled assistant, talking on the phone.

113

'Sorry to have landed you in that,' said Junpei Iseki, allowing Inspector Nobuo into his office before him.

Junpei Iseki's office always seemed too small for its occupant. Walls lined with filing cabinets pressed available space to a minimum. Files stacked on the floor required the Superintendent to climb in behind his desk. In an alcove there were photographs of a smiling woman and children, two framed citations and a vase of bright plastic flowers.

'Some tea, Nobuo?'

'Ah, excellent, thank you, Iseki-san,' Nobuo replied.

Iseki bent and plugged in a kettle, then from a press beneath the alcove he took out a tray laden with small cups, a teapot, a ceramic jar and scoop, and a kitchen cloth and spoon. As the kettle came to the boil, he poured water into the teapot, dipped in the spoon and washed it, then turned and tipped the waste water into the flower pot. Nobuo watched attentively as Tokyo's Chief of Crime wiped the spoon with the cloth, opened the ceramic jar and transferred four scoops of powdery green tea into the teapot. Pouring in boiling water, he whisked the concoction energetically with the spoon, put on the lid and served.

'Ahh,' said Nobuo appreciatively, resting his bowl on the palm of his left hand, then bowing once before sipping. 'Ahh,' he said again, 'excellent, Iseki-san, truly excellent.'

'What about that peacock from Imperial Security!' Iseki scoffed, putting down his cup and taking out a pipe in the shape of a bulbous-ended 'S'. 'Put some people into the palace and they think they're the ones with royal blood!'

'I hate to see Chiyaha involved,' Nobuo said.

'You tried long and hard to put him away in Kobe, did you not, Nobuo?' Iseki asked, puffing mightily.

'Not hard enough,' Nobuo said. 'My case fell apart when Chiyaha managed to intimidate the principal witness, although he did three years afterwards in Sugamo for mail fraud.'

'What sort of a hoodlum is he?' Iseki asked.

'With respect, that would be the first mistake,' Nobuo replied. 'He's not your traditional hoodlum at all. He's very bright. In Kobe they talk about him like he was chairman of Mitsubishi.'

'Praise indeed,' Iseki said.

Nobuo was thoughtful. 'We had some psychiatrists talk to

114

him back at that time,' he said. 'Their report is still clear in my mind. Chiyaha was acutely traumatized as a child by the death of his father, a small-time runner for the Kobe yakuza. After his death, the mother was forced into prostitution to maintain herself and the child; Chiyaha kept thinking each night that it was his father returning – evidently he still in a way believes this. Such beliefs lead to gross insecurity, and in turn to psychopathy.'

'So he's a psychopath?' Iseki asked.

'Yes, but at the same time, extraordinarily clever and capable,' replied Nobuo with measure. 'Here you have a man, reliving an unfulfilled part of his childhood – perhaps every day – and at the same time totally without scruple or conscience about how he achieves his ambition.'

'And what is his ambition?' asked Iseki quietly.

'To be the most powerful oyabun in Japan,' Nobuo replied.

Junpei Iseki tapped the pipe stem against his teeth.

'Sounds like it all adds up to an awful lot of trouble,' he said. 'Okuma's widow, the so-called Mama Yayoi is obviously the key. But is she still alive? Even if she is, with Okuma dead, she'll have gone into hiding. She'll never risk contacting us twice.'

Inspector Nobuo shrugged.

'Then we have to find her,' he said.

Seven

Ross took the Seventh Avenue local to 116th Street, walked east one block through Columbia and then north until he reached some cellar steps on the east side of Amsterdam Avenue. The bar smelled of disinfectant. Tommy Klein was at a back table, halfway through a pitcher of beer and a hamburger.

'Old habits die hard,' Ross smiled.

Tommy, check shirted, blue jeaned and sneakered, poured beer and pushed the glass towards Ross.

'We're all still workin' at Morales Magee,' he said with a little shrug. 'As if we didn't see enough of each other all week, we sneak out weekends and solve the remainin' problems of the world.'

'Good days,' Ross said.

'They're the ones I'll always remember,' Tommy nodded. 'It was a great team, everyone wanted the thing to work and it nearly did. You were the best team leader there was.'

Ross smiled. 'Thanks.'

'Arrivin' in Reesons was like a different world,' Tommy said. 'The people were warm the way corpses are warm – Bacik had them that way. I said, shit, this is about money, not people, but I was wrong. I'd often sit there and say to myself, I'm pickin' up the phone and callin' Ross and comin' back. Then I'd think of my mortgage, and Annie, and my car, and I'd think of what you might think, and I'd just blink and start again.'

'Life is about believing in yourself,' Ross said.

'I'll drink to that,' Tommy said and emptied his glass. He looked across the table. 'Let me tell you how I spent the last two nights. I stayed back, sayin' I needed to write up my order book and that I couldn't do it at home with the baby cryin'. Reesons uses one mainframe for all its trades, but each tradin' section has special access codes. Each trader has his own password and ID which lets him log into the machine. Therefore, guys on T-Bonds can't look in on metals, no more than guys tradin' the kerb stocks know what's movin' in oil.'

'OK,' Ross said.

'But they haven't changed the access code to metals since I moved out,' Tommy said. 'I went into the cage and accessed the machine for all platinum delivered by us on NYMEX goin' back three months. I won't mention the fact that I'm shittin' marbles that someone, Gerry Bacik, for example, is goin' to come along and ask me what it is I'm doin'.'

Tommy poured beer from the pitcher and drank a long draught.

'Your Kobe platinum was sold in the name of a Jap named Eiichi Eda. He's the head guy of a big outfit we act for on the corporate side named Sun Valley. Now I think it's about time you told me what the fuck is goin' on.'

At three the sun shone brightly on Columbia. They sat on the rim of a fountain.

Tommy said: 'So Eda sold the metal and Eda heads Sun Valley. Does that make him mafioso?'

A picture was flashing in Ross's mind: it was Gotō's face as he left the office building in Kobe. Godammit, he was so sure it had been Gotō!

'That's now what I've got to prove,' he said tightly. 'We've made the first link, now we need the second.'

Tommy said: 'Just think of all the people in Japan who buy and sell platinum. They go crazy for the stuff. Eda could be frontin' for an excess holder in any one of a dozen industries who wants to dribble metal out without disturbin' the domestic market.'

'In all those cases, the platinum would form part of existing statistics,' Ross said. 'I've looked in the Cresswels files, I've seen the statistics in Tokyo; this metal isn't there.'

117

'Cresswels make mistakes like everyone,' Tommy said. 'And business is not about tellin' the world your next move.'

'It's yakuza platinum, Tommy, I'm sure of it,' Ross said.

'Well, maybe it is, but this is as far as I can take it,' Tommy said. 'I'm just a trader.'

Ross was looking into the middle distance.

'I'm close,' he said quietly, 'hell, I know I'm close. I've got to get to Eda.'

Tommy shook his head.

'I don't know how you're going to do that, old buddy.'

'We're going to use our inside track,' Ross answered.

'Inside track? "We"?'

'You're the ex-head of precious metals trading in Reeson Rhoades,' Ross said. 'You're on your way out of Wall Street and into real estate. You're getting in touch with obvious contacts, buying them lunch, seeing if their portfolios need a little massaging from the real estate point of view.'

'Ross, forget it!' Tommy cried.

'Tommy, you're paid to buy people lunch. You've got a friend in town who needs to meet the shakers and movers; the introduction may *help* Mr Eda. He'll be grateful and may even start to trade T-Bonds with Reesons. That's the way the world goes round, isn't it?'

'Ross, if it ever came down to a trade-off between you and Gerry Bacik, you know for me there'd be no choice, right? But in a week I leave that place with six years' pension benefits and a lot of unused vacation pay. Don't make me screw it up, all right?'

'What are you afraid of?' asked Ross. 'That this guy Eda is going to call up Gerry Bacik and say: "Hey, mister! Get this guy Klein off my back! He's trying to buy me lunch, for Christ's sake!"?'

'Ross, I don't know Eda.'

'I recall times when ten-second encounters with strange ladies in elevators qualified them for weekend invitations to ski lodges in Vermont,' Ross grinned.

'How could I have forgotten that you are the most obstinate son of a bitch?' asked Tommy plaintively.

*   *   *

118

Traffic crawled in along the Hutchinson River Parkway after the sunny weekend. Tyler Wrixon eased the Lexus into line for the toll, winced in agony as something slalomed down his stomach, then tossing quarters into the basket, he gunned out on to the highway for New York.

He analysed the situation yet again. If the bid for Oxx collapsed, the Grand Bahama profit and all the downstream income would evaporate. And at what price then would the market value Oxx? In a pull-out by Sun Valley, would the market think twenty dollars? Less? Sweat began to seep from Tyler Wrixon. In another bank in Grand Bahama was another account, in the name of a John Tyler, the beneficial owner of five hundred thousand Oxx at twenty dollars, bought on margin through a broker in Freeport. The two million down payment had been borrowed from a secondary bank in New York, secured by a second mortgage on a mansion in Connecticut.

Wrixon looked at the dashboard clock. Twenty-two-forty. He rarely did business with the man he was going to see, their paths seldom crossed. It had been the insistence in the voice that had dragged Wrixon into town.

He turned up the air conditioning. At $21.50 he was still $750,000 up. Perhaps he should sell? But at $24 – the agreed bid price – he would net two big ones.

He took 125th Street to Fifth Avenue and drove downtown. He turned right on Fifty-fourth Street; one block west; right and right again. At 11.15 he walked through the doors of the St Regis Hotel on Fifty-fifth Street. The lobby was deserted. He turned into the men's rest room as he had been told to. He found if he took his body weight on the heels of his hands and leaned forward on the basin, the flame in his gut was doused momentarily. A cubicle open behind him and he busied himself with rinsing his hands.

'Tyler?'

Wrixon spun, his wet hands held out protectively.

'Did I startle you, chum?' sniffed Timothy Manners.

*   *   *

Ross sipped a tumbler of Freeman Oxx's Glenfiddich and simultaneously pressed out the number on the phone. Through the big picture window of the penthouse he could see the cars on the Queensboro Bridge begin to switch their lights on.

'Kyle? Ross.'

'Hey, it's Monday, I thought you were still in Tokyo,' said Kyle Spicer.

'I got back Saturday.'

'Any joy?'

'Nothing in Japan,' Ross replied. 'Here in New York I've managed to connect the platinum selling direct to Sun Valley, but now I've got to prove that Sun Valley are yakuza owned or, at least, yakuza led. I may know more later this evening. Anything your end?'

'Some answers on which I asked for clarification,' Kyle replied. 'Nothing that would shake the earth. How's your timing running on this project?'

'Tight,' Ross replied. 'I may have to put back this boat deal again and I'm not sure I can.'

'If you're still in town Friday, I'll buy you coffee,' Kyle said. 'I'm in New York ahead of a bond auction.'

'I'll look forward to it,' Ross said.

He stooped at the hall mirror to fix his tie knot; Tommy had come through an hour before.

'I guess I should have known I was important.'

'Oh, yeah?' Ross said.

'Twice this mornin' I called this guy Eda. Both times I get his secretary and each time I tell her there's a roller in town I want Eda to meet. She keeps tellin' me, Mr Eda's a very busy man, he can't see anyone.' Tommy paused. 'Can you use chopsticks? Suddenly Eda wants to entertain me and my friend to dinner. Tonight. In his apartment. What do you think of that?'

'I think you're a genius,' Ross had said.

He had picked up the phone to call Freeman, then put it back. Better to wait; better not raise the old man's hopes.

He thought of Freeman for the ten blocks uptown. Two weeks ago he had gone to California because of Misty and nothing else. Now he found himself looking out at night-time Manhattan and praying that Tommy Klein had come up with a winner.

The apartment building was in the seventies on Lexington and came complete with street awning and doorman in matching livery. Ross stepped out of the elevator on the twelfth floor and pressed the buzzer. The safety chain was slid back and suddenly he was face to face with a five-foot china doll.

'Irasshaimase,' she said softly, bowing.

Ross stared.

'I'm Ross Magee.'

Her hair was black and bobbed at the neck with bunches of flowers over each ear. Her face was a chalk-paste mask, her mouth a blood-red cupid. A silk robe – vivid blacks and blues chasing through a field of wine – was bound by a deep obi which wound from her breasts to her waist. She looked so perfect that she might break.

'Please,' she said, and Ross stepped in.

She walked before him down a narrow hallway and stopped at a screen. Ross drank in the sway of her hips.

'Please,' she bowed, indicating his shoes. 'It's Japanese custom.'

'Of course,' Ross murmured and his guide slid the panel.

'Ross Magee-san,' she announced.

It was like a set for a play. A big window with a bamboo curtain through which New York was twinkling; a low, lighted ceiling; in one corner, a tiny, black stove; in another, an alcove with flowers and a container of wisping incense. Tommy Klein was sitting at a low, lacquer table, his legs stuck out in front of him and a crooked grin on his face. Today it was back to the weekday wardrobe: double-breasted pin-stripe complete with budding rose in lapel. As Ross entered, Tommy and a man in a blue suit got up.

'Ross, good to see you,' beamed Tommy, shaking hands. 'Mr Eda, this is the man I've been tellin' you about, Ross Magee. Ross, Mr Eiichi Eda.'

Ross bowed and Eda returned it, lower.

'Ross and I have been friends for many years,' Tommy said cheerfully.

Eda indicated a pole which ran from floor to ceiling at the centre of the table.

'Please,' he said. 'We call this the kyakuseki, the seat of honour.'

Ross sank to his knees and drew one foot, then the other into

121

the lotus position. The spot from the alcove opposite made him narrow his eyes. Eda had seated himself, crosslegged, directly across. Ross saw a man in his forties, narrow shouldered, slim, no taller than five seven or eight. His head was domed and round and the front three-fifths of it was bald with the hair behind close cut. He wore large, thick-rimmed spectacles through which his tiny, black eyes darted, the only live features in a tight, impassive face.

'Did Tommy tell you, this is all for sale?' Ross asked and gestured generally towards Manhattan.

Eiichi Eda smiled thinly.

'Ross is in the investment advisory business,' Tommy said. 'In Canada.'

Eda raised his eyebrows politely.

'Ahhh,' he said.

'How are your markets today?' Ross asked Tommy.

'Cautious,' Tommy said. 'No one's willin' to bet heavy on which way interest rates will turn. It's all flat, dead in the water.'

'Precious metals?' asked Ross innocently.

'I told you, dead in the water,' said Tommy, busying himself with his napkin.

The smaller, rear door opened and Ross's guide of minutes before reappeared. Again he found himself staring.

'This is Yukiko-san,' said Eda formally. 'She is our geisha for this evening.'

Ross bowed and Yukiko modestly averted her eyes; Tommy had his most endearing smile in place.

Eda said: 'The meal which she will serve, she has also prepared.'

'Fantastic,' Tommy said.

Yukiko sank to her knees and drew a tray containing tiny glasses and a crystal bowl full of ice out along the ground. Reaching to the ice for a cut-glass decanter she poured from it. 'To America,' said Eda as they raised their glasses and drank.

'My God, that's good!' Tommy gasped.

'Vintage sake from some of the best rice fields in Japan,' Eda said.

'May I inquire, what line of business are you in, sir?' asked Ross.

122

'I work for a company you probably have never heard of,' Eda said, looking at him closely. 'It's name is Sun Valley.'

'Sun Valley,' Ross said, shaking his head. 'No, can't say I have. Is it part of a big Japanese group?'

'Ahhh, no,' Eda replied.

Yukiko reappeared and kneeling, began to transfer dishes from her tray to the table: bowls of lacquered wood and enamel, platters of raw wood and of earthenware, tiny plates of eggshell porcelain. To Ross, her hands were like small birds in flight.

'With respect, may I suggest that Yukiko-san explains these servings to you?' said Eda.

Tommy smiled at the girl. 'Otherwise we might start with the ice-cream, right?'

She inclined her head gracefully.

'In Japan we cook not just for the appetite,' she said in a lilting voice, 'but for the other senses too. We make the food look as beautiful as possible, at the same time remembering that the things you see here all began life in open air.'

Everything about her floated: her voice, her hands, her head. She lifted the lid from a steaming, black, lacquered bowl.

'Sumashi-jiru, clear soup,' she said, 'made from bonito and seaweed, with sake added.' She pointed to a deep dish. 'For many Westerners, the most Japanese part of a meal: sashimi, raw fish. Rub it on the little block of ginger.'

Tommy smiled: 'I just love raw fish.'

Ross followed the line of Yukiko's neck as she bent.

She said: 'Four different types of cooked fish: ayu, a rare small river trout, then hake, salmon and squid. The hake is steamed, the salmon is simmered, and the squid is agemono, deep fried.'

'Some people think Japanese cooking begins and ends with sushi,' Tommy said.

'It's a work of art,' Ross said.

Yukiko smiled. She edged back from the table, bowed, then came to her feet.

'Enjoy your meal,' she said and left the room.

Eiichi Eda gestured to the food and Ross took the lid from the soup and brought the bowl to his lips; the light taste was delicious; it reminded him of the girl who had just left. There was another feeling, hard to describe, but growing with every

123

second: he felt he was being minutely observed by Eda even though the Japanese appeared engrossed in his meal.

'You are based in Canada?' asked Eda, putting down his bowl.

'Yes,' Ross replied. 'But my work takes me around quite a bit.'

'So tell us, Ross,' Tommy asked mischievously 'what is your investment mood today?'

'A bit like your markets,' replied Ross dryly. 'Cautious.'

'Ahhh, cautious,' said Eda, bringing his rice bowl up and flicking rice at speed into his mouth.

'This country runs a simultaneous trade and budget deficit,' Ross said. 'Sooner or later things will go wrong.'

'As you can see, Ross is a real optimist,' Tommy remarked.

Ross looked at Eda and shrugged reasonably.

'You're a businessman, Mr Eda. You know that nothing lasts forever, particularly bull markets, although Wall Street and Tokyo would have us believe otherwise.'

Eda bowed. 'Very interesting. But one question, Mr Magee, then what do you tell your clients to put their money into?'

'Platinum,' said Ross as Tommy got a fit of coughing.

Eda inclined his head respectfully, picked up a tiny skewered fish and popped it into his mouth.

'May I ask, please, why platinum?' he asked.

'It's too low,' Ross replied. 'Any blip on the economic horizon and it could regain the fifty or so dollars an ounce that it's lost recently.'

A little smile appeared on Eda's face.

'If I may, I would like to tell you a story about platinum,' he said.

Ross had a peculiar sensation that he had met Eda before – all the more peculiar because he knew he hadn't.

'The owners of Sun Valley are mainly charitable foundations in Kobe,' Eda was saying. 'I cannot name them, you will understand, but charitable institutions have to invest their money like everyone else. Well, one of them had a large stock of platinum from many years ago, several hundred thousand ounces in bars, and they asked me three months ago whether the time was right to dispose of it – anonymously, you understand.'

124

'This was . . . old stock?' Ross asked.

'Over twenty years old,' Eda replied.

'I see,' Ross said. The peculiar sensation was even more persistent.

'I said I thought the time was right, so I shipped it over here and sold it on NYMEX,' Eda said. 'I got four hundred and seventy-five dollars an ounce for some of the metal – two weeks before the market collapsed. I think you say, "the timing was OK", yes?'

'The timing was impeccable.' Ross nodded. 'Wouldn't you say, Tommy?'

'Impeccable,' Tommy agreed admiringly. He shook his head. 'So the people you work for are . . . charities, Mr Eda?'

'That is so, ultimately,' Eda replied.

Tommy's head was going from side to side like a marionette.

'That's just got to be a tremendously satisfyin' job, Mr Eda. I can't think of anythin' more worthwhile.' He smiled crookedly. 'I guess it makes everythin' else us folks do, well, just crass, don't you agree, Ross?'

Ross didn't reply. He had identified the sensation: it had been precisely the same in Kobe, facing Mr Sakada, the head of the warehouse firm. Like Sakada, Eda was lying through his teeth.

Piping hot green tea came in tiny, handleless cups. Eda slurped every time he drank and Tommy did the same. Ross watched as Yukiko removed the last of the empty bowls. She embodied grace in even the simplest movement. He couldn't keep his eyes from her. Was there a relationship between her and Eda? If Eda was yakuza, did that make her yakuza too?

Somewhere in the apartment a telephone rang; Yukiko appeared and spoke to Eda who excused himself. Looking at her again, Ross felt himself surge.

'This has been unforgettable,' Tommy said to the girl. 'Did you really prepare it all yourself?'

Yukiko bowed her head demurely.

Tommy grinned. 'I'm extremely interested in Japanese culture. Would you be interested in giving me some lessons?'

Yukiko put her hand to her mouth and giggled.

'How's Annie?' asked Ross.

'Gone to stay with her mother in Denver for a week,' answered Tommy from the side of his mouth.

The screen slid back.

'I'm so sorry,' said Eiichi Eda, looking at his watch. 'A business call I've been expecting.'

'This has all been wonderful, Ross said, 'but if you'll excuse me, I've an early start tomorrow.

'Of course,' Eda said.

They got to their feet and he ushered them into the hall. 'God loves a trier,' said Tommy quietly.

'Excuse me, please,' said Eda from behind, 'but are one of you gentlemen going downtown?'

'I am,' Ross replied.

'Would it be too forward to ask you to share a taxi with Yukiko-san?' Eda inquired. 'Please, if it is inconvenient . . .'

Ross quickened.

'My pleasure,' he said.

'She is actually my secretary,' Eda said. 'A most talented lady. Very accomplished, I think you will agree.'

'Very,' Tommy said.

Eda slid back the door to allow Ross to precede him to the hall. A Japanese girl stood there. She was exquisite: she had very large and deep brown eyes, and a smiling mouth whose lips she had painted with a purple lipstick. Her hair came in a fringe to her forehead and was tied on the top of her head in a frizzy knot. She wore tight purple jeans and a black shirt which came down to near her knees. The effect was stunning.

'. . . Yukiko-san?' said Ross.

She smiled at him and this time held his eyes. Eda opened the door of the apartment and walked them all to the elevator.

'Don't forget real estate, Eiichi,' Tommy was saying. 'I can assure you of my personal attention in any inquiries you might have.'

'Enjoy the rest of your stay in New York,' Ross said.

'Thank you,' Eda smiled, joining his hands and bowing.

The cab swung east and then downtown on Third. Yukiko sat crosslegged on the back seat.

'How long have you been in New York, Yukiko-san?' asked Ross.

'I came from Tokyo with Eda-san four months ago, sir,' Yukiko replied.

She sat, the palms of her hands upwards, one on the other in her lap. She radiated not just health and beauty, but something additional.

'You like the type of work?' he asked.

She smiled at him serenely. 'I am just a secretary.'

They stopped at red lights on Sixty-eighth.

'You come from Tokyo?'

'No, I come from Miyagi. From the city of Sendai. I came to Tokyo to work.'

'To work for Mr Eda?'

'Yes, sir.'

'The name is Ross.'

'Then, yes, Ross.'

Ross laughed. She was looking forward, her face in profile to him. In the streetlights as they swept downtown, it was a profile of perfection, long eyelashes, petite nose, lips slightly parted. Maybe she was yakuza – but maybe not.

'Yukiko-san, I can imagine all the work which went into that meal. How would you like a nightcap someplace?'

Yukiko looked at her watch, then smiled.

'That would be lovely, Ross. And please call me Yukiko.'

There were dark little booths, all facing a floor which pulsed with lights in time to the beat. There were real vines overhead: arm-thick branches and deep green, glossy leaves. There was a fish pond and a grand piano and the whole place was below street level on Thirty-seventh and First.

'The last time I was here I drank some really old Irish whiskey,' Ross said. 'You should try it.'

Yukiko nodded and smiled.

'What's it like for a Japanese living in New York?' Ross asked.

'America has strange ways for us Japanese,' Yukiko replied. 'At home, we are a homogeneous society; over here we find we must act out of character.'

'Such as?'

'Such as the whole area of confrontation. In America, confrontation is an art form. You pound the table in negotiations.

127

You shout down the phone. A cab driver doesn't inquire where you wish to be taken, he shouts the question at you; you shout the answer back. In Japan these things would be frightening and serious. We are a consensus society. In Japan a raised eyebrow can mean a lot.'

The whiskey arrived and they raised their glasses. 'To a perfect evening,' Ross proposed.

'Cheers,' said Yukiko.

'You speak English fluently,' Ross smiled.

'I learned it at school,' Yukiko said, 'then later at night classes in Tokyo.'

'It's so different, Japan, isn't it?' Ross said. 'I wonder if we Westerners can ever really understand the country or the people.'

'Have you been there, Ross?' asked Yukiko and looked at him with big eyes.

'Once, but only for a quick visit,' replied Ross truthfully.

'The spring is the best time,' Yukiko said. 'It is neither hot nor cold and the cherry blossom is out.'

'Tell me about this cherry blossom thing,' Ross said. 'Do people actually race around with calipers, measuring the size of the blooms?'

She giggled and put her hand in front of her face.

'Sometimes, yes. What else do you know about Japan?'

'That you work hard, live to be a hundred and are taking over the world.'

'You know a lot. Tell me about yourself, your work.'

'Oh, it's all pretty routine stuff, really. Analysing proposals, making decisions about money. I would much rather be measuring the size of a cherry blossom.'

She giggled respectfully, then said: 'I could not help overhearing Eda-san say you live in Canada.'

'That's right. In Nova Scotia, the wilderness.'

'Ahhh. You are Canadian?'

'No, I'm American, but I've chosen to live up there.'

'Ahhh. You run your business from there?'

'Yes, I do.'

'What is it called?'

'I operate under my own name,' he replied casually.

'Ahhh. You have no partners, no one to look after things when you are away?'

'It's just me.'

'I could not help hearing Eda-san say that you think people should invest in platinum. Is it true? Is that where I should put my money, Ross?'

Ross shook his head.

'Two days ago I thought so,' he said as the music changed. 'Today I'm not sure. You like dancing?'

'Sure,' she said.

They went to the empty floor and began to slowly jive. Infrared strobe lights in the ceiling whirled and flashed and picked out Yukiko's mouth in the darkness like a floating kiss.

'What did Eda tell you to ask me?' he asked quietly.

She looked up at him. 'Please?'

'I think you know what I said,' he said gently.

'Is this not the way Americans hold polite conversation?' she asked, wide-eyed. "Hi! Where do you come from? What do you do? How much money do you earn?" I just asked you the same sort of questions as you asked me on the way here in the taxi: "How long have you worked for Eda? Do you like the work? Do you come from Tokyo?" Am I not behaving like a proper American girl?'

The music speeded up and she was away across the floor, elbows working, head down, the turtleshell comb in her topknot chattering furiously in the coloured lights. Suddenly Sun Valley and the Masisi seemed very far away; suddenly the last time he had enjoyed the company of a beautiful woman seemed very long ago.

'Let's make a deal,' he shouted to her over the noise.

She looked up as they both kept rhythm.

'No more questions, OK?'

She looked at him studiously, then a smile lit her face like a sunburst.

'A deal,' she said.

Midnight slipped by without a murmur. The club was much fuller now, the beat slower, the dance floor full. They ate two bowls of the house special – ice cream with honey and almonds – and drank glasses of the house champagne.

She leaned back and closed her eyes, her hands upwards in her lap.

'You look like you're praying when you sit like that,' Ross said.

'In a way I am,' she replied.

'Explain.'

She looked at him, listened to the music, smiled. 'You know what Zen is?' she asked.

'It's Eastern mysticism, flowers, swords, things we Westerners can't grasp,' Ross replied.

'Zen is mysticism, but with a very Japanese flavour,' Yukiko said. 'The very special cultural qualities of Japan spring from Zen principles, qualities like simplicity, asymmetry, stillness, emptiness. All our arts, both oral, written and visual, and all our physical disciplines including the martial arts have their roots in Zen.'

'Does it have an ultimate goal – like everlasting life, for example?' he asked.

'The qualities I mentioned are the outer forms of what on the inner plane we call satori, or awakening,' Yukiko said. 'Satori is Zen. It is the mystery and the meaning of you. You can only really understand it by experiencing it.'

'Could you call it "holiness"?' asked Ross.

'That risks confusing it with the Christian ethic and things like good deeds,' she answered. 'Zen is concerned with *the moment*; it may happen when you are riding the subway, or writing a letter, or peeling a carrot. Satori suddenly hits you like a thunderbolt and you are never the same again. You experience peace.'

Ross felt his senses do a cartwheel. Her face had the assurance of extraordinary beauty.

'In Eda's apartment this evening, I looked at you serving the meal,' he said. 'Apart from your being beautiful, I felt you had something extra. I think you've just told me what it is.'

She smiled without affectation. 'Zen is the peak of Mount Fuji. Most of us are just looking for paths in the foothills.'

'Tell me more,' Ross said.

Yukiko said: 'A Japanese poet once wrote:

> *How marvelous, how miraculous,*
> *I draw water,*

130

I gather fuel.

The waterfowl
Lays its beak in its breast
And sleeps as it floats.

An old pine tree preaches wisdom
And a wild bird is crying truth.

The poet was totally at one with himself and the world; he had discovered satori.'

'I need time to figure out what it means,' Ross said. 'But it's beautiful.'

'It's really about inner peace,' Yukiko said. 'Do you have such peace, Ross?'

Ross looked at her.

'Sometimes.'

'But not always?'

'I've found that life has a nasty habit, the moment you feel at peace, of coming along and screwing everything up,' he said.

'You've been hurt, haven't you?'

'Who hasn't?'

'Each of us is a well,' Yukiko said. 'Some are shallow, some deep. The shallow wells are easily filled; their requirements are few; the lightest shower satisfies them. The deep wells are more difficult: their streams go into the very heart of the earth so they need much water before they are filled; but when full, they will never run dry. You are a deep well, Ross.'

Ross looked at her for a long moment. In the background they were playing 'Rainy Night in Georgia'. She took his hand as they went out on to the small floor, then both her arms went up around his neck as they swayed softly with the music. Ross savoured her perfume and her soft, pliant body. He felt an exuberance which he had last felt looking at the hull of his *Mermaid*.

'I want to see you again,' he murmured.

'And I want to see you,' Yukiko whispered.

She turned her face up to his and he kissed her. She had even given him the word for it: he had got satori.

*

131

It was 6.15 and he was walking down empty Park Avenue, trying to wonder if at any moment he might float. Yukiko. Her fragrance. Her face. Her lips. Her body. Her femininity was still in charge of his system. Infatuation had last happened so long ago that he had forgotten the sensations that come with it: delirious irresponsibility, a hit from the body's own pharmaceutical department. He had sat in Central Park for over an hour watching the world come to life. He had seen the squirrels, felt the sun, waved to the first joggers.

He also felt a bewilderment which he needed time to analyse. Twelve hours ago, nothing had been more important than stopping Sun Valley and getting Freeman what he wanted; twelve hours later the urgency was no less but now it was complicated. Her smell was part of him. He brought his face down to his shoulder and inhaled her; she was there, he could bring his hand to stroke her hair and kiss her she was so close. But what if she were yakuza? Would that mean they were on different sides? He turned east on Seventieth. He had her address in Brooklyn. He had to see her again. He would. That was the complication. Was a uniquely beautiful woman like Yukiko worth sacrificing for the shares in a corporation? Was it a trade-off between her and Oxx? Could he bring himself to *use* her to help Freeman? Ross reached the apartment building. Yukiko . . . Flowers in an unexpected place, perfume in a wood after rain, sunlight through water, she was them all.

Yet he had promised Freeman. Could he be loyal to both if she were yakuza? Ross stepped from the elevator. Eda had been lying he was sure, but Ross now had no idea what the next step was or whether a next step was even possible.

In the curtained room, the green light on the telephone machine was winking at him like a serpent. He kicked off his shoes and rewound it.

'Ross, this is Orem Williams, Mr Oxx's personal assistant, calling you at four a.m. New York time.'

Ross blinked. Four a.m.?

'Mr Oxx has suffered a severe coronary. He is in the intensive care unit of the San José Clinic where I've just returned from. His condition is critical.'

Ross sat with a thud.

132

'The board of Industrial Oxx have held an emergency board meeting by conference phone. By unanimous vote, Mr Lascalla of Portfolio Trust has been appointed acting chairman. I'll be pleased to update you. Thank you.'

Something undefinable rose from Ross's chest into his throat. He rewound the tape and replayed it; then he walked to the window, shaking his head and pulled the cord so that daylight flooded the room. His doubt of moments before shamed him and sat like a harbinger of doom in the middle distance that was New York. He pinched his eyes but still the tears came.

Eight

The sides of the dōjō, the combat area, were lined with kneeling police cadets, each helmeted and visored into huge, curious ants. A squeak of twisting heel on pine signalled a lunge from the larger of the two barefoot competitors. Both turned and faced again, their shinai, their long swords of bound bamboo, presented.

'Yōi . . . hajime!' cried the referee. 'Fence!'

Inspector Nobuo saw Junpei Iseki's feint, parried it and immediately swung his shinai left. He anticipated correctly: the echoing clack of bamboo was followed by a deadly, swooshing roundhouse. Nobuo made a half step back; then sprang and cut to breastplate. There was an appreciative murmur from the spectators.

'Yōi . . . hajime!'

Iseki knew he was trailing. The split skirts of his hakama swirling, he came forward, cutting furiously. Nobuo ducked and parried, thwarting the bigger man's strength. He could see Iseki lift up from his heels, then bring the shinai mightily down. Nobuo sank with it to kill the blow, then came up on springs with a fierce counterattack. Iseki was off-balance now, retreating, using strength in place of skill.

'*Men!*' shrieked Nobuo, launching the winning cut from somewhere between his shoulder blades. The sword struck Iseki's steel helmet with a reverberating clang and Nobuo cantered past triumphantly.

134

The referee signalled the winner as applause broke out.

'Excellent, Nobuo-san, excellent,' Junpei Iseki gasped, dragging off his helmet.

'With you, win or lose, it is always work of the utmost difficulty, Iseki-san,' Nobuo bowed.

As they entered the changing room, a valet took their helmets and gloves. They peeled off, bodies steaming.

'I finished your report late last night,' said Iseki, sitting, towelled. 'I'm on the eighteenth floor later this morning. They're going to love us.'

'The facts are there,' Nobuo said. 'Early last November, Chiyaha flew to Manila. We've traced him to the island of Mindoro where he has a shabu plant. The local police are on a payoff, but my counterpart in Manila seems straight enough. A month back he pulled in a drugs dealer and got wind of a killing on Mindoro. The dates tally exactly with Chiyaha's visit.'

'A ninja,' said Junpei Iseki grimly.

'A ninja with skills in sul sa,' Nobuo affirmed. 'The yakuza fly whores out to the islands once a month. A year ago one of them came back and complained to the cops about the guard commander, a sul sa master. She described him in great detail – a "round eyes", a half-caste, very strong, very intricate body tattoos. She says he almost strangled her. Following my inquiry the cops looked her up again. She'd been back to Mindoro three months ago but the talk was that this ninja had left after the alleged killing with an unnamed yakuza oyabun from mainland Japan. Again the dates tally to Chiyaha.'

'A "round eyes",' said Iseki thoughtfully.

'Western in appearance but half oriental,' Nobuo said.

'Imperial Security will go crazy,' Iseki said, 'and all the flak will come down on us.'

Nobuo continued: 'In late November, we have at least six of Japan's main oyabun holed up in an hotel in Funagata Yama – including Chiyaha and Kazuhiro Kasumi, sworn enemies. Why? Is it the move Chiyaha has always wanted to make? But as for an onward connection that might threaten the Tennō, the Emperor . . .'

Iseki scratched his white-haired chest.

135

'Why can't we find Okuma's widow and have her tell us what's going on? Why do we have to guess every step of the way?'

'Every policeman in every prefecture in Japan knows we're looking for Mama Yayoi Okuma,' Nobuo said. 'I've been up to Sendai myself and evaluated all Okuma's contacts – the trouble is that old Abe from Hokkaido has moved into Sendai and people are scared out of their wits.'

'Do you think Mama Yayoi is dead, Nobuo?' asked Iseki directly.

Nobuo shook his head.

'Were she dead, why would there be so much silence?' he asked. 'No, Iseki-san, my humble opinion is that the yakuza have no better idea of where she is than we.'

*   *   *

Ross adjusted his eyes to the dim light. He no longer felt the discomfort of the mouth-mask nor the penetrating, sterilized smell of the hospital. He stared at the white face on the white pillow. A translucent cup obscured the mouth; a white cap collected the white hair.

'Freeman?'

Breathing was a sudden jerk, dictated by the battery of bedside machines whose tubes snaked everywhere.

'Freeman, it's Ross.'

Without its open eyes, its blue flames, the face was as dead as parchment. Had it always been so dead in sleep? What had the ever-present women seen? A face like this, a bloodless mask of something not alive?

Ross swallowed to clear the dryness from his throat. He had real difficulty in believing that the two men were the same: this ... person in the bed, and his Freeman. He blinked. His Freeman. He had said it. *His* Freeman! No longer dangerous, or overbearing, or scheming. Nothing. Ross looked down and tried to understand his doubts of two weeks ago. It might have been worse. He might have refused to come to Freeman's call, then as with Misty, a month later he might have read a throwaway line in a paper ...

136

'I haven't stopped them yet, Freeman,' he said aloud. 'But I will.'

A thousand people seemed to be screaming all at once. The vast auditorium on the seventh floor of four, World Trade Center, New York, could have been a gladiators' arena from a past age were it not for the electronic wizardry, or an asylum from the twenty-first century were it not that the doors were unlocked.

Picking his way through ankle deep paper, pushing through the surge of shirtsleeved, shouting bodies, Timothy Manners looked more like a prosperous undertaker coming to measure up the victims of Saint Vitus Dance than a metals broker. He liked the bedlam. It reminded him of the street in East London where he'd grown up with dozens of raucous kids like himself, living on their wits.

Manners sniffed and bared his teeth. The platinum ring looked dead – like nearby gold and silver. No wonder Cresswels, New York were going to have a piss awful year.

'We may have to reappraise, Timmy.'

The chairman's public school obliqueness had done nothing to soften the threat. Manners reminded himself of the time twenty years before when, overhearing a chance remark from a shipper, he had put every shilling he could lay his hands on into coffee. The market went up by a factor of ten. But at the time, he told himself, *at the time*, no one else believed except himself. No one.

He approached the Cresswels booth. The floor broker looked up in surprise from his salami roll.

'Mr Manners.'

'Anything happening, son?' Manners asked, although he knew the answer.

'Nothing,' the floor man said, 'August is still four hundred five bid, four hundred six a seller. There haven't been more than a hundred trades all morning. Gold and silver are the same. You tell me, what's going to move these precious metals up or down? Nothin'.'

Manners bared his teeth.

'I want you to work an order,' he said quietly. 'Sell twenty thousand ounces of the August down to four hundred and four dollars an ounce. Slowly, understood? No rush.'

137

'Sell it?' the broker asked. 'Mind of I ask why?'

'Because it's going down, son,' Manners said dryly, 'and when it does I'm going to buy it in again and make a fat profit.'

'I know that, sir,' said the floor man, colouring, 'but platinum seems to be at the bottom of it's range. I mean, has there been a new mine discovered or something?'

'Just be a good boy and sell it,' said Manners and turned for the doors of NYMEX.

Ross waited for the lights, then left the kerb and continued downtown. There was a little breeze, pleasant heat. Across the traffic, across Central Park, buildings floated over trees at the horizon. In the near trees he could see birds moving. Over the wall, inside the Park and about five hundred yards away, the headbands of joggers bobbed. Everything was moving: the joggers, the foliage, the birds, even the distant buildings bent and straightened in the haze. Movement was the secret. You live, you move. The man who stands still is dead. You take what you have and you go forward.

Espresso was a bustling coffee shop with timber floors halfway between Fifth Avenue and Sixth. Ross combed both his hands through his hair and walked through the mirrored door. She was sitting in the lobby. Her hair shot up in spikes and spilled on to her forehead. Apart from the pink on her lips, she wore no makeup. Perfect.

'Hello, Ross.'

His eyes searched her face; she held out her hand and he kissed it. A waiter led them across the clattering room to a table. Yukiko took off a cream coloured jacket, ribbed with curving lines like a seashell.

'How are you, Ross?'

'I'm just fine,' he smiled. 'I've been chasing around, trying to tidy up some things.'

'When do you leave for the north?'

'Too soon, I'm afraid.'

A girl wearing a toga and a garland of leaves in her hair brought the menu. Ross ordered.

'Is it very cold where you go?' Yukiko asked. 'I looked it up on the map and it seems if you go much further you are in ice caps.'

138

'It often seems like that,' Ross said. 'I guess it never gets really cold in Japan.'

'In Sendai where I come from, there is snow every winter,' she said.

'I bet you ski like an angel,' he said.

When she smiled, she shone.

'Do angels ski?'

'When they do they look like you.'

'We don't have angels in Japan,' Yukiko said. 'We have ancestors whose memories we venerate, we have gods, but no angels.'

'You may start a trend,' he said and she smiled again.

The coffee arrived; Ross pressed down the plunger, then poured.

'How much longer will you be in New York?' he asked.

'I'm not sure,' she replied, 'it is up to Eda-san.'

Ross nodded. 'I guess you've known him a long time,' he said.

She looked at him curiously.

'For a few years,' she said. 'Hmmm, this coffee is good!'

Ross watched as she closed her eyes in pleasure and breathed in the fumes.

Ross sipped.

'The menu says it's Colombian,' he said carefully, 'but I don't think that's true. For my money it's a blend of Mexican and Costa Rican.'

'Who cares?' Yukiko smiled. 'It's delicious.'

'But it's not Colombian,' Ross said.

'Is that so important?' she asked quietly, putting down her cup.

'Isn't that what we spoke of the other evening?' he replied. 'Satori? Enlightenment?'

'You would make a good zen scholar, Ross.'

Ross took her hands.

'Yukiko, I have thought about you almost continuously since we met two nights ago,' he said. 'There are things I must tell you.'

'I said then you were a deep well,' she said. 'Now the well is bubbling over.'

'Maybe so, but I trust my own instincts. If I'm bubbling over it's because you make me.'

139

'Then I'm happy,' she said.

'I want to see you again,' Ross said. 'But first I want you to make me a promise.'

Yukiko tilted her head. 'About what?'

'You must promise me that you trust me.'

She smiled. 'I trust you.'

'There are things you should know,' Ross said. 'My background for instance: it's commodities, things like precious metals, gold, silver. Platinum.'

She nodded.

'The reason I'm in New York is a long story,' Ross said, 'but let me just say that I've indirectly come across information that I want to share with you. It concerns Mr Eda.'

'Oh?' Yukiko said. 'Information?'

'Look, this may come as a shock,' Ross said, 'but I think Eda is yakuza.'

She sat perfectly still, a doe that has scented the air.

'Who told you that?' she whispered.

'Just trust me,' Ross said. 'Is it true?'

If Yukiko was breathing there was no sign of it.

'Sun Valley is yakuza backed, Yukiko,' he said quietly. 'Did you know that?'

'We had a deal,' she whispered. 'You said: "no more questions".'

'I know we had a deal,' Ross said fervently, 'but things have changed in the last two days. Now I'm caught between my regard for you and my loyalty to the man who gave me everything. I want you to help me; I want you to tell me if the people behind Sun Valley are yakuza.'

She blinked once.

'Why?'

'Because I want to stop the Sun Valley bid for Oxx,' Ross said. 'Because of an old man's promise. Because of the tribal beliefs of a people no one has ever heard of who live in a place called Bamolisi.' He tried to make her smile. 'Does that answer your question?'

But Yukiko wasn't smiling. She had freed her hands and was pushing her chair back.

'I'm sorry, but I've got to go.'

'Yukiko . . .'

140

'This has been a mistake,' she said.

'Yukiko!'

His voice stopped her reaching for her jacket.

'You promised me you would trust me!' Ross cried. 'Friends are for telling the truth. I had to tell you this.'

'Thank you,' she said, starting to get up, 'but I really have to go now.'

Ross's hand snaked over and made her arm part of the table.

'Yukiko!'

'Let go of my arm!' she whispered fiercely.

'What the hell is the matter with you?' he hissed.

'You're hurting me!'

'For Christ's sake, why can't we talk about it?'

'I don't want to talk, I want to leave!'

'You want to leave because you know what I'm saying is true, isn't that right? You won't sit here and listen because you already know!'

'You're crazy!'

'Am I so crazy?' Ross asked. 'Tell me Eda's not yakuza and I'll believe you.'

Her eyelids flickered, then she wriggled away and jumped up, her chair falling backwards. An oasis of silence spread out from their table as the diminutive figure strode across the room, her heels echoing on wood. Ross followed with the waitress in the toga close behind.

'*Yukiko!*'

At the door he corralled her against the wall. Her face was now streaked with tear lines.

'OK,' Ross said calmly, 'OK, I'm sorry. I'm sorry if what I said back there upset you. I can imagine the loyalty you must have to Eda. But please hear what I've got to say.'

'Are you going to let me out of this place?' Yukiko asked. 'Or do I have to scream?'

'For Christ's sake, why can't we talk about it?' Ross cried.

She opened her mouth and screamed a full-blooded scream that stopped all activity in that part of Manhattan.

Ross watched her, bag hitched on shoulder, walk through the door. He followed her out to the street.

'Yukiko!' he shouted, but she kept walking for Fifth, never

turning her head. Ross stood as the tiny figure became lost on the sidewalk.

The long Caddy with the blacked out windows on the far kerb were ten a penny in New York.

In an anonymous suite on the eighth floor of six World Trade Center, eight men perused copies of a one-page fax. At the head of the table, Ed Rich, the square shouldered Special Agent in Charge of the Secret Service Field Office in New York City – to everyone, the SAC – leant back thoughtfully. He looked at Special Agent Bernie Hutt, twenty-six and on his second year in the New York Field Office of the Secret Service. Hutt had dark sleep rings under his eyes. That kid is going to screw himself into the grave before he leaves New York, Rich thought ruefully.

'What's your impression, Mr Rich?'

The only black man present was Brandon Amis, a Deputy Chief of the New York Police Department (NYPD), a man of fifty plus with a round, intelligent face and greying hair. He was also Commanding Officer of the Police Intelligence Division.

'It's not a specific threat, Chief,' SAC Rich replied. 'It comes, as you see, from the Japanese Imperial Palace Security Force – Kokyo Kei Satsu, the KKS. There's a reference to possible yakuza, or Japanese mafia, connections. No suggestion is made that the threat is connected in any way to the US visit.'

'Nevertheless, a threat, at whatever level exists,' said a slim, reserved man. Eric Kruger was the senior field representative from the Foreign Office Section of the State Department. He looked up the table. 'Do we have any independent information?'

'Negative,' said SAC Rich. His hair was steel-brush grey; he had eyes like the water in the harbour outside: they changed colour with the atmosphere. He had come to the New York Field Office via the Presidential Detail. A CPA by training, he was married with two kids, boys, and lived in Manhattan.

'Gentlemen, I'd like to focus on numbers this morning. We need to agree on numbers, then build security around those numbers. After today, no extras, even if requested by the Emperor himself. Captain Levine?'

Zach Levine was sallow and bald and had active, observant

142

eyes. A Port Authority police captain, he was in charge of security at New York's airports.

'OK, we're talking S for Suki-yaki, Wednesday, May twenty-sixth,' he said. 'The Emperor is wheels down JFK at nine a.m. He goes straight into Hangar Fourteen where security will be the same as for the President of the United States visiting New York.'

'We've got a couple of lists at this stage,' Rich said.

Levine nodded. 'Incoming, the Emperor, the Empress, our own Secretary of State and his wife, the Japanese Foreign Minister, the Japanese Ambassador, the President of the Japan Foundation, and the Commissioner at the Agency for Cultural Affairs in Tokyo plus all their wives. Add to those, ten members of the Imperial Palace Police Security Force and half a dozen members of Kunai Cho – the Imperial Household Agency – and you have twenty-eight incomers, not including our own travelling security personnel and media.'

The other men round the table took notes.

'A lot of people on the plane,' remarked Chief Amis.

'Inevitable,' SAC Rich said. 'The exhibition has been dubbed the most important collection of Edo Period art ever assembled outside Japan.'

Levine continued: 'Present in Fourteen will be the Welcoming Committee.' He picked up a sheet of paper. 'The Governor of New York, The Mayor of New York, our two Senators and three of our Congressmen, the Japanese Ambassador to the UN and the US Ambassador in Tokyo. That's the front line, plus, of course, all their wives. Then you've got the Chairman of the Port Authority of New York, the Chairman and Chief Executive Officer of JFK International and the manager of the Japanese Air Lines office in JFK and their wives.'

'JAL are freighting the exhibition from Tokyo,' explained SAC Rich.

'Finally,' said Captain Levine, 'we have a group of sixteen schoolchildren from a Japanese school on Long Island, two teachers, and a Japanese poet who's lived in Boston for thirty years and who's flying down for the big occasion. The Emperor is a big fan. Including the arrival party, but again excluding US security personnel and media, that makes seventy-three people in Hangar Fourteen.'

143

'All passed by the KKS?' queried Kruger from State.

'Every man, woman and child,' Levine replied. 'That list is now closed.'

'Problems in and around JFK?' queried Chief Amis.

'At least two demonstrations,' Zach Levine replied. 'Japanese students and others protesting against the acquisition of farmland for Narita Airport, Tokyo, and a right wing group who want Japan to attack Russia. They'll be kept way, way back. The Emperor won't see them.'

'Good,' said Eric Kruger.

'Where are we at with Highway, Chief?' inquired SAC Rich.

'Of the seventy-three people in Hangar Fourteen,' replied Chief Amis, 'the school group, the poet and the JFK people all remain behind and the remaining forty-four travel into Manhattan by motorcade, departing nine twenty-five, allowing for usual delays.'

'Forty-four people?' asked Kruger, totting.

'The Governor and his wife have a local engagement upstate,' Chief Amis explained. 'The motorcade comes into town, route now decided by Highway District. We're budgeting thirty-six minutes, JFK to the Metropolitan.'

'Security on route?' asked a man sitting behind Kruger, a special agent from the State Department.

'I'd like to leave the technical security for another discussion,' Ed Rich said and smiled pleasantly at the men from Foggy Bottom. He turned around. 'OK, we're in the museum. How do the numbers look, Mr Hutt?'

Special Agent Bernie Hutt cleared his throat.

'Pretty numerous, sir. Forty-four dignitaries arrive from JFK. In the exhibition pavilion on the first floor of the Metropolitan, two distinct groups will be waiting: one Japanese, one American.' Bernie held up a list. 'These are the names who've been passed and vetted by both ourselves and Japanese security personnel. There are one hundred and eighty-six people.'

'That'll make over three hundred people in all, Mr Rich,' said Chief Amis.

'Three hundred and ten, Chief, including all US security personnel, museum employees and media,' said Ed Rich quietly.

'Where have they come from?' Chief Amis asked.

Bernie Hutt looked down his list.

144

'Far more have been left off than got on, sir,' he remarked. 'All the Japan Foundation and their Cultural Affairs Bureau are making the trip, plus architects and designers from Tokyo. Add the board of the Metropolitan Museum, their senior staff, subcommittees and advisors; and finally, half a dozen sundry luminaries including the Archbishop of New York.'

'And all their wives,' said Zach Levine.

'Except, presumably, the Archbishop,' Chief Amis observed.

Ed Rich smiled. This was his fifth such visit. He appreciated the professionalism of the men around the table, guys who would lay down their own lives if necessary for a man they would never meet.

'The Emperor opens the exhibition.' he said. 'A small reception area with a rest room off it has been provided for the royal party within the pavilion at the request of the KKS. The opening ceremony and reception takes one hour ten minutes in all. The royals have no further public engagements. They fly home next day.'

'Museum employees,' said Kruger of State.

'We will be issuing special passes,' fielded Bernie with Rich's approval. 'Since this exhibition has been insured for over a billion dollars, the underwriters have insisted that an armed guard be with the exhibits at all times – including inside the pavilion before the show opens. Security Ten, a firm known to us, specializing in art escort and protection, are in place.'

'After the museum, the Emperor retraces his route to JFK and flies home,' Rich said and looked around the table for questions.

'That just leaves the threat received from Tokyo,' said Kruger from State.

'I am proposing to keep closely in touch with our counterparts in Tokyo over the next thirteen days,' said Rich.

'So we're not raising the perceived threat level,' said Kruger, pressing for a formal decision.

Ed Rich knew the game very well: State would like a world in which all incoming dignitaries would be one thousand per cent safe in an environment which would suggest that a security apparatus did not exist. He'd dealt with Eric Kruger before. Put another sniper on the roof and the guy was talking police state.

'Not at this time,' replied SAC Rich.

'Our next meeting?' asked Chief Amis.

'Friday, May twenty-first,' Rich responded. 'Chief of Department's Conference Room, Police Headquarters, eleven a.m.'

He watched Bernie Hutt, the first to put his file away. That kid'll screw himself to death, he thought wryly.

At five o'clock, Yukiko boarded the subway at Seventy-seventh Street. She was exhausted. And confused. She had made a fool of herself with a man she should never have agreed to meet; and then she had returned to the office to find Eda in a very strange humour.

She composed her thoughts as the train doors closed. She had been foolish. Young and old, north and south, east and west: they were made apart for a reason. Western thought was too crude and simple, everything was reduced to banality in a ceaseless attempt to explain and justify. In Japan energies which existed in every country were harnessed and put to work for the good of the whole community; the West spent their lifetimes trying to deny that such energies exist.

For Christ's sake, why can't we talk about it?

Talk? She shook her head. How could he expect her to talk? But he had been different. His body had been enormous, but gentle, his hands understanding. When he kissed her she had tingled through every pore. She sighed. Forget him. Forget his clumsy intrusion. There were more important things to think of.

The doors opened at Twenty-third Street and the car filled.

She had come back to the office wearing sunglasses so that Eda-san would not see her red eyes. Eda-san was on the phone; he looked up.

'Ahh, konnichi wa,' he said, replacing the phone and inclining. He was sweating, she noticed; she had never seen him sweating before. And his eyes were evasive.

'Konnichi wa,' she replied cautiously.

'There is not much to be done here today,' Eda said. 'Please, if you wish, take the rest of the day off.'

'Thank you,' Yukiko bowed.

She turned to leave his office.

'Yukiko-san!'

'Hai?'

146

'The gaijin from the other evening, Ross Magee,' Eda said. 'Have you seen him again?'

'No, Eda-san,' Yukiko answered innocently.

'Ahh,' Eda said, almost sadly.

As she had left his office he had been standing behind his desk, looking after her with a strange expression on his face.

The train stopped at Wall Street and as many people as could fit squeezed on. Yukiko frowned. Eda-san's 'ahh', such a little sound, yet so full of disappointment. Why had she lied? She had done so with such ease that she had surprised herself. She had never lied to Eda-san before. Did it matter? But his reaction ... She shook her head irritably. Although she had lied, it was a lie about nothing, and anyway, how could Eda-san have possibly known?

She saw her own reflection in the window as they restarted. She felt a tug of regret. *Trust me.* She sighed. Forget Eda-san, forget Ross. She needed a good sleep.

Borough Hall, Brooklyn and half the carriage emptied.

Yukiko opened her bag and took out a rolled newspaper, *Asahi Shimbun*, the Tokyo daily that got to them three days after publication. She folded it out as the train drew away from Grand Army Plaza and looked at the front page. There was a photograph of a bomb site with a man's picture inset. Yukiko gaped. Her head jerked back and struck the back of her seat. Suddenly breathless, she sucked air like a fish. A girl on the opposite seat stood up nervously. Yukiko's arms and hands shook uncontrollably. On legs of sand, paper held out front, she staggered from the train as the doors opened at Brooklyn Museum.

'Hey, your bag!' shouted the girl but got no response. She threw Yukiko's bag after her and it hit the platform, spilling it's contents out.

The train pulled away. Moaning in shock, Yukiko sank down as people made their careful way around her. The keys from her bag lay shining in the platform lights: they had a white tag with her name: 'Y. Okuma.'

Ross crossed by the statue of a mounted General Sherman, walked up the steps of the Plaza and in through the lobby. The

Oak Room was busy; Kyle sat at a table with his back to Central Park South.

'Coffee?' he smiled.

'An Irish coffee,' Ross said, sitting.

'Two,' said Kyle to the waiter. He turned back, his green eyes shrewd. 'You look as if you've been hitting New York pretty hard, old buddy.'

Ross told him about Eda. About Yukiko.

'Eda's a liar, I just know,' he said, as two white-bobbed Irish coffees arrived. 'And as soon as I mentioned yakuza to Yukiko she got up and bolted like a rabbit.' He clenched his fist. 'These guys are taking over a major American corporation,' he said grimly, 'and I'm damned if I know how to stop them.'

Kyle took a drink and licked cream from his lip.

'You may be jumping the gun,' he said cautiously.

'Meaning?'

'You asked me to make inquiries about Sun Valley and about this Eiichi Eda, right?' Kyle said. 'I did. I put a top level inquiry into Treasury in Tokyo and eventually I got a response – or part of a response. Sun Valley are on the level, they're owned out of Kobe by foundations of some kind. There's nothing to suggest they're yakuza – or that they ever got a parking ticket.'

'And Eda?'

'I'm still waiting for word on Eiichi Eda, but it doesn't look too promising, does it?' Kyle asked.

Ross's breath came out in a long whistle. 'I don't believe it. It's impossible to find out anything in Japan if they don't want you to. Eda was lying. Why? Because he's yakuza, Kyle!'

'You want to stop the bid very badly, I know,' said Kyle gently. 'But there comes a time to face facts. What about this fishing boat? Where's the plan I heard about in Washington? Come on! Don't get sucked into something that has no future, Ross!'

'I saw Freeman yesterday,' Ross said. 'He's in a coma, he may be dead in a few days. What am I to do? Walk away from this thing? Somebody has to do this, Kyle!'

'Oxx is lost, Ross,' said Kyle with quiet insistence. 'Maybe Bamolisi will turn out OK in the end and you'll find that Freeman never had anything to worry about.'

Ross felt his senses do a cartwheel. If Kyle was right, then

148

Sun Valley was clean, there was no reason why the bid should not go through, and he had alienated the most beautiful woman he had ever met.

'I've got to catch the shuttle,' Kyle said and they stood up. 'Hey, cheer up! In a few days it'll be Captain Magee! Don't forget my invitation!'

'I won't forget,' said Ross as he stood on the steps of the Plaza, watching as Kyle made his way to the head of a line of cabs on Fifth.

Ross walked uptown. He passed the synagogue on East Sixty-second Street and ran his hand through his hair. He saw her beautiful face, shining as she spoke the lines of poetry, and he felt something plunge inside him. He could imagine her body as they danced. Infatuation. It blotted out all other senses. So long since he'd spent an evening with a woman . . .

Unfeeling and emotionless, that was the only way to survive. A prehistoric creature that slowly took in messages through its primeval antennae and digested them over a long time. Cold. A shell without a memory. But he had wanted her so badly.

He turned west on Sixty-ninth Street. He had to see her again. He might even explain to Freeman what he was doing. Could he ever talk to Freeman again? If Freeman did regain consciousness, what could he tell him? We've failed, Freeman, I'm sorry, but there was nothing I could do. Send the old man off on his journey, knowing that everything he stood for had ended in ruins? Was there an option? A lie? We won, Freeman, we stopped the bastards. Or: it's all right, Freeman, they've agreed to respect your promise to the Masisi. The old man might die happy. But what then of the spirit, the swallow that would fly free over Bamolisi or Santa Clara County? Would it dip over infinite years into countless pools seeking that one droplet of truth that had been denied it?

She had cried. Her eyes had filled and overflowed. How could he possibly fathom the size of the gap between them? She had frozen on the word 'yakuza' and he had never got her back. What did he know of her background or culture or the sensitivities which he had offended? The chemistry had worked that first night more powerfully than anything he had ever remembered – then as surely as night ends day he had thrown it away.

He stepped off the kerb to cross at Seventieth Street; a cab waited there, its 'For Hire' light on.

Impulsively, Ross opened the back door.

'Brooklyn,' he said.

Yukiko stumbled along the street, dazed, past men and women staring at her wide eyed, but nothing registered. She had to get home, to a phone, to call someone, Eda, Mama, anyone, she had to make sure there was a mistake, that it wasn't true, she paused and held a lamppost to get her breath.

Chichi. Father. His kindly face. It had smiled when she smiled; it had creased in concern when she cried. When she came home he would lift her off her feet. She set off again as tears rolled down her face and hands on to the rumpled clutched newspaper as a car's horn blared on top of her almost and she stepped back on to the kerb.

Control. This was insane. Like the newspaper story. Mad monkeys in her head; stoically she began to replace them with cool, impersonal digits; at the count of seven his face intruded and made her eyes well with tears again. She crossed.

In Winthrop Street, the last patches of street sunlight were being painted in by the dusk. She hurried, each forward step seeming to save her just from falling. She was a tiny child, he was by her bed, there were princes in castles in the clouds, fire-eating dragons and beautiful princesses who rode white horses through lands where the sun never set.

She couldn't talk on a phone like this. She tried zazen again. One. Two. Three. She thought of the numbers, of clear space, of void, of whiteness, of sky. She turned left on to Linden Boulevard and then left into Penn Street and took out her keys. She ran through the entrance. She never used the elevator, it was just a single flight to the one bedroom apartment. The bulb was gone on the first floor. She turned the key once in the lock and then again. It would not turn a second time. She shook her head. She had put on the deadlock that morning, she was sure. She pushed the door inwards, kicked it to shut, dropped her bag and walked straight to the telephone.

150

There was noise like wind. As Yukiko began to turn and opened her mouth to scream, the sound in her throat was stillborn, cut rigid. She was carried, mute, in. She saw round, empty eyes. She began to kick. He grunted and dropped her, then bowled her over with a slap. She grabbed at him reflexively and tore open his shirt; as she fell she could see swirling colours on his chest. Ninja! she thought in panic and screamed. She was almost on her feet when he hit her again. The blow careened her over the counter which held her cooking things. Everything came with her, deafeningly; she lay knees up on the floor, winded. He picked her up one handed, then methodically slapped her, left cheek, right cheek, six times each, till blood trickled out her lips and her eyes began to go. He dropped her. She saw him through red veils, smiling at her. He knelt, then unzipped his blue jeans. With the thumb and forefinger of his right hand he fastened on her gullet and began to slowly choke her, whilst with his left hand he tore her skirt from her waist in a single, powerful tear. Yukiko experienced extraordinary numbness. Detachment. She was slipping. He was entering her. The fingertips of her right hand searched frantically. He squeezed her throat. Her tongue was out. She felt him thrust hard into her. Her searching fingers fastened on something. She plunged.

'Araghhh!'

He sprang off, a kitchen skewer quivering from beneath his armpit. He tried to grasp at it. Yukiko crawled on all-fours down the hall like a wounded dog. She saw him tug out the skewer, zip himself and come at her, crazy. She got to her feet and bared her teeth. For a moment he checked. She stepped back through the open door of the bathroom as his hand came for her neck, straight as a spear. She fell backwards, pushing the door shut and his hand came through it. In the instant when he had to withdraw Yukiko turned the lock. She could sense him step back. There was a stool beside the tub: she rammed it between tub and lock as he launched. The force of his ramming shook the apartment, but the door held.

Yukiko began to scream.

His arm had come through the jagged hole and was groping for the stool.

Yukiko screamed.

151

A pair of nail-scissors lay on the basin, beyond the questing arm. His fingers touched the rim of the stool. Yukiko lunged for the scissors. His blind arm caught her throat. Trying to break her neck like a chicken's. Screaming, she stabbed with the scissors at the arm. Blood spattered her face. Her vision began to go.

The afternoon was pure May: it was sunny without being oppressively hot and where flowers grew they bloomed.

'This city is crazy. You live here?'

'No.'

'You're lucky, believe me. You want my opinion?'

They were crossing Linden Boulevard in Brooklyn.

'It's a shit hole,' came the opinion. 'Last month it was the garbage; next month it's the subways. You ever been here when the subways are on strike? I mean, have you any idea what it's like?'

Ross looked out the window and thought about Yukiko.

'In exactly three years and six months,' the man said, 'that's exactly forty-two months, we come to the end of the millennium. Whadaya think? The end of the fuckin' millennium! I mean, it only happens every thousand years, right? So for something that happens once every thousand years, do you think that I'm goin' to spend it in this cockamamie city? The hell I am, my good friend, the hell I am.'

Ross paid him off and walked into the empty lobby of the apartment building. Had she wiped her eyes dry and forgotten? Would she remember him from their first evening together or from today? He stopped by the wire cage of the elevator and frowned. At first he thought it was a child crying. He pressed the button to call the car, then felt himself electrify as he heard the scream again.

He took the stairs in threes, passing the elevator car as it came shaking downwards. On the first landing he paused, his ears pounding. He checked three doors before he found hers. He hammered on it.

'*Yukiko!*'

There was something happening at the other side, a scuffling. He stepped back three paces and came to the door with the flat of his right foot. Door and hinges flew inwards and Ross

152

tumbled on his head into a tiny, dark hall. He heard a wind sound behind him and flattened instinctively against the wall.

The downward blow caught him savagely on the shoulder. He kicked out as hard as he could at the dark shape and made the connection. He was dimly aware of a splintered door to his left as he came fully to his feet. Wind again in the dark hall. Ross put up his forearm and then felt a jackhammer strike it.

'Hey! What's going on in there?'

The shout had come from out in the building. Ross lunged and caught shirt in his hands. Head down he powered the other man into the wall and head butted him. He felt excruciating pain as the back of his leg, just above the knee was squeezed in a vice.

'Get the cops!' someone cried.

Ross felt himself thrown. Hands up to protect himself he landed, winded, in the living room of the apartment. It took him a second to realize that his attacker was no longer there.

'Yukiko?'

The apartment might recently have been in the path of a hurricane: plates and pots and upturned pieces of furniture everywhere. Ross was covered in blood, but not his own. He heard a moaning from behind the splintered door. It was jammed from its other side. The hole in it was just big enough for a man's arm. He reached in, found the stool and levered it up. He was aware of people in the apartment doorway.

'Did you see that guy's face?' someone was asking. 'He was crazy!'

'Yukiko?' Ross whispered.

She was rolled into a tiny ball between bath and wall, naked except for a torn blouse that she was trying to wrap herself in. Blood everywhere.

'Is she dead?' someone asked.

'It's all right now,' Ross said to her, hunkering down.

She stiffened and hissed like a cat. She had a pair of scissors clenched dagger-like in her right hand.

'It's me, Yukiko,' he said gently. 'It's Ross.' He got to his feet. 'OK, folks, it's OK now, thank you.'

He ushered the small group back down the hall, then

153

manoeuvred the hall door into place. She hadn't moved when he got back.

'It's me,' he said again and one by one unfolded her rigid fingers.

'I'm sorry, I'm sorry,' she whispered as he put his jacket around her, then picked her up like a child and carried her out.

Nine

Tyler Wrixon flicked back the bedcovers and made for the bathroom. His face looked back at him: pale grey flaps hung under red eyes, stubble dirtied the upper lip and chin. He winced with the change from the horizontal to the vertical. Dousing his face, he squirted out and kneaded on shaving cream, scraped the razor down his throat, and thought of the day ahead.

The board of Oxx had unanimously recommended the bid; the shareholders had indicated over eighty per cent acceptance. The only remaining obstacle – a time wasting, frivolous series of delaying tactics by the ex-chairman of the company – had been swept away by the courts. Truly, the meeting today at noon was a formality.

Wrixon also thought of Ross Magee, and he thought of the information he had been forced to trade with Manners, the Brit, just to find out what was going on. He'd passed it all on and the Japs would do the rest.

He gritted his teeth. He'd celebrate tonight. French food in the good place on Forty-ninth that always had a table for Mr Wrixon, and to hell with ulcers. Even a few days in the Bahamas to spend some of Mr Tyler's profit – not that he ever need have worried: Oxx shares on Friday had traded up to $23.50 in New York ahead of today's meeting.

Fifteen minutes later, fully dressed, Wrixon was leaving the bedroom when his wife awoke.

'What time is it?' she asked.

'It's three-thirty, I need to get in early this morning,' he replied.

'Have a good day,' she murmured as the door closed.

Henry Babbage, gingham-suited, bow-tied and carrying a trilby hat, was outside the door of the Oxx apartment at 9.30 when Ross opened it.

'Henry, thanks for coming,' said Ross quietly, closing the door behind the little man.

'How is she?' Henry asked.

'In shock,' Ross replied. 'They wanted to keep her in the hospital for the weekend, but I didn't want to risk it.'

Henry shook his head grimly.

'Poor girl,' he said. 'I can only try to imagine what she's been through.'

'And what she's still going through,' Ross nodded. 'Henry, it sounds callous, but this gives us – and I include Yukiko – it gives us the chance to stop these people, whoever they are.'

Henry winced.

'Ross, I'm sorry but I have to say this. It's not going to work.'

Ross stuck his jaw forward.

'Henry – come on!'

Henry sighed and they walked into the big living room with it's views of the East River.

'Ross I started making calls at seven this morning and all hell has broken loose. I spoke to Wrixon at Isaac Watson. The guy used language I haven't heard in twenty-five years.'

'That bastard is meant to be acting in the best interests of Oxx,' said Ross.

'He says the Oxx board are fully behind the Sun Valley bid,' Henry said. 'He says he'll vigorously counterattack any move we make by accusing us of sabotage. He says we have no role in the matter. He's got a point there, you know.'

Ross combed his hands through his hair.

'Can we take it from the top? Sun Valley is owned by the Japanese mob. The Oxx takeover is the brainchild of a yakuza called Rokuo Chiyaha, a godfather, a man who has killed and robbed his way to the top and who will do anything to stay there. Yukiko's father was part of this deal, but Chiyaha had

156

him killed. Three days ago, probably because she had lunch with me and later denied it, Chiyaha ordered Yukiko to be killed by a professional killer. If I hadn't happened along she would certainly be dead.'

'How can she say the killer was hired by this Chiyaha?' asked Henry softly.

'Because this morning she called her office and there was another woman at her desk!' Ross cried. 'Because her boss, Eda, wasn't expecting her back! He knew. He's yakuza – Yukiko says his real name is Tatsuo Eda and back in eighty-seven he ripped off Nomura Securities for over a million.'

A door opened and they both turned. Yukiko was dressed in blue jeans and a white polo. One of her eyes was still partially closed by a liver-coloured bruise; and although the polo jumper hid her neck, the tails of more bruises could be seen. She walked uncertainly across the room, then stood beside Ross and took his hand.

'OK?' he asked her.

She nodded.

'This is Henry Babbage,' Ross said. 'Henry, Yukiko Okuma.'

'Very pleased to meet you,' Henry said.

Yukiko sat into the corner of a large sofa and looked expressionlessly ahead.

'I'm very sorry for your loss, Miss Okuma,' Henry said quietly. 'I'm also shocked by what happened to you. Words are quite inadequate.'

Yukiko looked at him, then out in the direction of the river. Henry smiled at her, then turned to Ross.

'Does she speak English?'

Ross nodded. 'Yukiko,' he said, 'can you tell Henry what you told me?'

Yukiko took in her breath, then spoke, all her words a monotone, flat.

'The man who tried to kill me was a paid ninja. Chiyaha ordered him to kill me – like he killed my father.'

'Ninja?' said Henry and looked at Ross.

'A paid killer,' Yukiko said. 'Ninja kill without weapons.'

'Describe him,' Henry said.

'Very strong,' Yukiko said tonelessly. 'Body tattoos. Round eyes.'

157

'I've been telling Henry what you told me,' said Ross gently. 'About your father, and about Chiyaha and Sun Valley and Eda.' He looked to Henry, then to Yukiko. 'Yukiko will testify,' he said and Yukiko nodded.

Henry leaned forward, isolating Yukiko from the conversation.

'It's not enough, Ross. Look, I'm a thousand per cent on your side, but I've got to tell it to you like it is. This one has already been before the Southern District Court in Manhattan three times – twice when Oxx went in and got a TRO, a Temporary Restraining Order, against Sun Valley, and once last week when the board of Oxx went in and got the last TRO lifted. The judge in Southern District is Melvyn Graub. He's a son of a bitch. If he sees this coming through his door again I assure you he'll throw it out. We wouldn't last a minute – not when the board of the company are behind the bid to a man and there's less than two hours to the meeting.'

'We're bringing vital new evidence!' Ross hissed. 'We can't be thrown out!'

Henry was tight-lipped.

'There's no such thing as "can't". This young lady can swear on a stack of Bibles, but what proof can she give? We're asking the court to hold up a two and a half billion dollar takeover for the third time: there's got to be a reason. Miss Okuma, admirable though she is, will be cast by the other side as a tainted witness. What shred of evidence is there to support her story? How can the court know that her testimony is not simply an extension of her imagination?'

'How about the testimony of the person who recently headed up Reeson's bond department?' Ross asked. 'How about if we produce a guy called Tommy Klein who will swear that Eda sold Chiyaha's platinum?'

'Allegedly sold platinum that was allegedly Chiyaha's,' Henry said. 'There are too many open-ended issues in the case. For instance, from Miss Okuma's physical appearance she's clearly had a very distressing experience, but unfortunately that may mitigate against her – who's this person she says tried to strangle her? Why hasn't she been to the police? What exactly was her relationship with Eda? Do we know for sure that Eda is someone who defrauded Nomura nearly ten years ago? To be quite plain, Miss Okuma's testimony smacks of that of the embittered ex-employee out to screw her boss.' Henry shook his head in resignation. 'I'm sorry.'

'The girl's father has been murdered by these people,' said Ross, refusing to let go. 'She's in a strange country, she comes from another culture. She admits that her own background is yakuza and in Japan yakuza have the same regard for the cops as the Cosa Nostra have in the United States. A person like that doesn't walk into a precinct station.'

'So, are you suggesting our case should rest on the fact that she's yakuza?' asked Henry gently. 'Hardly likely to swing Melvyn Graub, that, is it?' He leaned forward. 'Sun Valley hasn't broken any law. No crime has been committed, no regulations infringed. The court would look at the record, see that Oxx himself had tried this scam twice before, then ask Miss Okuma here to substantiate her allegations. She can't.'

Ross ran his hands through his hair and thought of Freeman Oxx, three thousand miles away, breathing through a plastic cup.

'Henry, I don't care how you do this for me, but you've got to do it,' he said.

'I can't walk on water, Ross,' Henry said. 'I'm sorry.'

'Mama Yayoi will have the proof.'

Both men looked at Yukiko.

Yukiko said: 'Mama Yayoi, my mother. She kept my father's books.'

'She was the . . . business person?' Ross asked.

Yukiko said: 'My father called her his rejigakari, his cashier. She handled all the money.'

'Even for something like Sun Valley?' asked Ross.

Yukiko spoke flatly: 'Certain cash transactions took place. Large amounts were involved. Father subscribed his cash into a trust set up in Kobe by the accountants, Hirano-Maeda. That trust ultimately owns Sun Valley. Mama-san will have a receipt from Hirano-Maeda. The trail will be there.'

Ross turned to Henry.

'Can we go into court and get a TRO on the basis that the evidence *will* be produced?'

159

'Hold on, hold on,' Henry said. 'Young lady, do you understand what a court in this country means by evidence?'

Yukiko said: 'I understand you want the truth. Mama Yayoi will have the truth.'

'And where is she?' Henry asked.

Yukiko bit her lip. 'I do not know. I have been unable to contact her since I learned of my father's death. She is no longer in Sendai.'

Henry looked hopelessly at Ross.

'But she's somewhere, right?' Ross pressed. 'I mean, I'm sorry to have to say it this way, but she's not dead.'

'She is not dead,' Yukiko said, 'but I think she is hiding for her life.'

'And if we were to find her, would she testify?' Ross asked. 'Provide the proof we need?'

'Yes.'

Henry's eyes motioned Ross to one side.

'This is insane,' he whispered. 'We're now talking about promising the court the testimony of a witness who is not simply the widow of a crime boss but is currently on the run from the mob in Japan. I always knew the world was crazy, Ross, but this is giving me an entirely new perspective.'

'Could it work, dammit?' Ross snapped and suddenly realized that it could have been Freeman Oxx talking.

'Who's case would we be representing?' Henry pleaded. 'We're the only people who want to stop the takeover and we've no legal interest in the matter.'

'How about if I brought the case as a shareholder?' asked Ross.

'Are you a shareholder?' asked Henry.

'No,' said Ross, reaching for a phone, 'but I'm just about to be.'

Henry sat back and smiled benignly at Yukiko as Ross made the call.

'Crazy,' he repeated. 'Absolutely crazy.'

'Hold on,' said Ross to the broker on the other end. He turned to Henry. 'I'm asking them to send the contracts by courier, right now. Where will we be? Southern District Court?'

Henry shook his round head in bemusement.

160

'Tell them to meet us in Cadman Plaza, Brooklyn – at the Federal District Court for the Eastern District of New York.' He took a deep breath. 'Nothing in the book says that we have to appear before that son of a bitch, Melvyn Graub.'

Ross spoke the instructions rapidly, then looked at his watch and pressed for the dial tone again.

'There's a banker in Lunenburg called Harry Warren, and he's not going to believe this,' he said.

Two security guards, each six and a half foot high, stood either side of the doors on the third floor of the New York Hilton. Behind them, at a desk set up in a lobby, sat two men from the Isaac Watson internal audit staff, and the lady who kept the share register at Industrial Oxx.

'No one, no matter what the excuse, no matter who they are or what they say, no one who's not on that register gets in,' said Tyler Wrixon. 'And when the doors are closed, that's it, get it?'

The guards, the men and the woman all nodded.

'It's going to be all right,' said James Lascalla, walking back with Wrixon into the West Ballroom Foyer, laid out with rows of chairs and a top table covered in green baize. 'You know the Sun Valley people have taken a suite on the second floor? I saw Gerry Bacik go in there thirty seconds ago.'

Wrixon nodded tightly.

'No word from our lawyer?'

Lascalla pushed back a white cuff to see his watch.

'He should be in court right now. Look, Tyler, it's going to go our way, OK? Even the market agrees. Oxx traded at twenty-four this morning.'

Wrixon nodded.

'What would the market be if Sun Valley had dropped the bid?' he asked.

'Twenty?' said Lascalla grimly. 'Eighteen? But that's academic now, in less than forty minutes everything will be over and Freeman Oxx's crazies can do what they want. I mean, there comes a point when they just can't screw around with other people's money anymore.'

'It defies belief,' Wrixon said, opening his mouth wide and

drawing in air. 'With less than an hour to go, it defies belief that they're going into court again.'

'Did you get an idea of the substance of what they're saying?' Lascalla asked.

'I listened to Babbage and I listened to a man hallucinating,' Wrixon said. 'They're claiming that Sun Valley are a front for the Japanese mob. That was one of Freeman Oxx's crazy allegations three weeks ago.'

He looked at the door as a solitary man in a dark suit entered the room holding the motion paper he'd been given on his way in.

'Good to see you, George,' said Lascalla, recognizing a banker who would be voting nearly three per cent of the Oxx stock.

'James. Tyler,' the man nodded, taking his seat. 'End of a long haul, huh?'

'That's for sure,' Lascalla smiled back.

For some reason the presence of the first shareholder to arrive made Wrixon feel better; it was concrete proof of the day and the time and the business about to be done.

'Who's representing the Oxx shares?' he asked the acting chairman.

'I don't know – a proxy of some kind?' Lascalla shrugged. 'It's quite possible his shares won't be voted. How does a guy in a coma arrange a proxy?'

'Not that it matters,' Wrixon said. 'There'll be over eighty per cent for the motion.' He looked at his watch, then to the door. 'How long will it take?'

'Four or five minutes,' Lascalla said. 'I call them to order, read the resolution authorizing the meeting, then I read the motion itself. A show of hands is all I need – how long does it take a hundred guys to stick their hands in the air? Five seconds? Quit worrying, what's happening in Brooklyn is a sideshow.'

'You need to be prepared for an attempt to delay,' Wrixon said.

'I am,' Lascalla said. 'I've got Meshnick primed for that eventuality – he's quite happy that any attempt to further stall company business is out of order. I'll rule accordingly.'

'It's filling up quickly,' Wrixon observed as he saw two of the board members of Oxx take their places at the green table. The small man who managed the portfolio at Mid West Star entered

162

the room and Wrixon felt something inhuman happen to his stomach.

'Do you have a problem of some kind, Tyler?' Lascalla asked.

Wrixon shook his head impatiently.

'Look,' he said, 'even though the official starting time is noon, if everyone is here before noon, can't you ask the floor to take the business there and then?'

'I don't know, Tyler,' Lascalla said, 'I don't want to leave myself open . . .'

'Mr Wrixon!'

One of the Isaac Watson audit staff was at the door, pointing to his ear. Wrixon went to the West Promenade and took the phone. Lascalla followed him. There was now a line waiting to be cleared through the lobby.

'Good, *good!*' Wrixon said in satisfaction. 'That's what I like to hear!'

He put down the phone and nodded a grim smile to Lascalla.

'That was Brickell, our lawyer, calling from his car,' he said. 'The judge has ruled that because of the history of the case, the application can't be heard until both sides are represented in court.' He looked at his watch. 'Even if he heard them in the next ten minutes, which is most unlikely now, and even if the judge rules for them, it will be physically impossible for them to get an order over here.'

'Could they phone it through?' Lascalla asked.

Wrixon's eyes narrowed.

'Like fuck!' he snarled. 'Excuse me!'

One of the big guards from the door turned to the clicking fingers.

'I want something done, fast,' Wrixon said. 'I want all the telephones in this area disconnected.'

'Disconnected?' the guard said. 'I don't know how to disconnect telephones.'

'It's easy,' Wrixon said, 'look.' He wound the flex from the phone on the table around his wrist and with a sharp tug ripped it from it's socket in the wall. 'Do it!' he said to the staring man. 'I'll take full responsibility.'

Then he strode ahead of Lascalla, into the rapidly filling room.

*   *   *

163

The night mountains became foothills in the first light and the foothills swept down into the cultivated plain of Kobe, with its houses and its rice fields and its crisscross of cable-bearing pylons. Immobile, Chiyaha sat by the pool in the noiseless garden that became gradually black and white with the rising light. Black: large boulders of granite that looked as if they grew where they lay; white: white pebbles, carefully raked. The moon and the sun shared the sky equally. They made gentle contrasts, soothing aspects that brought many things to mind: the futility of life, for example: the boulders and stones had been there since the start of time and would still be there long after Chiyaha had gone. Or man's place in the universe – man being the pebbles caught in the race of life, the boulders being the planets which govern everything. Or the symmetry and order which is the keynote of any successful business; a man came every day and raked the pebbles' surface with a wooden rake, always in the same direction, making great sweeping circles of the stones, each whorl growing into another so that the whole was a careful series of never ending currents.

Everything was preordained: wealth, power. Some men crossed the surface of life like ants, leaving no mark, others were giants, secure in their destiny. The ant scurried; the giant sat and waited.

With his boulders as companions, Chiyaha sat. Waiting.

*   *   *

Timothy Manners tapped the keys on the desk consol and peered at the green numbers on the screen. August platinum winked back at him: $402 bid, $402.50 a seller. Manners swivelled away and sniffed. At $402 an ounce he was two dollars under his sell price of the previous week. Put otherwise, Cresswels was making two dollars an ounce on the twenty thousand ounces which Manners had sold for the firm in anticipation of the market falling. He felt himself tingle down to his shoe leather. It was happening.

He watched the screen hypnotically. Two dollars by twenty thousand was forty thousand.

The screen wrinkled as the price changed: $401.50. Platinum

164

was slipping inexorably towards $400 an ounce, the psychological barrier from where it had bounced countless times before. Once through $400 then where? The abyss.

That morning at eight, Tyler Wrixon had been edgy.

'Oxx changes hands at noon today,' he had said. 'What more can I say?'

The screen blipped as Manners watched and he felt the hairs on his neck do something: $401 bid. He hit the tie line to NYMEX.

'Sell me another thirty thousand of the August down to four hundred dollars,' he snapped.

Looking warily over his glasses, Federal Judge Charles Murphy tapped his gavel on the bench of Court 2. He had just left over a dozen disgruntled lawyers, plaintiffs and defendants in Court 1 for the second time that morning, promising to be no more than fifteen minutes, the maximum time his clerk had been assured by Henry Babbage it would take to hear his application. Judge Murphy nodded at a lawyer named Brickell who had arrived out of breath two minutes before, then looked down as his friend of forty years rose to his feet.

'As we're all here you can now proceed, Mr Babbage.'

'Your honour,' Henry began, 'I represent Mr Ross Magee, a shareholder in the Industrial Oxx Corporation of Santa Clara County, California with offices registered in Wilmington, Delaware.'

'I object,' said Brickell. 'I represent the said Industrial Oxx Corporation, your honour. No such shareholder appears on my client's share register, a notarized copy of which I'm now pleased to lodge in court.'

Ross was sitting directly behind Henry with Yukiko beside him. He had called the clinic in San José from Henry's limousine just before they got to the courthouse. No change. Neither better nor worse. Ross looked at Yukiko. He covered her hand with his and pressed it, but there was no response; Yukiko was functioning at a basic, mechanical level only. Henry was getting to his feet.

'May it please your honour, here are original contract notes, executed on the New York Stock Exchange this morning to

165

show that my client is indeed the owner of a thousand such shares.'

'I object, your honour,' Brickell said. 'A contract note is merely a transaction outside the company. No shares have yet been issued to Mr Babbage's client.'

'I've never bought shares in a company that haven't subsequently issued,' observed Judge Murphy. 'Carry on, Mr Babbage.'

Ross made a fist. We're fighting, Freeman!

'Thank you, your honour,' Henry was saying. 'May it please the court, my client has come into the possession of information regarding the proposed takeover of the corporation in which he is a shareholder. He believes that a bid for the entire capital of Industrial Oxx by the Sun Valley Corporation of New York, or more correctly, of Kobe, Japan, infringes the fundamental anti-fraud provisions of the Securities Exchange Act and in particular SEC rules Nb 5 and 14 D. He believes that as a shareholder he has been given incorrect information as to the true nature of the persons who control Sun Valley Corporation and their intentions. My client further believes that these people are engaged in Japan in activities which we in this country would describe as organized crime.'

'Your honour, I strenuously object!'

'Let Mr Babbage finish, Mr Brickell.'

'Thank you, you honour,' Henry said. 'I have here the sworn affidavit of Yukiko Okuma in support of our application, which I now lodge in court. As your honour can see, the allegations raised are of the most serious nature possible.'

'Your honour . . .'

Cutting Counsellor Brickell off, Judge Murphy accepted the pages from Henry and began to read.

On the other side of the courtroom Ross could see Brickell whisper urgently to a younger man who then hurried out. He caught Henry's glance. They're worried, Freeman! Hell, are they worried!

Judge Murphy cleared his throat.

'Pretty serious allegations, Mr Babbage,' he observed.

'Extremely serious, your honour,' Henry responded. 'Time is now crucial. In literally minutes, the shareholders of Industrial Oxx propose to vote on the takeover bid mentioned. I would beg the court to issue an order restraining that meeting from taking place until my client can place evidence before the court supporting his belief that Japanese yakuza or organized crime are behind Sun Valley.'

Brickell was on his feet.

'Your honour, I have never heard such malicious rubbish in my thirty-five years at the bar,' he stormed. 'My colleague's motion is outrageous, damaging and totally unsupported. I would respectfully remind the court that there have already been two extensive reviews of the facts relating to this bid in the court of the Southern District of New York when Judge Graub was prevailed upon to hand down a TRO on each occasion. An application last week by Oxx itself asked that court to remove the TRO as no further impediment to the takeover existed. This application is therefore time-wasting and frivolous and I would ask you to rule on it with the disdain which it deserves and to allow the real shareholders of Industrial Oxx to make up their minds on the matter.'

Judge Murphy nodded several times as if a weighing process was taking place. Then he took a deep breath.

'I can't just ignore an allegation of this kind, brought by an American citizen and supported by a sworn affidavit, against what are, let's face it, foreigners come over to buy one of our companies,' he said quietly. 'I mean, Mr Brickell, have you anyone here in court who can testify that what Mr Babbage's client alleges isn't true?'

'If your honour would adjourn the proceedings for twenty-four hours, I would be pleased to produce such testimony,' Brickell replied.

Ross closed his eyes.

'But in twenty-four hours the issue won't exist, your honour,' Henry cried.

Judge Murphy peered at Henry Babbage. 'What exactly are you proposing, Mr Babbage?'

'That a temporary injunction be granted against Industrial Oxx, restraining that company from voting on the bid to take it over until my client can produce evidence which will satisfy the court that the injunction should be made permanent, your honour,' Henry said.

167

'What sort of evidence is it envisaged will be brought?' asked the judge sceptically.

'Documentary evidence, your honour, showing receipts of investment by undoubted yakuza in the trust company which ultimately owns Sun Valley,' Henry replied.

Judge Murphy looked down his glasses.

'You're asking me to stop a two and a half billion dollar takeover, Mr Babbage,' he said. 'I need to know where this evidence is going to come from.'

Ross stood up.

'From Japan, your honour!' he cried and there was an outburst of chatter throughout the courtroom.

'Silence.'

'You may approach the bench, Mr Magee,' Judge Murphy said.

'Your honour, with respect . . .!' Brickwell began, but the judge silenced him and the lawyer resumed his seat.

'How's the evidence going to come from Japan, Mr Magee?' Judge Murphy asked Ross, now standing directly in front of him. 'I've read the girl's affidavit. If I believe that, then we're dealing with particularly bloodthirsty criminals in another jurisdiction.'

Ross saw that the judge had small, brown unwavering eyes, not unkind, but eyes that had seen it all.

'I will go to Japan and bring the evidence back here, your honour,' Ross heard himself say.

Judge Murphy raised his eyebrows, then looked at Henry.

'On that basis, I'll rule in favour,' he said. 'What time frame had you in mind, Mr Babbage?'

'At least four weeks, your honour.'

'Your honour . . .!' Brickell was shouting.

The judge peered at his diary. 'I'll hear you again at twelve noon, June 1st,' he said. 'That gives you almost two weeks.'

'Your honour . . .'

'I have taken the liberty of preparing the order,' said Henry, charging on. 'In the light of the time constraints, I would ask the court to give leave that the order may be served on the directors of Industrial Oxx by facsimile machine.'

168

'Granted,' said the judge and signalled Ross to return to his seat.

'I would also ask the court,' Henry pressed, 'in the light of the appalling allegations contained in Miss Okuma's affidavit, to impose restrictions on the details of this morning's hearing being reported in the Press.'

Judge Murphy looked up to get Counsellor Brickell's response to Henry's proposal, but Brickell had already gathered his papers and was leaving the court on the run.

'Granted,' said Judge Murphy and brought down his gavel with a smack. 'Mr Babbage, can you see me in my chambers, please?' he asked as the court rose.

Ross felt himself glowing all over. He would call San José. Freeman wouldn't be able to hear, but they could bring a phone and put it by his ear and Ross would say: 'We won this time, Freeman, you and I, we won!'

He looked at Yukiko. If the outcome of the proceedings had registered with her, her face gave no sign. Ross caught her hand and they walked down the centre aisle of the courtroom.

Henry Babbage followed the usher through the door behind the bench. Judge Murphy was standing, hands behind his back, glaring.

'Charlie?' said Henry pleasantly.

'Henry, not for anyone else in the world would I do that,' Charlie Murphy said. 'Melvyn Graub will dance a jig when he hears what I've just granted.'

'It was a good decision, Charlie.'

'I'm warning you now, Henry,' said Charlie Murphy, his finger upraised, 'your client had better produce this evidence by June 1st, or so help me, I promise you, I'll never hear you again.'

'Don't worry, Charlie,' said Henry with a confidence he suddenly didn't feel. 'We'll be here.'

The guard watched as his colleague pulled the double doors to shut.

'Godamn,' he said, pushing his cap back, 'I've been asked to do a lot of things but never to vandalize the fittings.'

169

'Forget it,' said his colleague with a derisory shake of his head. He turned to the audit men who were packing their files. 'How long is this show likely to run?'

'If Tyler Wrixon has his way, about ten seconds,' replied the auditor for the benefit of his colleague. 'Ten, fifteen minutes, I guess,' he said to the guard and clicked his briefcase closed. 'Just make sure no one else gets in there, OK? The list is complete. Nice to have met you.'

The guards nodded as the auditors made their way down the West Promenade. The keeper of the Oxx register was tidying her desk. From behind the closed doors came the voice of one man. A woman stepped off the escalator forty yards away and strode purposefully towards the guards. They exchanged glances. She was middle-sized and middle-aged, had thick, curly black hair and wore glasses with purple frames shaped like devil's eyebrows.

She stopped in front of them and said: 'I am here to serve a court order on the board of Industrial Oxx.'

One of the guards shook his head resolutely.

'I'm sorry, ma'am, this is a restricted area, you'll have to leave.'

'Didn't you hear what I said?' asked the woman. 'This is a court order to be served on the board of Industrial Oxx,' and she made to walk through, but the guard stepped in front of her.

'Didn't you hear what *I* said? There's a meeting on in there and no one goes in.'

From beyond the doors came the sound of raised voices.

'Are you a court official?'

The question came from the lobby, from the lady who had been packing files into her briefcase.

'My name is Demi Zougrafou from the firm of Babbage and Kellaway, Attorneys at Law,' answered the woman firmly. 'I have in my hand an order of the Federal District Court of the Eastern District of New York, made in the last ten minutes by Judge Charles Murphy of that court to be served on the chairman and the board of Industrial Oxx.'

A single, raised voice could be suddenly heard from the other side of the doors, then a chorus of protest.

'I don't care who you are, you're not going in there,' said the guard.

'Do you understand the penalties for contempt of court?' Miss Z asked.

'Lady, we got our job to do. Now please leave this area.'

'I'm going to ask you one more time to let me in, in front of this lady whom I will call as a witness to what I am doing,' Miss Z said. 'If you still fail to obey the order of the Federal Court of the United States, I intend to see that you are both charged with contempt.'

'I think you should at least let the chairman know she's here,' said the share register woman.

'We got our orders . . .' said the guard, turning as he replied.

Diving between the men, Miss Z flung herself at the doors.

Orem Williams was getting to his feet for the third and what he knew would be the last time when the explosion happened. A dark haired, shouting woman and two uniformed guards crashed into the meeting room. Immediate chaos ensued. Over a hundred people jumped to their feet. A banker, coached in anti-terrorist and kidnap manoeuvres, rushed at a service door behind the green table, kicked it open and leaped out. There was a stampede. James Lascalla stood speechlessly at the top table, trying to comprehend what had occurred. Someone was standing beside him, screaming. Lascalla's intake abilities overtook his shock.

'Stop them!' Tyler Wrixon screamed. 'Stop them leaving!'

Lascalla took a step backwards as the woman shook off her guards and approached him.

'Are you the chairman?' she panted.

Lascalla nodded, open mouthed.

'Well, you are hereby served,' said Miss Z and fell in a faint.

Rudi Meshnick read the court order with an expression of growing disbelief. Wrixon was looking around the emptying room. His gaze stopped at the door to the lobby: Gerry Bacik stood there with a dark suited, bespectacled Japanese. The look on their faces showed that they had come expecting a scene entirely different to the one they were witnessing.

One thought only dominated Wrixon's mind: it was the traded share price of Industrial Oxx, twenty-four dollars a share on the opening this morning, a value that would still be intact.

Unminding of the other people in the room, Wrixon dived for

171

a phone in the corner and stabbed out the digits. Panting, he waited. Suddenly realizing the phone was dead, he threw it down with a little cry and crashed through the bewildered crowd out to the lobby where he grabbed another phone. Dead.

'These fucking phones are all dead!' Wrixon screamed at the hapless security guards.

The call came through to Chief Tshubisi just after nine p.m., Southern African time. The caller was Orem Williams, Freeman Oxx's assistant. Walking out the back door of his two-bedroomed house, the Chief sat into his pickup truck and drove west.

It was a special night. The great plain of Bamolisi stretched unbroken in all directions to the night horizon. No lights were needed for the journey: the guidance from the stars made lights unnecessary.

At a waterhole used by the Masisi people since before time, Chief Tshubisi drew up and parked. Kneeling beside the spring, he cupped his hand and then washed his whole head in it. Walking now, still due west, he felt the rise of ground against him and then his eyes picked out the contours of Gotsube. It took him twenty minutes to reach it's flat top. He saw the poles there with the tribe's totem, the kweena, the crocodile; and the mounds of rocks strategically placed to attract rain; and the rings of stones inside which on the nights of the new moon fires were lighted so that the spirits of the Masisi wandering the Bamolisi plain could find their way home.

Kneeling, the chiefman bent his head. Gradually, into the great theatre of which he was now the central part he soared, away up and over Gotsube. He heard the laughing voice of his father, and of his grandfather, the man who had barehanded fought and killed the kweena and given the tribe the totem which would always be theirs. He roamed the skies with them and with a host of other relatives and friends whose bones lay deep under the hill on which his body knelt. It was a celebration. They swooped and soared and at their heels, yapping and barking with excitement were dogs that had died at the other end of the century and who had been placed with great tenderness beside the masters they had served.

172

The merrymaking went on all night, but Chief Tshubisi had no time to think of exhaustion, such were the huge numbers of people who had come to hear the news. To each of them in turn – and to some who asked twice or three times – his message was the same.

'Sleep in peace. Sleep in peace.'

BOOK FOUR

THE BARBARIAN

Ten

The Cadillacs began arriving after dark. Up the narrow, neon-clad Kabukicho backwater they crawled like huge, deepwater fish lost in a twisting, inland stream.

The restaurant was no longer fashionable; the ageing geisha who ran it was glad to close for the night and had raised her price accordingly. A door from the kitchens led to an alleyway which in turn connected with Yasukuni-dōri. Out front, armed kobun in parked cars faced each other off from both kerbs for five hundred yards. As the last limousine made it's way into the alley, signs went up on Shinjuku citing cable repairs and road closed.

The kyakuseki was occupied as age demanded by Ichirō Abe. Chiyaha looked at Abe's smoking cigarette and thought: over six months since we have last met; now our numbers are less by one and you have added Sendai to your fiefdom. You will soon die, old man, when your belly is full and you least expect it.

'I have come a long way, Chiyaha-san,' Abe began hoarsely. 'This is vacation and tourist time. The night spots are busy, my girls work like sweats to keep up with demand. We must all harvest with the sun.'

Chiyaha bowed gravely and said: 'You have all heard about the latest delay in our bid for Industrial Oxx, many of you have phoned me; you have spoken with each other. This meeting is

177

to address the question you want to ask. The answer is: the delay is temporary. The plan goes ahead.'

There was an outbreak of discussion.

Abe: 'Kasumi-san.'

Kasumi's eyebrows met in a clump on the bridge of his nose.

'I am reliably informed,' he said, 'that our late brother, Okuma-san, the oyabun of Miyagi, may not have taken the sacred vows he made last November as seriously as the five of us now present.'

Chiyaha looked at Kasumi. The greatest danger, only held in check by a single thread of fear. What are you planning against me, Kasumi-san? How will you die? By the bullet, or by the knife held in your own hand?

'You have a point to make, Kasumi-san?' asked Chiyaha politely.

'When Okuma was killed the word is that he had an important rendezvous in Tokyo,' said Kasumi. 'The word on yakuza lips throughout Japan is that he was talking to police.'

The table turned as one to Chiyaha.

'I too have heard such rumours, Kasumi-san,' he said, 'but first let me ask you, since when have the actions of a traitor made you run?'

'I have scars on my body to show that I have never run,' Kasumi snapped. 'But only a fool leaps from a cliff. Okuma's wife – perhaps the true oyabun of Okuma-kai – is still at large despite all efforts to find her. She knows our plans word for word. She is the hole which will sink this boat in which you have put us, Chiyaha-san.'

'Maybe we should be thinking again, Chiyaha-san,' Abe rasped. 'The brave shogun avoids the battle in order to fight all the better another day.'

Chiyaha faced him.

'I acknowledge the danger, but how grave is it? If Okuma's widow was talking to police, would she not now be in their protective custody? We know she is not – on the contrary, we know they are looking for her as diligently as we are. We will find her first and cut the tongue from her throat.'

Shigeru Ōmori nodded gravely.

Kasumi spoke: 'You want to know the truth? The truth is

178

that even as Okuma was planning to betray the sacred trust, who was sent to New York, to work at the very heart of this whole enterprise? I'll tell you who!' Kasumi drew himself up like a bullfrog. 'None other than the daughter of the traitor Okuma!'

Everyone wanted his say.

'Let Chiyaha-san reply,' said Abe, tapping his glass.

Chiyaha spoke evenly: 'Yukiko Okuma had a yakuza background, no one was more qualified for the position. In New York, she was sent as bait to a man called Magee-san, an agent working for Oxx, a spy. But treachery obviously runs in Okuma blood, for Yukiko Okuma has now joined this yaban-jin, this barbarian, against us.' He paused. 'And within the last six hours they have left New York for Tokyo in a desperate attempt to find Mama Yayoi Okuma. They are seeking her testimony to halt our bid.'

Kazuhiro Kasumi: 'Was I therefore wrong? This is all too fraught with risk!' He became reasonable. 'You are not to blame, Chiyaha-san, for the actions of a traitor, something that none of us could have foreseen. No face has been lost. We are all still brothers in yakuza.'

Abe murmured his approval; Ōmori and Egusa looked to the oyabun of Kobe. Chiyaha saw them all, not as flesh and blood, but as tools to his purpose.

He said: 'Have you forgotten why we are doing this? We *need* the money, just to survive! Do you turn your backs on one of the great deposits of platinum in the world, just when the market is about to soar? Just when we are about to change the whole basis of the relationship between Japan and the US? We *need* the money! We cannot turn back now!'

'How can you be sure that the Socialists will do as you predict?' asked old Abe. 'I would rather breed my wife to a snake than try to understand the mind of a politician.'

'As Ōmori-san can vouch, I have helped many men over the years, Abe-san,' answered Chiyaha softly, 'including figures that now vie for leadership of the Socialists. With the outrage will come the change, believe me.'

There was the sudden sound of Kanji Egusa expelling his breath.

'I vote we abort,' he said. 'Our money is still safe, after all. I want my portion back.'

179

Chiyaha sighed. Egusa-san, you have just put your name to your own death certificate.

'Unfortunately, Egusa-san, that is no longer possible,' he said smoothly. 'The crucial move has been made and cannot be reversed.' He met their nervous eyes. 'Let Okuma's daughter lead us to her bitch mother and then let us all watch the unfolding drama that we have put, irreversibly, in place.'

The oyabun looked to each other.

'Let us vote our confidence in Chiyaha-san,' said Shigeru Ōmori. 'It is from his efforts that we will all benefit.'

'Or be destroyed,' said Abe darkly.

Ōmori said: 'I support my brother, the oyabun of Kobe. I now call on you all to do the same.'

'I want my money back,' said Kanji Egusa. 'I abstain.'

Ichirō Abe wanted to go home. He hated big cities, pressure, heated meetings and dissent. And he hated the ground that Rokuo Chiyaha walked on.

'I support Chiyaha-san,' he said.

Kazuhiro Kasumi knew he was again beaten. But he saw the look of loathing in Ichirō Abe's eyes and he knew that he was not alone.

'Chiyaha-san knows that at the end of the day I will always do my duty,' he said.

*   *   *

The supervisor in the loading bay off Fifth Avenue was a beefy ex-cop with a short fuse. He strode from his office and stood, hands on his hips, facing down the driver of the forty-foot container-truck, who had hooted from the other side of the barrier.

'You lookin' for someone?'

The driver produced a freight manifest.

'Delivery,' he said, 'to Metropolitan Museum, sealed container from JAL Freight, Kennedy.'

'Oh yeah?' the cargo bay chief nodded. 'Not by any chance the container that should have been here five hours ago?'

'Yes,' the driver nodded, 'sorry, I got lost in Queens.'

'You got lost in Queens. Just like that. In the meantime I got

180

a schedule that's fucked out of it's mind waiting for you, buddy. I got men standing by to strip your box since noon. I got a three-container sculpture exhibition stacked on the second floor, waiting to go, but I can't allow freight in because you might turn up, Columbus. That means trucks standing off somewhere, charging their time to the Metropolitan. And I got a hundred thousand cops crawling all over the place, saying that because your exhibits are late they may not even be allowed into the fucking exhibition for security reasons, how do you like that?'

'Sorry,' said the driver dejectedly.

'Looney Tunes,' said the supervisor activating the barrier. 'Looney Tunes.'

Taking the manifest, he began to check it against a list of his own as museum employees went to work with a forklift. He ticked crates labelled lacquer boxes, and painted wooden panels, and an eight-foot stone buddha from the thirteenth century. He never considered the value of the items he was handling – they were wooden crates on a freight manifest. As the last one was lifted out he checked inside the forty-foot, signed his copy of the docket and handed it wordlessly to the driver. The truck turned, the barrier was raised and the empty container rattled up the ramp.

The supervisor went back to his office, shaking his head. Looney Tunes.

Eleven

Yukiko dozed most of the way in from Narita. To Ross the suburbs and crowded streets held little familiarity and although he thought he recognized a building or two, it wasn't until they hit neon country and ducked and weaved and doubled back and eventually arrived at the hotel that he knew for certain this was where he had so recently been.

He thought of his call from New York to Captain Belliqueux. 'Now you 'ave gone too far, Monsieur Ross. Now I sell 'er to first man who gives me three 'undredsousant.'

'This is the final delay, I promise you, Captain. We close Monday, June 2nd, or you keep her.'

'I keep 'er right now unless I get tensousant more.'

'Five.'

'Ten, that's it or forget.'

Henry Warren said he would send the cash, although he sounded cool, up there in Lunenburg.

Then Tommy had called.

'Hey! You know this tribe you were tellin' me about? The one with all the platinum?'

'The Masisi,' Ross said.

'Yeah, the Masisi. D'you think after all this they might want a talented guy to look after their financial side?' Tommy had asked.

Ross smiled as the cab came to a halt. If only he could have spoken to Freeman; if only Freeman knew the breathing space they had won and the fight that was being fought.

Yukiko had a blankness to her that made Ross ache. It was as if each step the nearer to her homeland, the more she hurt. The cab pulled into the kerb and she blinked her eyes as the door was opened and a porter said, 'Irasshaimase, welcome to Tokyo.'

Hours seemed not to matter to Kerry O'Brien. Before leaving New York Ross had faxed him; within half an hour of their arrival there was a knock on the door of Ross's room.

Kerry was smiling. 'I knew you liked Tokyo, but not this much.'

He sat on the only chair as Ross uncapped two beers from the fridge. He saw crow's feet stamped around the edges of the bulky American's eyes.

'This is beyond the call of duty,' Ross said, raising his bottle.

'Forget it,' Kerry said. 'Cheers.' Lighting a cigarette, he blew smoke in a thin trail. 'Sounds like you've been busy.'

Ross filled him in.

'They tried to kill Yukiko, probably a decision taken here in Japan by Rokuo Chiyaha after he'd murdered her father. She's already testified about the yakuza's part in Sun Valley. We need her mother's evidence to sew it up.'

Kerry's eyebrows went up.

'Rokuo Chiyaha? You realize that regardless of what happened in a New York court it won't open doors over here? Remember the brick walls we came up against on your last trip? Tarai-mawashi, the runaround? Everything is still in place.'

'But Mama Yayoi exists,' Ross said. 'She's the key. If she can produce evidence showing her husband's investment in Sun Valley, then I think we've won.'

Kerry made a pained face.

'I got your fax.'

Ross looked at him.

'I've been making some discreet inquiries,' said Kerry quietly. 'Since Senko Okuma was killed, it seems his territory has been the subject of a yakuza succession battle. I don't quite know

183

how you're going to tell this to Miss Okuma, Ross, but from what I hear, her mother is almost certainly dead.'

The hope which had sustained Ross across the Pacific plunged.

'"Almost certainly"?'

'They haven't found the body, as I understand, but when yakuza wars flare up, the cops here stand back and let them beat the living shit out of each other. She's unlikely to have escaped.'

Ross went to the window. Same air-conditioner. Same building outside, so near you could touch.

'What about Eiichi Eda?' he asked. 'Can we even confirm that he's Tatsuo Eda who ripped off Nomura back in eighty-seven?'

'I'm trying to get hard information on Eda,' Kerry said, 'but so far, I can't get your story confirmed.' He shrugged with the air of someone used to being beaten by bureaucracy. 'Have you thought of going to the cops here?'

'That's difficult,' Ross said. 'Yukiko believes that the cops set her father up for Chiyaha. She won't have anything to do with them.'

'They may be your best bet,' Kerry said.

'Do you have a contact?' Ross asked.

'I can get one,' Kerry said, lighting another cigarette. 'Look, you told me you were a fisherman. Let me bring you out for a night on the town, tomorrow morning you talk to the cops, then climb back on a big bird and go home. Back to the boats and the fish. Forget this scam.'

Ross sighed.

'I can't do that, Kerry. Too much hangs on finding Mama Yayoi.'

'I can't get too much more involved, OK?' said Kerry reasonably. 'This whole business is spilling into an ugly area: yakuza, mob warfare, the daughter of a dead godfather. Nothing personal, but if you insist on pursuing this, I've got to give you a warning – official, you understand? You're a free citizen, you do exactly what you want within the bounds of the law; but you get your ass in a sling over here, don't expect any help from Uncle Sam.'

Ross nodded.

184

'I appreciate everything you're doing.'

Kerry looked somewhat sadly at Ross. 'Is there no other way you can do this?'

Ross replied: 'We're keeping up the pressure back in New York, even though the entire Oxx board are against us. I've got a friend who'll testify that Eda sold platinum through Reeson Rhoades. We'll ask the court to insist on definite proof that the platinum was owned, as Eda says, by a charitable trust in Kobe. My hunch is Eda won't be able to do that.'

'Who's the witness?' Kerry asked.

'A trader named Tommy Klein. He used to work for me, now he works in Reesons.'

Kerry stood up.

'I hope things work out the way you want them.'

'I gave Henry Babbage, my attorney, your fax number,' Ross said. 'He may want to contact me.'

'My pleasure,' Kerry said. 'I'll keep any messages.' He handed Ross a card. 'Here's my unlisted number. Memorize it. Call me any time, OK? And good luck.'

Ross felt drained. The frantic calls before they left, the long flight, somehow he had hoped for more than what Kerry O'Brien had just said. Cigarette smoke like fog clung to the ceiling. He tried to open the window but it's designers had had other ideas. Turning the air-conditioning up full cold, he collected the empty bottles, dumped them and the ashtray and sat down again. What was he going to tell Yukiko? He couldn't bear to see her hurt again.

There was a knock. She was standing there in jeans and a jumper. Sometimes, like now, her vulnerability was all he saw.

'You don't look as if you've just got off a fourteen-hour flight,' he said cheerfully.

She came in.

'What did he say?'

'That we're crazy,' Ross replied.

'What else?'

Ross caught both her hands in his and brought her to sit with him on the bed.

'Yukiko ... this is a nightmare for you, I know it,' he

185

said, 'but Kerry O'Brien's information is that Mama Yayoi is dead.'

Yukiko blinked just once and stood up.

'He's wrong.'

Ross saw sudden anger and determination in her face.

'I called my home in Sendai,' she said grimly. 'A man's voice answered, a strange man. Then I called a girl-friend in Izumi I have known since childhood. Ichirō Abe has moved into Sendai.'

'That's what O'Brien said, that there was a succession battle going on,' Ross said.

Yukiko shook her head with a new impatience.

'The kobun on the phone in my father's house had the accent of someone from Aomori – Abe's country. It means Mama Yayoi is alive. Abe's men are in the house waiting for her to come home. It means she's alive but they can't find her.'

Whatever way she arched her head, her fragility fell away like a dead skin.

'Can . . . we find her?' asked Ross.

'It will mean contacting people who will trust me and convincing them of who I am. But we can find her,' Yukiko nodded. 'We have to find her, Ross, before Chiyaha does.'

'O'Brien suggested we ask the police for help,' said Ross quietly.

She looked at him with scorn.

'You don't understand, do you? The police are the omawari, the yakuza's enemy. My friend in Izumi told me there's a rumour my father was on his way to see the police in Tokyo when he was murdered. I would not be surprised to learn that the omawari are the guilty ones.'

'I want to stop Rokuo Chiyaha taking over Sun Valley,' Ross said. 'I'm sure the police would want the same.'

' '"Ahh, Sun Valley, Magee-san," ' mimicked Yukiko. ' '"So, Chiyaha owns this company? Please, where is the evidence for this? Ahh, so you have no evidence; ahh, so the evidence is what you are here to look for . . ." ' We may need the police, but they don't need us. They won't help us.'

'Yukiko, I know it goes against everything you ever believed in,' Ross said and drew her down beside him. 'But time is moving on and we need all the help we can get. If there's a

186

chance the police can give us some help, then it's smart to at least ask them.'

Yukiko shuddered and looked away.

'O'Brien can set it up,' Ross said gently.

'There are many paths to the peak of the mountain,' Yukiko whispered. 'OK, if it's what you want, call him.'

Sergeant Bando held the door and Inspector Nobuo walked through. The windowless interview room smelled and sparkled clean as an operating theatre. Nobuo saw a very pretty Japanese woman in her mid-twenties with facial and throat bruising, and a tall gaijin, a foreigner. Both got to their feet.

'Hajimemashite, Nobuo desu,' said Inspector Nobuo, bowing.

'Okuma desu,' bowed Yukiko Okuma formally. 'Kochira wa Magee-san desu. This is Mr Magee. Ross, this is Inspector Nobuo.'

Ross and Inspector Nobuo exchanged bows.

'Pleased to meet you,' Ross said.

'Dozo yoroshiku,' said Nobuo correctly. 'Kochira wa Bando-san desu.'

Everyone bowed again to each other and they sat, two either side of a table. Nobuo concentrated on the woman. He could straight away sense her hostility. Once yakuza, always.

'How can I help you?' he asked in Japanese.

'I understand that you are in charge of the investigation into the murder of my father, Senko Okuma.'

'That is correct.'

'May I ask, have you found his killers?'

'Unfortunately, no,' Nobuo replied, bowing his head respectfully. 'But we are following certain leads and given time, we will find them.'

'Have you arrested anyone?'

'Ahh, no, no one has yet been arrested.'

Sergeant Bando was writing notes.

'Does the fact that one of Rokuo Chiyaha's kobun was found dead at the scene not mean something to you? You do know that a kobun of Chiyaha-gumi was there, don't you? It was in *Asahi Shimbun*, after all.'

She's angry, this one, Nobuo thought, she's like a beautiful angry hawk. Let's see if we can make her lead us to her nest.

187

'We have identified all the dead,' Nobuo affirmed without expression.

'Do you at least suspect anyone?'

'We have some ideas.'

'But just ideas . . .?'

'The police inquiry is proceeding,' said Nobuo affably.

He saw a glance pass between Yukiko and Ross. Who is this huge yaban-jin, this barbarian, Nobuo wondered? What's his involvement. Are they lovers? Why is he here? And the girl: in the last five days someone tried to strangle her.

'This is hopeless,' Yukiko said to Ross in English. 'They have no idea who killed my father.' She saw Ross look in Nobuo's direction. 'Don't worry, he doesn't understand a word.'

Nobuo's face was an uncomprehending blank; but inside he tingled. Three years of getting up an hour early and going to classes; three years of tapes and movies and practising words that were beyond pronunciation. Lead on, pretty bird!

Yukiko spoke: 'Please, in your investigation, have you come upon any trace of my mother, my father's wife, Yayoi Okuma? I am concerned for her safety.'

Nobuo looked suitably abashed. 'Again, unfortunately not, but be assured, we would very much like to talk to your mother.'

'What steps have you taken to find her?'

'She has not come forward, if that's what you mean,' Nobuo replied unctuously.

'The woman is obviously missing. Her husband has been murdered. Surely you have tried to find her?' Yukiko asked.

'Your mother has not committed a crime, Okuma-san,' said Nobuo as blandly as he could. 'Unfortunately, as you will appreciate, with so many other cases pending . . .'

'My father is dead, his men either murdered or dispersed. As we sit here there are kobun of Ichirō Abe in his house in Sendai, waiting in case my mother should come home. Isn't it obvious that her life is in danger?'

'No one has made a report . . .' Nobuo said sympathetically.

'This is a total waste of time,' said Yukiko to Ross. 'They couldn't care less if Mama Yayoi is dead or alive.'

Nobuo blinked appropriately at Yukiko's words. Oh, she's alive, pretty bird, but only you know the way to find her.

'Ask him if any unidentified bodies have been found. Ask him if he thinks she is dead,' Ross was saying.

The yaban-jin knows just as much as she does, Nobuo thought. But who is he? The US Embassy might know. Who was the contact who set up the meeting?

Yukiko was relaying Ross's question in Japanese.

'No bodies have been found that would fit the description,' Nobuo answered. 'Personally I believe that if Okuma-san had died, then we would know by now.' He leaned towards Yukiko, his hands joined. 'May I ask, please, if you had any contact with your late father in the weeks immediately before his death?'

'I had no contact for ten weeks,' Yukiko said.

'Or with your mother?'

'No contact. I have been working in the United States for the last three months.'

'Ahh,' Nobuo said, then looked pointedly, first at her bruised throat, then at Ross. 'May I ask, please, if your work in the United States – and Magee-san's presence here today – might in any way be connected to your father's death?'

'There is no connection,' Yukiko replied.

'Your father did not explain to you why he was going to Tokyo, for example?'

'I thought you might know the answer to that, Inspector.'

'Please . . .?'

Yukiko sighed. 'I already told you, we had no contact for ten weeks. I'm just here to find my mother. Magee-san is simply a friend.'

'What are you discussing?' Ross asked.

'He wants to know why we're here, why you're here,' Yukiko replied.

'Have you told him?'

'Of course not. What's the point of getting into Sun Valley and that whole thing? This is just a cop pretending to investigate the murder of an old yakuza. It's a waste of time.'

Nobuo's face was like a mask of poured wax. Sun Valley. That whole thing. This was like a magic chest his little son had been given for his birthday: each time you thought you had opened the last door, two more doors appeared.

'Ask him will he help us try and find your mother,' Ross said.

Nobuo listened respectfully to Yukiko and then put on his best bureaucratic face.

'There is a procedure for finding missing persons,' he replied. 'To date no one has reported your mother missing – but if you would care to make a report to Sergeant Bando and to fill up the appropriate forms . . .'

Yukiko had risen to her feet.

'He wants us to fill up forms before he can look for her,' she said to Ross. She turned to the policemen who were also on their feet. 'One final question, Inspector,' she said bitterly. 'Some people have said to me that it is possible my father's trip to Tokyo was arranged by the Tokyo Metropolitan Police. What would you say?'

Nobuo looked stuck for words.

'Thank you very much for your help,' said Yukiko dryly. 'I shall certainly remember my first – and what I hope will be my last – visit to Keishicho.'

Nobuo stood aside and bowed low as they left the room. This was a gamble all right. Strictly, by the book, he shouldn't be doing it. But this pretty bird was yakuza, she would never let him help. Now he had better be sure not to lose her in her flight.

'Sayonara,' Inspector Nobuo said.

Ross turned back once to nod goodbye, but Yukiko was already through the doors of Keishicho.

Sunlight dappled through glossy, leafy trees. Ross could see the tears brimming into her eyes. Opening her bag she fitted on a pair of round, wire-rimmed dark glasses.

He said grimly: 'You were right. I'm sorry.'

'Now we must do it my way, Ross,' she said shakily.

'If Chiyaha is even half as smart as I think he is, then he already knows we're in Tokyo,' Ross said. 'How do we find your mother without leading Chiyaha to her as well?'

'We go to the burakumin,' Yukiko said.

*   *   *

Finishing her coffee, the duty nurse rinsed the cup. She tried not to get too close to the patients in the clinic's Intensive Care, it

190

wasn't worth it. Take the man who'd been in the near bed the morning before: a nice person, told her he'd been in business in California all his life, smiled at 7.15 and at 7.30 he could have been dead for a week.

She divided patients into fighters and others. Bed one was a fighter. Six days on the heart-lung machine, white hair spread on the pillow, no family, his only visitor a young man in a suit. Looking at his yellowing face she wondered what his life had been. Whatever he'd done, he'd always been a fighter; few people would have put up the battle he had since they'd brought him in. She walked from her station to check his monitor and blood pressure. As she got there, without warning, both the eyes opened suddenly wide.

'Oh,' she said, catching her breath, 'I never guessed you'd have such beautiful eyes.'

'What day is it?'

Another surprise: although weak, the underlying voice was firm.

'It's Monday,' she replied, reaching for the phone beside the bed to call the duty doctor.

She felt her arm caught.

'It's all right, honey,' she smiled down. 'You're going to be just fine.'

'Where's Ross?' asked Freeman Oxx.

*   *   *

Ueno: a sudden, torrential downpour halted traffic, boiled the street drains to overflowing and brought out umbrella sellers like mushrooms.

Tokyo's northern station was a human zoo: be-gloved porters and ticket collectors; tiny children being marshalled into line; middle-aged couples with the anxious expression of country people; a hundred or so Swedes, towering like giraffes; and a clutch of Americans, distinguishable by clothes and girth, standing beneath a departure board like souls lost in outer space.

Yukiko, dark glasses on, led the way down an escalator, checking constantly behind. The Swedes were also northbound; five minutes later Ross and Yukiko hurtled out of Tokyo, face to

191

face at the window of a carriage which reverberated with the sing-song accents of Stockholm.

'I know it's a risk going to Sendai,' she said, 'Abe may have men watching the station. But I would never have been told to come if it wasn't a step closer.'

'Who are these burakumin?' asked Ross as suddenly the rain ceased and the sun raised the colours on faraway mountains from black to deep, tropical green. With a loud whack of colliding air, the train met a tunnel.

'In Japanese society,' Yukiko said, 'the Tennō, the Emperor, is at the top and everyone else is in layers underneath. At the bottom you have the peasants, but they are not the lowest. There is another, invisible group that no one ever speaks of, an almost subhuman species of outcasts. They are the burakumin.'

She bought them each a miso biscuit and a cup of scalding, green tea from a passing trolley.

'Thousands of years ago they were probably slaves, forced to wash corpses, boil offal, do all the filthy jobs despised by the Shinto priests. But yakuza accept them.'

A patchwork of brilliant green paddy fields bordered by mountains was unfolding.

'Where do they live?'

'Like all untouchables, together. In ghettos, in makeshift villages on the outskirts of towns. They still do the despised jobs; they intermarry. They have a network stretching all over Japan.'

There was a sense of purpose about Yukiko; the drained husk of sorrow that Ross had brought from New York to Tokyo had been replaced by a woman with singular resolve. Yukiko finished her tea and looked out the window of the train.

'When my mother married she came with her own jochu, her maid. She was burakumin. Her name was Ko-san and she came from Hokkaido. In summer when Ko-san went home I was sent with her. It was a fairytale. A house on the edge of a cliff. A line of washing. A garden with flowers and vegetables. I remember thinking: this is where I would like to live, out here with the gulls and the sea and the burakumin.'

Bright sunbeams flooded in and lit her face. A rusty-headed Swede smiled to them and got up to stretch his legs.

192

'You think burakumin are hiding Mama Yayoi?' asked Ross.

Yukiko nodded. 'Why else would I have been told to come to Sendai? The burakumin were my parents' natural allies.'

Clipping over bridges and through short tunnels, they sometimes curved with the contour of a mountain or valley and Ross could look back and see the snaking, silver tail of the shinkansen. The tunnels became longer and the Swedes gave tongue to rousing songs.

'The Funagata Mountains,' Yukiko said, looking out. 'My father taught me to ski here.'

Ross ached for her.

'We had status and privilege,' she said. 'Now, I'm in a race to save an old woman from a pack of wolves.'

'You miss your father terribly, don't you?' asked Ross quietly.

'He was a simple but proud man,' Yukiko replied. 'He gave us a nice home, we were a happy family. Those are the sort of memories no one can take away.'

'You've lost your father,' Ross said, wishing he could do more. 'I've found mine. Is that nature's idea of balance? Does it tell us something about ourselves?'

'I have suddenly seen myself in a way I would never have thought possible,' Yukiko said. 'Everything I stood for has been changed. Why does life turn upside down so quickly? I believed that as a yakuza I would be safe – instead, the people I would have laid down my life for sent an animal to rape and kill me.' The look came into her eyes. 'I think of that and I want to die,' she whispered.

'It will pass,' said Ross gently.

'They know nothing about dignity when it comes to serving themselves,' she said. 'Now I can see their evil: how Eda had it arranged the night you came to dinner that you drive me home so that I could find out exactly who you were and what you knew. I was just a whore in his eyes.'

'But you weren't,' Ross said gently.

'I can't do that,' Yukiko said. 'Maybe looking back I will see that as the moment when I ceased to be yakuza.'

'You were never yakuza,' said Ross.

The countryside gave way to factories and houses; the train began to lose speed. They cruised through an urban area of parks and spanking clean houses.

193

'We're almost in,' Yukiko said, wrapping a scarf around her head. 'I'm going to check the station. You are too obvious.'

Ross nodded.

'You are a good man, Ross,' she said without warning. 'If anything happens I want you to know that I have valued our short friendship more than almost anything I have ever known.'

She disembarked quickly and disappeared down steps. Ross made his way off with the Swedes who were dragging their luggage down from racks. He thought of what she had said and realized again how remarkable she was; in a matter of days she had transformed the way he looked at life.

The terminal was sparkling and white-tiled, domed with a glass roof and home to fat pigeons that might have come from Grand Central. Green lines and numbers on the platform matched up precisely with carriage numbers on the bullet train. Ross walked down the platform and watched as the Swedes and their luggage were formed into untidy groups by Japanese girls who smiled like immaculate figurines. With a whistle blast the shinkansen edged out northwards.

There was a line of payphones. Ross checked his watch. He wanted to keep in touch with the clinic in San José to see if there was any improvement. He lifted a phone, then froze. Even from thirty yards – the distance to the top of the steps – he could see that something was wrong. Yukiko was running, looking over her shoulder. Ross took a step towards her. The vanguard of the tour group had reached the steps and was streaming downstairs.

'What . . .?' he began.

'Yakuza!'

Ross snatched the suitcase, caught her elbow and powered her back the way she had come.

'Take off your glasses!' he hissed. 'Act like a guide!'

The Swedes were shuffling down steps, chattering. Yukiko distanced herself from Ross and began ushering the tourists in front of her, just as a Japanese man in dark glasses squeezed up against the downward crush of bodies. Ross turned to a girl with a magnificent, blonde plait and blue eyes level with his own.

'You having fun?' he smiled broadly.

'Ga tack!' she responded. 'Stockholm?'

'Sure,' Ross answered as the kobun passed them. Yukiko was five steps back.

'Jōgi Spa?' smiled Ross's new friend as they spilled out into a concourse.

Directly opposite the stairwell two further men in dark glasses were scanning. Putting his free arm around her waist, Ross drew the girl tight to him.

'I love you,' he smiled.

'Ga tack?' she asked with bright incredulity.

Ross kissed her on the mouth as they were borne along in the crush, past the yakuza and out through glass doors into the bright morning. There were three blue buses and some cars.

'Het kalla,' said the Swede and gave Ross a squeeze and the biggest smile he could ever remember. 'Hot springs.'

'You said it,' he replied as they walked up the steps of the first bus and he saw that Yukiko too had made it and was following.

*   *   *

Special Agent Bernie Hutt walked briskly beside SAC Rich, out the door of Six World Trade Center, down the steps and across Church Street at the A T & T Building.

'It could mean anything, it could mean nothing,' said Rich, turning east along Fulton Street. 'What it does mean is that no one gets a moment's peace until Tuesday next, lunchtime.'

'What are Washington's thoughts, sir?' Bernie asked, springing around two people on the kerb to keep level with SAC Rich.

Rich looked at him and wondered about the wisdom of young men.

'With a possible ninja on the loose, as you might expect, Mr Hutt, they've upgraded the threat level to "high",' Rich replied. 'Security in Washington hasn't been tighter since the Gorbachev summits in the eighties.'

'You've covered everything up here pretty much completely, I would say, sir,' said Bernie.

SAC Rich nodded. 'Nevertheless, there are many questions that the Japanese police seem either unable or unwilling to

195

answer. Where's the threat from? Who might want the Emperor dead? Who would hire a ninja, a contract killer? Ninja means we're not dealing with a nut but with a cold, premeditated plan. But whose?'

'Our own people in Tokyo haven't come up with anything?' Bernie queried.

'The Japs are playing it so tight no one knows what's happening,' Rich said and looked sideways at Bernie as they walked uptown on the west side of Broadway. 'I want more information, Mr Hutt.'

'Sir?'

'Read up on ninja. On sul sa. Make a short list of every organization and club in Manhattan that comes close to the category. Look at the new members who have joined from the time this ninja went missing from the Philippines. See if the police files might help. Report to me in the morning.'

Rich saw Bernie blink; I guess some weekend plans have just been put on hold, Rich smiled to himself. How do these kids do it?

'Get a line into Tokyo on who exactly in their police there is investigating this thing,' he continued. 'Get a name. I want to get closer to the way they're thinking.'

'Yes, sir.'

They crossed Broadway, forking right up the back of City Hall on Park Row.

'The two most vulnerable points of this visit are JFK and the museum. On Wednesday, I'll take the museum, but I want you out in Kennedy, Mr Hutt, right there in Hanger Fourteen to make sure there are no mistakes.'

'Yes, sir,' said Bernie Hutt as the outline of Police Headquarters came into view.

*　　　*　　　*

Sendai shone. Motoring along tree-lined avenues and past symmetrical parks, the bus hummed with the sound of on-winding Swedish film. Ross's friend of the blonde plait brought back two cans of Stockholm beer and little plastic boxes of hot noodles. With a knowing smile she left them as the bus began the climb into foothills.

196

Ross said: 'In America when we say "mafioso", people have a certain reaction. They think "hoodlum", "criminal", something they will never have anything to do with. It doesn't seem that way in Japan.'

Yukiko said: 'Yakuza is like a religion you are born into; you may not practise it, but you never actually leave. My father would never have stopped to think that his was an unusual occupation.'

'And yet he was yakuza.'

'Yakuza is an integral part of Japanese life, almost impossible for the Western mind to understand,' she replied. 'It is an enormous family – the gamblers, the street stall operators, the labour unions, what we call the mizu shobai – nightclubs, bars, restaurants, hostess bars – most of the entertainment industry and the speedboat racing industry, the list goes on and on.'

'The image we Westerners have of Japan is of a country largely free from crime,' Ross said as they passed under soaring, volcanic peaks formed in the recent memory of the world and crossed a wooden bridge.

Yukiko tilted her head.

'It is because of yakuza that what you say is indeed the case,' she said.

It was dusk as the luggage was unloaded and brought in through the flapping doors. Vending machines lined the low-ceilinged lobby. As Yukiko went to sign them in, Ross returned the curious bows of tiny, bespectacled ladies strolling about in kimonos and flat sandals.

The bedroom was at the end of a corridor on the second floor. Large by Japanese standards, there was a central area partitioned off with paper screens and two futons, side by side on the ground, their sheets folded back neatly. Ross threw down the suitcase, walked over and opened the window curtains. Stars were popping out above the pines.

'I'm afraid to make this call,' Yukiko said, sitting on the bed.

Ross watched her as she tapped out the digits, then waited, her lips parted.

She looked up, frowning. 'No one answers.'

'Try it again.'

She did as he suggested, pressing each number carefully. After thirty seconds she replaced the phone.

197

'That's bad,' she said shakily. 'Chiyaha's got to the bur-akumin. Worse, he's already got to Mama.' She began to bite her lip in an effort to control her feelings.

'It's OK, it's OK,' Ross said. 'Look, what time is it? Seven-thirty? It's a safe number, right? They were expecting you to call hours ago. Now there's no one there. Call again in the morning and they'll answer.'

She came to him at the window and he held her, looking out at the stars that were everywhere. They had followed him halfway around the world.

'Just look,' he said softly.

'My father told us that each star was an ancestor,' Yukiko sniffed. 'He said they would protect us.'

'We were told they were our guardian angels holding candles,' Ross said.

'Do you believe in a God?'

'I believe in myself.'

'To believe only in yourself leaves you unable to fully share in the wonder of the world,' Yukiko said.

'The world is OK,' Ross smiled, 'it's man that screws every-thing up.'

Yukiko shook her head.

'Look at the moon,' she said. 'It appears everywhere, over a crowded city, a sleepy village, an ocean, a mountain; it is seen in the depths of a pond, in a jug of water, in a drop of dew hanging on a leaf. That such a thing could be is wondrous, but it took man to appreciate it.'

He stroked her cheek.

'I love you, Yukiko,' he said.

She looked at him. 'For me mankind is intrinsically good and always will be, no matter what, Ross. We are two very different units.'

'There is no gap between us,' Ross said.

'I believe that I am part of this great universe,' said Yukiko. 'It is a thing of fantastic beauty. And since all men are essentially the same, if I am part of the universe and it's beauty, then so are all men. Therefore, if I do not believe in the intrinsic goodness of mankind, how can I believe in myself?'

Ross left the tiny figure at the window and went to the

bathroom. He felt more passionately for her than he had in New York, but now in addition, he saw in her an integrity that reminded him powerfully of Misty. This link suddenly reared in him an ugly foreboding; it surged and made him grit his teeth as if by doing so he might frighten away demons. He took off his clothes, showered, grabbed a toothbrush, savagely brushed his teeth, then took one of two check-patterned kimonos from behind the door and belted it on.

Outside, she was sitting, waiting.

'I'm sorry,' she whispered. 'My thoughts are selfish.'

'Don't be sorry,' he said. 'I understand.'

She looked at his kimono, then her hands came to her mouth and she began to giggle.

'What's the matter?'

'You . . . you remind me of your friend, Mr Klein,' she laughed. 'That night in Eda-san's. He sat with his legs stuck out – so!'

She sat stiffly, legs out like a rag doll. Ross cocked one eyebrow.

'What do I gotta do? I'm in this weird hotel with this beautiful doll, we've been travellin' all day, runnin' from guys who all graduated by killin' their grandmothers; I visit the bathroom – I tell you, I've been in bigger payphones – I slip into the lingerie provided, I come out and what is she doin'? She's laughin'.'

Yukiko's eyes were streaming.

'Oh, it's so wrong to laugh at such a time, but it's so good,' she said. 'He liked me, I think, Mr Klein?'

'Tommy's in love with all the beautiful women in the world,' Ross said wistfully. 'He's one of the real, good guys. Beneath all that New York tough trader speak, he's a warm loveable person.'

Yukiko took one of Ross's hands.

'So is his friend,' she said.

With his thumb he wiped tears from her cheeks.

'I haven't seen you smile since the night we first met,' he said.

'I could never not smile with you,' Yukiko answered. She looked at his kimono again, then at her watch. 'Give me five minutes,' she whispered and went to the bathroom.

'What are we doing?' Ross asked.

Her head came around the door.

'Your first night in Funagata Yama must start with a visit to the springs,' she said.

Except for a man at the desk, the lobby was deserted. Steps led down to a dark, winding corridor. Yukiko pushed through a door and found the light switch for the anteroom where neatly towelled massage tables awaited bodies for kneading. There was hissing steam and the echoing sounds of dripping water.

Ross entered a tiled washroom; rows of stools stood over a shore grid, each stool facing a shower nozzle and a plastic mirror. He wiped a mirror of steam, pinched the bristle of his chin, then lathered up and drew the BiC across his face. Glowing, his hair slicked to a tail point on his neck, he walked through to the onsen.

The only light was from the night sky shining down through an enormous, glass roof. The humidity was tropical. With hissing noises all around him he could see jet trails of steam dispersing overhead past jagged outcrops and tumbling clumps of vegetation.

'Hi.'

Ross turned. He hadn't heard her. He didn't care if he was staring. The gloss of her body, the round of her breasts, the downward flow from her waist through her hips and thighs and legs was unforgettable.

'You are incomparably beautiful,' he said.

They descended steps and waded between cliffs of rock into an amphitheatre and waterfall. Ross felt the warm strength of it ripple through him. Yukiko's back was long and glistening like an otter's as she stood, face up, where the fall was heaviest.

Wading on, the water deepened and they swam away. All at once everything was blue, the blue sides and bottom of a kidney-shaped pool. Yukiko rose out, water clinging film-like to her skin.

'You OK?' he asked.

'OK,' she said and the steam, rising, seemed to melt away the bruises at her throat.

Steps wound circularly, first up, then down. A jetty of flat-topped rocks ran into the middle of a steaming pond with lily-leaves and pods floating on its surface. Yukiko walked out on the jetty and stepped down. Without warning the surface of the water broke two feet from her and a massive bullfrog leapt up, croaking.

'Ahhhh!' she screamed.

They sat on the rocks, shaking with laughter. Ross stretched in his foot and touched the bottom: the mechanical frog again broke the surface, it's manic croak echoing in the humid cavern.

Ross slipped into the water and as he struck out she put her arms around his waist and let him pull her. They inched across the steaming pond, past the plastic lilys, beneath an arch that sagged with plastic jungle. Approaching a shore, Ross turned on his back and kicked them gently in as she transferred her hands to his neck.

'We must keep going,' Yukiko whispered. 'We mustn't cool down.'

'Are you kidding?' he murmured, kissing her.

Up steps again, visibility improving with height, Yukiko ducked under a bough and into a round cavern. She cried out in little gasps. Ross followed; the scalding water burned into his ankles.

'It's impossible!' he cried.

Yukiko turned, up to her breasts to show him it wasn't.

'Expel the air from inside you,' she said. 'Each time you feel you can't go any more, empty your lungs.'

Ross tried again, drawing in his smarting breath.

'Breathe out!' Yukiko cried. 'Look! *Ah! Ah! Ah!*'

'AH!' Ross said, following her. 'AH!', but he found he could take it, and suddenly he was beside her, kneeling, a sensation of uncanny relaxation sweeping through him.

'Good?' she smiled, wiping sweat from his eyes.

'Unbelievable,' he said.

'This is the hottest spring, but you mustn't stay in it too long,' Yukiko whispered. 'After more than two minutes, men lose their fertility at this temperature.'

'*What?*'

He left the pool like a pink water buffalo bitten by an eel. Yukiko lay, head back, laughing.

'You . . .' he began, wading back.

She struck out for a vertical ladder on the other side. Ross reached it in two strokes and lunged, but she was already half way up and all he could see were the pink soles of her feet. He scrambled for the top, on to a platform overlooking everything. Yukiko was sliding back a glass door.

'I'm sorry,' she laughed, 'I promise . . .'

He scooped her up and she covered his face with tiny kisses, her mouth darting like a hungry bee. He carried her outside to a ledge of rock where a small, deep pool was cut, fed by a steaming stream from the mountain. He sank them into it and she swivelled in the water to face him. Her breasts rode the water between them. Effortlessly he lifted her, felt her rise, then come slowly down.

'Incomparably beautiful,' he whispered into her ear as all around pines sawed in a wind that was less a wind, more a sigh, and overhead the sky was lighted by stars that were less stars, more candles held by kindly guardian angels.

*   *   *

The office of Deputy Assistant Secretary for Domestic Finance is located on the second floor of the United States Treasury Building and looks west, straight out at the White House.

Phone jammed between ear and shoulder, yellow pad on knee, Kyle Spicer scribbled down the numbers, then threw the pad on his desk and sat up.

'It all sounds a little ragged,' he said.

'It is,' said his counterpart in the New York Federal Reserve, the man who directly managed the quarterly auctions which refinanced the United States debt. 'The markets suspect something – I don't know what. We could see a push on interest rates next week.'

Kyle shook out and lit a cigarette. His recent visit to New York hadn't suggested anything other than a normal auction.

'What are you hearing?' he asked.

'I dunno,' replied the man in the New York Fed. 'We won't have the whole picture for another four, five days, but I get the feeling that the Japs may have been less active than usual.'

Kyle looked down Pennsylvania Avenue.

'We need to talk again next week,' he said. 'I'll call you Monday.'

He put down the phone and drew thoughtfully on his cigarette.

Eighteen months ago you were a nobody in Washington if you hadn't produced half a dozen 'What If?' scenarios involving the new Japanese government. What if they stop buying our bonds?

Looking out over sunny Washington, Kyle could hear Ross's voice.

What if the yakuza are moving into US corporations? Wouldn't that send a shiver down a few spines?

Kyle drew a one page fax across the leather topped desk. It had come in the evening before from the Treasury office in Tokyo:

Reference your recent query on Eiichi Eda, a.k.a. Tatsuo Eda. Subject is known to Tokyo office as sarakin, *that is, loan shark operator, funded in main by yakuza syndicate chief, Kanji Egusa. All relevant departments Tokyo now briefed. Ends.*

Kyle bit his lip. It didn't solve the Sun Valley problem for Ross since Eda was just an employee, but 'all relevant departments Tokyo' had to include the US Department of Commerce.

Kyle thought of all the hours Ross and he had spent together. Ross had been the leader. Always. Naturally. There was an integrity about the guy that would shine through any darkness.

Kyle lit another cigarette.

*   *   *

The red sun rose from the bowels of the Funagata Mountains. It edged up from behind the surrounding trees like a huge, impossible balloon and filled the bedroom with heat, even though the time was just 4.00 a.m.

Holding her to him on the futon, he watched the sun and tried to understand the thing he was part of. Not since Misty had he felt this way. And never with Ashley. Ashley had been like a high-stepping filly; or a diva; you could love her but there was always tension. Except with sex. Sex she understood as a two-way trade – it was the sex with Ashley he best remembered. Misty seemed like someone who had always been there – sex

203

with Misty had been as natural as waking, but it wasn't what he best remembered. She had always been for him. She had tried to heal the dark places within him that had made him turn his back on so much; she had wanted to warm his cold wastelands, to make him whole where he was fractured and see life as fully as she did. There was much of Misty in this strange, sad, tantalizing girl, lost in her own country. He felt suddenly buoyed by this knowledge. His mind seemed clean as stone washed by water over time. Doubt, or its residue, no longer existed. The sun warmed his skin as it inched nearer the tree tops and prepared to cut its tie-lines with the earth. Somewhere a door banged. Another day had begun at Jōgi Spa.

Tiny, Japanese women, all in kimonos and chattering like geese, streamed towards the onsen area. In the souvenir shop, a bespectacled man in a bright T-shirt browsed. A desk had appeared in the lobby, advertising day trips from the hotel.

Ross made his way to the elevators. Earlier Yukiko had ordered for them and he had eaten seaweed and pickles and drunk green tea to dreams of eggs on toast and strong, black coffee. As he had left the room she had tried to call her contact in Sendai but the number had been busy. Encouraging. He waited for the elevator; outside he could see the buses that had brought them the previous evening and some parked cars.

'God morgon!'

The girl from Stockholm stepped out. She was wrapped in a silk kimono, her long, brown legs stuck into wooden sandals. She had yet to braid her hair and it fell in a golden cloak around her shoulders.

'Hi,' he smiled.

'We take the springs, the het kalla, now, ga tack?' she said and linked him to her.

'Normally, that would be a great idea,' Ross said, 'but this morning there are problems for me.'

'That's OK,' she said brightly. 'Later?'

'Later, no problem,' Ross said.

'I love you, mister,' she said and kissed his lips.

Upstairs, Yukiko was sitting, dressed.

'I got through.'

Ross sat beside her and saw the resolve of the evening before, now etched in clean, bold lines by the daylight.

'I was asked the favourite name by which my father called me. He always called me Mio-chan. After that I was told everything. It's bad. Mama and Ko-san are hiding for their lives. Last Saturday Sendai became too risky and they went north to Sapporo, in Hokkaido.'

'Are they OK?' Ross asked gently.

'They were OK when they left Sendai,' Yukiko nodded grimly. 'My contact was terrified. He gave me a number to call when we get to Sapporo. That's all.'

Ross took out a map and spread it on the floor.

'I don't want to scare you, but we may have a problem downstairs.'

Yukiko looked at him.

'A red Nissan compact,' Ross said. 'It's parked outside. I'm sure I saw the same car yesterday at Sendai Station. Also, there's a customer in the souvenir shop who don't look as if he's enjoying his stay in the mountains.' He turned the map to him. 'Is there any other way of getting to Sapporo except by train from Sendai?'

'We could drive,' Yukiko said, 'but that would take a day and it would also mean going back to Sendai to rent a car. There may be a flight to Sapporo from the airport in Sendai . . . What is it?'

'Furakawa,' Ross said, following the shinkansen track north from Sendai with his finger. 'There's a bus trip this morning for our Swedish friends to Furakawa. Can we pick up the train from there?'

'I think so,' Yukiko said. 'But how do we get out of the hotel without being seen?'

'In the best tradition of eloping lovers,' Ross said, grabbing their case and sliding open the window.

The police station in Sendai, the headquarters of the Miyagi prefecture, was located in a brand new building overlooking the River Hirose. These policemen, two hundred miles from Tokyo, although ever-smiling and infinitely courteous, seemed to move in a different gear to those in Tokyo.

205

'Telephone, Inspector-san,' bowed the Assistant Inspector who had been assigned to Nobuo. He went so far as to lift the receiver for Inspector Nobuo, wipe it and hand it to him.

'Hai?' Nobuo said.

'It is Bando, sensei,' said the apprehensive voice of Sergeant Bando from the Funagata Mountains.

'Yes, Bando-san?' said Nobuo, frowning.

'I don't know how to tell you this, sensei,' said Sergeant Bando, 'but they've disappeared.'

Twelve

Total darkness. Movement restricted to three inches. Every two hours for fifteen minutes he exercised each of the main muscles of his body in turn. Flexing, relaxing, flexing again. Fifteen minutes rest. Then the joints, each one it's turn. Turning, returning. Ankles to neck. The back was the hardest because he could not bend.

Time presented no problem. His mind, already committed and at peace, was free to soar, away from this darkness to the land of memory which in many ways he had never left.

The fertile plain around the River La-nga stretches north to the distant peak of B'nom M'hai and south to Xa-muong-man. The wealthy landowners build their houses on the elevated sites so that in summer they may catch the little breezes.

He wriggled up his right hand and from a pouch around his neck he thumbed some rice grains to his mouth. Everything had to keep moving, however slowly: muscles, joints, blood, the juices of his mouth, the functioning of his digestive tract. From the other side of the pouch he took a square of ginseng and began to chew.

The poor man's wife is bent of back and old before her time. The rich man's wife is milk-skinned and unlined. From her alligator purse she takes a little book and makes notes to tell her servants what to do.

Working in hot fields the whole family of Dinh Thack. His

mother wore a white maku, a veil wrapped around her hat and face, but even so, men passing on the dirt road would stop to admire the fineness of her features.

The poor man builds his house with timber, bamboo and straw. The rich man builds his house with brick. The poor man plants every rood of land with rice; the rich man has lawns and pleasure gardens, things that yield him not one grain of money but which exist for the entertainment of his eye.

A car had driven in one day with black suited men from the State bank in Ho-Chi-Minh City. Is this the farm of Dinh Thack? His mother, frail from a lifelong chest infection, began to cough and tremble. His sisters took Rex to feed the carp bred in the holding pool behind the house; the fish swam darkly back and forth, their supple tails propelling them through the muddy water. All his life he would hear the soft, slurping noise they made: a water noise. Like the sobbing coming through the paper-thin walls of the house.

He was ready for what he was about to do. For six months he had trained the muscles of his sphincter for denial and reduced the issue of his bladder to minute, concentrated quantities which passed to the urinary pouch strapped to the inside of his leg. His hands, plunged remorselessly into gravel, were wings of steel. His hands.

His mother's sobbing was as real as the day he had heard it. His sisters laughed as they tried to humour their stocky little brother whose eyes were so different from their own. Half-caste. Round eyed. But loved. Sobbing and coughing. The whole world had stopped: men and women in nearby fields; birdsong; the traffic on the high road; time. The half-caste had to repay their love in time.

He'd plunged his hands into the pool and caught a carp.

He'd beat the carp to jelly on the ground. Dead. Dead. Dead.

Another hour passed. He recommenced. First with the muscles. Flexing. Relaxing. Flexing again.

*   *   *

They rattled northwards through deep and ever-changing green. The tunnels were frequent, blinks of darkness and daylight. It was an old train – the shinkansen had not been due for over an hour and rather than wait they had decided to go. The lights in the uncrowded carriage didn't work and in the darkness of the longer tunnels Yukiko reached for his hand. At Ichinoseki a hard faced man entered the carriage – dark, business suit, briefcase, rolled *Asahi Shimbun* – registered Ross's presence and took a seat facing them, just one from the door.

Leaving the bus in the morning sunshine of Furakawa, saying goodbye to the Swedes, had been an unaccountable watershed. It was as if a link had been cut, that now they were really on their own, speeding north in pursuit of a woman who sometimes seemed like a ghost.

The topography was changing: less tropical forest, some cattle in sloping fields, crops of gently swaying corn. The towns of Mizusawa, Kitakami and Shin-Hanamaki came and went. Hitching her bag on to her shoulder, Yukiko smiled as she got up and walked down the carriage. Ross watched her go. Feminine. He'd never before known the meaning of the word. Light, lightness, floating, sensitive, all these words did nothing to truly explain her or what he felt. And underneath these words, something else: steel, bone, worth, truth. Truth? Ross shook his head. You had to dig under mountains of words to find real people.

They shot into another tunnel and the train noise doubled in the darkness. In the thundering blackout Ross was suddenly swept again by his foreboding of the night before. The tunnel was longer than the others. He imagined he felt a momentary breeze, and found himself sweating. The train's noise, the steel revolution beneath him, seemed gross. Daylight flooded again. Ross looked up the car and took all of a second to register the empty space. The man with the hard face who had boarded at Ichinoseki was no longer there.

Two strides took Ross to the empty seat. Nothing. No briefcase, no newspaper. Then Ross remembered the little breeze of a person passing. He began to run to the other end of the carriage, the way Yukiko had gone, his body now swamped in the sweat that his sixth sense had begun in the darkness. The interconnecting doors were power operated, slow. Cursing them he squeezed through. Another carriage, faces upturned in puzzlement to his.

'Yukiko!' he began to shout. '*Yukiko!*'

Halfway through the next car there was another tunnel and he powered on, using the backs of seats to direct him, sometimes feeling a head under his hand, leaving protesting cries in his wake, shouting 'Yukiko! Yukiko!' as he ran flat out and hit the already opening next door with a crash.

Where on a train would a killer choose? A toilet? An empty corridor? The swaying, no-man's-land of trains where two carriages coupled?

Light again and he was in a service carriage. A toilet was showing its red engaged sign.

'*Yukiko!*' he cried, banging on the door, aware that an audience had followed him. 'Stand back!' he shouted and half a dozen figures drew back as one.

He saw the lock change to green and raised his clenched fist.

'Hai?'

The dark suited man from Ichinoseki stood there, quizzically, the cubicle behind him glaringly empty. As Ross brought his fist slowly down, the door of the adjoining booth opened and Yukiko emerged.

'Ross?'

'Are you all right?' he swallowed.

'I'm fine,' she said cautiously.

Bowing curtly, the man with the hard face made his way back through the staring crowd.

'What's the matter?' Yukiko asked. 'You're wet.'

'Nothing,' he said, 'I'm just ... come here, will you, and don't go off like that in the dark again.'

She came into his arms and he wrapped her close and held her as tightly as he could as yet another tunnel engulfed them. He looked out to see his own head and big shoulders framed by the window, replaced when they shot out overland by rice fields peppered with tiny, veiled figures and tube-like tea-bushes snaking into the hills.

*   *   *

Henry Babbage picked up the telephone.

'Who?' he frowned.

210

'Tommy Klein,' repeated Miss Z. 'A friend of Ross Magee's?'

'Ah, right,' Henry nodded as the call was put through. 'Mr Klein? Henry Babbage. Are you calling about an affidavit?'

'That too, Mr Babbage.' Tommy Klein sounded uncertain. 'I think I need a lawyer. Ross told me you were handlin' this whole Jap affair, so I figured maybe you could help me.'

'Have you got a problem?' Henry inquired.

'I work in Reesons, OK?' Tommy said. 'I got in this mornin', usual time, there's a guy called Anderson from Bacik's office – that's Gerry Bacik, the man? – waitin' in the tradin' room lobby. He's one of these MBA rabbits that sits in an office next to Bacik's all day playin' with himself.'

Henry blinked.

'He says he's actin' under instructions from Bacik,' Tommy went on, 'and that he's been told to tell me I'm out. I thought it was some kind of joke. I said, OK kid, very funny, now back to your lettuce, I got bonds to trade. He said, I'm sorry, Tommy, but you can't go in there. I said, what is this shit, Anderson, this is my production, I trade the bonds in this place! He said, Tommy, you're fired and if you try and go in there I'm authorized to call security. I saw red. I said where's the great shithole himself, how come he's not down here for the execution? I mean here we are standin' there, and here's the guys I work with all comin' in and sayin', hi, Tommy! and here am I bein' fired by this kid.'

'Was there any reason given?' Henry asked.

Tommy shook his head. 'I know I'm long and bonds are goin' south, but that's only in the last two weeks. My desk should make anywhere between eight and ten million for the year.'

'Do you think there's a connection between what happened and the Sun Valley business?' Henry asked.

'You bet your ass, Mr Babbage,' Tommy replied. 'These guys want me out because they're afraid I know too much about them and about their platinum trades. But they can't just throw a guy out after six years, can they? I want to sue.'

'I think you should come in and see me, Mr Klein,' said Henry, then thought of Yukiko and added, 'and I would also counsel you to be extremely careful.'

*   *   *

211

Downtown Sapporo stretched, clean and sparkling, into the distance. The station plaza, the junction of three, wide avenues, was a leafy, relaxed place where people sat or strolled or stood in line for ice-creams. The ambience followed a relaxed pace in harmony with the day and suggested that Sapporo had it's priorities in order.

Yukiko said: 'I'll make the call,' and went ahead to a row of payphones.

Sitting on a seat at the base of a tree, Ross felt the sun on his face. Comforting normality: young couples holding hands, women rocking baby carriages, not a goon with dark glasses in sight. There would be an end to this thing and the business of living could be resumed. But it would never again be the same.

'Ross.'

He looked up. Yukiko's eyes burned with urgency.

'They've gone,' she said.

Ross stood up and felt the urgency pulsing from her.

'What's happened?'

'Suddenly an old woman is the most dangerous person to know in Japan,' she hissed. 'Everyone is asking questions, everyone: burakumin, omawari, yakuza.' She bit her lip. 'Chiyaha has offered a reward of a hundred million yen for Mama.'

They walked briskly off the plaza, Yukiko's eyes ahead.

'They came through Sapporo four days ago, Mama Yayoi and Ko-san,' she said.

Ross held her arm at lights as they waited, then crossed.

'You remember Ko-san's house I told you about?'

'I remember,' he replied. 'The sea, the gulls.'

'That's where they've gone, I'm sure,' Yukiko said. 'The burakumin I just spoke to is terrified. No one can be trusted with money like that being offered.'

'How far is it?' Ross asked.

'North of Ishikari, about fifty miles,' Yukiko replied grimly.

'Is there a train?'

'The nearest train station is Tobetsu,' Yukiko said. 'But even if we take a bus from there to Ishikari, Ko-san's house is still twenty miles out of town. We have to drive.'

'There's a Hertz office fifty yards from here,' Ross said.

212

'We may as well call Rokuo Chiyaha and tell him our plans,' said Yukiko impatiently. 'All the car hire offices and taxis in the area will have been alerted by yakuza.' She looked at children in toy cars twenty yards away being pushed by their mothers. 'Tada,' she said suddenly. 'My father's driver, Tada, comes from Sapporo. Now that Abe is in Sendai, Tada may have come north.

Ross was dubious.

'Can you trust him?' he asked. 'Think of Chiyaha's reward.'

'Tada was Okuma's driver for fifteen years,' Yukiko said restlessly. 'He's known me since I was a child.'

'Times have changed,' Ross said gently.

'Tada is old school,' said Yukiko. 'If he has changed sides he won't be in Sapporo, he will be still in Sendai, working now for Abe.'

Ross looked at his watch. It was 5.45. Less than two hours of light remained.

'Call him,' he said.

Mannequins in the window of the shop beside the coffee house drank coolers whilst men in plus fours teed off. Traffic on the main, downtown avenue rumbled by.

'Why is it taking him so long?' Yukiko asked.

Ross watched as shops closed and Sapporo's rush hour came off the boil. The coffee shop was full of businessmen finished for the day and women with bags of shopping. A yellow, two-doored car pulled up outside and a man jumped out.

'Tada-san!' Yukiko waved.

They hurried across the sidewalk and Ross climbed in the back; as Yukiko closed the door, they drove away at speed.

Tada might have been thirty-five but the digits could easily have been reversed. His eyes, perched on a pair of jutting cheekbones, were yellow where one expected white. Yukiko spoke animatedly, pointing to herself and back to Ross. Tada inclined solicitously. Ross heard the name 'Mama Yayoi' several times. Tada spoke in a rapid, sing-song voice.

'Tada-san has been hiding with his mother in Sapporo,' Yukiko explained. 'He says that his whole life was devoted to my father and that he is honoured to be able to help.'

213

They were leaving downtown Sapporo, crossing intersections at blocks of wasteland and downmarket apartment buildings. Tada asked Yukiko something and she shook her head.

'What's he saying?'

'Tada-san asks, have we be followed?' Yukiko said. 'He asks, does anyone else know we are in Hokkaido? I have told him only he knows.'

Stopped at traffic lights, Tada made a calming motion with his hand, then pointed to Yukiko's seatbelt. As she buckled it, he checked his mirror, then squealed away, right-handed across the intersection. No following car could possibly have made it in the face of the approaching traffic. They made a sudden left. At what appeared to be a dead-end, a narrow alley appeared, the back of an old warehouse, and Tada screamed along it at sixty. With a lurch and a bump they bounced from a kerb and were suddenly driving at sane speeds through a peaceful suburb.

Yukiko took off her dark glasses and put them in her jacket pocket. Turning to Ross, her eyes shining, she said: 'Tada-san was not the driver of Senko Okuma for nothing.'

They hit open road and drove through countryside of the Western variety – railed paddocks, grazing horses and a field of cut hay. Yukiko sat forward, chatting quietly. Ross began to relax. Tada reminded him of P'tit Pol, a man who claimed his appearance was his undoing. And Yukiko's confidence had suddenly returned; with Tada at the wheel again, Ross could see that she was back as rightful heir in her father's territory.

They made good time through Teine but approaching Ishikari there was heavy traffic and Tada tapped his fingers on the wheel. Yukiko asked him something and Tada replied at length. Taking out a tissue, she dabbed at her eyes.

'What's the matter?'

'I have been asking Tada-san about the night Okuma died,' she replied quietly. 'He said they never had a chance. A grenade launcher of some kind was used.'

'How did he escape?' asked Ross.

'Tada-san had left the car to go to the toilet,' Yukiko said. 'When the fighting started, he ran into the darkness and hid in the countryside until they had all gone. In the days that followed, he made his way north to Hokkaido.'

214

Ross puts his doubts aside and concentrated on the task ahead. What form of evidence would the old woman be able to give them? Ideally a receipt from the accountants Hirano-Maeda in Kobe. Henry had been specific about what should happen then: the receipt should be translated, the translation notarized and both documents faxed to New York. Maybe Ross wouldn't have to go to New York, but could catch a flight from Tokyo to San Francisco and spend some time with Freeman before going north to Lunenburg.

Tada swung left, off the main road. Abruptly the tarring ended and they were on a dirt track, a cutting through a field whose grasses brushed the bodywork. The way became progressively narrower and the cutting deeper till it was almost a tunnel. They bumped along, twisting and turning, for over thirty minutes.

Yukiko suddenly cried: 'Look!'

A blood-red carpet of flowers stretched out to the middle distance.

'Safflower,' she said, winding her window down. 'In the old days it went all the way south to Kyoto as rouge for ladies of the Emperor's court.'

Dusk gathering they drove by the edge of the red meadow and, when the meadow ended, on across a wide heath of scrub and gorse and twisted Acacia trees.

'Hai,' Yukiko nodded, pointing the way, 'hai.'

Occasionally the tinny belly of the little car scraped earth. Rising ahead of them, as big as the sun that morning, an enormous, ash white moon had appeared, it's gullies and craters a stone's throw away. After fifteen minutes and a number of horizontal ridges they shuddered to a stop. Yukiko exchanged words with Tada.

'Tada-san prefers to stay here with the car,' she explained. 'He will wait for us here.'

Salt on the air. Up a steep hill to a cliff top, its contour ahead visible for a hundred yards. Below, surf pounding throatily and left, a great expanse of corrugated darkness, bisected by moon and sprinkled with the bobbing glow from the masts of fishing boats.

As they left the safflower plain behind, Ross stopped once to

215

turn in Tada's direction, but the car and Tada had been swallowed up.

Inspector Nobuo looked out at Central Sapporo from the second car of five in a convoy complete with sirens and outriders.

It had taken the usually meticulous Sergeant Bando a precious hour to discover the bus tour that had left Jōgi Spa that morning for Furakawa – and then a further, agonizing two hours before Miyagi prefecture police found the bus and questioned it's driver. Furakawa train station. Yukiko Okuma and the gaijin. But had they taken a train? And if so, had they gone north or south? The ticket clerks in Furakawa station had changed at midday and so another frantic search had begun.

The phalanx of wailing cars hurtled past the wooded expanse of Hokkaido University.

A call made by Yukiko Okuma from Jōgi Spa had been traced – to a poor family of tallow makers, burakumin, on the outskirts of Sendai. When Nobuo arrived at the address, a mobile home beside a yard full of sulphurous vats, the gates were chained. It was two o'clock and he was prepared to accept defeat. Then a shout from the driver brought Nobuo running. Sergeant Bando from central Sendai: the chase for the Furakawa ticket clerk was over: the petrified girl had been found in bed near Enkōji with the owner of a hairdressing salon, a woman twenty years her senior, but the vital detail had been established: Morioka. North. By slow train.

They screeched back to Sendai and Nobuo cursed himself that no helicopters were laid on. He and Bando caught the north-bound shinkansen at 2.39.

As they shot north like a silver arrow, Bando kept an open line to Morioka. The slow train that Okuma and the gaijin had taken had arrived there over two hours before. Nobuo's shinkansen was met by half a dozen policeman from the Iwate prefecture; the local men shook their heads. They had questioned extensively; all the station staff had been interviewed; no one remembered a gaijin of the description . . .

The shinkansen whistle sounded.

'Come on!' Nobuo cried to Bando and jumped on board. 'They're going north!'

But now, in the absence of a firm destination, the whole of northern Japan seemed to confront Inspector Nobuo like a lotus flower going to seed. They arrived in Aomori, the last stop on Honshu, and it was the same story. The ticket office had been busy; no gaijin had been seen.

'North,' said Nobuo grimly, stepping back on board, trusting in his instinct in a way that the Keishicho handbook had never dealt with.

In the Seikan Tunnel, twenty minutes out of Sapporo, things had begun to turn Nobuo's way. Down in Sendai, the tallow maker's wife came home, found herself face to face with six policemen and became hysterical. When they calmed her down, she brought them to her husband who was hiding only a block away. The tallow maker was petrified. He had seen the kobun of Abe at work in the aftermath of Senko Okuma's death and feared that Yukiko's presence would spell disaster for him and his family. But he talked.

Nobuo's train pulled into Sapporo and he and Bando hit the platform on the run. Downstairs and outside, across the wide plaza where people were enjoying ice-creams in the evening sun, the red-strobing, black and white convoy had waited at the kerb like champing horses.

Inspector Nobuo swore at himself. An hour behind could add up to a lifetime. Or two. How could Bando have missed something as obvious as the bus? There was no point in blaming Bando. How had it taken them an hour in Miyagi prefecture to find the bus driver and then another hour to find the clerk? There was no point in blaming the men in Miyagi or Iwate or Aomori. The thought of Superintendent Iseki facing the Deputy Chief – perhaps at that moment – came to Nobuo's mind. He gritted his teeth and looked at his watch. As the second hand swept through seven, the sign for Teine flashed by.

A wind got up behind the sea, heightening its roar and blowing cloud scraps across the moon. They both heard the sound and stopped. A door was banging. Ross peered downhill. A cottage, long and low was set in an indentation of the cliff.

'Just as I remember it,' Yukiko whispered.

'No lights?' asked Ross.

217

Yukiko stopped ten yards short of the cottage and tilted her head. The unattended door banged. The wind made the pampas sing.

'Mama? Ko-san?'

A small porch faced inland and east. Yukiko walked on to it and called again. She was answered by the banging door and the sound of stones dragging on a surging tide.

'Mama?'

Ross pushed the front door and it swung inwards.

'Mama, Yukiko desu,' Yukiko called.

'There's something wrong here,' Ross said.

A paraffin lamp hung from a hook and beneath it a match holder. Ross put flame to wick and a swarm of green-bodied flies rose from nowhere to smatter themselves against the lamp's glass.

Yukiko shook her head.

'They're not here,' she said in bewilderment.

The kitchen was neat and tidy: a scrubbed table and chairs and a dresser with blue and white plates. Yukiko began to walk through the house, calling softly. Everything was musty and dead. The lamp threw giant shadows, adding to the eeriness. There were two doors off a hallway; Yukiko pushed in the first; it was a pantry or storeroom of some kind, empty of furniture. The second room contained a rudimentary washstand, a table and chair and, in a corner, a narrow bed. Ross held the lamp high.

'My God . . .'' he said.

A corpse lay on the bed. Although the hair was as black as Yukiko's, the face was the colour and texture of dead cod. The mouth was open, the full set of teeth showing, boosting the impression of an embalmed skull.

Yukiko went on her knees.

'Ko-san?' she whispered.

Ross stared. A vein running in a half moon from ear to forehead had pulsed.

'Ko-san,' Yukiko whispered, 'Ko-san, Yukiko desu.' She turned to Ross. 'Quick! Some water!'

Ross returned to the front of the house. The suicidal insects were frying on the lamp glass and filling the house with a sickly

218

smell. Ross took a cup from the dresser, filled it from the tap, then, as he turned to bring it back, paused. A muffled, thumping sound had come from somewhere outside the cottage door. A footfall. Putting down the cup, he eased the door quietly open. The pampas sang; cicadas had come to life; and moon shadows played across the dunes and up over the heath as surf thumped in and sucked away, rattling distant stones with it. Ross came back in, closed the door and brought the water to the bedroom.

'How is she?'

'Nearly gone.'

Taking off her jacket, Yukiko dipped the hem of its sleeve into the cup and dabbed the bloodless lips.

'Ko-san, Yukiko desu.'

Yukiko drew the blanket down; Ko-san was no bigger or smaller than her; except for the hands; large and claw-like from years of physical work they lay revealed on her breast.

'Ko-san,' Yukiko crooned and dabbed.

'. . . ah . . .'

It was a tiny noise and it came from her throat. Yukiko bent her ear.

'Hai! Hai!'

Ross watched as the lips came painfully together.

'Hai!' Yukiko nodded. 'A fisherman . . . a fisherman from Uozu,' she said to Ross.

Ross heard the sound again. He stood. Yukiko was straining to hear Ko-san's words. He took up the lamp and walked through to the kitchen. He stood in the flitting darkness, listening. Sea, he knew. Buzz and fry of flies, he heard. Thump of blood in his ears, of dust in his throat, he heard and tasted. Across the window a black form darted. Outside. As Ross took one step to the door, it crashed open.

Two hooded men jumped through. Reflexively, Ross flung the lamp and caught the first one chest high. Flames flew up as the man sprawled back and smashed out through the window, lying half in, half out, the curtains around him suddenly ablaze.

The second man readied a gun and Ross dived at him. A clip spewed into the ceiling as they fell. Ross was aware of shattering glass, way off.

'Ross! ROSSSSS!'

219

Everything seemed so suddenly hot. The attacker was up first. Ross swung his foot from where he lay, but the hood sidestepped and leaped, landing like a cat on his chest. Steel glinted. Ross caught the downward sweeping knife arm at the wrist. The man's free fist slammed his ear. Ross rolled them both right, butting upwards with his head. He heard the man grunt with pain. He bent the wrist back until there was a crack, then a cry. He slammed his knee full forward into the face and the fight died.

Gasping, standing shakily, Ross realized he was in an inferno. Lungs on fire. He charged for the door of the bedroom, then dived as it was raked from the other side by gunfire. There was a chatter-chatter noise which he could not identify. He rolled for the front door and through a wall of flame he saw the lights of a helicopter sweeping up into the night.

'Yukiko!'

There was no way out. The walls of the kitchen had ignited as if they had been built just for special effects. Ross looked wildly around for something to wrap in. Everything was ablaze. He turned and tried to force out but the flames sprang from the shirt on his back and he ripped it off and dropped down, gasping, as air was sucked from the room.

Yukiko. Yukiko.

He thought he could hear another noise, a wailing, rising and falling.

The roof took and little lumps of flaming debris began to fall like hot snow. Ross made a run for the inner door again, regardless of guns, over the floor crisscrossed with bars of flame. Flames scorched his legs and thighs viciously and he shouted out in pain. As his face kindled, he wrenched the door of the tinderbox. He lurched crazily into where Yukiko and the old woman should have been, but he could see nothing, just fire, fire, and it hurt like nothing he could ever remember. And he saw where the bedroom window had been as his eyebrows scorched and then he screamed without control as his hair took and he was clawing like a thing demented out over spikes of glass and running for the only thing he knew, every part of him a torch, out over the cliff into the void and down into the cool, blessed sea.

220

Thirteen

Timothy Manners stared at the screen on his desk and watched sickly as August platinum changed from $406.50 an ounce bid to $407. He grabbed the phone and hit the button which connected him directly with the Cresswels platinum booth on the floor of NYMEX.

'What the fuck is going on?' he hissed.

'Your guess is as good as mine, Mr Manners,' cried the floor broker over intense, background noise. 'Every time a seller comes out, he's swallowed up. Volume is well up too. Looks like the market wants to get back into the teens.'

Manners's small eyes swept the screen and saw that both gold and silver had also moved up.

'What's the talk?' he asked.

The floor man dropped his voice: 'The buying has been coming from Buckley and Schmidts, maybe acting for Japanese buyers. Other than that . . .'

There was a roar.

'Shit!' the broker cried. 'Four hundred eight bid August platinum! I think you should stop out.'

Stops were a device to cut a losing position.

'I'll let you know when I want your opinion,' Manners snapped and threw down the telephone.

Everything he had ever learned about markets screamed at him to abandon the position. But abandoning it meant taking a loss of nearly quarter of a million that would be automatically reported in the weekly cash figures to London. With the position open, he could still fudge it for a day or two more.

That morning he had finally got through to Wrixon.

'I'm in conference,' Wrixon said and Manners could sense he was about to hang up.

'Wrixon!' he cried. 'You hang up and so help me, you'll live to regret it.'

There was a pause.

Wrixon's voice: 'What do you want?'

Manners wondered if the call was being recorded.

'You know,' he replied thinly.

'We go into the Appeal Court this morning,' said Wrixon quietly. 'If they don't shove a red hot poker up that Brooklyn judge's ass, then the best legal advice in New York means nothing. My best guess is we'll see Oxx change hands, middle of next week, latest. Now don't call again, get it?' he had said and disconnected.

Manners watched the screen. Buying from Japan? Right when they should be selling? It didn't make sense. The bid at $408 eased half a point to $407.50. Manners swallowed. It was going to be all right.

*   *   *

Rise and fall. Mesmerizing, each wave, exactly the same yet unique.

Air and spray washed and rewashed him.

He would never leave the sea again. She had been a mother to him, all those years ago when he had left the old man, left those blue-lantern eyes and run . . .

The water was an anointing. It caked his lips and eyes and chaffed his skin. It dripped from the black thickness of his beard . . .

Many things remained a mystery. Silly things. Like his name. But it didn't matter. She, whose face he knew but not her name, was in charge of his soul, layering on healing for the traumas of times past.

The old man was smiling and Ross was smiling back and he

222

was happy because it had been days since they had smiled like that to one another.

He opened his mouth and felt fresh water on his tongue, droplets exploding in the most exquisite sensation ever known.

Soaring music of seabirds.

* * *

Inspector Nobuo could see the leaves of the maple trees in Odori Park. Each leaf seemed distinct in the Hokkaido sunlight. The conference link monitor flashed suddenly and Superintendent Junpei Iseki's large image beamed into Police Central, Sapporo.

'Iseki-sensei, ohayō gozaimasu,' Nobuo said, bowing.

'Ohayō, Nobuo,' Junpei Iseki responded.

'I trust you received my faxed report of events, Iseki-san.'

'Events have overtaken you, Nobuo,' Iseki said without preamble. 'Information has came through to the Deputy Chief from International. Yukiko Okuma worked in New York for a company called Sun Valley and on Monday last she was in a New York court saying that the main shareholder in Sun Valley is Rokuo Chiyaha.'

'Chiyaha?'

Iseki nodded grimly.

'A takeover bid has been halted. This case has suddenly solved itself, Nobuo. Senko Okuma got in the way of a yakuza takeover and Chiyaha had him killed. Okuma's daughter was out for revenge. It's all an inter-yakuza feud about money and power and nothing else.'

'But there was Mama Yayoi's call to Superintendent Nishikawa of Imperial Security . . .' Nobuo said, suddenly feeling very cut off in Hokkaido.

'The Okuma's *knew* Nishikawa from his time in Sendai,' Iseki said. 'He's the only cop they knew so they went to him for help. The threat to the Emperor – our deduction, remember? – was a ruse to get to Nishikawa, or Nishikawa picked it up wrong, one or the other.'

'Chiyaha . . .?'

'Chiyaha made a trip to the Philippines,' Iseki said patiently. 'He's got shabu plants there, you recall. Was there a ninja

223

involved? If so, he was probably used by Chiyaha to kill Okuma.'
Junpei Iseki closed a file. 'I have also been making inquiries
through the US Embassy Commercial section about this gaijin
you've fished out of Ishikari Wan,' he said dryly.

Nobuo leaned forward.

'Yes?'

'Ross Magee. He's trouble, Nobuo. Three years ago he was
involved in a bankruptcy on Wall Street – the New York police
tried to get him on fraud but there wasn't enough evidence.'

'I see,' said Nobuo slowly, then frowned as he thought of the
looks he had seen pass between the gaijin and Yukiko Okuma in
Keishicho, Tokyo.

'But please, Iseki-san, was there not a . . . relationship between
this Magee-san and the dead girl?'

Iseki shook his big head deliberately.

'She was yakuza, Nobuo,' he said. 'She picked him up in New
York a week ago to suit her purpose. I've seen her photographs,
I'm not surprised he fell for her. You know these yakuza
women . . .'

Nobuo did not reply; he was trying to replay the scene in
Keishicho again from the point of view that Iseki had just given
him, but it was not working.

Superintendent Iseki leaned back.

'It's a weight off my chest, I can tell you,' he said. 'There's
been unholy pressure from the eighteenth floor, but it's over
now and if all we've ended up with is three dead including the
daughter of a yakuza oyabun, then, I won't say I'm happy, but
I can think of worse outcomes.'

Nobuo inclined his head.

'Iseki-san, with respect, there are aspects which have not
been solved. We have identified the body of a Kasumi-rengo
kobun and that of Yukiko Okuma. A third body is so badly
burned that forensic cannot yet comment on it. I have to ask:
how is Kazuhiro Kasumi involved? It was his helicopter that left
the scene as we arrived, the markings have been confirmed.
But where is Mama Yayoi Okuma? I am still officially looking
for her, after all.'

Iseki's face showed irritation.

'These are not issues that concern us, I'm glad to say, Nobuo.'

224

'But, Iseki-san,' Nobuo persisted, 'why did Kazuhiro Kasumi come all the way from Tokyo to kill Yukiko Okuma? Even old Abe is involved – it was an ex-Okuma kobun, a man named Tada, who tipped Abe off about Yukiko Okuma. Abe in turn informed Kasumi. There is too much activity to be explained away by a mere takeover bid – especially since Chiyaha is involved.'

Superintendent Iseki reached for his pipe.

'A lot of face has already been lost, Nobuo. We alerted people to a yakuza threat to the Tennō which never made sense, to a supposed ninja on the loose. Now we learn that it was all a yakuza row about money. The Deputy Chief is embarrassed – you know as well as I do what that means.'

Nobuo saw a face in his mind's eye: the Tennō's, polite and kind, looking out from the back of a car.

Nobuo said: 'None the less, I would like to try and conclude what I began: the finding of Mama Yayoi Okuma. I would like, therefore, to remain in Hokkaido to question the gaijin, Magee-san.'

Superintendent Iseki looked ominously at the camera.

'At the specific request of Deputy Chief Amemiya, a separate report has been requested from your counterpart in Sapporo,' he said with measure. 'The gaijin has already been questioned, Nobuo-san.'

The earlier feeling of being cut off from events rose like stale rice in Nobuo's gullet.

'Iseki-san . . .'

'That is all, Nobuo-san,' said Iseki firmly. 'When we start to worry about yakuza warfare, that will indeed be a dark day.'

'Questioning the gaijin may remove any remaining doubts,' pressed Nobuo forlornly.

'There are no remaining doubts, Nobuo-san!' Iseki cried. 'The case is closed! And there is to be a review next week of our performance in the whole matter on the eighteenth floor here in Keishicho! Now is *that* clear? Please return to Tokyo. Ohayō gozaimasu, good morning.'

*   *   *

Henry Babbage never brought home his work. Mrs Babbage had seen to that many years ago and had extended the sanction to

225

cover not just the physical bringing home of such things as briefs and files, but also the mental conveyancing of anything to do with Babbage and Kellaway. Such division had served Henry well and was yet another example of Mrs Babbage's wisdom.

Thus, early on Saturday morning when the bell rang downstairs, Henry had no reason in the world to believe it wasn't the kid who delivered the *New York Times*, that is until Mrs Babbage appeared like thunder.

'Did they say what for?' Henry asked when she had explained.

'*I* wasn't told anything,' she retorted.

'Tell them I'll be five minutes,' Henry said, climbing from the bed.

The two detectives from the New York Police Department looked impossibly young.

'Gentlemen,' Henry said, indicating chairs. 'To what do I owe this honour?'

'Sir, we're sorry to disturb you,' said one of the men whose card named him as Hennessy. He took a file from a briefcase and handed a photograph across the desk. 'Is this man familiar to you?'

Henry squinted down his nose at the photograph. He saw a youngish man, smiling crookedly, wearing a hat.

'I never saw him before in my life,' Henry said.

'He's not a client of yours, sir?'

'I gave you my answer, officer,' Henry said. 'What is this? Who is he?'

'His name is Thomas Klein,' answered the other detective. 'His body was found last night in his car in a wood in Westchester County. He had your number written into a diary and a note of an appointment at your office yesterday.'

Henry sat back with a start.

'Jesus, Tommy Klein,' he said. 'He never showed.'

'So you do know him?' Hennessy said.

'I told you I don't know him,' Henry snapped, 'but I know of him. What on earth happened?'

'He was murdered, sir,' Hennessy replied.

'Murdered,' Henry echoed, feeling light-headed.

'Yes, sir. He was killed by a single blow to the head,' Hennessy

226

said. 'The medical examiner says it's unusual, he's almost sure no weapon was used.'

The man who tried to kill me was a paid ninja. Ninja kill without weapons.

'Ninja,' Henry said aloud.

*   *   *

Sergeant Bando held the door and Inspector Nobuo walked out. His feeling was of great unease, of unfinished business.

'It has been a great privilege,' bowed his Sapporo counterpart on the front step of Sapporo Central Police Station. 'I hope one day to have the honour again.'

Nobuo returned the courtesies quietly, then got into the patrol car that would take them out to Okadama Airport. He fought to put the case from his mind as he had been trained to. Tokyo Police was a microcosm of Japanese life: densely peopled, well ordered, an organization which functioned on conformity. Like a clipped hedge, the piece sticking up was lopped off. In rare cases of individualism, those that resulted in success were quietly tolerated; those that failed . . .

The car drew away into downtown Sapporo's traffic. There were rules: leave yakuza to fight their battles; never question unless yakuza step over the invisible line drawn centuries ago between them and the rest of society. Custom replaced logic. Logic begged to hear from Mama Yayoi's own lips why she had called Nishikawa. Logic begged for explanations: why was Kasumi involved? Why did he kill Yukiko Okuma? How had Yukiko Okuma got the bruises on her throat that Nobuo had seen the morning he met her in Keishicho? He looked up and saw they were stopped outside a two-block-long building with a sign reading 'SAPPORO CITY GENERAL HOSPITAL'.

He said: 'Pull in here.' He saw Sergeant Bando's surprised face. 'I will be five minutes, no more.'

The hospital lobby was done in antiseptic blue and white. Nobuo showed his shield at the reception desk and was directed to an elevator. The flight from Okadama to Tokyo was in fifty minutes. There would be no report of this meeting, this one was for logic – and his own curiosity if he was honest. One last chance to get answers to questions that would never be asked again. He took the elevator to the fifth floor.

'Dozo yoroshiku,' bowed a little nurse correctly as he showed his shield. 'The gaijin-san? Hai. This way, Inspector-san.'

'How is he?' asked Nobuo as they walked down a shining corridor.

'Quiet now,' the nurse replied. 'We had to sedate him, he became very violent.'

'Yes, I know,' Nobuo replied. 'Is he conscious?'

'Maybe just,' the nurse replied.

'How bad are his injuries?' Nobuo inquired.

'His arm did not require a graft and the head burns will mean frequent painkillers,' the nurse replied. 'He's a big man, very strong and fit.'

They turned a corner and Nobuo saw an armed policeman from Sapporo prefecture on a chair outside a door. The little nurse drew herself up and faced Nobuo.

'But there are wounds far deeper than burns, Inspector-san,' she said primly. 'Although I have forgotten most of the English I learned at school, I know that this poor gaijin is bleeding in a place that medicine cannot reach.'

The policeman got up; he saw Nobuo's shield and bowed. The nurse looked through a small window in the door.

'Five minutes,' she whispered. 'No more.'

Motioning the cop to sit, Nobuo went in. Semi-darkness. He walked on the balls of his feet, blinking his eyes to adjust. He could make out a big form, head turbaned, bandaged right arm held across the chest, and a drip of some kind running from a frame-mounted bottle to the left arm. The chest rose and fell with the regularity of sleep. The little nurse's words had made Nobuo even more confused. As a woman, the nurse had picked up, even through the wall of a foreign language, the fact of the gaijin's grief for Yukiko Okuma. Grief? Nobuo thought. How could a man grieve for someone that Iseki-san said he had met only ten days ago? Nobuo looked down at the big figure and remembered his own grief when his father, a rice farmer on Hyōgō, had died without warning. Nobuo had been twenty. Twenty years of love and understanding. Twenty years, Nobuo could understand, but a week, ten days? He shook his head.

228

Maybe, after all, some questions were better unasked. Nobuo began to creep from the room.

'Who are you?'

Nobuo stopped and turned. The unexpected voice was thin. Nobuo licked his lips and drew on the suddenly pathetically small reserves of three years' morning lessons.

'Nobuo,' he said, then added, 'I am.'

He felt himself being examined.

'You're the cop from Tokyo.'

'Yes.'

'You speak English.'

'. . . Thank you.'

'What are you doing here?'

'I . . . want . . . to ask you,' Nobuo said, approaching the bed.

Ross was on his elbow.

'I told your buddies who were here earlier: I want an American lawyer, I want a telephone, I want clothes! I want that gorilla away from the door of this room and I want out of this place! Now!'

'Please.' Nobuo drew with his finger in the air as he fought for the words. 'I want to . . . help you.'

'Help me like you helped Yukiko find her mother?' Ross asked, sinking back. 'She was right. Yakuza can wipe each other out a thousand times and to you guys it's all water off the deck. Go screw yourself.'

Nobuo was getting about fifty per cent of the words.

'She came over here like an outcast, running from yakuza, hiding in the countryside she'd known as a kid, then she was betrayed by her father's driver, a man she thought was a friend. She was betrayed like her father was betrayed.'

Nobuo nodded grimly.

'So you know all this, do you, Nobuo?' Ross cried. 'Did you also buy stock in Oxx before the bid? Come on! Don't be ashamed! Everyone else's doing it!'

Nobuo felt a sudden shaft of anguish in response to the savage grief. Feeling like this had to have been reciprocated or else it could never have come about. Something far deeper had existed between this man and the dead girl than Iseki-san had concluded. Like all the circumstances of the case, far more complex truths lay hidden than at first appeared.

229

'Mr Magee,' Nobuo said fervently. 'Tokyo, you and Okuma-san . . . I no help. I wish to follow Okuma-san . . . her mother-san . . .'

Ross stared at him.

'You . . .?'

'I wanted Yukiko-san to lead me.'

'You didn't help us because – because you wanted Yukiko to lead you to her mother?'

'Yes.'

Ross jumped up, crashing the drip over so that the needle tore from his arm. He led with his left fist, but Nobuo sidestepped the wild blow, caught the wrist, then sat him down on the bed. The door flew in and the little nurse stood there, hands to her mouth.

'Inspector-san!' she cried.

'I still have three more minutes,' Nobuo said, facing her down. 'It will be all right now.'

The nurse backed out, shaking her head.

'Please, Mr Magee . . . I trying to help.'

Ross's chest was heaving.

'You killed her, you bastard!'

'I took a gamble, I lost,' Nobuo nodded.

Ross looked at him, ashen. 'Why?'

'I must find Mama Yayoi-san.'

'I wouldn't trust you to tell me night from day,' said Ross, looking away in disgust.

Nobuo looked at his watch. There was a shadow as the cop out in the corridor peered in.

'Mr Magee.' Nobuo pointed to his own face. 'Please here look. No lies. Incidentally, I promise. OK?'

Ross closed his eyes.

Nobuo said softly: 'Do you too still really want to find Mama Yayoi-san, Mr Magee?'

Ross took a deep breath. 'Yes, I do.'

'Then I can ask . . . please?' Nobuo said. 'Mr Magee?'

Ross looked at him. 'Go on.'

'Once,' Nobuo began, 'please, was Mama Yayoi-san in Ishikari?'

'No,' Ross answered and Nobuo saw him screw up his face as if the question had tapped a vein of information, somewhere very deep. Ross said: 'No, but we thought she would be.'

230

'OK,' Nobuo said, 'twice, did Yukiko-san know Kasumi-san?'

'Who?'

'Kazuhiro Kasumi, oyabun of Kasumi-rengō.'

'The name means nothing to me,' Ross replied. 'Who is he?'

'Kasumi is the great rival of Chiyaha,' Nobuo replied. 'For some reason Kasumi too wants Mama Yayoi before Chiyaha, before police. I think it was Kasumi's men and not Chiyaha's who attacked you in Ishikari.'

'And killed Yukiko?'

Nobuo nodded. 'Please, Mr Magee,' he persevered, eyes closed, drawing words from books and tapes long forgotten. 'Third time, I know Sun Valley . . . and all that thing. And about Okuma-san, the father . . .' He pointed to his own throat. 'Yukiko-san . . . dabokushō . . .' He pointed to the black of his jacket sleeve and again at his throat. 'Yukiko-san, face . . .' He clicked his fingers. 'Pain, face . . .'

'Face?' Ross asked.

Nobuo pointed to his own neck, then made a throttling motion with his hands at Ross's throat.

'Kill.'

'Kill?' asked Ross, then suddenly understood. 'The bruises on Yukiko's throat?'

'Hai! Yes!' Nobuo nodded vigorously. 'How?'

'How did she get the bruises?' asked Ross. 'It's in her affidavit. Chiyaha tried to have her killed in New York. By a ninja.'

Inspector Nobuo leaped up. '*Ninja!*' he exclaimed in a long, shuddering sigh.

The door flew in and two women came determinedly into the room: the little nurse and an older woman in dark blue.

'Inspector-san . . .' began the more senior, firmly, but Nobuo caught one at each elbow and marched them back into the corridor. He could see the puzzled expression on the uniformed cop's face.

'Admit no one else!' Nobuo snapped to him and shut the door. 'Mr Magee . . .' Nobuo had to fight the noise he was hearing in his ears, ten thousand people shouting that he was right. Carefully he drew up his chair, hands bracketed in front of him. '. . . Mr Magee, you say "ninja", New York, how Yukiko-san knows this?'

231

'She just knew he was ninja,' replied Ross. 'She said he moved like a professional killer. He tried to rape her and she saw that his body was covered in tattoos – dragons, flowers . . .'

'*Rape her?*' Nobuo exclaimed as the circle from Manila was suddenly closed. 'Tattoos?'

'Heavily tattooed,' Ross nodded. 'Now what the hell is this all about, Nobuo? Are you going to get me out of here?'

Inspector Nobuo quietened the voices in his head, blotted out the image of the Tennō riding in a car beneath the Empire State Building and joined his hands in composure.

'I will get you out,' he said doggedly, 'if you will help me on.'

The brown eyes and the grey held each other.

'If I answer your questions,' said Ross softly, 'will you take me with you to find Mama Yayoi?'

Nobuo glanced towards the door. 'Police business . . .' he began.

'Do we have a deal or do we not?' Ross asked, defying the other man to refuse.

Inspector Nobuo looked into the haggard face and saw the pain the little nurse had spoken of. He was trained never to allow the facts or personalities of any case intrude emotionally on his own judgement, but he knew that he could never again love warmly if he did not respond to the plea for help that he saw there.

'We have . . . a deal,' he nodded slowly as he realized for the first time in his life that in love and pain all men are of the same race. 'Please, Magee-san,' he asked, 'what happened in Ishikari?'

Ross shook his head. 'It's not clear.'

'You must . . . work.'

'I'm trying, dammit, but it won't come.'

'Tell me the pictures you see,' Nobuo said.

Ross was sweating. He drew in his breath. 'An old woman,' he said suddenly.

'Old woman,' Nobuo nodded.

Ross hyperventilated as he forced his memory. 'The maid, Ko-san.'

Nobuo, standing, was still a head shorter than Ross. 'Alive?'

'Yes, she was alive when we got there.'

'Talking?'

'Talk? No, she couldn't . . . wait . . .' Ross hammered his fist against his head. 'Godammit!' he cried.

'Ko-san can talk?' Nobuo asked, struggling mightily. 'Does she know where Mama Yayoi is?'

'She was burakumin,' Ross replied willing it out. 'They hid Mama Yayoi in Ishikari.'

'You can see Ko-san, Mr Magee?'

'She'd nearly gone,' Ross said and frowned, wondering why he had said it.

'She,' Nobuo pointed to his lips and traced the word, 'spoke?'

Ross shook his head. 'I've told you, she couldn't speak, Yukiko tried to get her to . . .' He got to his feet. 'Wait, I . . .'

'Mr Magee? Yes?'

'I'm going to the front of the house. I'm getting her some water.' Ross pressed his head. 'The kitchen. The tap. A thumping sound. A footfall. The sound makes me go out and listen. I'm outside . . . Singing grass . . . Cicadas . . . Nothing. I'm walking back to the room with the water . . .'

'Water,' Nobuo said. 'You bring Ko-san water. How is she, Mr Magee?'

'Nearly gone,' Ross said again, his breath coming in gasps.

'Keep on!' Nobuo cried. 'Nearly gone. What is Yukiko-san doing, Mr Magee?'

Ross clenched his fist, with Nobuo now on every halting word. 'Kneeling.'

'Speaking?'

'Yes, speaking.'

'She says, Mr Magee?'

'She says . . . she says . . .' Ross shook his head in frustration 'She says Hai! She says Hai! Hai!'

'*Yes! Yes!*'

'The noise again . . . Out front . . . I'm taking the lamp . . . I'm looking back at Yukiko's face. Her lips are moving and she's turning back to Ko-san . . .'

'*Yes!*'

'A fisherman from Uozu,' said Ross clearly.

Nobuo thought his head would burst. He flopped down on the chair as the door opened and the uniformed cop came in.

'Inspector-san, forgive me but your driver says that you will miss your plane if you do not leave.'

'Hai, hai, thank you,' Nobuo said as the man backed out.

233

'Uozu,' he said, getting up, taking out a white handkerchief and wiping his face. He began to pace the small room. 'Uozu.'

'Where's Uozu?' Ross asked.

'Sea of Japan,' Nobuo replied. 'South of Niigata.'

Nobuo couldn't stop sweating. The Tennō in his car. His kind, slightly puzzled face was as familiar to Nobuo as his own. But after what Iseki-san had said, to go back to Keishicho with this information would be like taking the pick of the sake harvest and pouring it into Tokyo Bay. Nobuo stood at the door, looking through the tiny window across the corridor where the cop was speaking urgently into a wall phone.

'Nobuo, remember we have a deal,' said Ross warily.

'I remember, Magee-san,' Nobuo said, turning, ' but now we must leave here very quick.'

*   *   *

Freeman Oxx turned his head to the door of the room as Orem Williams entered.

'Sir,' Williams smiled, 'each time I come in here, you look a ton better.'

Freeman lifted both arms, hoisting tubes into the air.

'I'll be one hell of a lot better when they un-plug me from these things,' he growled. 'When are they going to stop treating me like a baby? When are they going to let me out of this bed and give me a fax and a phone?' He scowled at Williams. 'What's the news on Ross?'

Williams made a reassuring face.

'Nothing firm yet,' he said, 'but it shouldn't be much longer now.'

'Come on, dammit!' Freeman snapped. 'Cut out the invalid-speak! Where is he?'

'They . . . don't know, sir,' replied Williams under the penetrating stare and abandoned the instructions he had been given by the young doctor outside. 'On Thursday morning, Ross and Yukiko Okuma left Tokyo by train for northern Japan.' He sighed. 'We can't get a fix on them, no one can – that includes the embassy in Tokyo.'

'This is Saturday,' Freeman said and thought of a broad little

234

boy with black hair holding Misty's hand. 'Something's happened or he would have called in by now.' He gave Williams a dry look. 'I know about the latest court decision on Oxx,' he said quietly. 'And I know what happened to Ross's friend in New York, Klein.'

Williams stared.

'Henry Babbage was here this morning,' Freeman said and managed a faint grin. 'A cardiac specialist from New York, he told the nurse outside.' Freeman's head rocked from side to side. 'Ross can't be left at risk. These guys place no value on human life. He's got to get out. He'll call me, I know he will.'

'Don't worry yourself, sir . . .' Williams began.

'I want a phone, Orem,' Freeman commanded, 'here, right beside me, I don't care what they say I can or can't do, I want a phone and I want it now.'

'Sir, you know . . .'

'I know shit, Orem,' Freeman snapped. 'I know I looked death in the eye and I won – this time at any rate. Now do I have to rip these things out and get the phone myself?'

Williams sighed and thought of the doctor.

'One phone on the way,' he said.

*   *   *

The night shinkansen to Tokyo swept south at over two hundred miles an hour.

Ross ached. How hollow everything seemed now. He tried to imprint her profile on the retina of his mind as a storehouse for the empty days and years ahead when the moments they had had together would be all he had to draw on. He wanted to tell Mama Yayoi about Yukiko and him. She would always be there now, right through those northern nights where night and day have called a truce and man is ushered quietly off the stage.

He tried to think clearly, to wash the clutter from his mind. He imagined a boat's thick mooring line winding endlessly around a stanchion. Circular, soothing motion. How else might Oxx be saved? Freeman had tried everything, but was there a fall back if Mama Yayoi too was dead? Ross thought of the Masisi, bewildered children, trying to save their sacred hill that sat astride such riches. Circular hill. The Masisi's. And the platinum below it. The Masisi's.

235

'That's it!' he cried and sat up. 'That's it!'

He was wide awake now. Inspector Nobuo sat opposite; across the aisle, Sergeant Bando looked at him, bowed, then looked away.

'How much longer to Tokyo?' Ross asked and looked down the almost empty carriage and then at the windows, closed by blinds.

'Less than one hour,' Nobuo replied. He offered Ross a little bottle of orange juice, screwing it's cap open for him.

'Thanks,' said Ross.

He felt unshaven. The skin beneath his arm bandage itched and his head under the cap that Nobuo had given him – along with the ill-fitting clothes – was on fire. But he also felt excited now. He needed to think it through, then to phone Orem Williams at Oxx.

'You are . . . married man, Mr Magee?'

'I was,' Ross said. 'Divorced.'

'Ahh, divorced.'

'How about you, Inspector?'

'No, not divorced.'

Ross smiled. 'Do you have a family?'

'Family,' Inspector Nobuo nodded. 'Two boys.'

'How old?'

'Ten years and eight.'

'That's good,' Ross said.

'We play football,' Nobuo smiled. 'Ikebukura Park, Saturday. And kendō. I teach.'

'Kendō?'

Nobuo brought his hands down to show a blow. 'Sword,' he said. 'Japanese sport.'

Their eyes held each other's for a moment in a silence.

'I am sorry,' said Nobuo quietly. 'Sorry that you are sad.'

'I didn't think I would ever meet someone who would so quickly become the centre of my life,' Ross said. 'She had remarkable qualities.' The train sang them through the night. 'Do you think she had much pain, Inspector?'

Nobuo shook his head emphatically.

'In fire, people first . . . sleep.'

'Become unconscious.'

'Hai. Their lungs, they cannot breathe . . .'

236

'I hope someone pays for her death,' Ross said without emotion. He looked at the broad shouldered cop. 'You never answered my question back in Sapporo. Why do you so desperately want to find Mama Yayoi?'

Nobuo looked in Bando's direction, but the bespectacled sergeant was looking uncomprehendingly ahead.

Nobuo sought the words: 'Mama Yayoi tried to speak with Imperial Police. She say, threat to life of Tennō, Emperor, from yakuza,' he said quietly.

'From Chiyaha?'

'I think, Chiyaha,' Nobuo affirmed. 'Chiyaha went Manila. Philippines. I find he take ninja out. Ninja with body colours. Tattoos.'

'Christ,' said Ross softly.

'But Amemiya-san, Deputy Chief, he heard about Sun Valley.' Nobuo cut the air. 'Case is closed.'

'The ninja is in New York, Inspector,' said Ross. 'He's there, believe me.'

'And in a few days, so is the Tennō,' said Nobuo, his eyes clear and steady.

'Why?' Ross asked. 'Why would Chiyaha want the Emperor killed in New York?'

'Chiyaha's mind . . .' said Nobuo simply and with his finger made convoluted circles in the air.

He reminded Ross of himself: cut off, maverick, chasing the elusive. Was there a plot to kill the Tennō? If so, why? Why the Sun Valley bid? Why had Yukiko died? Ross sighed deeply. Why had he ever come south to Santa Clara that morning . . .?

Sergeant Bando opened the window blinds and Ross could see that they were drifting in through the sleeping suburbs of northern Tokyo, into Ueno which he and Yukiko and a gaggle of laughing Swedes had left only three days ago. A lifetime ago. Nobuo had said they would have to change stations for Uozu. Before they did, Ross would call California. He felt his legs weaken. He didn't want to hear that Freeman too was dead.

A clock over the platform read 3.30. The empty station echoed with every noise. A lone porter stood to one side with a baggage cart as Ross walked ahead of the two policemen to the first in a line of empty payphones.

*

237

Inspector Nobuo waited at the upper level. Thirty minutes to Tokyo Station at this hour. Two hours thirty minutes to Niigata. The authority of a Keishicho CIB inspector would get him all the help he needed in Niigata, no questions asked. No one would dream that he was acting outside orders. Orders didn't matter now, something visceral had taken over, something as old as Japan itself. If everything went well he could be before the Deputy Chief with the new information – and with Mama Yayoi-san – before sunset. He wasn't afraid anymore. He was following instinct and he knew the instinct was right.

And the gaijin? It was most irregular, but then the whole exercise was most irregular. Orders deliberately ignored. Initiative taken and no clearance obtained. Americans were meant to be loud and crass and to lack feelings. Nobuo would take with him from this case an impression of depth and sensitivity far greater than he had ever imagined possible in a gaijin.

Nobuo turned to the elevator. First, Magee-san's head appeared, then his shoulders. Nobuo was puzzled. The face had changed from downstairs; in addition to pain and exhaustion there was now an element of despair that Nobuo had not seen before.

'Magee-san – is there something . . .?'

Ross's eyes brimmed, red-rimmed. Struggling to breathe, his face was changing as great swells of emotion crossed it. Nobuo stepped forward.

Ross tried to speak: 'A great guy, a friend, in New York, Tommy Klein . . .'

Nobuo caught Ross tightly at the arm and watched the agony with a distress of his own.

'Magee-san . . .'

Ross's head sagged and the little policeman pressed his cheek up against the rough stubble.

'Magee-san . . .'

Ross cried out: 'The ninja has killed Tommy Klein.'

*   *   *

Kazuhiro Kasumi stroked the back and tail of a large cat and smiled. He liked cats, despite the fact that as a child his mother

238

had always forbidden one in the house, saying they were cruel creatures that ate their young.

There had been a wall which the young Kasumi had climbed. At the other side was the yard of a rice merchant, a wealthy man. This yard was the province of a magnificent old orange coloured cat which lay in the sun and preyed off the rats that came up from the river. Kasumi remembered him well. The sun shone and the cat appeared to sleep. But when his eyes were closed he was at his most dangerous, springing at the ultimate moment to impale a screeching rat. When he'd crippled the rat, he'd let it off, crawling to the centre of the yard. Then he'd hide until a companion rat, drawn by whatever communication passed between them, braved it out from the fence. The cat would strike and kill. He'd bring the dead rat out of sight and hide again, leaving the cripple to roast kicking in the sun.

One lazy afternoon young Kasumi had watched as nine rats were so trapped by the great cat. It was a lesson he had never forgotten.

*   *   *

Sea mist rode the gunwale. Ross stood at the deck hatch of the coastguard launch as a yawl appeared from nowhere, it's dirty-red jigger limp in the still air. His unreal detachment was like the morning: dead: the same that had taken him over three years ago when Jim Morales had cut his wrists and the piranha moved in; the same as when he first read about Misty. He fought the feeling. Life was a grotesque ledger where the debits and credits always balanced if you had the time to wait. Freeman had made it, and Ross, in his excitement, had barely been able to relay the thoughts about Oxx and the Masisi that had come to him on the train. Then Freeman had quietly told him about Tommy.

Ross looked through the mist. You found people in strange ways. Like Yukiko. Like the Japanese cop standing beside him whose only concern since Tokyo was that Ross should not suffer too much.

Life in Uozu port had not yet started: boats with deck awnings and hung with washing; dogs barking; a baby's cry. The

239

coastguard in Uozu had confirmed to Nobuo that the boats recently in from Ishikari numbered four. One was burakumin. The captain – a tall man, all knees and elbows in white shirt and shorts – cut back the engines and brought them sideways on to a wooden pier. Half a dozen men carrying semi-automatic weapons hurried out from the quayside.

'Magee-san, please.'

Nobuo motioned Ross to remain on board, then jumped off as the men on the jetty snapped him salutes. Ross watched as Nobuo led them at the crouch, gun in hand, out along a line of trawlers, two cops either side of him, guns readied.

Ross stepped off the launch. Families moored finger-like were all taking quiet stock of the sudden activity as he crossed the decks of boats reeking of stale fish and diesel. Vaulting to the deck of the final trawler, Ross saw Sergeant Bando, gun in hand, and Nobuo, sitting under the awning, talking to a small, undernourished man whose hair straggled over his ears and down his bare chest. A young woman with high cheekbones sat beside them, holding a baby in the crook of her arm. The fisherman was crouched, knees either side of his head like a black haired cormorant. Nobuo questioned. The fisherman shook his head. Nobuo raised his voice threateningly. The fisherman hunkered down even more, whimpering and rocking from side to side. Nobuo stood up and came over to Ross.

'He say he knows nothing of Mama Yayoi,' Nobuo said. 'He say he come here for the fish.'

Ross crossed the deck to where the man and his wife sat with their baby under the awning. They stared up wide-eyed at him.

'Tell them I was in love with Mama Yayoi's only daughter, but that yakuza killed her,' Ross said to Nobuo. 'Tell them I want to tell Mama Yayoi how Yukiko died honourably and bravely.' Ross nodded to the couple. 'Please say, Yukiko Okuma said that the best friends she had ever had were burakumin.'

Nobuo translated rapidly, gesturing to Ross, pointing north. The fisherman said something to his wife, then getting up on his knees to Nobuo he slit his finger over his throat.

'Yakuza!' he cried and rolled his eyes.

'Leave him some protection,' Ross said. 'Tell him you'll leave a cop here until he puts out of port.'

240

Nobuo relayed what Ross had said, but the fisherman resumed his crouched refusal to communicate.

'May I?' Ross asked the woman, reaching with his good arm for the child.

The mother drew back, but Ross smiled at her. Very slowly she placed the baby in his arm.

'Inspector,' Ross said, 'I need some money.' He rocked the child gently. 'Fifty thousand yen.'

Nobuo took out a wallet and handed over the notes. Tucking them into the child's fist, Ross handed it back.

'Tell them it's for luck,' he said. 'Tell them it's from one fisherman to the child of another.'

Nobuo translated and the husband and wife looked at the money, then back to Ross, open mouthed.

Nobuo spoke again. The fisherman looked at his wife, then he suddenly reached out and drew Nobuo into him.

'Hai?' Nobuo said, listening.

'Hai!' the man said. 'Hai!'

Nobuo jumped up.

'Let's go!' he cried.

He led the way back across the trawlers, rattling off instructions to the local policemen, jumping deck to deck past the eyes of the floating families.

'Where is she?' asked Ross, catching up.

'In the Imperial City, in Kyoto,' Nobuo whispered. 'She is in the care of the monks at the temple of Shoren-in.' He passed the coastguard launch on the run, looking at his watch. 'We can be there in three hours, still a.m.,' he said. 'Every second now is golden.'

They reached a car where Sergeant Bando was holding open the door.

'Inspector!' Ross called. 'I need to call Tokyo. The US Commercial Attaché is a guy called Kerry O'Brien. He can meet us in Kyoto and arrange to take a deposition from Mama Yayoi about Sun Valley.' He saw Nobuo look again at his watch. 'It's important to me, Inspector.'

'Please, Mr Magee, yes, but hurry,' Nobuo said. 'I think we may not be very far ahead of Chiyaha.'

*

241

Chiyaha bit his lip. The tension had come and with it, noises.

Feet on the stairs, wood noise, wooden clogs on the wooden risers. She had had a perfect, round face.

'Roki, to your room now, to your room.'

A mask of rice paste and her lips like drops of blood.

'Is this chichi come to see us, mother? Is tonight the night he comes?'

'I asked you not to talk of chichi, Roki. Now to your room!' A fist softly struck the door, bone noise, bone on wood.

'It is chichi, I want to see him! I want to see my father!'

'It is not your father, child! Now go! Quickly!'

Inwards bundled little Roki, to a tiny room.

Feet on floor, closing door. Tinkling mother laughs. Silence through the rice paper, giant shadows rear and plunge, Roki's own picture show. Rhythmic rustle of her futon, straw noise, straw on wood. Her scream of strange pain. Woman noise. Steel in flesh. His hands to ears could kill all noise. Silence.

'Roki? Are you asleep?'

He was like a sleeping angel as she kissed his little cheek.

'Goodnight my little angel.'

Even as she left the tiny room he heard the next feet on the stairs as the next giant shadow had arrived.

The ringing phone made him blink.

'Hai?' he spoke.

'He's back in contact,' the caller said.

The cop on the Uozu jetty heard the cars before he saw them. They screamed around the corner below the pilot's station and slewed to a stop twenty yards from him. He unclipped his gun with one hand and reached for his belt radio with the other.

Things happened fast. Car doors flew open and men hit the ground, rolling. The cop's mouth dried out; his hands froze for a fatal second; he heard explosions before toppling backwards into Uozu harbour.

Kazuhiro Kasumi emerged from a rear car and strode reverberatingly down the jetty, chest out, the centre of a moving square whose four corners were men with guns. Heads disappeared down hatches. Six kobun of Kasumi-rengō ran out

242

across the line of trawlers. There was a scream. Kasumi propped himself on the shoulder of one of his men, jumped heavily down, then made his way outwards.

'Lord Kasumi!'

A wakashira-hosa was standing at the hatch, pointing into the hold. Kasumi looked down and could see a small, bony man and a young woman crouched there. Reversing his bulk into the square of space, the oyabun of Kasumi-rengō descended.

'Ohayō gozaimasu,' he bowed, out of breath. 'I am Kazuhiro Kasumi, oyabun of Kasumi-rengō. I am seeking Mama Yayoi Okuma in order to bring her into my sincere protection. I know you brought her here from Ishikari. Please, where is she now?'

The fisherman and his wife clung to each other.

'I will pay you a hundred thousand yen for this information,' Kasumi said, 'but I must know – and I must know now!'

'I do not have the information, my lord,' the fisherman whispered. 'I do not know what you ask.'

'So you don't know,' Kasumi nodded, his jaw working. 'Very well.' He clicked his fingers and took a 9mm Beretta from a kobun. 'Very well,' he repeated and discharged the gun into the fisherman's face.

The shot boomed around the hold. The man went back on his heels, blood spraying. The wife began to scream.

'I know Mama Yayoi came here with you,' said Kasumi to her patiently. 'I know you know where she has gone. Do you want to follow your husband, or will you tell me?'

The woman lunged at him but a kobun stepped in and felled her with his gun butt.

'Korose!' the woman screamed from the floor. 'Kill me!'

'Take her up,' Kasumi said, handing back the gun and climbing the steel ladder.

He reached the deck and paused to get his breath. Mama Yayoi was the counter he needed to foil Chiyaha. With her in his power, everything was safe; without her, Chiyaha would ruin them all. He looked at his men, a blank-faced circle.

'Lord Kasumi!'

Kasumi turned. A kobun had come from the forward deck, awkwardly holding a crying baby. Kasumi waited until the sobbing woman had been brought to face him, then he addressed her.

243

'Where has Mama Yayoi Okuma gone?'

The fisherman's wife spat into his face, then she saw her baby.

'*Watashino-akachan!*' she screamed. '*My baby!*'

Kasumi turned to the kobun.

'Drown it,' he said.

The kobun caught the infant by a heel, lay on the deck and plunged it into the sea.

'*Stop!*' the woman screamed, scrambling forward. '*My baby!*'

Red blotched from the heat, Kasumi looked at his watch.

'Is it dead yet?'

The kobun lifted his arm and the baby came up, spluttering feebly.

'Not yet, Kasumi-san,' the man replied and returned the child to the water.

'Stop!' the mother screamed. 'She has gone to Kyoto, to the temple of Shoren-in.'

'That was very simple,' said Kasumi. He jumped briskly to the adjoining boat. 'See if she can swim as well as sing,' he called back, then continued for the jetty as, laughing, the kobun threw the child as far out into the harbour as he could and the mother leaped over the side.

Ten minutes later, from a wooded area south-west of Niigata, a helicopter rose into the morning sky and began to thread it's way west on a flight path which would bring it to the Imperial City.

Fourteen

SAC Ed Rich looked to the door of the Command and Control Centre of Police Headquarters and noted the absence of Special Agent Bernie Hutt. Rich thought of himself twenty years before, first as a young, eager CPA in Saint Paul, Missouri, then, four years later, the Special Agent on the Presidential Detail who always had an eye for a pretty woman. He sighed, looked at his watch and then at the upturned faces of the five Department Chiefs and Agency Heads of Station and their assistants.

'Gentlemen, good morning.'

'Mr Rich,' nodded Eric Kruger, the Field Man from the State Department. He held up a piece of paper. 'I'm sure we're all aware of this report which came in Saturday from Tokyo. It seems our ninja scare was just that – a scare. I guess we can now back the tanks away from the museum.'

Although Kruger smiled at his own joke, Ed Rich knew that there was a vein of seriousness within in it.

'For the record,' Rich said, 'we're standing down the threat level from "high" to "mid-level". Are there any questions before we proceed?' He looked around the faces, then to his file. 'In that case, Captain Levine, do you have any comments to make on arrangements out in Kennedy?'

'Wednesday morning, nine a.m., will be a standard top security arrival and departure through Hangar Fourteen involving the people already listed,' Zach Levine said. 'The ninja threat gave us an excuse to push the demonstrations back another mile, which suits everyone – except a few screwballs, that is. I'd drafted in a little extra sniper cover from the Emergency Service Unit which I'm leaving in place.' He saw Kruger's face. 'These guys will be invisible to anyone taller than a blade of grass.'

Ed Rich nodded his approval.

'So, the motorcade.'

Deputy Chief of Police Brandon Amis looked at his file.

'We're all ready to go,' he said. 'We move forty-four dignitaries from JFK to midtown Manhattan. They travel in eight bullet-proofed limousines. The Emperor and Empress go in the first car with the Mayor and Mayoress of New York. Second car: the Secretary of State and his wife, the Japanese Foreign Minister and his wife. Then they go in sixes, led by our senior Senator, the Japanese ambassador and our ambassador in Tokyo, plus their wives, and so on. Eight limousines in all.'

Ed Rich looked at his watch. Where was Hutt?

'Three cars with Highway Patrol and Secret Service personnel will sweep the route five minutes ahead of the motorcade,' Chief Amis said. 'The motorcade itself will be led by six motorcycle cops, then a marked patrol car, then an unmarked car carrying the Commander of the Highway District and myself, then the Emperor flanked by four, motorcycle outriders. Immediately behind the Imperial car will be a CAT van – a Counter Attack Team from Police Intelligence riding in a black, Chevrolet truck with blacked-out windows – and behind it, a similar van carrying Secret Service counterattack personnel. Cameras on the first van will film the entire motorcade and send pictures to both our car and back here into this Command Centre.'

The Chief consulted his file.

'The other limousines follow, led by the Secretary of State. There are two further counterattack teams in the motorcade, two further unmarked cars carrying detectives, an ambulance and a repair truck with two mechanics. After them come the accredited media, a car from the Highway Patrol and four cops on motorcycles.'

'What about the air?' asked Kruger of State.

'Two NYPD choppers, one filming the whole event, one with snipers and rocket firing capabilities,' Chief Amis replied. 'Air space has been restricted in the area. Coast Guard are on alert. Of course every component part of this operation will be linked in here by radio.'

He turned to a floor plan of the Metropolitan Museum pinned to an easel-mounted board. He continued: 'Tuesday morning, the Metropolitan is closed to the public. When the Emperor arrives, the invitees will be inside. Each person will have entered on specially issued passes which will combine proof of his or her identification. Each one will have passed through the magneto-meter and have been physically searched, if appropriate.' He pointed to the map. 'The podium and stage has been constructed by a joint team made up of personnel from our own Bomb Squad and Mr Rich's office. The podium has transparent, semi-invisible, bomb proof screens running around it in a one-eighty degree arc. In front of the podium there is a ten foot deep, cement-lined bomb drop, incorporated into the stage. Special Agents and detectives will continually scan the audience, as will two video cameras which will relay the picture to a control booth located in the exhibition gallery.'

The door was opened by a beefy cop and Bernie Hutt hurried in.

'Windows and doors have already been replaced and reglazed with bomb-proof materials,' Chief Amis went on. 'Wednesday morning, we'll have swept not only the immediate area but the entire building, the buildings opposite and on either side of the museum, and the relevant area in Central Park . . .'

The discussion went on, but Ed Rich's attention was on a one paragraph page which Bernie had handed him. It was an extract from the computer in the Crime Analysis Section of the New York City Police, detailing a homicide reported four days before. Part of it was underlined and in the margin, in Special Agent Hutt's writing, was the word 'ninja'.

There must have been three hundred children on the steps of the Metropolitan. SAC Rich led the way past the gushing fountains, then stopped to survey the façade of the huge building through narrowed eyes.

Bernie Hutt said: 'A sul sa master can be classed as a one-man army, sir. Their abilities include survival in alien terrain and

247

self-hypnosis using principles of Zen Buddhism.' Bernie caught the SAC's glance. 'The army teach sul sa on a selected basis in Fort Bragg, North Carolina, sir,' he added.

Rich took in the umbrellas of the ice-cream vendors on the kerb, the shrubs either side of the entrance doors and the massive cloth banners hanging between the four twin columns that made up the entrance façade. The central banner, in brilliant yellow, proclaimed in red letters, 'GREAT JAPAN'.

'Who exactly is Babbage?'

'The senior partner in a firm of Wall Street attorneys named Babbage and Kellaway,' replied Bernie. 'I ran a check through the New York Bar Association. They're blue bloods.'

'Let me get this straight,' Rich said, moving towards the steps. 'Babbage represents a guy named Magee who's trying to stop a takeover bid for a US corporation called Oxx by a Japanese outfit, Sun Valley? Magee is claiming that Sun Valley is yakuza owned and he's produced a yakuza witness, a woman called Okuma, in support of this contention? Okuma claims that yakuza have tried to have her killed by a ninja?'

'Right, sir,' Bernie replied as they made their way up by the brass hand rails, through the crush of children. 'Babbage gave me a copy of the affidavit he'd lodged in court. Okuma claims this ninja would definitely have killed her if Magee hadn't arrived at her apartment.'

Ed Rich showed his credentials to a uniformed policeman.

'The Executive Director and his staff are all assembled for your briefing, Mr Rich.'

'Thank you, officer,' Rich responded. 'Please say I'll be five minutes.'

They passed between the narrowly placed pillars which housed the electronic counting eye. The vastness of the Great Hall reduced people to the status of ants. Rich led the way briskly up marble steps to the second floor, past a gift shop and back towards the Fifth Avenue windows.

'A Tommy Klein who has worked for Reeson Rhoades, Sun Valley's bankers, is due to swear an affidavit in Babbage's office but doesn't show up,' he continued. 'He's found murdered. He's been dead for twenty-four hours and he was killed by a ninja-like blow to the head.' He paused with his back to a panel

248

which listed the names of benefactors to the museum. 'The cops haven't come up with a motive. Where's our threat, Mr Hutt?'

'We're on alert for a ninja attempt on the Emperor, sir,' answered Bernie. 'The attempt on Okuma's life and the killing of Klein were both by ninja. We have a ninja in New York.'

Rich stroked his ear.

'Have you tried to get a fix on Okuma?'

'Through our contact in Tokyo, Superintendent Iseki,' Bernie nodded. 'Babbage says Okuma and Magee are in Japan endeavouring to get a deposition from Okuma's mother. Babbage says it will prove the yakuza assertion against Sun Valley.'

Rich said: 'Is this the same Superintendent Iseki who reported, forty-eight hours ago, that we could forget about the ninja threat to the Emperor?'

'I'm still waiting for his reply on Okuma,' Bernie nodded lamely.

Steel mesh gates ran from ceiling to marble floor at two entrances either side of a banner with the 'GREAT JAPAN' sign. SAC Rich pressed a bell inset in the wall and after some moments a section of curtain hanging the other side of the gate was pulled back. The guard in dark blue uniform and cap wore tinted glasses. He scrutinized the men's ID, then unlocked the gate and slid it partially open to allow them in.

Soft lights in the anteroom gave an impression of delicate intimacy. Six-fold screens, their pastel silk almost fragrant, stood between the visitor and the inner galleries.

'Everything all right in here?' asked Rich, walking through.

'You bet, sir,' answered the guard.

Bernie said: 'I've read a lot about sul sa, sir – and about how these ninja operate. When they self-programme they're meant to be unstoppable. They kill without weapons, which means that they have to operate at close quarters.'

'Like this, Mr Hutt?' asked Rich and lunged, flat hand whistling, halting half an inch from Bernie's startled face.

'Yes, sir, I guess so,' Bernie swallowed. 'I've been thinking on the way here, trying to put myself in the shoes of this . . . of a ninja, were he to exist.'

SAC Rich nodded pleasantly, his back to the inner pavilion.

'I'm sure that was interesting, Mr Hutt.'

249

Bernie raced on: 'I've thought about the airport. The numbers in JFK are small, Hangar Fourteen is inaccessible to the general public, they're used to security out there. Levine's an expert, no ninja is going to get into his show. I even thought about the Japanese poet who's coming from Boston, but the guy is eighty.'

SAC Rich was amused.

'Very good, Mr Hutt.'

'I've thought about the motorcade,' Bernie said. 'There's plenty of ESU cover and the journey into town will make the Emperor think he's in the Indy 500.' He paused for breath. 'It's got to be in here, sir.'

SAC Rich nodded reasonably.

'We have recognized the vulnerability of this building, Mr Hutt. That is why the place is tighter than a drum. That is why we've closed it down and gone through it with a fine comb. That is why we know the pedigree of every single person who'll be here on Tuesday better than their mothers do. There's no way for a man like you describe to get in, no place for him to hide.'

'I don't know, sir,' said Bernie uncomfortably. 'Maybe you're right. It's just that, well, this is a place used to protecting things, not people. Perhaps I'm over-reacting.'

Rich looked at his watch.

'You've obviously had a very good look at the martial arts scene in New York, Mr Hutt,' he said slowly. 'I would estimate that there are probably a hundred people in New York who call themselves ninja and can kill with a blow to the head, would you not agree?'

'Yes, sir,' answered Bernie quietly.

'The Japanese themselves have admitted that the initial threat to the Emperor was unfounded,' Rich continued. 'Here in New York we've got the tightest security operation in place that I've ever experienced. It would take a lot more than this, Mr Hutt, for us to revert to high-level threat status again, especially with people like Kruger from State breathing down my neck.' He looked coolly at Bernie. 'I suggest you get a good night's . . . sleep, Mr Hutt,' he said hanging on the word. 'I'll see you tomorrow.'

Bernie watched the gate closed behind the SAC, then made his way back into the pavilion. The inner gallery was carpeted

250

underfoot and had been conceived in a colour that reminded Bernie of the sun at dawn. The exhibits in the long, rectangular room were arranged to create a sense of space: along the walls, hanging scrolls and silks were interspersed with wood panels depicted in gold leaf and lacquer; a man's outer robe and a decorated fan stood side by side; running down the centre of the room were objects of sculpture in metal and wood and, before the podium was reached, alone like an island in a cold, hushed sea, sat a brooding stone buddha.

Bernie strolled round the buddha and stood between it and the stage. The top of the buddha's head was fully two feet over Bernie's and dominated the aspect back to the door. Bernie stood there and suddenly for no reason he could explain, his flesh began to crawl. It was a chill feeling where all his body hairs stood up and the pores of his skin distended. It was a feeling he used to get as a kid on dark nights and later, in the army, on combat exercises. It was an involuntary, chemical thing and it meant danger. He shook himself and looked over to a side table where the guard was reading a book.

'Has anyone else been in here today?' he called. 'I mean, apart from security and museum personnel?'

'You and Mr Rich are the only ones,' the guard answered.

Bernie wiped the back of his neck as he recalled his reading of the last two days. *In ancient times, sul sa were regarded as being almost magical* . . . He climbed the three steps to the stage and podium. The feeling would not go away. Ninja. Here. *It was said of them that they could scale the sheerest castle walls with ease and camouflage themselves to the point of being invisible* . . . Bernie stood at the lectern and looked back down the gallery, over the bomb drop. The arc of transparent screens that would surround the Emperor were more visible at this angle. The feeling subsided.

Rich was right. He needed a night's sleep. He made his way down again. At the buddha he froze again as all his neck hairs bristled for the second time in a minute. There was something. More than a feeling. Less than a smell.

'Do you smell anything?' he asked the guard.

'Sure,' the guard said 'it's those bomb dogs. They're using bitches. They smell when they're in heat.'

Bernie nodded slowly. 'OK,' he said and made for the gate.

Fifteen

They left Uozu to the north, joined the Hokuriku Expressway at
Toyama and drove due east along the base of the Noto Hanto
peninsula. The Sunday traffic was thin; the unmarked car from
Toyama prefecture averaged fifty, weaving through carloads of
families headed for the beaches of Chirihama. Ross sat in front.
Behind, Nobuo and Sergeant Bando were hunched over a map.
Ross drifted into sleep and when he awoke, sun hot on his face,
they were passing a row of weeping ash on the bank of a river.

'Kyoto?' he asked.

'Kyoto,' Nobuo said. 'This, the river Takano.' He leaned
forward. 'Mr O'Brien said, Nijō Castle?'

Ross nodded. 'Nijō Castle – he said everyone knows it.'

Over a bridge, past a park where roofs peeped through trees
like graceful bells, Kyoto was more graceful than Tokyo, more
serene. Ross saw Nobuo look at his watch and sensed the
tension in him.

'Are you expecting trouble, Inspector?' he asked quietly.

'Maybe trouble,' Nobuo nodded.

'From Chiyaha?'

'Yes, from Chiyaha,' Nobuo said. 'Always trouble from Chiyaha.'

'You sound as if you know him well,' Ross said.

Nobuo smiled thinly. 'I know him.'

'What sort of a man is he?' Ross asked.

Reaching inside his jacket for a wallet, Nobuo took out a photograph.

'Like this.'

Ross saw two standard shots, face and profile of a man wearing glasses. The mouth was large and prominent and in the picture of the full face, the gaze into the photographers lens combined arrogance with cold indifference. Ross looked at Nobuo: the cop's eyes had become hard. Who was it who had said that you always carry with you the picture of your enemy?

'He looks a mean piece of work,' Ross said, handing the picture back. 'Do you think he knows where Mama Yayoi is?'

'Maybe . . .' Nobuo said. 'Maybe also . . . Kasumi-rengō.'

Ross frowned.

'That's the name you asked me about back in the hospital in Sapporo. Kasumi. You asked me, did Yukiko know a Kasumi. Who is he?'

'Kazuhiro Kasumi. Oyabun of Kasumi-rengō. Like Chiyaha, Kasumi is yakuza.'

'How is he involved?'

'We find Kasumi's kobun in Ishikari burned house. I do not know why he was there.'

Ross remembered the door. The two kobun in black. The lamp as he crashed it at the first of them, flaming the man back and out through the window, starting the fire that had . . .

'You must have found two men,' he said. 'Two yakuza.'

'Two?'

'Two,' Ross said, holding up two fingers. 'Two yakuza attacked me. One I knocked through the window, the other could never have made it out of that fire, he was unconscious.'

'We find, one,' Nobuo said, holding up his finger. 'Half outside house . . . dead.'

'That was the one that went through the window,' Ross nodded. He waited, looking at Nobuo's open face. Then he turned right around in his seat.

'How many bodies did you find, Inspector?'

'Three bodies.'

Ross shook his head like a horse ridding itself of flies. 'Two dead kobun, Ko-san and Yukiko,' he said. 'That makes four, Inspector.'

253

Nobuo frowned and said, 'Two kobun,' as the car turned left into a crowded street. 'Nijō,' he pointed.

Tour buses were parked on the right-hand side, nose to tail, and as one of them drew out, Ross had a glimpse of the stone wall around Nijō Castle.

'Kerry O'Brien said to meet him at the castle gate,' Ross said and Nobuo repeated it to the driver.

The further down the road, the thicker the crowd, a mixture of Japanese and Western tourists, getting into or out of buses, or forming lines, or taking photographs. A loudspeaker blared. Hawkers were out with trays of souvenirs swinging from their necks; there were uniformed parking attendants, arms flapping, then the gate of the castle came into view, an arched pediment towering over the street. As they pulled in a cop tried to wave them on, but then he saw Nobuo's shield and saluted. Ross got out and strained to see over the milling heads.

'Everything OK?'

Kerry O'Brien, smiling, emerged from between buses, his dark suit correctly buttoned. His face dropped.

'Hey, what have you been doing to yourself?"

Ross shook the outstretched hand.

'It's a long story. This is Inspector Nobuo from Tokyo – Inspector, Kerry O'Brien, Commercial Attaché, US Embassy, Tokyo.'

'Hajimemashite,' Kerry bowed.

'Hajimemashite.'

'Where's Miss Okuma?' Kerry asked.

Ross shook his head.

'Yukiko . . . she's dead,' he said quietly.

'Jesus, Ross, I'm sorry,' Kerry said. 'What happened?'

Traffic was backed up behind them and now buses were beginning to hoot.

'I'll have to tell you later,' Ross said.

'OK – it's Shoren-in Temple, right?' Kerry said and put a hand of comfort on Ross's arm. 'You sure you still want to do this deposition?'

Ross nodded.

Kerry looked at Nobuo. 'Has he got a big operation in place?'

'You'd better ask him.'

Kerry exchanged words with Inspector Nobuo.

'He's not anticipating trouble,' Kerry nodded. 'That's good. Look, Ross, you and I need to go right away to the consulate and meet the guy who's going to swear up this thing, OK? It's Sunday – he's come in specially.'

A bus blared, trying to find a way through. Ross looked at Nobuo, then back at Kerry.

Kerry said: 'And your Mr Babbage has come up with a few things that you and I should discuss – about the bid for Oxx.'

'The bid for Oxx?'

Kerry nodded and looked at Nobuo as if it were better that the cop didn't know.

'OK,' said Ross cautiously. 'Inspector Nobuo, I'm going with Kerry here. To the US consulate. Can you bring Mama Yayoi there before you leave for Tokyo?'

More horns sounded and the traffic cop began to walk back across.

'Mr Magee,' Nobuo said. ' I try.'

Kerry O'Brien made to lead the way back across the street, but Ross stood where he was.

'Inspector, I want to thank you,' he said. 'You're a friend.'

'My pleasure,' Nobuo bowed, then he put out his hand and Ross shook it.

The horn of the bus echoed from the Nijō gates. They crossed over, Ross behind Kerry, and walked downtown by the castle walls.

'He's been one hell of a help to you by the look of things,' said Kerry dryly. 'This is bad, bad news you just gave me.'

'I should have taken your advice,' Ross said. 'I should have put Yukiko and myself on a plane and gone home.'

'What happened?' Kerry asked.

'We got attacked by yakuza,' Ross said as they turned right.

'In Hokkaido?'

Ross looked curiously at him.

'Yes, in Hokkaido.'

'And?'

'There was a fire,' Ross said. 'Nobuo thinks the yakuza were Kasumi-rengō.'

'Kasumi,' said Kerry tightly as they came to a car.

A Japanese driver jumped off the bonnet where he had been sitting and opened the back door. Ross sat in and Kerry walked around the other side. Ross's head buzzed in a way he could not account for.

'Kerry,' he asked as they pulled away, 'how did you know we were in Hokkaido?'

Kerry O'Brien turned in the seat. His face had the bitterness that Ross had last seen in Tokyo, except now it seemed far uglier. And he had a gun.

'Relax,' he said, 'just relax.'

'Jesus Christ,' Ross hissed.

'Don't try anything,' Kerry said. 'I don't want to mess up this car – it's not mine.'

'Whose is it?' Ross cried. 'Rokuo Chiyaha's?'

'Shut up,' Kerry said gently but the barrel of the snub-nose quivered.

Ross's ears were screaming but all the little questions he should have asked were now answered.

'Of course the inquiries on Sun Valley were slowed down in Tokyo!' he exclaimed. 'Of course all the Eiichi Eda queries came back whiter than white!'

'When I put you on a plane two weeks ago, I was doing you a favour,' Kerry said. 'I tried to tell you then the magnitude of these people's power. A week ago I did my level best one more time to get you to turn around. You're dumb, Ross.'

'Mr Gotō of the Noble Metal Society!' cried Ross and shook his head in disgust. 'I was right all along, wasn't I? That was him that day in Kobe. You know I don't speak Japanese – it could have been anyone on the phone.'

'You know how long I've been over here, learning to live with these people, surviving in this jungle?' Kerry asked. 'It's a system of give and take. Who cares what happens to Oxx or to a bunch of niggers someplace? Who cares?'

'Jesus . . .' gasped Ross as he remembered what he had told O'Brien in Tokyo. 'Because of you, they killed Tommy Klein. You told them he was going to testify against Eda!'

There was a glimpse of a narrow river.

'I've just delivered Mama Yayoi on a plate to Chiyaha, haven't I?' Ross said in disbelief. 'He's probably in Shoren-in Temple at this moment. How much is Chiyaha paying you, Kerry? What's your price?'

256

Kerry's eyes seemed to soften for a short moment.

'You'd never understand,' he said quietly.

'You're crazy if you think you can make me disappear and get away with it,' Ross said. 'An inspector from the Tokyo crime squad has just heard you say that you're taking me to the US consulate.'

'You're a pain in the ass, Ross,' Kerry said wearily. 'So is Nobuo. He's not even meant to be here, he's acting against orders. But when he gets to Shoren-in Temple he's going to realize – like you – that people's patience runs out in the end.'

They were halted at lights on a busy avenue. A hundred yards away Ross saw the outline of a fairground wheel silhouetted against the sky. A blood mist swam up in his eyes. As they drew away, the car tilted him towards centre and he led with his bandaged arm, driving for the gun. O'Brien fired. Ross felt his arm buck but he kept going until he found O'Brien's throat.

'*You bastard!*' he shouted.

'Uuuuuh!'

O'Brien tried to throw him back. Ross's bandaged arm jammed the gun so that it pointed up between them. He head-butted O'Brien frantically and tried to fumble the door-catch open. The car swerved as the driver also with a gun, tried to train it on him. O'Brien fired again and the shot went straight into the roof. The door swung open.

Ross took the fall on his shoulder. Rolling over and over he was aware only of screeching wheels and car horns. He put his good arm beneath him and stood; cars zipped past a foot away. Then he saw O'Brien, fifteen yards out; and the car, two wheels bounced up on the far kerb, the driver climbing out, buttoning his coat; and, from nowhere, two other men in dark glasses, weaving through the traffic. He ran straight across the wide street, leaving scraping metal and tinkling glass behind him. Panting, he came to steps and took them in two strides. There was a barrier in his path. A little man came out of an office and made negative signs. Ross looked back and saw O'Brien and the three men in a bunch, closing.

'Police!' Ross cried to the ticket man. 'Call the police!'

The man pointed to the barrier but Ross leapt it and ran over a gravelled area towards shuttered stalls, past uniformed broom handlers, paused in their work. He was under the fairground wheel which he had seen from the car. There were further steps and he took them, pausing at the top, head reeling.

'*Magee! You're crazy!*'

O'Brien's voice echoed in quadraphonic around the enclosure. A foot from Ross the rail sang sharply and he saw a kobun, levelling at him again, two handed. He took the steps at the other side in twos. Hitting the ground – soft, multi-coloured, rubber granules – he ran blindly, down a corridor of identical wooden panels, open to the sky. At a T-junction with two identical options, left and right, he chose left, then right and straight on and left again and thought in panic he had arrived back to his original position when he realized he was in a maze.

The wooden walls were eight feet high. The underfoot surface made for complete silence: only the Kyoto traffic was audible in the middle distance.

Ross tried to guess the extent of the maze, jinking along, into and out of dead-ends. The sameness of each passageway was dizzying. He stopped and leaned, hands on knees, panting, blood thumping so loud he could no longer hear the traffic. He looked up to find the sun. His chest burned: he looked down and saw a red, ten inch weal that O'Brien's second shot in the car had caused but that Ross had not felt until now. There was a cooing sound somewhere to his left, a bird sound, a wood pigeon. It was answered ten yards away. Ross ran again. The coos followed, nearer to each other.

'Ross!'

O'Brien's sudden voice was twenty yards off. Ross stopped before a corner, then sprang around it to be greeted by an empty path indistinguishable from the one he had left. He ran, sun on his shoulder.

'Ross, I want to talk.'

The voice was much nearer as if both of them had been tacking together.

'Look this thing is bigger than either of us OK? We can talk it out. You want to deal? OK, we'll deal. You have my word.'

Ross wiped sweat from his eyes. Another corner. Was the traffic noise louder?

'Ross, you're there, aren't you? I know you're there.'

O'Brien behind him; ahead, wood pigeons.

'Ross?'

Ross rounded the corner and froze. Five yards away, walking noiselessly backwards towards him, a broad shouldered kobun held an automatic weapon waist high.

'Right here, Kerry!'

Ross dived. As he rolled, gunfire raked the junction and opened a jagged, twenty foot crescent high in the panelling where he had been standing.

Ross leaped up and sprinted. He didn't bother with the corner, just went through it, head first, hit a steep grass bank painfully and rolled down. A flower bed, the smell of cut grass, the smell of high-octane gasoline.

He picked himself up. Another broad street. Streaming cars. Looking back he saw kobun leap through the splintered maze wall and slide down the grass after him. Three men but not O'Brien. Ross had a thirty-yard lead. A cab pulled in ahead, it's back door swinging open. Ross sprinted but another man was stepping from the kerb. Ross could hear the leather soles of the kobun on the road behind him. Would they risk shooting out here? He tried to weave as he ran. The other customer for the cab was a large man with bushy, black side whiskers and a topknot. Ross skidded up.

'I'm very sorry,' he panted and ducked for the back seat. An arm blocked him. 'Come on!' Ross cried.

The kobun were closing, forming a confident line. The man stamped his foot, then flattened Ross against the car's door. Ross tried to push him away, but the man was solid as a barge. The cab driver was shouting. Ross's opponent lifted him bodily and tried to swing him outwards.

'I'm sorry about this,' Ross said and closed his teeth on an ear.

With a shriek he was dropped into the back seat, just at the moment that the driver hit the pedal. As the cab screamed away, Ross rolled to the floor and watched the back window implode to the chatter of gunfire. He clawed up with his hand and saw the driver's terrified eyes in the rear view mirror.

'Go to Shoren-in temple,' Ross cried. 'And go fast.'

*   *   *

Freeman Oxx eased himself from bed to wheelchair, waited a moment to get his breath, then rolled himself to the larger of two desks by the window. He checked his watch. Not yet six p.m. The Oxx jet had touched down in San José International thirty minutes before: they should soon be here.

The activity that had taken place since very early morning – since two hours after Ross's call – had more in common with a busy trading floor than a hospital. CPA's from a firm in Los Angeles had arrived at nine with desktop computers and set up in a room down the corridor. Orem Williams manned two phones and a fax; he stacked the calls and Freeman took them. The numbers men were in and out like waiters from a kitchen as each fresh set of projections was presented to Freeman. He felt his old juices flow. He could still spot the aberration in a cash flow in one fifth the time of the younger men; they scurried back to re-work the figures as a batch of lawyers in weekend clothes arrived hastily from San Francisco.

On the phone, a New York banker, dragged from his barbecue said, 'It's too late, Freeman.'

'It's never too late, dammit!' Freeman cried and a nurse had come in clucking and fussing and shaking her head.

Ross had called to say that the chances of getting Mama Yayoi to testify were getting slimmer by the hour; then he had given Freeman a wild, crazy idea which, if everything else failed, might just – just, dammit! – succeed.

Freeman smiled grimly. No matter what happened now, it was no longer the end of a line, they could bury him and he would go down happy that the person he had tried to love for all those years would carry on. Whether at the helm of Oxx or not, it didn't matter now. What mattered was that the spirit was passed on and would continue down the generations. The Masisi again? Spirits flying hand in hand across the great plain? Yes, dammit! Yes!

He heard voices. The door opened and the towering figure of Chief Tshubisi came through, followed by a haggard Orem Williams and a doctor in a white coat.

260

'Mr Oxx,' said Chief Tshubisi deeply, 'truly never have I met a warrior such as you.'

*   *   *

Wide stone steps cut straight up into the mountain from the street. It was impossible to see up more than halfway due to tourist numbers and at street level there was the usual jam of buses and hawkers and sidewalk photographers. Twenty yards back from the base of the steps and to one side, Inspector Nobuo saw the black, windowless van and the patrol cars, as an inspector from Kyoto CIB in helmet and flak jacket came forward to meet him.

'Inspector-san,' the Kyoto man bowed.

Nobuo bowed quickly, then looked around him.

'What information have you been able to get?' he asked.

'We have spoken to a contact within the temple,' the local inspector said quietly. 'Although no name was mentioned, we believe that an important woman guest arrived early yesterday evening – and is still here.'

'Yoi desu-ne,' said Nobuo, 'good.'

'As you requested, no one has gone up, not even my men here have been given details,' the inspector said. 'However, the superintendent-san is keen that formal authorization from Tokyo be established before . . .'

'This is an emergency at the highest level!' Nobuo cried. 'Is that authority enough? Now, how many men do you have here?'

'Twelve, all armed, awaiting your instructions, Inspector-san!' the inspector said and stood to attention.

'Thank you,' Nobuo said. 'We can't risk frightening her at this stage.' He looked to the tourists streaming up and down the steps. 'There are too many civilians here,' he said to Sergeant Bando.

'It's a problem,' the Kyoto inspector responded. 'We estimate no fewer than two hundred up in the main courtyard. Do you think, with respect, that we should consider clearing the area first?'

'We can stop people going up, but there's not time to clear the temple itself,' Nobuo said tightly. 'Besides, from what you told me on the radio, there's a problem sealing the grounds.'

261

The Kyoto inspector nodded and produced a large-scale plan which he spread on the bonnet of the car.

'Hai. Here are the steps leading up to the quadrangle,' he said, pointing. 'Here is the prayer house.' A large, shaded square stood to the left of the open space. 'The public area is bounded by the prayer house and cloister on one side and the garden wall on the other.' He pointed to a square inside the garden wall, near a small lake. 'Our information is that the important woman guest may be installed in this house beside the lake.'

Nobuo's face furrowed as he looked to the immense area north and west of the garden.

'This is all mountain and wood?'

'The mountains of Sakyo-Ku,' the local inspector affirmed. 'They run right into the gardens. It's why any exercise to completely seal Shoren-in would require at least a hundred men, but at such short notice . . .'

'Have you had any evidence of yakuza in the area this morning?' Nobuo asked.

'None,' the inspector replied, 'but yakuza might have entered in the crowd, I cannot say absolutely . . .'

The distinct whine of a helicopter could suddenly be heard, somewhere above them, in the mountains of Sakyo-Ku.

'We'll have to take the garden as best we can!' Nobuo cried. He took a .38 Magnum from inside his coat, broke it open and scanned the chambers, then returned it to its place.

The Kyoto inspector barked an order. The van door opened and armed men in flak jackets and blue helmets began to jump out.

'Don't shoot if there's any danger to the woman!' Nobuo called, running to the base of the steps.

The sign said Yoshi-Ima. The streets were so narrow that the inhabitants of the wooden houses on one side could lean across and almost touch those of their neighbours on the other. Ross crouched between the two front seats as the cab nosed out into busy traffic. He didn't want to think of what had happened. It was as if his brain was a sponge that could not soak up further horror. He could not speculate anymore, he had to deal in certainties: Yukiko and Tommy Klein were both dead, an old woman had to be found and Inspector Nobuo was a friend.

The sidewalks were crowded with Sunday afternoon strollers and hawkers blocked the roadway. The cab drew up at steps where two, blue helmeted, armed policemen were on duty. People were being allowed down but not up.

'Shoren-in,' said the cab driver, looking at his back window.

'Where?' Ross asked. 'Shoren-in – where?'

'Shoren-in!' the distracted man cried, pointing at the steps.

Ross jumped out and the cab screamed away in a tight arc, back the way they had come. Everything ached for Ross: head, arm and now the flesh on his stomach and chest from the heat trail of O'Brien's bullet. He had lost his cap and his head, shaven and plastered, drew looks from the passing tourists. On the bottom step the cops crossed the barrels of their semi-automatics as he approached.

'Tojiru!'

Ross said: 'I need to get up there! I need to see Inspector Nobuo!'

'Tojiru!' the cop repeated. 'It's closed.'

People were backing up the other side of the two policemen, tourists trying to come down. The cop on the left swept Ross to one side with his arm and opened the gap so that the downward stream could resume. Seizing his wrist, Ross pulled him sharply into the street and foot tripped him. The cop sprawled, yelling, but Ross was already five steps up with a dozen people between him and the other blue helmet.

He climbed as fast as his heaving chest and clumsy arm would allow. He could hear shouts behind. People drew back as he charged up and suddenly he was at the top step, gasping for breath, confronted by a square which was dominated by a carved, wooden building of massive proportions. A temple or shrine, familiar in miniature, at this size it was breathtaking. Swarms of people crowded it's wide steps and it's verandahs. To Ross's right a high wall incorporated wooden doors.

'Tomare! Stop!'

He could see the shine of the blue helmet. He ran for the temple with no idea of where he was going. He heard firecrackers. For a moment they brought the whole, enormous square to a standstill. Then Ross realized it was gunfire and had come from the other side of the wall.

263

'Sochi! Tomare!'

The blue-helmeted cop had reached the square. Beyond the wall, the gunfire repeated.

'Stop!'

Ross took the temple steps diagonally. The main verandah separated the steps from an inner sanctum; the smell of incense; a glimpse of shaven heads, bowing; a mantra, chanted. A red, swag rope at the end of the verandah limited public access. Ross ran the length of the façade, jumped the rope and turned left, down the north side of the building with the garden wall still to his right.

The gunfire crackled again but this time it seemed higher up the mountain. He kept running, down a covered passage, it's floor boards chirping like nightingales. Rounding a corner, he jumped down three steps. A heavy door. He tried it. Locked. He heard the nightingales chirping. He stepped to one side and as the cop came down the three steps, he kicked him up between the legs, then used the point of his knee to clip his falling chin.

Ross stood back and came to the locked door with the flat of his foot. It crashed inwards. Faces upturned from prayer: monks in a stone-flagged enclosure. Through a gate, Ross could see a garden.

'Excuse me,' he muttered.

He was in the garden's furthermost corner where hills and manicured grass met. The firing was coming from over to his right and was being returned from higher up the wooded hillside. He had entered the battle at no-man's-land. Another volley was loosed off. Ross began to scramble. Vegetation was dense: thickets of bamboo interspersed with scrub and briar. The two-way firing was regular: not far above him he heard a bullet hit a stone and wing away. Streaming sweat, sore all over, he clawed up and rocks dislodged, rolling noisily down the mountain. Sudden movement to his right. He dropped behind a tree stump. A big man with a drooping moustache came into view through the scrub, gun in hand, twenty yards away. Then two kobun, climbing behind the big man like cats. Then Rokuo Chiyaha.

The familiarity was instant. The spectacles, the prominent mouth and forward thrusting head were exactly those of

Nobuo's photograph. As Ross stared, Chiyaha paused for breath and seemed to look directly at him. Then he continued his climb.

More firing from the right was exchanged again from higher up the mountain and Ross realized that Chiyaha and his men, like him, were between the two shooting parties. The police must have been behind the shots from the right; but if so, at whom were they shooting if Chiyaha was here?

Ross resumed his upward, one-handed crawl. Flies had discovered his raw head and were feeding on it with gusto. He fell out on to a narrow path which ran right to left, dividing the mountainside. Lurching up it, feet slipping on flat stones, he heard a sudden cry. A woman's cry. He rounded a bend.

He was on a shoulder of mountain. Opposite him, across a valley, was a plateau and on it, it's blades revolving slowly, sat a shining helicopter. Half way up the side of the valley as he looked at it, an extraordinary scene was being enacted: two kobun with rifles, firing repeatedly to Ross's right, gave cover to a man at their centre, a big-chested man with heavy eyebrows and a beard. He was climbing backwards towards the chopper, firing a pistol intermittently, as either side of him, two women tried to climb towards the helicopter.

'Kasumi-san!'

The warning cry of the kobun rang out clearly and the burly Japanese ducked as a bullet winged over his head. Ross stared. Kasumi bent to the smaller of the women and tried to pull her up the faster, but gunfire caused him to crouch and shoot back. She stumbled. The other woman turned and stooped to help her. Ross's head burst.

Yukiko. He couldn't say the name. Yukiko. He stood, unprotected and water flooded his eyes and prevented him focusing. Yukiko. He couldn't speak. He was stone. He was dead. He was mad. He was crazy. Yukiko.

'Yukiko!'

He ran down in huge leaps. Kasumi began to shoot at him.

'Ross!'

He reached the bottom of the valley and began to tear upwards with his only hand. He could see her now, see her beautiful face. He clawed. Kasumi aimed down very deliberately. Ross was shouting wildly.

265

'Ross!'

Three booming shots. Kasumi sank with exaggerated slowness, first to his knees, then, as if abasing himself, bowed his head ever so slowly, then rolled, one entire revolution, head over heels, ending feet to the valley, face to the sky.

Ross turned in the direction of the shots and saw Inspector Nobuo making a zigzagging run from fifty yards. Ross could see Mama Yayoi now, her mouth working. The kobun with the rifles had broken cover and as Ross looked, one of them was cut down. Something made Ross turn. The big man with the moustache was leaping down the hill in huge bounds, gun held two-handed above his head. Ross shouted but the man ignored him. Yukiko was trying to get to cover, dragging Mama Yayoi with her. With all the time in the world the gunman stopped and put two shots into Mama Yayoi, both high. Ross saw him actually wait until she had arched up and back, hands raised to what was left of her face, before he swivelled on to Yukiko.

'Yukiko!'

Ross was scrambling like a crazy man, but the yards between them were as miles. He picked up a rock the size of a melon and launched it. Yukiko was screaming. The rock hit the gunman's shoulder as he pulled the trigger and caused him to stagger, losing the shot harmlessly into the air. Ross leaped the last yards, bowling Yukiko to the ground, then rolled them both, over and over, downwards. A boulder twenty yards down stopped them, kicking the air from his body. Looking up he could see the gunman, silhouetted by the sun, readying. Yukiko never stopped screaming.

'No! No!'

Ross's only instinct was to survive. Where was Chiyaha? He saw the big gunman uphill of them. Three thumping reports echoed one after another and the man's pistol flew straight up as he twitched once and fell.

Ross suddenly saw Chiyaha, diagonally across the mountain, so near that Ross could see the colour of his eyes.

'No, no! Not you too, Mama! No, no!'

Nobuo was fumbling to reload, calling something out. Very deliberately Chiyaha shot him. The bullets hit the policeman in

266

mid chest and puffed his cheeks out like miniature balloons. Ross caught Yukiko tight to him and flung them rolling further down the valley.

There was noise and shouting and the clatter of blades, and if the last minute of their lives was to be this one, then it would be well spent if they could just be left like this, together, clinging to each other, screaming and weeping. Ross heard the helicopter lift into the air. He heard sudden birdsong. Yukiko was scraping frantically at handfuls of earth and her hands had begun to bleed.

Ross came slowly to his knees. Fifty yards up the slope he saw the flies of Sakyo-Ku, already swarming on the dead face of Inspector Nobuo.

Book Five

TENNŌ

Sixteen

New York slept. There were parts of Manhattan where life only began at midnight, but up here in the east eighties where the Metropolitan Museum of Art shouldered its way off Fifth Avenue to sit hulking, half in, half out of Central Park, sleep was the order.

The routine of the Security Ten guard inside the Great Japan Exhibition was the same each night: he came on at ten, relieving the man who had been there for eight hours; he stayed eight hours and at six in the morning he was replaced. The night man sat at a desk equipped with a light and a telephone, reading. Putting down the book he stretched, yawned, then got to his feet and began a stroll around the pavilion, more to exercise his legs than part of any security routine.

For over a week he had been looking at panels and silks and screens with pictures of swans and women with long necks and curling hands. They did nothing for him. He halted at a silk screen where a kimono-clad man and woman were ambiguously intertwined. He wouldn't come in here and look at this stuff for five minutes if he had the choice.

He walked into the inner reception area that had been incorporated specially into the pavilion for the Imperial opening. The rest room doubled as a kitchen for the guard during his night-long stint. It had walls done in thick, button-down velvet, and the chandelier hanging from it's temporary ceiling matched

271

the chandelier in the reception area. The guard plugged the kettle, made himself coffee and strolled back out. At one end of the exhibition area was a stage and podium where he could see the lip of the bomb-drop, but only because he knew it was there. Like the transparent, bullet-proof screens around the lectern. They'd even replaced the windows. He shook his head. You had to see it to believe it. At the end of the central aisle he stopped at the buddha.

'How you doin' tonight, my friend?'

The buddha he could relate to. Three-dimensional. The face and prayerful attitude of a lonely person, condemned to sit forever in stone. He rubbed the stone nose affectionately as the telephone rang.

'Security Ten, logging in,' said a girl's voice when he picked it up.

'All OK here at the Metropolitan,' the guard replied.

*　　*　　*

Deputy Chief of Police Amemiya was in full uniform. He got to his feet, flanked by the Tokyo Police Superintendent Supervisor and by Keishicho's Chief Police Superintendent, and bowed stiffly as CIB chief Junpei Iseki came into the room.

'I must state, Iseki-san,' Amemiya opened, 'that this meeting is being recorded.'

As they sat down, Amemiya nodded to the Superintendent Supervisor who depressed the record button on a tape recorder.

Amemiya cleared his throat and recited the place, the time, the date, and the names of those present.

'I have received a preliminary report from the Chief of Police, Kyoto prefecture,' he said tonelessly, 'about events in that city, Sunday, May 23rd. Ten people died in two gun battles, one at a fairground in the city, the other in the grounds of the temple of Shoren-in. The dead include two members of the Kyoto Crime Bureau, Inspector Nobuo Imai from Keishicho CIB, the Commercial Attaché at the US Embassy in Tokyo and six others, yakuza. Although Kyoto CIB state that Inspector Nobuo assured them he was acting with the full authority of Keishicho, it appears that Inspector Nobuo was in fact acting in direct contravention of specific orders.'

272

Amemiya put down the report and looked ominously at Superintendent Iseki.

Iseki looked at his notes and spoke: 'On Saturday, May 22nd, at four p.m., I spoke with Inspector Nobuo Imai by audio-visual conference link to Police Central, Sapporo. I instructed him that the case involving Mama Yayoi Okuma was closed. Despite his considerable protests in the matter, I ordered him back to Tokyo. I never spoke to him again.'

'Were your orders to Inspector Nobuo ... clear, Super-intendent-san?' asked the Chief Police Superintendent.

'Completely,' replied Junpei Iseki.

'Inspector Nobuo had something of a fixation about the yakuza, Rokuo Chiyaha, had he not?' Amemiya prompted.

'Yes, so it would seem,' replied Iseki. 'It dated from Inspector Nobuo's previous posting in Kobe when he unsuccessfully brought charges against Chiyaha.'

'Would you say that Nobuo was obsessed with Chiyaha?' asked the Superintendent Supervisor.

'Inspector Nobuo was an excellent policeman,' Superintendent Iseki answered, 'but events in the last two days have shaken my confidence in his impartiality.'

'What is the present status in the search for Chiyaha?' Amem-iya asked.

'It will be most surprising if he is not captured in the next three or four days, Amemiya-san,' Iseki answered. 'There are six hundred officers throughout Japan directly assigned to his arrest.'

Amemiya looked at the tape recorder.

'There has been widespread yakuza activity throughout Japan in the last forty-eight hours,' he said.

Junpei Iseki nodded.

'The oyabun, Ichirō Abe was shot dead yesterday evening as he left a restaurant in Sendai,' he said. 'The sarakin, Kanji Egusa, has disappeared, and the word from yakuza circles is that he will not be found. In both cases, Chiyaha-gumi is suspected.'

Amemiya sighed: 'We understand the presence of the American, O'Brien, is being investigated by the US Embassy.'

'O'Brien was in debt to yakuza and not a CIA agent as we

273

first thought,' Iseki said. 'In the last few hours we have received reports of a relationship between him and a high class prostitute of Ichirō Abe's – a girl of no more than sixteen.'

The Deputy Chief looked down at his file.

'The events in Ishikari, Hokkaido, that preceded events in Kyoto, are now more clear,' he suggested.

'Three dead,' Iseki confirmed, 'two kobun and a female burakumin known as Ko. She was previously thought to be Yukiko Okuma due to the presence of sunglasses frames near the body. The mistake was understandable. The woman's body and one other were so badly burned that recognition was nearly impossible.'

Amemiya looked around his men grimly.

'I have asked the Chief Police Superintendent to take statements in Hokkaido, in Niigata and here in Tokyo. His work will take at least five days. We will meet then again to assess the outcome.'

The Superintendent Supervisor switched off the tape recorder, then getting to their feet, he and the Chief Police Superintendent bowed to the Deputy Chief and to Iseki and left the room. Amemiya sat back and exercised his neck inside the gleaming collar of his white shirt.

'Nobuo had lost his grip,' he said quietly.

'Perhaps,' Iseki responded, then shook his head. 'I find it hard to believe. He was the best cop I ever came across – a future head of Bureau, without a doubt.'

The Deputy Chief coughed.

'Word is coming through of nervousness in the financial sector,' he said quietly. 'Hard to pin down, political uncertainty, that sort of thing.'

Junpei Iseki said: 'Could it all be related? The Okuma girl is bringing up this whole Tennō business again. She says Nobuo spoke to Magee-san about it . . .'

Amemiya looked balefully at the CIB superintendent.

'Please, Iseki-san . . .'

'What am I to do with her?' Iseki pressed. 'There are no charges to be brought. She's demanding continually to see the gaijin, Magee.'

274

'I take it you have made the necessary arrangements for the gaijin, Iseki-san?' said Amemiya thoughtfully.

'Hai, Amemiya-san. Tomorrow morning. Everything is arranged between us and the Embassy,' Iseki said.

'Then, does that not provide an opportunity to solve two problems in one?' asked Chief Amemiya.

*   *   *

Kyle Spicer waited as the Under Secretary for Domestic Finance re-read the one page summary. Kyle's immediate boss was a small, natty man, a Wall Street banker by training with a reputation as a conservative. It was 10.00 a.m. and Washington was already enjoying a sunny start to the week.

'So,' the Under Secretary said with deliberation, 'the Japanese participation in the last T-Bill auction is confirmed as down by a factor of twenty-five per cent, isn't that the bottom line?'

Kyle nodded.

'Down four billion, sir,' he replied. 'Some of their banks and institutions seem unaffected, but others either just did nominal business or stayed out completely. It's as if Tokyo is expecting something.'

'And the dollar's gone south,' the Under Secretary mused, 'and interest rates went up a full half point this morning.'

'The market said the yield had to rise,' Kyle shrugged. 'So did the Fed. Bonds will follow the dollar.'

The Under Secretary looked down Pennsylvania Avenue.

'It's political,' he said, 'it's got to be. But where's the Jap money gone, that's what I'd like to know? Dammit, they have to do something with it.'

'Transferred into precious metals, perhaps,' said Kyle quietly. 'Gold, silver, platinum, they're all up.'

The Under Secretary looked at him speculatively.

'Kyle, you got an egg you want to lay?' he asked.

Kyle spoke for fifteen minutes. When he was finished, the Under Secretary picked up a telephone.

'I need to see the Secretary – this morning,' he spoke.

*   *   *

The wooded hillsides encroached further with each passing second. Ross could see floating lilies, heavy with buds, breaking the landscape of water where sedge-fly fed and the questing mouths of carp showed. Evening song and the drone of insects were the only sounds: even the city traffic was blanketed out by the all-pervading peace.

Ross turned from the window. The room was square, built in cement block and whitewashed. There was a grey carpet, an iron bed, floor-bolted, a table and chair similarly secured, and in one corner, screened by a five-foot wall, a toilet and wash basin, both cast iron, both cemented in place. He went to the part of the wall where the flush door was and pounded it.

'I want a lawyer!' he shouted. 'I'm an American citizen! I demand to speak to someone!'

He beat the door for three minutes – as he had done every half hour since early morning – and when there was no response, returned and lay on the bed. He had let them dress his arm and head, but had refused either shots or capsules. The pain was more bearable than the thought of awaking some place, not knowing where. He knew he was still in Kyoto, brought handcuffed and wedged on the back floor of a patrol car by two cops who had been in no mood for discussion. Yukiko was dragged away from Mama Yayoi's body; Ross saw her manhandled into the back of a black van at the base of the temple steps. He tried to call out to her, but he had been doubled by the cop and folded out of view.

That was over twenty-four hours ago. But she was alive, that was all that was important because it meant that no prison was strong enough to keep them apart. Somewhere on earth there was a place they could meet and when they did it would be for all time. He wanted to be near her in her grief. He worried what might happen to her, now that Nobuo was dead. Would there be a cover-up? Would she be swept beneath a mat because she now represented an inconvenience?

Ross got up, walked to the window, then to the door. He had to contact Freeman as well. Somehow there was a link between everything – between Nobuo's obsession with Chiyaha, the Emperor and the Sun Valley bid for Oxx. Somehow, Freeman had just to hold out.

276

He was about to bang the door again when it opened. Two cautious policemen stood there, a third brought in a tray of food and placed it on the table.

'Just a second,' said Ross amiably. 'Just hold it for a moment, OK?' He beckoned to the two men at the door. 'I just want you to listen – listen, OK?' The tray bearer straightened warily. 'Forget about me,' Ross said, 'I'm crazy, but Inspector Nobuo – Nobuo, Tokyo, yes? – he's dead. He died because there's a ninja – yes, a ninja – in New York. The ninja works for Chiyaha. He's going to kill your Tennō in New York.' He slit a finger over his throat. 'Tennō – New York – dead.'

The policemen backed away.

'I need to talk to someone who understands English!' Ross cried. 'Why am I being held here? Where is Yukiko Okuma?'

The door began to close.

'Godammit, I'm trying to help you people!' he shouted, picking up the tray in his only hand and flinging it against the closing door.

The marriage between hillside and lake was almost consummated. The song of birds was replaced by the whir of cicadas. Peace reigned over Kyoto.

*   *   *

A voice again. So near he fancied he could feel the breath on his face. What would it be like to feel again? To see? To move . . . How he could move! He was like the wind, something that was there but that you could not see. He happened! A painting could never capture the freedom he felt when he moved in attack. He could fly. He could leave the branch of a tree and fly weightless like a bird to his target. He had killed many men whose eyes were still looking for the source of the wind sound, even as they died.

For the first time ever, he had felt fear. The man with the young man's voice had stood a foot from him and there had been direct contact between them, an electric circuit as strong as if they had touched each other's flesh. Then it was that Rex had emptied himself of all feeling and ceased to breathe. For eight minutes. When at last he had heard the man with the young man's voice leave the pavilion and he had sucked in his first gulp of new air, he had shook with fear at what nearly had come about. Of failure. He had almost never failed.

Nearly over now. Not just a long, dark week of waiting, but a lifetime. He still lived in that earlier time: in the fertile plains around the River La-nga, working in hot fields, his mother wore a white maku . . .

*   *   *

Tyler Wrixon looked up in surprise as the door of his office swung open and Timothy Manners appeared, unannounced. Wrixon's secretary stood in the doorway, flapping her hands.

'It's all right,' said Wrixon and smiled his best as the door was closed. 'You want to see me, Tim?'

'Have you seen platinum?' asked Manners.

Out of breath and chalk white, he looks like an albino rat, thought Wrixon.

'I don't follow metals, Tim . . .'

'It's four hundred and thirteen dollars an ounce bid,' Manners said, breathing hard. 'Four hundred and thirteen dollars and I can't even get you to take my calls, you shit.'

'Hold it right there!' Wrixon said and inched his hand towards the phone to call house security.

'Hold it my bollocks!' Manners cried and slapped Wrixon's hand away. 'Now you listen to me, Tyler, my old chum. I've made a bloody fool of myself over you. I've a fifty thousand ounce short platinum position, or my firm has, that's losing over half a million, waiting for your nasty little friends to tell the world about their new platinum mine in Bamolisi.'

All Wrixon wanted to do was to get out of the office.

'Tim,' he pleaded, 'what's the problem? The deal goes through in two days, Wednesday. Platinum will fall. There's no problem. Relax.'

'There's never a problem with you, is there?' Manners hissed. 'You see, Tyler, there are people in London who won't like it one bit when this loss gets reported. But it won't, will it, because the real owner of the position is a nominee account somewhere, anywhere you like – does Toronto suit? – and the entry in Cresswels name was a book error all along, wasn't it?'

Wrixon reckoned he knew a screwball when he saw one.

'Sure,' he said, 'sure, Tim.'

'The only trouble is,' Manners snapped, 'the chap in Toronto can't pay his deposits. He needs a loan of half a million, and he needs it right now, Tyler – from your pissing bank.'

'You're out of your mind,' Wrixon said.

It was Manners's turn to grab for the phone. Very carefully he pressed out seven digits.

'SEC? Your fraud investigation section, please,' he spoke calmly.

Wrixon leaped to his feet and disconnected the call.

'What the hell are you doing?' he snarled and suddenly he was as pale as the little Englishman.

'I'm going to sing like Pavarotti,' Manners spat, shaking. 'I'm going to tell them everything I know about Oxx, about you, about me, about Magee. And when that's all over, I'm going to get an obnoxious shit I know in Miami to come up here and cut your balls off.'

'Sit down,' swallowed Wrixon.

A sudden squall in the sky outside advanced the evening by thirty minutes.

*   *   *

The first hint of daylight came when they opened the transport's rear doors and led Ross out, handcuffed to a cop, through a side door and down an empty passage. The journey had taken six hours, beginning when Kyoto slept and ending here with the whine of jet engines. They came to a door and the cop led Ross in. There was a man in a suit behind a desk and two military police in uniform. No windows. The suited type stood and read staccato-like from a document. Concluding, he bowed in Ross's direction, signed the document and handed it to the cop.

'Do you speak English?' Ross asked, but he was being led on again, through a door to the front of the office, into another room. Here were windows: they looked straight out on the

279

apron of Narita Airport where a Pan Am 747 was parked diagonally, fifty yards away.

'I want someone who speaks English!'

'I can probably do that.' A man in his thirties was standing to the back of the office. 'Tony Waddel, US Embassy, Immigration.' He came forward. 'We don't have much time.'

'Time?' Ross said. 'Time for what? Do you know what's been going on here? Do you know that Kerry O'Brien, your Commercial Attaché, tried to kill me two days ago in Kyoto?'

The cop opened the handcuff on his wrist and transferred it fluently to that of Waddel.

'I'm sorry about this,' Waddel said, as the door was opened and they walked straight out, 'but handsome is as handsome does.'

'Hey, what's your name? Tony? Waddel? Wait!' Ross strained the American to a halt, then saw the four cops behind him. 'What the fuck is going on?' He could see faces at the portholes of the jumbo, two male attendants at the top of the steps and half a dozen soldiers in combat gear dotted around the plane, pointing semi-automatics.

'They've taken you pretty seriously, as you can see, Ross,' said Waddel affably. 'Now are we going to do this thing with dignity?'

'What's happened to Yukiko Okuma?' Ross cried.

'Please,' Waddel said and they resumed for the steps.

The cops stayed on the ground as Waddel led the way upwards.

'A word of advice,' he said, pausing halfway. 'Any trouble and they'll sedate you, OK?' He smiled. 'But why cause trouble? Enjoy the flight – you're travelling front cabin.'

At the top step Ross looked down and saw a semi-circle of cops and soldiers looking up at him. An attendant stepped forward.

'Good morning, gentlemen.'

He led the way in and to the left. Waddel guided Ross to the very front window seat of the empty first class cabin, unlocked the cuff and clipped it to the armrest.

'Sorry, but the Japanese authorities insist on this until you're out of their airspace,' he smiled. 'Enjoy your flight.'

'Waddel . . .'

280

Ross looked around but the Immigration official had disappeared through the door, the door was swung closed and spun locked, outside the steps had already been rolled away, Waddel on them, and the jet's engines rose in pitch as she nosed out for take off.

'Would you care for a cocktail when we're airborne, sir?'

'Go to hell,' Ross growled.

They went straight out, by-passing half a dozen other planes waiting in line.

'Thirty seconds,' said a voice on the intercom.

The engines screamed. The plane hurtled forward and Ross thought of how much he had wanted to be with her for her grief. He could have helped her over it, used his love to help her as she had helped him. Other people too were grieving: the Nobuo family, the wife and the two little boys who played football with their father in a park somewhere in Tokyo, and learned kendō from him, the way of the sword. Not anymore. Was there an end to grief? Was there more to come, the grief of a whole nation perhaps, if Nobuo was right? Did it matter? Ross closed his eyes as the plane took to the air. He felt it climb and wanted to open his eyes and have a last look out at the country that he would never see again, but a massive weariness had taken him over and he craved an oasis of normality where he could start to think sanely again.

They climbed for fifteen minutes and he wandered along the borderline of sleep. Then he smelled something indescribably sweet and felt his lips touched by angels. He turned and opened his eyes.

'They would not let me in here until now,' whispered Yukiko.

*   *   *

At 5.45 a.m. the relief guard with the tinted glasses came up into the morning out of the subway on Lexington and Seventy-seventh and walked three blocks west before turning uptown along Fifth. Traffic was sporadic as he crossed to the north side of East Seventy-ninth Street. He could smell summer in Central Park. He envied people with outdoor jobs on days like this.

Passing the empty cycle rack, he entered the museum by a

door marked 'Uris Center'. A cloakroom area was manned by two regular Metropolitan attendants in air force-blue.

'Good morning,' the guard said, showing his pass.

'Hi,' said one of the men and nodded him through.

Taking off a nylon jacket, pinning his ID to his uniform lapel, the guard put on his cap and made his way left, out and up two flights of narrow marble stairs to the first floor. When would the Bomb Squad arrive? The whole building would be swept yet again, every square inch sniffed by dogs that could smell an explosive device at twenty yards, although no one could have smuggled a box of matches in here for over a week.

He walked down a corridor of sculptured busts. Torsos lacking limbs, heads lacking eyes. He passed the shuttered gift shop, entered the Great Hall and paused; few people saw it like this: arches and domes like an empty church. He made his way to the main stairs. Today would be different. Today would be all NYPD and goons from the Secret Service whispering into their lapels. His job was to protect exhibits, not people, exhibits whose combined value he had heard was over a billion dollars. A billion dollars. He reached the second floor and turned right. How much was he being paid? Two hundred for eight hours? And later this morning, how much would it cost the City of New York to look after one man? Dogs, men, cars, guns . . . A million bucks? Ten? Sick.

He rang the wall bell on the second floor and waited as the inside curtain was pulled back and the metal grille raised.

'Hi there,' said his colleague, sleepy-eyed, stubble-chinned. 'All set for the big day?'

'With any luck they'll let me go home,' the guard said as the grille was brought down and they walked back to the desk.

'Quiet?'

'Not a cockroach, all night.'

'All logged in?'

'Here's the record,' the night man said. 'You're due a call –' he looked at his watch, '– in ten minutes, I guess.'

'Any plans for the day?' asked the guard as they walked back out to the pavilion entrance.

'How about sleep, sleep and sleep?' said his colleague, ducking out. 'See you on TV.'

282

The guard locked the gate where it met the floor and drew the curtain across it. The aisles looked exactly as they had done the morning before and the one before that. Ten minutes to a log call. Thirty minutes before the guys with the dogs arrived. Coffee time. He walked towards the inner reception area and stopped dead. Maybe it was the dim light after the bright morning, but something had caught his eye. A movement. Impossible. His throat dried out. A shadow, had to be. He unclipped his gun holster. Shadow from what? He'd drawn over the gate curtain and only artificial light remained in the room. Suddenly he couldn't hear over the hammering of his heart.

'Hey! Is there someone there?'

It was crazy! The guard who'd just left had been in here on his own for eight hours ... He walked the length of the aisle, gun in hand, till he came to the buddha. The statue's face seemed to be trying to tell him something. His nerve snapped. With a cry, he turned for the phone, then stopped dead once again. A silver quarter was rolling out across his path, left to right. He spun, looking wildly for a target. He heard a wind noise. He saw the buddha's slow smile ...

Eight minutes later the phone rang.

'Security Ten, logging in,' said the girl's voice.

'All O K here at the Metropolitan,' came the level response.

*   *   *

The wing-tips of the plane were unzipping the darkness of the world. Ross could see great deserts of polar ice, red-tinged with dawn, sprawling underneath them.

'They won't believe us,' he said. 'They'll look at us and think we're crazy.'

'This is the point my parents had reached,' said Yukiko. 'They could not live with the knowledge that Chiyaha wanted to kill the Tennō. My father gave his life for the Emperor. My father was not crazy.'

Ross looked at her and knew there were sides to her that he still did not know. They had talked for six straight hours; Yukiko had cried and clenched her fists and told Ross about her

283

abduction from Ishikari and how Kasumi had used her to get Mama Yayoi out of Shoren-in.

'She would have rather died than let him take her,' she whispered. 'Kasumi told her that he would kill me if she caused him trouble.' She began to weep again. 'Oh, I wish he had, Ross! I wish he had!'

Ross held her to him and rocked her gently. Kasumi had wanted Mama Yayoi so that he could use her as a weapon against Chiyaha. It made the evil of Chiyaha even more real.

'I talked about this with Nobuo,' Ross said aloud. 'Why? Why would Chiyaha do it?' He looked at Yukiko. 'What would happen in Japan if the Emperor was assassinated on a visit to New York?'

Yukiko replied slowly: 'It would depend on who did the killing. If the killer was an American, for example, there would be an outburst of anti-American hysteria – which is never far from the surface in Japan.'

Ross blinked as something fell into place.

'The ninja,' he said softly. 'Describe him again.'

'Very strong,' Yukiko said, 'very elaborate body tattoos, moved and fought like a ninja . . .'

'Yes, but his face!' Ross pressed. 'You described his face to me and Henry.'

Yukiko frowned.

'He had round eyes,' she said.

'Round eyes,' Ross cried. 'In other words, he doesn't look like an Oriental?'

Yukiko was puzzled.

'I thought of him as Oriental at the time,' she replied, 'the way he moved, his smell, the tattoos. I am sure he *is* Oriental. But no, now that you say it, he could pass for a Westerner.'

'So,' Ross cried as the other pieces found their place, 'the killer looks like an American! He kills the Emperor and he in turn is taken out. Let's say he has papers on him suggesting he's some sort of fringe CIA groupie, a Lee Harvey Oswald type. Hysteria in Japan. Yes? Huge pressure on the government to do something, for Japan to save face, to show it's muscle. That's it, isn't it? What muscle does Japan have? Financial. The government makes some financial reprisals against the US as a sop to public opinion! It's brilliant!'

284

Yukiko was staring at him.

'How does it help Chiyaha?' she asked.

'Precious metals,' said Ross, shaking his head in wonder. 'They'll go through the roof and Chiyaha will own Oxx; he'll be sitting on one of the biggest platinum mines in the world.'

Yukiko's eyes were like the twin moons of their first night together in New York.

'What do we know about this ninja?' Ross asked, pacing the cabin. 'What can we tell people when we get to New York?'

'He is very strong,' Yukiko said. 'He will not use a gun or bomb. He will make his move somewhere crowded, somewhere he can actually touch the Tennō.'

'Like at a reception,' Ross said. 'Or a meeting of some kind. What's the Tennō's itinerary?'

Yukiko unfolded a copy of *Asahi Shimbun.*

'Today, Tuesday, is his last day in the United States,' she said. 'He comes to New York from Washington to open an exhibition of Edo Period art at the Metropolitan Museum. According to this report, he then flies home.'

'Then if it's going to happen today it has to happen in the museum,' Ross said and bunched his fist in the air.

The pain in his head was the only thing preventing him from thinking that he was losing his mind. Was this trip reality? Or was reality some other state from some other time when he had lived in a house on Staten Island with an attractive woman, taken the ferry twice each day, worked with normal guys, buying and selling, drinking beer after work, shooting the moon? Were the last three weeks part of some bizarre fantasy? Ross thought of Nobuo's square figure taking Chiyaha's bullets. He thought of the cop's cheeks puffing out as his lungs collapsed. No fantasy, that; just the bitch of reality at it's best.

'They'll think we're crazy,' he said simply, as the endless white deserts unfolded in the ever-rising light.

*   *   *

Shigeru Ōmori's weekend villa overlooked the blue waters of Sagama-Nada, outside Kamakura, south of Yokohama. The villa was a five bedroomed, wooden structure set in half an acre of

285

gardens in an area where land was sold by the square foot. No fewer than ten armed kobun guarded all access to the property while another five men sat in cars strategically parked on the approach roads.

Ōmori sat, traditionally robed, crosslegged on cushions, one side of a first floor verandah; Chiyaha, similarly robed, sat across. As they watched, a flock of early morning guillemot buzzed the shoreline, banking, sometimes black, sometimes white.

'In 1945, there was no greater criminal in Japan than Kodama,' said Chiyaha quietly. 'Yet within a few years, all was forgotten and he was the boon companion of the Emperor's brother.'

'So it always was, so it will always be,' said Ōmori.

'Very shortly, the omawari will have far greater problems than me,' Chiyaha continued. 'Public disorder. Street scenes like after the war. Very soon.'

Shigeru Ōmori's black hair glistened in the reflected light of Sagama-Nada. Was this man a satan come to ruin them all? Ōmori full knew the penalty if the omawari came; for now he was the only oyabun whom Chiyaha had left. They had all gone in one way or another: Okuma, Abe, Egusa and Kasumi. Only Ōmori remained. As a bakuto, it was time to hedge his bets.

'Look at the price of platinum,' Chiyaha smiled. 'Already others have got the word and are climbing on board. It is the shinkansen, going to the moon.'

'Hai,' Ōmori nodded wisely, but inwardly he was calculating how many extra kobun he could get into place without Chiyaha's knowing.

*   *   *

Captain Zach Levine took his job seriously. Seriously meant living on Rockaway Boulevard, ten minutes from JFK International. Seriously meant a track suit and sneakers at 4.00 a.m., driving his Chevy station wagon on to the Southern State Parkway which led into the airport. Zach wanted a last look at the on-ground situation at Hangar Fourteen, he wanted to check out the crowd barricades that had gone up thirty-six hours previously at Braisley Pond Park where protestors with

286

camping equipment had arrived on Sunday. The Emperor might just catch a glimpse of a distant banner protesting about God knows what; which as far as Zach was concerned was just fine.

Airports were eerie places at this hour, full of shadows and pools of yellow light. Planes winked red and white alternately from the apron. There was a constant noise of generators and the whine from freight jets, working through the night.

Five hours to wheels down, thirty minutes of intense activity. Another flurry next day as the royal party flew out. Zach drove down a service road and halted at a gate. The men from the ESU, the Emergency Service Unit – pros with large calibre sniper rifles who could divide hairs at half a mile – were due to report at five. He would place each of them.

A guard came out, looked at the car, checked his pass and waved him through. Four-o-five. He could check out the hangar, then the barricades at Braisley Pond, get home, shower and change into his uniform and still be back to grab some breakfast before the ESU men arrived.

'Captain!'

The big desk sergeant manning the Airport Security office was at its door.

'What is it, sergeant?'

'I've just got this from the control tower, sir,' the sergeant replied. 'It's been patched through from one of the Pacific stations, but there's a guy on a 747 on it's way here from Narita, and he says that someone is going to try and kill the Emperor today in New York.'

*   *   *

The G-VI made its final approach to La Guardia at 8.30 a.m. Freeman had slept up forward for the last two hours, leaving the non-stop conference of lawyers, bankers and numbers men to continue in the back. He looked out as they sank under the New York skyline. This was Ross's city. This was the furnace he had gone into and conquered, only to be thrown out again like pit waste. Ross had a real talent for the world of deals and money, an understanding that Freeman had understood only fully when Ross had called him from Tokyo. But Ross also had a talent for another side of life: for wide open spaces, for life lived almost

287

alone, empty of men. Without Freeman, is that the Ross who would have emerged – a back street dreamer, but happy? Had Freeman imposed an imperative of money as god, simply by being there? He looked down derisively at the legs that wouldn't serve him anymore. Had he screwed up both Ross and himself?

The runway came into view. This would be Ross's day, he was sure. Every bolt and nut and red cent was screwed into place; now it was up to bankers, then a court to decide; now, even without the evidence that the court required Ross to find, because of Ross's talent they had one last chance.

'Sir, thirty seconds to touchdown,' said Orem Williams, slipping into the opposite chair and buckling up.

Freeman's inquiring stare needed no explanation.

'The picture isn't exactly clear, sir,' Williams said. 'The embassy in Tokyo have brought down the shutters – we have word that a skirmish of some kind involving yakuza, and maybe Ross, took place in Kyoto, that several people were killed but that Ross was not one of them. We've urgently requested more information on his safety at the highest level.'

'And the mother?' Freeman asked. 'Mama Yayoi?'

'We're not being told at this time, sir,' Williams replied.

They landed and taxied to the private aircraft bay. New York summer warmth flooded the cabin as the door was opened. Chief Tshubisi came through from the back and dismissing the male steward's offer of help, scooped Freeman up without effort and carried him down the steps to a wheelchair, where a small, round man in a spotted bow tie awaited.

'Mr Oxx, I'm Henry Babbage,' he smiled brightly. 'Welcome to New York.'

SAC Ed Rich stood on the kerb of Fifth Avenue with his back to the main entrance of the Metropolitan Museum of Art. The buildings opposite were mostly turn of the century townhouses with elaborate, Italian-style cornices in the best Fifth Avenue tradition. Rich scanned the roof lines which might hide an army of snipers but which right now he knew were staked out by men from the ESU of NYPD.

The call had come through at six on Rich's cellular. Zach Levine out at Kennedy had begun apologetically.

'I'm sorry to disturb you at this hour, Mr Rich.'

'I'm on my way to the Command Centre,' Rich responded. 'Is there some problem?'

'I don't know,' said Zach Levine. 'We've been radioed by the flight deck of a Pan Am jumbo on it's way to New York from Tokyo. They have a guy on board named Ross Magee – evidently he's the subject of a deportation order by Jap immigration.'

Rich's eyes went still.

'Go ahead.'

'Seems he's travelling in the company of a female Japanese national named Okuma,' Zach continued. 'They're insisting they speak to someone in New York about an attempt on the life of the Emperor of Japan which they say will be made today.'

SAC Rich said: 'Have they given details of this attempt?'

'They're saying that the Jap mafia have hired some type of contract killer, a ninja,' replied Zach Levine. 'Magee says it'll happen in the Metropolitan, although how he has come into this information I have no idea.'

Ed Rich's jaw set doggedly.

'What time is their flight due?'

'O-nine-thirty,' Zach replied.

'I don't propose to get into ninja territory again at this late hour,' Rich said firmly. 'As Magee's a deportee, I suggest you put a temporary detain order on both him and the woman when they arrive. We don't want trouble.'

'Will do,' Zach Levine had said.

Rich looked uptown. Pedestrian access had been pushed back north of Eighty-fourth Street and south of Eightieth and the streets leading on to Fifth Avenue from Madison Avenue had been closed for four blocks. He turned to survey the museum itself. Over the doorway the banner for GREAT JAPAN billowed like a sail in a sudden breeze; either side of the door the wings of the massive building floated away like ships gliding out of port. A limousine pulled up and let off its passengers who hurried over a red carpet across the empty sidewalk and up the steps. As Rich made his way after them he pressed a switch on the mobile radio unit hooked to his trouser belt and a comforting belch of static emitted: the Command and Control Centre in Police Plaza had been operational since 5.00 a.m.

Inside the doors, three NYPD cops manned an inspection table beside a magnetometer. Showing his pass, Rich stepped over a rope and walked around the security operation. Two patrician looking men stood waiting in the centre of the Great Hall. Rich nodded to a plain clothes officer standing to one side.

'How are numbers?'

'The entire invitee list is now present, sir.'

Rich could take a professional satisfaction in the way all the pieces were smoothly interfacing – the further into the day they got, the more the various anxieties began to reduce into proper perspective. But why did the ninja thing refuse to go away? Who exactly was Magee? Hutt was out at Kennedy; later he could question Magee. Rich reached the top of the stairs on the second floor and frowned as he saw at least fifty men and women who had spilled out on to the balcony from the Great Japan pavilion. Kruger from State hurried towards him.

'It's a furnace in there,' he said. 'The TV people have set up and the air conditioning isn't functioning properly, something to do with the new windows. There just isn't air for all these people.'

SAC Rich weaved through the crowd and stood at the door. The exhibits which had been designed to give a sense of space were now almost lost in the crush of bodies. He could see NYPD officers forming a human barrier between the room and the podium and keeping the central aisle open. It was stifling.

'The people out here will have to go right back, now,' Rich snapped, pushing with both hands in the direction of Fifth Avenue.

'I'll handle it,' Kruger nodded.

Rich re-entered the pavilion and walked down the central aisle, reflexively touching the gun on his hip. He passed the stone buddha, squeezed between the line of cops and climbed the steps to the podium. TV lights dazzled him. Putting up his hand to shield his eyes, he scanned the crowd: faces of a dozen hues looked back up. He could see his own men in various parts of the room, and detectives from the NYPD, and a few faces from Japanese security whom he had memorized from the KKS file. The faces he didn't know were reassuringly normal – men and women chatting quietly, out for the day. The place was as tight as a place could be. Should he try and get Hutt to talk to the Magee guy sooner? What would be achieved? Nothing could be altered now – to alter the schedule in any basic way would be contrary to safety principles. Kruger from State would just love a change in the schedule at this hour. But why was Magee insisting?

The mobile unit on SAC Rich's belt erupted and he brought it to his ear.

'All stations,' said the voice of the cop in Police Plaza. 'Suki-yaki is wheels down Kennedy.'

Ross looked incredulously at the two cops and then around the bare room and out through the steel-grilled window where he could see small planes and helicopters parked.

'Say that again.'

'Our orders are to detain you here until further notice.'

'Are you arresting us?'

'Do you want to be arrested?'

Ross looked at Yukiko, then shook his head from side to side in dismay.

'On what basis are you detaining us?'

'Under the Immigration Code,' replied the big sergeant whose belly spilt out over his belt. 'You've just been deported from Japan, mister, and you're in poor shape so I suggest you sit down and relax until this thing is sorted out.'

'Look,' said Ross, 'you're a bright guy. There's a State visit in New York today. The Emperor of Japan is opening an exhibition of art and a professional assassin is going to try and kill him. Did you hear that? Kill him. Yukiko Okuma is the only person who can recognize the killer. Do you understand what I'm saying to you? She can try and prevent this thing happening. Now I want you to take us to someone involved in the security for this visit – now, right now, OK?'

The sergeant exchanged glances with the other cop.

'Just take it easy.'

'Come on!' Ross shouted.

'Mister, they know you're here,' the sergeant said.

'Who?' Ross queried. 'Who's "they"?'

'The Secret Service know you're here,' the sergeant nodded.

291

'They know we're here?' Ross cried. 'Well then why in hell isn't someone here listening to what we have to say?'

'Mister, there are a couple hundred security personnel right now in this airport with an awful lot more to do than to sit down and listen to you,' the sergeant said.

Ross took a deep breath and saw Yukiko looking at him.

'I want a telephone,' he said.

'I'm sorry,' the sergeant said and shook his head.

'I want to make a telephone call!' Ross cried. 'To my lawyer! I'm allowed one telephone call, dammit!'

The cops made for the steel door and Ross made to follow but at the door the sergeant turned and put his hand on Ross's chest.

'Take it easy, mister.'

'You're talking about a human life!' Ross shouted.

The cop gave him a little push but Ross caught the man at his shirt collar and pulled him back into the room.

'HEY . . .!'

In the empty outer office, the other cop began to turn. Ross hit him with his left fist on the chin and the man's legs went as if all the air had been let out. Ross threw the telephone receiver on to the desk and began to stab out Henry's number.

'Ross!' shouted Yukiko in warning.

Ross pivoted and struck, but the big sergeant was quick on his feet. He blocked the blow with his left forearm and hit Ross a piledriver into the face. Ross fell across the desk and hit the floor on the other side.

'I said you were in poor shape,' the cop panted.

The six-motor-cycle vanguard dropped speed to leave the Van Wyck Expressway in safety, then gunned down the ramp, gathering speed as they reached Forest Hills. Two cars behind, separated from the six-bike spearhead by a strobing patrol car, Chief Amis bent over a small screen. There were ongoing bursts of static from a dashboard-mounted radio.

'At this speed, we'll be there on target minus five minutes,' he said to the Highway Patrol Commander.

On his screen Chief Amis could see the Imperial limousine, immediately behind their car with a motor-cycle cop at each corner. He could also see the blacked out Counter Attack van behind the Imperial limousine and the first of the next seven limousines as the motorcade roared under the Long Island Expressway. He reached for the hand-held.

'Suki-yaki delivery to Control, K,' he spoke.

'Suki-yaki delivery, go.'

'We're now passing through sector two and will soon be in sight of the Bridge,' Chief Amis said. 'ETA the kitchen, ten-o-five, K.'

'Ten-four, Suki-yaki delivery,' Control replied.

The last vehicle carrying media personnel disappeared across the concrete. Someone was marshalling the group of school-children into line for the walk back into the public area and out to the car park. Zach Levine looked around Hangar Fourteen, saw Special Agent Bernie Hutt walking towards him and suddenly remembered the detainees from the Pan Am flight out of Tokyo.

'That went very smoothly, Captain, congratulations,' said Bernie.

Zach's radio crackled and he put it to his ear, nodding to Bernie as he did so.

'Captain, this is Levinski in the station.'

'I hear you, sergeant.'

'We've had major hassle from this guy Magee,' the sergeant said. 'I've had to use force.'

'I'm on my way,' Zach replied. He turned to Bernie. 'Sorry, Mr Hutt. That was my sergeant in the airport station. Have you been talking to SAC Rich?'

'Just briefly,' Bernie replied.

'Then he's told you about our two detainees?'

'What detainees?' Bernie frowned.

'We've got two detainees off a Tokyo flight,' Zach said, walking for the doors. 'A Ross Magee and a woman called Okuma. Magee's a lot of trouble – he's got a fixation that a ninja is going to kill the Emperor this morning. Crazy.'

Bernie had stopped three paces back.

'What did you say?' he asked.

*

He heard the sirens. So did all the guests and a sudden hush fell over the pavilion. He had entered a minute before from the inner reception area. Eyes hidden by tinted glasses. Body hidden by the uniform. Walking like a guard walks. Confidently. He had been a guard commander on Mindoro for three years and knew the way to stand and act and the way to display arrogance. He stood five yards from the pavilion door, slightly hidden by a partition, a single pace from the backs of the cops separating the crowd from the red carpet. He could see a man out on the balcony, roping back the crowd overflow towards the Fifth Avenue windows.

Confidence was his greatest asset. Then peace of mind. Few people were so privileged. On the plains around the River La-nga, the name Dinh Thack would be spoken again. The old people would nod their heads knowingly and say, 'Ah, Dinh Thack, of course,' as if it had simply been an inevitable matter solved by time before the sons of the father returned.

The sirens got nearer, coming right to left, uptown.

A great house went up, visible from the high road from Xamuong-man. It had a flower garden high above its rice fields and sheltered in the gardens, a carp pool. A stocky little boy came down before supper with his parents: the father, tall and dark haired and handsome; the mother, milk skinned and so fine featured that men talked of her beauty in hushed tones.

He flexed the fingers of his hands. Wings of steel. When it happened, even he did not fully understand what was at work, the nature of the power that was unleashed, although he was in perfect touch with every nerve-end and extremity of his body.

The stocky lad knelt and reached in and caught a carp by its tail whilst his parents and their servants clapped and laughed for his happiness.

He would come in on the soft point just beneath and behind the lobe of the left ear.

The round eyed child beat the fish's head on a sharp stone until it's blood flowed back down to the water. Dead. Dead. Dead.

From outside came the sound of clapping.

They screamed along a narrow road in Zach Levine's car, bypassing the freight sections and the airline terminal area and

294

came to a halt at a grey, nondescript building, twenty yards from the perimeter fence.

'What's the SAC's order on them?' Bernie asked.

'Hold until further notice,' Zach Levine replied. He ran ahead, into the outer office where Sergeant Levinski was sitting at a desk. 'Can you please open the detention room, sergeant?'

'He's a pretty big guy, Captain,' said the sergeant cautiously.

'Just open the door!' Bernie cried.

The sergeant led the way, keys jangling, and halted at the steel-sheeted door. He checked through a peephole, then turned the double lock. Bernie walked into the room.

'Mr Magee?'

'I'm Ross Magee.'

The face was lined and drawn; the right arm was in a sling; the head looked as if someone had used paint stripper on it.

'I'm Special Agent Hutt, Secret Service.'

'I'm glad you're here. This is Yukiko Okuma.'

Bernie nodded.

'I understand you have something to tell us,' he said directly.

'We believe that a Japanese yakuza named Rokuo Chiyaha has hired a ninja to assassinate the Emperor,' said Ross quietly. 'I understand the Emperor is opening an art exhibition in New York this morning. You've got to stop him.'

Bernie felt his neck hairs rise. *Once programmed, a Sul Sa ninja will not think of his own safety . . .*

'I can't stop him,' Bernie said. 'He's almost in Manhattan by now. This opening has been planned for months.'

'You've got a chopper out there,' Ross said. 'Fly Yukiko and myself in – she can recognize the ninja.'

Zach Levine was wide eyed.

'Is there something going on that I've missed?' he asked the young Secret Service Agent.

'Just bear with me, Captain,' said Bernie, hoping the cop didn't notice the shake in his hand. 'Mr Magee, I appreciate both your concerns, but you should recognize that during visits of this kind there are always scares. We've already heard about this ninja threat and as a result, security for the Emperor is so tight that no one will be able to get near him.'

Yukiko spoke quietly: 'In olden Japan, the shōgun slept in a room in the centre of his castle. The castle was surrounded by two wide moats; there were men on the battlements, constantly vigilant; all the windows had thick bars and the doors were locked. Outside his room the shōgun posted his most trusted men, and locked inside with him was his wakashū, a man who would lay down his life for his master.' She looked at Bernie. 'Still the ninja could make his way into the bedroom and kill the shōgun whilst he slept.'

Bernie's skin crawled all over.

'Captain, I need a chopper,' he said.

Ross looked down and saw the sprawl of limousines, vans and trucks, and the bunches of men, and the flash of bulbs near the red carpeted steps of the Metropolitan. Bernie brought the Bell in steeply, stood it on its nose before the main portico, then levelled out and put down with a bump ten yards from a line of fountains. He opened the door, jumped out and helped Yukiko down the two steps. Ross followed. Heads bent, the three of them ran for the red carpet. Ross held on to Yukiko. Bernie drove through the stragglers, knocked the retaining rope beside the inspection table and held his arms out to allow them in. Looking up, Ross could see a procession nearing the top of the stairs at a dignified pace. Everything seemed so orderly, so calm. Life had become a tableau and he an onlooker, watching life being played without him.

'Come on!' Bernie shouted to Yukiko.

A cop cleared a way up one side. As they hit the second section of steps, Ross could see a number of dark suited Japanese at the top of the stairs turn and look down. But Bernie was at the top step now, and Ross saw another man run out, a broad shouldered man in his forties with flinty blue eyes.

'This is not going to be popular, Mr Hutt,' he hissed.

The people behind the newly roped-off area in front of the Fifth Avenue windows had begun to clap and the Imperial party paused short of the pavilion door as the Emperor stopped to acknowledge the reception.

'Just walk in here with me, Miss Okuma,' said Bernie and walked Yukiko through the door in the diversion.

Ross was cut off by a surge of bodies.

'Yukiko!'

Ross saw her look back. He was less than ten feet away as the Emperor turned and their eyes met. Ross saw a polite, inquiring face, grey flecked hair, a man in his fifties, slightly stooped, then the party was moving right to left past him, the circle immediately around the Emperor closed off by plain clothes Japanese security men.

'Right back! Right back!' said a uniformed cop and put his hand on Ross's chest.

'Just a minute . . .' Ross protested.

'Right back, godammit!' the cop snarled. He looked at Ross's jacket then pulled out a gun. 'Hey, you've got no ID! Hold it right there, mister!'

The crush at the door was intense. The ropes and the crowd either side meant the Emperor went in first. Yukiko walked backwards to one side, Bernie's arm firmly around her shoulders. It took some seconds for her eyes to adjust. So many faces, men and women, mostly smiling, a mixture of Japanese and caucasian.

'Take your time,' said Bernie, 'have a good look at all the faces.'

One by one. Their eyes first, then their smiling faces began to turn as the Tennō came to the door and they began to clap as one, their hands making a rippling, wave-like motion as she looked at them.

And stopped.

At one pair of hands poised as if to clap. But unclapping. She looked up. The mouth. Unsmiling. The round eyes behind their glasses. As the Emperor stepped forward, Yukiko screamed.

Everything halted. The Emperor began to turn, questioningly towards his own security. Yukiko was thrown forward on to the red carpet as Bernie moved. Yukiko was trying to point. Bernie dived. There was a simultaneous whistling as if of wind. The ninja came, airborne, straight out, hands ready to cut. Bernie took the blow and went down.

Only three seconds had elapsed. People were unaware that anything had happened. The Emperor stepped back as his men, shouting urgently to each other now, pressed him unceremoniously to the ground and readied sudden guns. More shouts. The

297

cops at the door were straining to see. The ninja was coming to his feet.

Outside the door, Ross and the uniformed cop holding him both heard the commotion at the same time. Ross rammed his elbow into the cop's throat and sprang forward.

'Hold it!' the cop cried, but Ross was through the press of bodies and the man had no clear shot.

Yukiko knew the ninja would come for her. She lurched away and put up her hands to protect herself as he lunged, then she fell backwards on to the stone buddha, toppling it. The back of the statue fell away and the face of a dead man could be seen within the hollow stone. The force of the crowd pressing forward from the back caused the ropes either side of the aisle to give way and people spilled forward. Women began to scream.

Ross flung his way through, shouting, but now the din was at hysteria level as the crowd made for the door and the security people tried to get the Emperor out first. Sheer strength carried Ross against the tide. Suddenly he saw Yukiko, sprawled on the ground beside a fallen statue, kicking at a man in uniform who was reaching for her.

Ross's impetus carried him the final few yards. The ninja sensed the danger and began to turn in a fluid, almost poetic movement. Ross's blow came from the bed of the ocean. He felt nothing only craziness as his fist hit the turning man between the eyes. The ninja went backwards, eyes gone, landing between a dead man's body and Yukiko.

Ross felt a gun rammed into the small of his back.

'You're under arrest,' panted the uniformed cop who had made it in from outside.

Seventeen

Federal Judge Charles Murphy looked down the court and nodded at Henry Babbage. Beneath Judge Murphy's bench, the court officer was on his feet.

'This is an application by Ross Magee, a shareholder in the Industrial Oxx Corporation of Santa Clara County, California . . .'

Judge Murphy could see a black man with snow white hair behind Henry's table, beside a man in a wheelchair with skin the colour and texture of smoked hide. There was a twinkle in Henry Babbage's eye that reminded Charlie Murphy of good times together an awful long time ago. On the defendant's side were five lawyers, led by Rudi Meshnick of Bastin and Nazareth, no less. The Press box was overflowing and Judge Murphy had been told of at least one TV team outside.

'. . . to show that the Temporary Restraining Order should be made permanent,' the court officer concluded, handed the order of business up to the bench and sat down.

'Your honour.' Meshnick was first up. 'I represent the Industrial Oxx Corporation. I will not try the court's patience with a review of the facts of this case to date, other than to say that I believe your honour's good nature was prevailed upon on May 17th to grant a TRO in this matter on the basis of baseless allegations.'

Judge Murphy swivelled to Henry Babbage but if Rudi

299

Meshnick had expected to provoke an outburst, he was disappointed. Henry beamed.

Meshnick continued: 'I have here sworn affidavits from impeccable sources in Japan, your honour, proving the ownership of Sun Valley Corporation of Kobe to be vested in registered charitable trusts and pension funds of impeachable pedigree. The plaintiff's allegations have been of the utmost damage to the shareholders in Industrial Oxx and I now move that the TRO be lifted.'

Rudi Meshnick sat.

'Mr Babbage?'

Henry Babbage seemed as relaxed as a father, giving away the bride at a wedding breakfast.

'Your honour, my learned friend may be pleased to know that I do not intend to oppose the motion.'

Rudi Meshnick's mouth fell open.

'May it please the court,' Henry went on, 'but ten minutes before we came in here the Sun Valley bid for Oxx was withdrawn by their bankers, Reeson Rhoades, after it was learned that the main consortium of Japanese banks may no longer support the project.'

There was a huddle at the defendant's table and reporters scrambled to get out of the courtroom to telephones.

'Your honour,' said Meshnick, on his feet, 'I beg for a recess.'

'Recess?' snapped Judge Murphy. 'After all's been done to get this case in here today? Motion denied, Mr Meshnick.'

Henry was on his feet again.

'Your honour, an investing group comprising interests in Bamolisi, South Africa, have arranged a five billion Deutschmark facility, secured on the revalued assets of Industrial Oxx, which I understand include rich deposits of platinum, hitherto unexploited.'

The black man with the snow white hair looked to the man in the wheelchair, then nodded impassively.

'The Bamolisi group propose to pay seventeen dollars in cash and seven dollars in subordinated, ten year notes for the entire, issued share capital of Oxx,' Henry said.

'Your honour . . .' began Rudi Meshnick weakly.

Henry said: 'The Bamolisi group have already got acceptances

300

in principle from over fifty per cent of the shareholders in Oxx
and I would guess that after this morning's developments, those
numbers will greatly increase.'

Judge Murphy looked up; a fleshy man with black hair
retreating behind a high forehead had scraped back his chair
and was lurching for the court doors. He looked to have something wrong with his stomach.

Henry was saying: 'I therefore agree that it is entirely reasonable for the TRO to be put aside and for the shareholders of Oxx
to be allowed to conclude their business. Of course,' he added,
'what the new owners of Oxx, the Bamolisi group, actually do
with their newly discovered resources is very much a matter for
them.'

'This court's order of May 17th is set aside,' ruled Judge
Murphy. He beckoned Henry. 'Dammit Henry.' he said quietly,
'Magee brought this application, he should be here. Where is
he? Where's the Okuma girl?'

'I understand they have an engagement elsewhere that can't
be broken, your honour,' Henry smiled.

The Pierre was like a fortress. Access to the hotel itself was
rigorously controlled; access to the penthouses on the top floor
was forbidden.

Ross raised the cup to his nose appreciatively, then sipped.

'Jamaica Blue Mountain,' he said knowingly to Kyle Spicer.
'How do you do it?'

Kyle smiled.

'You join the Marines the same day as a guy, you sail with
him, you learn little things . . .'

A batch of Japanese officials moved hurriedly across the lobby
to the elevators.

'I guess the Emperor will fly home today after his unscheduled
stopover,' Kyle said.

'That's the word,' Ross nodded.

'How long has she been up there now?' Kyle asked.

'Over an hour,' Ross said. 'She said there were things the
Tennō should hear; like how her father, a yakuza mobster, gave
his life for him; like how some of the most decent folk in Japan
are outcasts called burakumin.'

'Burakumin?' frowned Kyle.

'It's a long story,' said Ross and for a moment his eyes were somewhere else. 'What's the official word from Tokyo?'

'Official? Zilch,' Kyle replied. 'Unofficial? Well, State are forecasting a Japanese cabinet reshuffle – that's like, totally unofficial. The Deputy Chief of the Tokyo Police has resigned for health reasons. And there's been a yakuza gun battle somewhere near Yokohama.' Kyle nodded grimly. 'CIA say that your friend Chiyaha got shot in the back of the head by one of his yakuza buddies.'

'Chiyaha,' Ross said, half to himself and thought of a cop on a mountainside, a man with an open, sincere face. He could still feel the smooth warmth of his cheek against his stubble.

'The markets have cooled down,' Kyle was saying. 'Platinum is back at four hundred five, but a lot of people got roasted. And this morning we got an absolute assurance from the front line Japanese banks that they would all be participating fully in our forthcoming bond auctions.'

'He nearly succeeded,' Ross said. 'The love-hate line between us and the Japs is so thin, Chiyaha nearly pulled it off.'

'You're dammed right he did,' said Kyle quietly. 'How's that Secret Service kid?'

'Bernie Hutt? His neck is broken, but I'm told he'll be OK,' Ross answered. He shook his head. 'I wish the ninja, whoever he was was alive to stand trial. We might all have learned something.'

'I doubt it,' Kyle said.

Their attention was drawn to the door of the hotel where a wheelchair was being pushed through.

'Ross!'

The voice was as strong as it ever was and Ross felt something warm and good run right through him.

'Seventy-eight per cent acceptances,' Freeman grinned and caught both Ross's hands in his. 'It's all over.'

'You did it,' Ross said.

'Me? I did nothing,' Freeman said. 'You're the one who did it, laddy.'

'Ross.'

Ross turned at Kyle's voice, then looked towards the elevators.

She came across the lobby to him and went straight into his arms.

'What did you tell him?' Ross asked.

'Everything,' she smiled.

'What did he say?' Ross asked.

'He says, now he wants to talk to you,' Yukiko replied.

'*Me?*'

Ross became aware of the three, courteous Japanese standing a few feet away.

'He's waiting, Ross,' Yukiko said. 'He's already delayed his departure twenty-four hours.'

'Yukiko's in good hands, buddy,' said Kyle and winked.

'I'll be just a few minutes,' Ross said.

'Before you go up there,' Freeman said, 'think of what you're going to answer when he asks you, what do you do, Ross? What will your reply be? Do you tell him, I'm a fisherman? Or do you say, I run the Industrial Oxx Corporation for its owners in Bamolisi, South Africa? Which is the answer, Ross? Which do you say?'

They were all looking at him, Freeman, Kyle, the Japanese. Yukiko. Rise and Fall. He smiled at her.

'We haven't decided that one yet, have we, Yukiko?' he said. Then he turned with the three Japanese and walked to the elevators.

Author's Acknowledgement
and Note

I am most grateful to Eric Bettelheim of Rogers and Wells, London, for his explanations of US corporate law and also for his general comments on the manuscript.

Joe Lisi of the New York Police Department brought me through the multiple stages of a State Visit to that city and briefed me on the current state-of-the-art protection which goes into place. His suggestions were indispensable.

Patrick Massey, ex Chief Correspondent for Reuters in Tokyo, provided crucial encouragement at an early stage and his knowledge of the contemporary Japanese scene gave me a solid base on which to build the story.

I must also thank John M Abbott, Financial Attaché and Treasury Representative at the American Embassy in London; Elizabeth Murray; Yoshi Ishii; Keiko Matsusaki Brophy; Hiroaki Sasaki; Kimiaki Sasada; Yoshiko Ushioda of the Chester Beatty Library, Dublin; Paul Majendie; Dick Warner; David Grossman; and my wife Carol and my children who had to live with two years of yakuza.

Many others are due my thanks but their names are too many for mention here.

Of all the books I read on Japan and the Japanese underworld, perhaps *Yakuza* by David E Kaplan and Alec Dubro (Macdonald, 1987) was the most helpful.

It is difficult for a Westerner to understand the cozy co-existence between yakuza and the rest of society in Japan. Most Japanese simply ignore the reality, but it may explain how the Liberal Democratic Party (LDP), has held unbroken power in Japan since 1955, despite endemic scandals that no political party in the West could weather for more than a few months.

The Liberal party was born in 1953 and backed with the wealth of Yoshio Kodama who had been jailed as a war criminal by the Americans in 1946. Kodama remained the most influential figure in Japanese politics for the next thirty-five years. He was arrested for tax evasion in 1977 and was subsequently accused of wide-ranging criminal activities including protection rackets, smuggling and corporate extortion.

A Kodama protégé, Kakuei Tanaka, resigned as Japanese Prime Minister in 1974 and was subsequently jailed for taking bribes of up to $2 million in the Lockheed scandal. In 1982 Tanaka succeeded in having Yasuhiro Nakasone follow him into the highest office. Nakasone, later heavily tainted by the Recruit scandal, resigned in 1987 and was replaced by Noboru Takeshita, Prime Minister until his resignation over insider-dealing in 1989. Takeshita's successor, Sousuke Uno resigned in disgrace the same year in a scandal linked to sex and money.

Uno was followed as leader of the LDP and Prime Minister of Japan by Toshiki Kaifu who was swept back to power in 1990 with a comfortable majority.

Glossary

Asahi Shimbun: Respected daily newspaper.

Bakuto: Gamblers. One of three historic types of Japanese gangster.

Bosozoku: Motor bike hooligans.

Burakumin: Japan's ancestral class of outcasts.

Chi-Chi: Father.

Futon: Straw mattress placed on floor.

Gaijin: A foreigner – usually a non-oriental.

Gumi: A suffix denoting association or gang.

Ha-Ha: Mother.

Haiku: Traditional skirt worn in kendō.

'Irasshaimase': 'Welcome'.

Kai: A suffix denoting association or society.

Karaoke: Sing-along machines found in bars.

Keishicho: Headquarters of the Tokyo Metropolitan Police.

Kendō: 'The Way of the Sword'. A popular sport in Japan, where contestants use shinai in place of swords.

Kobun: 'Child role', used in conjunction with oyabun. 'Soldier' in yakuza sense.

Korose: Kill.

Men: The helmet worn in kendō.

Mizu shōbai: Lit. 'water business'. Bars, clubs, anywhere drink is sold over the counter. Prime yakuza protection targets.

Ninja: Contract killer.

Omawari: Cops.

Onsen: Volcanic springs.

Oyabun: 'Parent figure'. Similar to 'godfather' in the Western, criminal sense.

Pachinko: Slot machine games.

Ryokan: Japanese inns.

Sarakin: Loan sharks.

Sayonara: Goodbye.

Sensei: Literally 'master'.

Shabu: 'Speed'. Amphetamines.

Shatei: Helper (Lit. 'younger brother').

Shinai: Bound staffs of bamboo used in kendō.

Shinkansen: High speed train.

Sul Sa: Martial art originating in Korea.

Tekiya: Street stall peddlers.

Tennō: The emperor.

Wakashū: Captain (Lit. 'young men').

Wakashira-hosa: Lieutenant (Lit. 'assistant young leader').

Yabin-jin: A savage – someone without appreciation of Japanese etiquette.

Yakuza: Somewhat similar to 'mafioso'. Loose term to describe organized crime in Japan.

Yūgen kaisha: Small, private company.